THE

DEAD

AND THE

MISSING

A.D. DAVIES

ALSO BY A. D. DAVIES

Adam Park Thrillers:
The Dead and the Missing
A Desperate Paradise

Alicia Friend Investigations:
His First His Second
In Black In White

Standalone:
Three Years Dead
Rite to Justice
The Sublime Freedom
Project Return Fire *(co-authored with Joe Dinicola)*

For all those out there fighting the good fight

Prologue

I live my life with a gun behind the fridge. That'd snag me a five-year prison sentence, just for owning it. Even though I'm sure the danger has passed, and the decisions I made can no longer bite me, I can't seem to let it go. Tucked away as it is, I can't even make an argument for self-defence; it's there in case I feel the need to break it out, and go where the law cannot.

That isn't a thought I would have considered a couple of months ago.

A couple of months ago, I was afraid of a fight, even one I knew I could win.

A couple of months ago, I had never killed a man.

But ask me if I regret taking the case, and the honest answer is "no." Because I don't care about the part of me that died this summer. All I care about is the outcome, and the good things I achieved.

The bad things do not haunt me. The mistakes I made do not weigh upon me. I wish they did, because that would prove I was normal. So maybe I'm not normal. Maybe that's why I survived. And why I will survive in the future.

UNITED KINGDOM

Chapter One

As the ocean swelled under a grey sky, my board rose higher than it had all day, and I started to question if I should really be out here at all. The five-foot wave rolled away, curling as it prepared to break, and half a dozen younger surfers scrambled to catch it, surging towards the beach in a line, to be greeted by the whoops and cheers of their friends waiting in the shallows. Like the other regulars, I'd been unable to resist the strengthening troughs and peaks that heralded a twelve-to-fourteen hour storm, a "weather-bomb" the tabloids predicted would destroy every town and village in its path, flooding the southwest back to Biblical times.

I might be exaggerating that last bit. But only a little.

It *was* a grey day, though, the wind picking up steadily, and it started spitting about ten minutes ago.

In Britain?

Yeah, in Britain. At the seaside.

My fellow hardy souls were all younger than me by a good decade and a half, and I shivered in my thermal wetsuit. I was pretty sure the next decent wave would be my final run of the day, so I had to make it count.

On the beach, a woman studied the horizon, stock-still amid the small audience. Strands of blond hair fluttered in the wind as if it escaped from a ponytail and, even from here, I could see she was dressed in sensible trousers and a padded jacket.

My curiosity ended, however, when an incoming roller chal‐
lenged me as only the ocean can. I lay on my front and
paddled. This was the wave. *My* wave. I found my focus‐point
and scooped faster and faster, shoulders heaving against the
water. My speed and the sea's roll fell into sync. I popped up
on my board and carved through the wall of water, nature's
hand embracing me and guiding me toward the sand. I'm a
shade under six foot, but this wave curled over me by another
head. It should have been terrifying, but I allowed the ocean to
propel me forward while all I had to do was not fall off; this
illusion of control, this *delusion* that nature could not simply
swat me from existence, it was enough to bring me home.

As I hopped off my board in the foaming shallows, a smat‐
tering of applause sounded and a couple of the youthfully‐
smooth girls trotted over. Late teens, early twenties. Bikinis
under hoodies. I picked up my board and returned their
smiles. They ran straight past to a kid peeling off a wetsuit
with purple‐swooshes, his sculpted hairless torso drawing even
my eye. Sure, I was in as good shape as any of the younger
guys, but at thirty‐six I needed to remember I wasn't some
"Bodhi"‐type figure from the original version of *Point Break*; I
was the old dude who turned up on their beach one day, and
just about earned his place.

The only person who noticed me was the mommy‐type
blonde in the padded jacket. Hands in her pockets, shoulders
hunched. About my age, perhaps a tad older, but if she said
she was thirty I wouldn't argue.

She said, "Adam Park?" Plummy, upper‐middle‐class. Not
quite aristocracy. Poking out of her coat was the corner of a
brown envelope about an inch thick.

I stripped off my hood and upper part of my wetsuit, per‐
haps hoping to compete with the young stud‐muffin and his
admirers. They all jogged by without as much as a glance.

Philistines.

"No," I said to the woman. "I'm not who you're looking for."

"Well that's odd." She fussed with her zip and slipped a portrait photo from the envelope. "You look an awful lot like him."

Even though it flapped about in the wind, I could see it featured a nasty bastard in a thousand-quid suit. The picture used to adorn the lobby to an office, beneath which was printed my name and position within the company—*director*. I was clean-shaven in the photo and my hair was a sensible length.

"That's not me." I snatched up my kit-bag and headed for the showers at the top end of the beach.

She scrambled in front and pushed the envelope into my bare chest. Which did surprise me. You see, I didn't really look like the sort of guy who people can push about. As well as my physique, my facial hair grows thicker and more quickly than the average person, so after five days without shaving, I sported a near-full scraggly beard. Still, it matched my hair that hadn't seen a barber in two months, yet this prim-and-proper lady wouldn't let me leave.

She said, "Can I at least buy you a drink? If you're still not interested, then fine. I'll go."

I carried on up the sand, the woman striding to keep up. "How'd you find me?"

"Harry."

"Of course Harry."

"He said you were hiding down here but I should try anyway."

More of the surfers were coming in now, my wave being the first in a succession of six-plus footers, a rarity in this part of the world. The horizon had darkened as black as night, although it was only four o'clock in July.

"I'm not hiding," I said. "I've been on holiday."

"For two years?"

It took me a moment to calculate but yes, she was correct. I'd now seen two Christmases with only myself for company.

"I needed a break," I said.

We paused by a row of showers at the foot of the access road. I said, "Daughter?"

"I'm sorry?"

I flicked on a shower and stood beneath it, one eye on the blue-grey clouds. "Someone's missing and Harry's obviously out of ideas. Your daughter? Son?"

"My sister," she said. "She just turned eighteen."

I glanced at the envelope through the stream of fresh water. "Why are you talking to Harry and me instead of the police?"

"Because the police say she stole a bag of cash and went on the run. And we don't think she is still in the country."

"How much did she steal?"

"*Nothing.* She wouldn't do that. She's either been kidnapped or hurt or she's … I need to know."

No one's loved one is ever to blame for criminal acts. They've always been coerced or kidnapped or threatened.

"Fine," I said. "So who did she *allegedly* steal from?"

"Her boss. She was working in a strip club, of all places. Harry thinks he's the one obstructing the investigation."

"Got a name?"

"He's called Curtis Benson."

Curtis Benson. I'd never met the man, but I'd heard of him. Investigators at my company had encountered his businesses in the past, but it was difficult to get a firm read on him. The grapevine gossips whispered that he'd risen too quickly to be an honest man, and opinion was divided as to whether he was just a dodgy entrepreneur who from time to time indulged in a spot of brown envelope action with the powers that be, or a serious *playa* in the crime community.

"Bloody Harry," I said. "He's supposed to be retired. Jayne'll be doing her nut."

"He's my uncle."

I almost laughed. "Came out of retirement to help a niece I've never heard of?"

"My father was Harry's brother. When my mother remarried we didn't really stay in touch, except for Christmas cards and birthdays, that sort of thing."

Harry had a brother who died back in the eighties—the Falklands War—so there was no reason to think this woman was lying. It happened before I started working with him, meaning I had no definite frame of reference. Except—

"But if your sister is only eighteen…"

"My half-sister, then. But still my sister. Please. My mother isn't with us anymore and Sarah's dad left a long time ago. Harry was willing to look into it if I paid his expenses, but now we're seriously short. He thought you would help."

I switched off the shower and toweled down as best I could. "Why would he think that?"

"He said you have more money than God, and you are soft as shit, and you'd probably take pity on me if I cried."

"You're not crying."

As I rubbed the towel over my scruffy hair, she fixed her eyes on mine and, through what looked like sheer willpower alone, a solitary tear rolled down her cheek. She said, "Do you have a hankie?"

Okay, I thought. *That was impressive.*

I said, "*One* drink."

I recommended Sanjay's Bar, a fifteen-minute stroll to a perch far enough back from the cliffs to be safe but sufficiently exposed to observe the approaching storm. I threw on a Fat

Willie fleece and, with practiced ease, dressed my nether-regions under my towel. When suitably decent, I gathered my things and set off up the steep, narrow road, trying not to show how difficult it was to walk in a straight line with the wind buffeting my surfboard like a sail. I think I did okay.

"Right," I said. "Let's hear it."

"The last I heard from Sarah was an email." She slipped a sheet of A4 from the envelope wedged in her coat. I had no free hands, so she gripped it in both hers, flapping close to my face. "She said she went on holiday. Didn't say where, but promised to be home soon. Then she stopped communicating altogether."

The name of the sender was Sarah Stiles. The recipient Caroline Stiles. I assumed the woman before me was Caroline. Sarah wrote that she was sorry for causing any worry over the past week and that, yes, as Caroline said, she'd be home soon. Actually—

"It says '*we* will be home soon'," I said. "Who's 'we'?"

"I don't know. Harry doesn't either."

"Boyfriend, then?"

Caroline folded the email and slipped it back in the envelope. "She never mentioned one, but Harry said we should work to that assumption."

"She sent it 22nd of June. That's nearly a month ago. The police still weren't interested?"

"I explained that already. They don't believe she's a victim. They think she's a *thief*, on the run with her accomplice."

"Right," I said. "The 'we'."

She adopted a "duh" voice. "*Miss Stiles, youngsters do this when they're in trouble. She'll come home when the money runs out.*" Back to normal. "All they've done is put her photo on their missing-persons website and told me to start a Facebook campaign."

"Bullshit," I said. "Not even the prime minister can phone up a police station and say, 'Hey, stop investigating this will you?' At least not without a compelling national security issue. Presumably Harry doesn't think the boyfriend is a terrorist?"

"Do you believe Harry would let it lie at that? Do you think *I* would? We went to our MP and she parroted the same nonsense. I tried the press, and they ran a story about how Sarah's lovely boss was now struggling to pay his staff because the money was gone. So I did the Facebook thing, and some other sites. But all the *horrible* people who post comments and false leads, it's … it's *horrible*, there's no other word for it."

"Trolls," I said. "They're called trolls."

We reached the car park of what looked like an Edwardian London abode, all grey brick and tall white-framed windows. *Sanjay's Bar*. The smokers' enclosure was empty, and the only remaining outdoor furniture was the bolted-down tables. We carried on round the side where Sanjay kept a space for my VW Camper, a burgundy 1974 beauty with a white roof and chrome wheels.

I said, "So no leads at all from social media?"

"Maybe one. A woman who thinks she met Sarah in Paris shortly before she sent that email. But she didn't leave a contact number or anything, so…"

I opened the VW's back door. "If she's with a boyfriend, she's probably fine."

"No." She set her mouth and eyes firmly. "If someone else is involved, some *guy*, it was *he* who put her up to it. Forced her to take part."

I maneuvered my board through the gap between the fold-out bed and kitchenette. I guessed Harry told her to emphasize what a turd the boyfriend must be.

"I'm sorry to be such a pest," Caroline said, "but I've virtually run out of money. Harry looked as deep as he could and found enough evidence leading out of the country, but—"

I wedged the board in place. "She definitely left the UK?"

"She definitely obtained a fake passport."

"Phone?"

"Turned off. No records in the digital cloud, no photos, nothing."

I shut the door. "Look. Caroline. They say it's a small world, but really … it isn't. It's huge. I mean ridiculously big. Even if she's still in Paris, that is one colossal city."

"Are you willing to help us?"

"Let me get this straight. Your sister goes missing a month ago. Possibly with a boyfriend. But no one else, I assume, is reported missing?"

She nodded reluctantly.

I said, "*Maybe* she stole a bunch of cash from a reputed criminal, *maybe* a case of mistaken identity. You can't afford to keep your detective, so you hop on a train in the hope of convincing an *ex*-private investigator to take over. For free. Do I have that right so far?"

"Almost," she said. "I couldn't afford the train. I used a coach."

"From Leeds?"

She nodded.

Leeds to Cornwall. That's a long journey.

"Bloody Harry," I said.

As the drizzle graduated to full-on rain, I hurried toward the pub's entrance, the wind blowing my hair every which way.

"Where are you going?"

"Inside," I said. "If Harry sent you, I never really had a choice. I'll look over the case. But you're buying me that drink."

The original Sanjay's Bar overlooked Aragon Bay, a white-sand beach in what Sanjay thought of as his wife's special corner of Sri Lanka. But when the 2004 tsunami smashed that to a billion splinters, Sanjay sold his ruined land to the government, and followed his university-bound kids to England. Pictures from before, during and after the tsunami adorned the walls even now. Sanjay says he likes Bude almost as much as he did Aragon Bay, but he still misses his wife. Now he runs this pub in a small town on the North Cornwall coast. It's like any other in this part of the world: a fire, booze promotions, quiz nights. Like any other pub, that is, except the main food menu sizzles with garlic and ginger, boasting twists on British staples as well as the traditional fare of pie and mash. Which leaves Sanjay himself—leather-skinned and fifty years old—who still dresses in sarongs and sandals, as he did back home, and insists on the same over-the-top welcome as when I first plodded up from the beach and flopped onto a beanbag on his deck.

"Adam, my good friend!" he called from behind the bar.

Caroline and I eased through the thin crowd, an odd mix of surfer dudes and gals fresh from the ocean and local drinkers who thought surfers were birthed by some demon to destroy society. Sanjay recommended the local brew, Bude-iful Day, and Caroline ordered two pints.

Sanjay eased back the pump, squirting bitter into the glass. "Good waves today?"

"Big ones," I said. "A little scary."

After our regular exchanges, I snagged a table near the window, and for a good minute or so Caroline and I watched the clouds sweep in. Others formed the same idea, and when lightening forked on the horizon, it drew an "Oooh," from the gathered drinkers.

Caroline slid the envelope into view and took a pull on the bitter. I sipped mine too.

"Smooth and strong," I said. "And a bit nutty. Exactly how I like it. Coincidentally, it's how I like my women too."

Not even the flicker of a smile. *Fine*, I thought. *Business it is.*

I said, "Did Harry tell you why I don't do this anymore?"

"He said you were good at it. Literally good enough to make a million."

"A lot more than a million." I detected that old bragging smugness in my tone and called a halt to it.

She nodded, like she'd heard it before. "He also says you have some resource, a tool that can help. Illegal, but…"

"It's called DDS," I said. "I don't have it. But I can get hold of it."

"Okay. Why give up your business if it was doing so well?"

"Talk to me about Sarah."

"Talk to me about why you gave up your business."

Sanjay delivered two menus, flashed a look Caroline's way, grinning like a teenager. *Subtle, mate.*

When he was gone, I said, "This is about your sister, not my employment history. *I'm* supposed to be interviewing *you*." I concentrated on my pint. "I need to be sure, and *you* need to be sure, that me getting involved will be beneficial."

Caroline used one finger to push the envelope towards me. I opened it.

A photo presented Sarah Stiles as a dark-haired girl with wide blue eyes and light freckles; an eighteen-year-old who looked fifteen. With her father departed and mother dead,

Caroline put her through high school. She left aged seventeen to work her first job in a department store, where she commenced a relationship with a man two decades her senior, but her condition meant she would not concede the boyfriend could possibly be a bad person.

"What condition?" I asked.

"What they euphemistically call 'learning difficulties'. Non-specific, but closely related to Asperger's."

"Like an extreme form of OCD?"

"That's something of a simplification, but not a million miles away. On the surface she is perfectly normal. But she does some things very, very well, while other things confuse and frighten her. And she has a near-eidetic memory too, which is tough."

"Eidetic? You mean photographic?"

"There's actually no such thing as a photographic memory, but yes, her ability to recall minute detail is remarkable."

"What does she do very, very well?"

"She is the best at spatial-relations. She can beat the world at Tetris, or organize a room to be more efficient in seconds. And her art ... it's so detailed. She can look at a building or a bridge, and sketch it out, exactly proportioned. Here."

Caroline took over the file and thumbed to a couple of pictures. The first was a black-and-white cityscape of Leeds, the town hall's dome rendered in intricate detail. The other was a color painting featuring the rock formation on Ilkley Moor known as the Cow and Calf. Again, stunningly accurate. I also noted there were no actual people in either.

Caroline said, "A gallery told us they were too clinical to ever sell well, yet she keeps trying." She slipped the pictures back into the envelope. "But when anything goes even slightly wrong, well ... she goes into what I call 'mission mode', where she becomes incredibly practical and focuses on solving the problem before her. Pure tunnel vision. If I'm running late, she leaves without me, or—".

"Is she medicated?"

"She was," Caroline said. "This man, he introduced her to something that helped but wasn't exactly legal."

"Heroin?"

"Marijuana."

"There are worse solutions than a little medicinal weed."

Without a reply, I concentrated on Harry's case file.

After the spat, Sarah showed up on her true love's doorstep, her way of solving the problem of betrayal. Unfortunately, her true love, being freshly divorced, "needed his space" and sent her away. She refused to go home, so had to make money quickly. Mission mode kicked in and she took the job where she could earn the most in the shortest time ...

"A table-dancing bar for Heaven's sake," Caroline said. "A *strip-club*." She hushed her voice at the final words there, as if anyone nearby gave a crap. "I finally got hold of her on the phone one night, and I told her she was right, that she should make her own decisions. We both had a bit of a cry and she told me she loved me, and she'd be home eventually. No. *Soon*. She said 'soon'."

Lightning cracked over the ocean, its twin fingers stabbing the water. The sky was a blue-grey blanket, so dull that rows of night-activated bulbs twinkled on outside.

Caroline said, "But then she stopped calling altogether. And I contacted Harry."

Harry tracked Sarah out to a terraced house in the district of Birstall, but it was in darkness and all its utilities were cut off. After much cajoling of Sarah's boss, and a strict promise of confidentiality, he was also allowed to interview Sarah's fellow dancers and other staff.

On Sunday 17th June, Sarah showed up as usual, and some-where between one and three a.m., while everyone was out front servicing the peak-time customers, Sarah vanished off the face of the Earth. The next morning, the safe was empty, and all who Harry interviewed seemed oddly aware of the fact that Sarah knew the combination.

All those accounts of that night, though, *each one*, were so similar, so word-perfect, that the witnesses had obviously been coached, which lead to Harry digging out a snazzy shirt and paying the club's admission. He found only one girl he didn't recognize from his interviews, a pixie-like blonde called Lily. A higher-than-usual tip meant the unprepared witness took Harry into a private room with no music, but as soon as Harry assured her about confidentiality, three meat-head security types muscled in and demanded to know what the fuck was going on.

I said, "No clue what she was going to say?"

"No."

"Any idea how much was taken?"

"The owner says it's between him and his insurers. But the people Harry spoke to estimated anywhere between fifty and two-hundred thousand."

A few bum-numbing stakeouts furnished Harry's file with a grainy photo, taken from a distance, of Lily exiting onto the street, but more importantly sent him to a forgery expert who paid a lot of visits to the club, an ex-copper who made IDs for some of the underage Eastern-Europeans. In a sales-tease, the forger admitted to Harry that, *sure, he'd made a passport for the little cutie*, but Harry could not afford the bribe that would reveal the identity issued.

I hate to brag, but I would have no such trouble in the brib-ery department. And Harry knew it.

A troubled girl falls for a violent ex-con.

The pair steals the contents of a criminal's safe.

Then they abscond abroad, probably to Paris.

The police are ordered to cease investigating by sources unknown.

No communication for three weeks.

I said, "I'm not Indiana Jones. I'm not some super ex-government special agent. I'm just a guy who's good at finding people."

"So *find* her," she hissed.

She seemed to shock herself at the outburst, but didn't apologize, just shakily lifted the glass to her lips again.

I said, "You have to understand, if she isn't in trouble, I will not drag her back to Blighty kicking and screaming."

"But you'll tell me she's okay? If you find her?"

"Yes," I said. "I can do that."

Outside, night-lights twinkled up and down Bude Bay. Thunder boomed overhead and another fork of white split the vista in two. I suggested we eat here before getting some shut-eye. Sanjay's B&B was full so she would have to share my VW. It was going to be a rough night, and we had a heck of a journey back to Leeds the following day.

Chapter Two

We set off before dawn. Rain lashed my camper van all the way up the A30, a road that feels like it loops around and around in a Groundhog Day-style procession of sameness, switching between dual carriageway and single-track road on a whim. The worst of the storm was over, but Caroline still fidgeted, hand gripping the passenger seat with every wind-assisted swerve. In the absence of a radio, voice raised over the chugging engine, her small talk felt forced.

"So what was the big thing Harry mentioned? What sent you away the first time?"

I said, "It was when my dad died. I took off with a rucksack and explored the world a little."

"A little?"

"Okay, eight years. Almost nine."

The wind changed direction and the van almost took off. Each time the vehicle aquaplaned or veered to one side, the chatter seemed to calm her. She asked how a guy like me—a "beach bum and thrill seeker"—came to specialize in tracking down lost people. For her benefit—absolutely *not* because I love talking about travel—I told her how, aged eighteen, I journeyed into Europe, where I met new people and drank foreign beer and took recreational drugs, and got mugged and pickpocketed, and learned how easy it was to meet someone in Marseille and bump into them six weeks later in Dubrovnik. I probably shared too much when I said I made love on beaches and up mountains, but it was such a release. I was a citizen of the world, a free man and, as far as I was concerned, the wisest person on the planet. And so it went, until three years later when I'd lived in South Africa a couple of months, and I met a young woman called Sophie, who became my first ever "client."

Being twenty-one and handsome, I decided to hit on her in a hostel bar, but after a little probing I learned she was on the road with her boyfriend during their university gap year. I kind of looked down my nose at her then because—y'know—I was *sooo* superior having lived Out There for so long. But they planned to rendezvous here once she'd done her thing in Jo'Burg, and now he wasn't where he was supposed to be. Still hoping, I suppose, to impress the pants off her, I used my ever-so-superior experience to analyze all the ways in and out of the town and traced his movements from there, eventually discovering him on a sand-and-palm-tree island, doped up on acid and weed, shagging a Russian girl whose assets and free-spirit made him temporarily forget Sophie even existed. Literally. I had to remind him. He felt bad. But not bad enough to leave the free-spirited Russian, so it was up to me to convey the news to Sophie.

"And no," I said, "she still didn't sleep with me."

After that, though, as soon as I understood the tribal nature of humanity, I gained something of a knack for tracing people. Even in a friendly country, our subconscious tells us it's enemy territory, so almost everyone acts in a way they wouldn't in a familiar place. I tune into that. Methodical investigation, logical deduction.

Detectives in Britain and the States would find me via this newfangled thingamajig called "the internet" and recruited me as their eyes and ears, and even though the vast majority turned out well, I still located a couple of subjects in morgues and, in one case, their hotel room with fourteen stab-wounds. Ultimately, though, the good work—putting parents' minds at rest—outweighed that tiniest fraction of humanity that is wired so differently to the rest of us that they might as well be a separate species.

In time, I convinced myself I was not only wise, but also tough. A hard-man. Turns out, I was wrong about that.

"Harry told me you got involved with some goons."

"Goons," I said. "Yeah, 'goons' is fairly accurate. Poked around somewhere I shouldn't have. Bangkok to be precise."

"And that's the reason you came home?"

"Yes," I said. "I guess I needed my mummy."

She wrinkled her nose in a chuckle, but it died quickly, as if she had no right to be happy at this precise moment. She needed to keep talking. "And the business? You wouldn't tell me last night why you gave it up."

"I didn't like it anymore," I said. "In a nutshell, after I came home to the UK, Harry and I started up together. We tracked missing people, and one day we took on a corporate client to locate a financial officer who ran off with a pension pot. We got recommended to other high-end companies. We grew from there. Harry said it wasn't 'proper' work, though. He'd been on about retiring for years, so he let me buy him out and I took things to the next level. I brought in actual executives to push the business side, made sub-contractors full-time employees, and hired accountants to invest our income. And you know what?"

"They invested badly."

"They invested *brilliantly*. Private investigations became 'corporate security', and the investment portfolio? It made ten times what the core business did. I was running an investment bank with a private investigation business tacked on the back." I shook my head and steadied the wheel again. "But we were investing in companies who … let's say I wasn't comfortable with their worldview."

"Couldn't you have stopped? Done something else?"

"I owned fifty-one per cent of the company. But when I tried to sack the senior VP, it turned out he had more friends on the board than I did." I braced myself as a sixteen-wheeler roared past, drenching the windows in spray. "They made me an offer."

"Resign?"

"Sell my shares and live a long, wealthy retirement. I negotiated. I let a prick called Roger Gorman take over running the place while I could veto certain clients."

"Roger…"

"Gorman," I said. "With a G. Not the filmmaker. Now all I can do is take the money they make and pour it into good causes. And keep a hefty chunk for myself, of course."

"Doesn't explain why you don't start a new firm. Help people like me."

"Non-compete clause. I'm not allowed to work as a private investigator unless it's through the company. Not here, or anywhere in the world. I'd forfeit all my shares and position. I've tried everything I can to get rid of the current board. I still hope to."

"Hope to?" she said. "While you bum around on a surfboard?"

I often asked myself the same thing. Many evenings I stand there on a beach, watching the sunset, envisaging scenario after scenario where I gutted the company and put it to work for good. The sun would go down without me seeing it, and I suddenly find myself bathed in twilight, and only the waves lapping at my ankles ever sparked me back to reality.

I said, "When inspiration strikes I'll know what to do."

A long silence ground itself out. I hoped she was finished with the interrogation. She wasn't.

"Is it true you failed your psychology degree?"

"I didn't fail," I said. "I got a third. A new exec suggested a qualification might add prestige. I excelled in the practical stuff, but I couldn't write for shit. Kept going off-topic. 'Too fond of introspection,' was how one professor put it." That and—what did my professors call it again? Oh yeah—my "moral judgments." Only Harry often added the adjective "sanctimonious."

We hit the M1 and the further north we travelled, the brighter the sun shone, and a full English breakfast and a couple of extra-shot-infused coffee-stops later, I was playing songs in my head, tapping the wheel, and my feet danced when not on the pedals. Caroline hadn't indulged in as much coffee as me, so she slept most of the remaining four hours. When I passed the sign confirming I had officially returned to Leeds, I wound down the window and felt the city's air on my face, the summer sun hot, the breeze cool and clean.

I dropped Caroline at her house out in the sticks, and headed for home, a newish building on the south edge of the city center. My parking space was still reserved in the underground lot and I ascended to the twentieth floor in my board-shorts and fleece, jittery from the caffeine and ready to go, go, *GO*! I entered my apartment, a split-level affair, the open plan kitchen-diner leading to a carpeted lounge, with a staircase to my bathroom and two bedrooms. On a clear day I could see all the way to the industrial landscape of Bradford. The apartment was cleaned once a month by an agency, so it smelled fresh and left no nasty surprises.

Once I'd unpacked my rucksack, I shaved my face smooth, showered, and changed into a designer suit and a shirt that felt a bit tight. No tie. My hair was clean but scraggly, yet it went well with the suit, like I was trying to emulate a GQ model. I didn't really need this getup for my planned meetings, but I wanted to avoid the attention of entering such an environment in a t-shirt and flip-flops.

I took my three-year-old BlackBerry out of a drawer, plugged it in and booted it up. Still worked. I needed two things before commencing my investigation in earnest: the Deep Detect System, and a chat with Harry. I sent Harry a text asking him to meet me here at three p.m., then fired off an email to Roger Gorman to say I'd be in his office at two. It was currently shortly after midday.

Sitting on a beach, up a hill, on top of a mountain, I could watch nature shift and sway for hours; I'd happily read a novel cover-to-cover, lying in a sunbeam, purring like a cat; I could listen to music as rain pounded outside all evening; all simple, do-nothing activities. But there was work to do here. Even lacking the data I needed from Harry, even without DDS, there were leads to chase, people to contact, a trail to pick up.

No, sitting on my arse was not an option.

Chapter Three

Blazing Seas was well-known as Curtis Benson's favorite table-dancing bar, or rather "gentlemen's club" as the sign proclaimed. Its nickname, Blazing *Sleaze*, was well-earned: gaudy orange neon, three stages hosting floor-to-ceiling poles, and an array of faux-leather chairs and sofas. Approaching lunchtime on a Friday and already a full complement of dancers sashayed about the place, gliding from one group of men to another.

I ordered a beer and sat on a barstool and pretended to be a punter. I referred three beautiful young women to the drink I was nursing so very slowly, and once the third girl wandered away, her colleagues seemed to figure I was only there for the stage-show.

About three-quarters through my pint, a woman of around twenty strode down one of two wrought-iron spiral staircases and through a cloud of dry ice that swept from the stage. She wore a see-through baby-doll nightie over white lacy bra and panties, and had long red hair and a petite body. She might have tempted me to fork out for a legitimate dance if I didn't find the whole panto-mime so boring.

As she approached, her smile showed she hadn't heard I wasn't paying for dances today. She placed her hands on my thighs and leaned into my ear and in a soft but discernible Yorkshire accent said, "It's ten pounds for a dance, love. Fifty for half an hour in the

VIP room," then stood back to allow me to perv over her a little longer. She added, "Limited touching in the VIP room. *Limited*."

I said, "I'm looking for someone called Lily."

"I can be your Lily if you want."

"I'll pay more than a VIP fondle," I said. "Finder's fee for you too. She came highly recommended."

Her eyes rolled up and to the left. "Lily...?"

"Youngster, quite small. Short blond hair."

"Oh, *that* Lily." Eyes back to me. "Yeah, I heard she moved to Manchester." The girl looked toward the large, shaven-headed barman. "Why don't you take me to the VIP room?"

I played along and handed her fifty pounds, which the barman exchanged for some sort of voucher. The young woman led me up the spiral staircase down which she had come minutes earlier, then to a compact room with its own stereo and a stiff leather couch, all surrounded by mirrors. She selected a Katy Perry track and went to work.

"How limited is the touching?" I asked.

"Hips and legs. An extra fifty to me gets you my ass too."

"Hair?"

"Stay off the hair. And my tits."

As she straddled my lap, I reached out for her hair and gently gripped it. As I suspected, it came partly away.

"Hey!" she said.

A wig. Attached to her real hair with metal grips. The grainy photo in Harry's file revealed her build and the shape of her nose. I'd taken a gamble here.

I said, "Lily, right?"

"Fuck you, prick." She climbed off and removed the wig entirely to reveal she was blond underneath. The boyish style gave her the pixie quality that Harry had described, although her Yorkshire accent had now developed a booming *ey-oop* timbre that really didn't suit her stature. "All I have to do is pull that chord and you'll be picking your teeth out of the alley."

The alarm was one of several strings made to look like sparkly decor.

I said, "I'll give you a hundred pounds if you tell me everything you were about to tell Harry before he got booted out."

"That hairy bastard? Get fucked. You know what they'll do to me?"

"Sarah's in trouble, you know?"

"I don't care. I *can't* care."

"You know she's not normal, don't you? Vulnerable. If she was put up to the theft, I need to know." I made my best *I'm desperate* face. "Please."

She stared at me.

I said, "No one will ever know. I won't note your name anywhere, or indicate where I got the intel. Not even that you were a friend." I saw that hit a nerve. "You *are* her friend, aren't you?"

"Two hundred," she said.

"One-sixty. That's all I have on me."

I took out my wallet and showed her eight twenty-pound notes. She snatched them, stashed them in her shoe, then took off her nightie and threw it in my face.

I said, "There's no need for that."

"Last time someone saw me chatting to a detective, I got proper threatened. If anyone comes in now, it needs to look like business."

In her underwear, she leaned forward, rolling her shoulders, her cleavage at my eye level. I couldn't pry myself away as I listened.

"Sarah, she was, like, this 'Rain Man' type. Rain *Girl*, or something. Memorizing the order of a deck of cards, or she could look

33

out over the bar for five seconds, and tell us how many people were in there. Crazy."

"Did you get on?"

"As well as any of them. Listen, love, I know you don't want this, but we've been here a while."

She unhooked her bra, slid it off, and I looked to the side as she straddled me again. I hadn't been with a woman in over a year, so a pretty dancer in nothing but panties meant the reason I crossed my legs was painfully obvious. She leaned in so close that my breath radiated back off her soft, tanned flesh.

I said, "What wasn't my colleague told?"

She writhed, taking pleasure in my discomfort. "One of them tricks. Sarah would hear the clicks of the safe and memorize them. She showed some of us girls one day as a joke, and the head security guy, this midget prick called Mikey, he made 'em change the combination and banned Sarah from going near it. When Gareth started banging Sarah, he must have convinced her to show him again."

I held her hips to stop her gyrating. "Wait. Who's Gareth?"

"Get off me. Now." I let go and she resumed her dance. She said, "Gareth Delingpole. Doorman here at the Sleaze. Started seeing her after she moved into his spare room."

"He was her landlord too?"

"Yeah, she rented a room in his house up in Birstall. Big terraced place, you know, four bedrooms, a cellar."

The house Harry found. Now empty, the utilities disconnected.

I said, "You think Gareth put Sarah up to it?"

"Of course. Sarah didn't do nothing bad, ever. That's why we thought it was odd, y'know, her ending up with him."

"Why odd?"

"Well, she's so nice and Gareth … he's got a reputation, okay? Jealous type. Heard he used to slap his wife around. Someone said he went to jail for it."

She performed a pirouette and paused in a commanding, hands-on-hips pose for a bridge in the music.

"Gareth brought a camera to work one morning, some new hobby, and, I dunno, we heard shouting. Guessed Gareth'd been takin' pictures of the girls or something. When we came out from getting changed, Curtis had Gareth's camera and took out that card thing that stores the photos."

"The SD card," I said.

When the singing resumed, so did she. "Right, that. Curtis threatened to fire him if he did it again. Gareth knew we saw what happened. And you could tell ... you could *tell* he wanted to hurt Curtis."

Embarrassed in front of a roomful of women. Could have been a trigger for revenge. I thought about the SD card Benson confiscated. If there was anything incriminating on there, it would have been destroyed, surely.

I said, "Money was stolen, but no one really knows how much."

"Reckon they got about two hundred grand, maybe two-fifty." With her back to me, she hooked her thumbs into her panties. "But we all know Curtis likes his shady deals, so it coulda been a million for all the tax man knows."

"I assume that Gareth isn't around anymore?"

"Nah." Her panties came down, then off entirely, twirling them round her finger before flinging them into a corner. "He disappeared the same night as Sarah."

The file specifically mentioned that no one else but Sarah was reportedly missing from the city, no one who could be connected to her, anyway. Her landlord, boyfriend, work colleague; Gareth was connected alright. And yet still the police hadn't made a move. I couldn't keep it all straight, partly thanks to Lily.

Still dancing, she said, "When they found out, Mikey summoned Curtis on the phone. Curtis came in, we all saw him. Shitting his pants, he was." The song ended. She stopped moving and sat on my lap. "So that's it. Some cash went missing, and the insurance is dealing with it. That's what the girls were told to say if anyone came asking questions. We shouldn't mention that Sarah and Gareth were in it together, or else."

A second high-tempo track boomed out and she shifted her weight side-to-side. I moved my thigh to hide my physical reaction.

She said, "You really don't like this, do you?"

"I really *do* like it," I said. "That's the problem."

"Wife?"

"Morals."

"Nature trumps morals, Mister… what's your name?"

The music died and a man's voice said, "Adam Park."

The door was open, revealing a short bald man, flanked by two bouncers with black goatees and leather jackets. *Goons,* as Harry would call them. The pair looked almost like twins, but one was in his forties, the other his twenties.

Lily said, "I'm busy, Mikey."

"We know," said the little man—Mikey, I assumed. He was about fifty, his face as craggy as granite and his t-shirt gave away not an ounce of flab. He was so short, I could easily have rested my chin on his smooth, dull pate.

Without a signal, the two men advanced and Lily scurried to one side, and my penis shrank to the size of a vole.

"Hi." I rose to my feet as four hands gripped my arms. "Is there a problem?"

"Might be," Mikey said. "Lily, what have you and Mr. Park been discussing?"

"Nothing?" she said.

Mikey took another step toward me. "Care to raise her on that, Mr. Park? Nothing?"

I said, "The booths are bugged, aren't they?"

THE DEAD AND THE MISSING

Mikey smiled. "It'll be easier if you just tell us."

I nodded to myself. "But you can't hear much above the music. Otherwise you'd be in here a lot quicker."

"Bob and Daz are gonna take you to see Mr. Benson."

I glanced at Bob and Daz. Cock-sure grins. Hands clasped, chests puffed. I wondered if I really was on my way to see Curtis Benson or if I was simply being removed to a place where they would brutally incentivize me to stay away.

Like most people, I watched the Jason Bourne films a while ago, and as much as I'd love to be able to take down my opponents with a quick flurry and leave them with nothing but a headache, the Bob/Daz twins were bigger than me, steroid-enhanced if I wasn't mistaken, and—trust me—punching a guy in the head often hurts the punch*er* more than a solid punch*ee*.

Still, I had to do something. I was not *prey*. I would never be prey again.

I launched my foot toward one of their knees—Bob, the older one. The crack was hard but didn't dislocate the joint, just hurting him enough to loosen his grip. I levered him around and shoved him into Mikey.

Lily pressed herself into the corner, screaming at the top of her lungs.

I spun to Daz and grasped his elbow, and shoved it toward his eye. His fingers opened. I threw my palm into his windpipe and crashed an elbow through his jaw. He went down; classic glass jaw, as so many of these pumped-up meat-heads proved.

They'd both be fine. In about five days.

Mikey threw Bob off him and prepared to fight me, but I raised my hands and said, "I give in."

Lily's screams deflated to a whimper, nightie held against her body.

I winked at Lily, and to Mikey I said, "Take me to your leader."

Chapter Four

It was always a shock, this violence. An evolutionary reaction that, in some people, comes naturally; in others it's a struggle to summon that willpower. Having once been beaten to a pulp in a foreign land, I learned that lesson more thoroughly than most ever will, an experience that would give the most ardent pacifist the impetus to really learn how to fight, to build up the strength required. I was a prime example of that.

The year I returned home from Thailand, I joined an athletics meet for the cardio, a meat-head gym for strength, and a Krav Maga club to learn the bastard-tough martial art used by Mossad. To my mother's dismay, I even sculpted my appearance to that of how I thought a "hard-man" should look: I allowed my over-active beard to grow out and clipped it into a goatee, shaved off my hair, and snapped a stud into one ear, and between the martial arts, athletics, and the meat-head gym, I was ready to face anything this evil world could throw at me. At the peak of my training, I prepared to hit the road again, launch myself back out into the world, and track down the Bangkok thugs who had hurt me so badly. My rebirth would have been complete. Then, a few days before I was due to fly out, the owner of the meat-head gym learned his fourteen-year-old daughter had run away to London with a detailed and well-thought-out plan:

To, like, become a singer?
And marry a footballer?

Because I was unfamiliar with the process in the UK, I called private detective Harry Riley, my late father's old mate. We located Darla physically unharmed, and although extracting her was something of a chore, it was a chore that enabled me to beat the living shit out of some would-be pimp's enforcer, a bruiser who would have destroyed me a year earlier. It confirmed that my efforts had borne fruit, but the act of breaking another human being had an unexpected effect on me: I felt truly sick. The blood, the twisted limbs, the pleading with me to stop …

The only outcome that left me remotely happy was freeing that girl from the mini-harem into which she'd been inducted, and so—with all thoughts of revenge shelved—Harry allowed me to come work with him. On one condition: I forget all about violent fantasies and use my brain instead. I agreed, and he made me shave my goatee and grow out my hair and remove the stud from my ear, ostensibly to make me less conspicuous when tailing someone, but also—he said—because I looked like a dick head.

Still, today, Daz and Bob had no doubt broken a few bones in their time, so I tried not to feel too guilty about using them as psychological leverage.

My pondering ended at a steel door as Mikey knocked and opened it. He held out his arm as an invitation and I adopted a manner that suggested I didn't give a crap what happened next, like this was routine. I kept the word "glib" in mind. I liked glib. Glib helped establish authority, even though it usually made the glib person unlikable. It could, however, rile up the wrong adversary, so I also kept in mind to not push my luck.

Inside, from the middle of a glorified storeroom, a desk and a leather chair greeted me, plus a couple of seats slightly less inviting than those in a trucker's cafe. I noted the exits—only the one I came through—potential weapons—boxes of beer bottles, those two chairs—and human threats—only one: Curtis Benson.

In a purple suit, black shirt and close-cropped dyed-blond hair (yep, on a black guy), he could have been an attention-seeking Premier League footballer on a night out.

Mikey stepped outside and closed the door.

With heavy eyelids, an expression that hovered somewhere between anger and boredom, Benson said, "Fucked up two of my men." He had no discernible accent, just a low voice that sounded similar to how rappers talk during interviews. How things turned next would depend on how much of his "gangsta" act was for show.

"Your 'men'?" I said, repeating the *keep it glib* mantra to myself. "What are you, a James Bond baddie?"

He scowled.

I said, "I mean a Roger Moore James Bond baddie, not Daniel Craig. Who has 'men' these days? Apart from royalty?"

"You think this is some sorta open mic comedy night?"

I sat on a plastic chair. Smiled. "And that's your best comeback is it?"

"You're overconfident," Benson said. "You got any idea how much shit you in right now?"

"You saw what I did to your, heh, 'men' back there. That's nothing. My own people know where I am, and they do not take kindly to small-time gangsta-wannabes beating up on their boss."

"Your … 'people'?"

"My people."

"If I'm a James Bond baddie, guess that makes you Moses."

"Now *that's* a better comeback," I said.

"I'm ek-*static* you approve. But you really are misinformed about the dynamic of this situation. You think I'm some gangsta-punk-wannabe, and you say you got some badass people backing you up. If that was true, I'd be impressed and you'd be walkin' outa here in about thirty seconds. But let's talk about your … 'people'. These would be…" He lifted an iPad from his desk, tapped a couple of icons. "Park Avenue Investigations, right? Those the people you mean?"

Did you see what I did there? Adam … *"Park"* … plus *"Avenue."* Known as *PAI* to those in the business, it was basically a play on words whilst sounding prestigious to clients from all over the world. *Park Avenue.* Cool, huh?

"That's right," I said.

"The same people consulting with Herman Yorrick Solicitors on how to *delete* you from the board. How to *dissolve* your majority interest an' kick you the fuck out on the street? *Those* your 'people'?"

He handed me the iPad and let me whizz through a couple of screens. Emails, contracts with Roger Gorman's signature, counter-signed by Sylvia Thorne, Gorman's right-hand pit-bull. They dated back a couple of months. Clearly, Roger wasn't satisfied with taking over the running of *my* business. He wanted me gone completely. Herman Yorrick specialized in negotiating people out of contracts that were otherwise cast-iron, and had consulted psychiatrists about my "erratic behavior." I was the person with legal responsibility over my shareholders' cash and I'd spent two years surfing, snowboarding and skydiving around the country. If proven mentally incompetent, Roger Gorman could, eventually, force me to sell my shares at current market value. So far, the responses from three psychiatrists insisted upon a full consult with me in person before passing judgment. They were waiting on a fourth psychiatrist. An email between Herman Yorrick himself and Roger Gorman suggested it would be fourth-time-lucky if some form of "bonus" were awarded for "a speedy turnaround." I'm pretty sure I knew what that meant.

I handed the iPad back to Benson.

"So," he said, "you still think they're gonna back you up with ninjas or some shit?"

"The chairman wants me out," I said, "but that doesn't mean my staff won't follow my instructions."

He dabbed the screen and showed me more emails. I didn't read them, so he narrated.

"You got a meetin' with the head honcho today, so I'm guessin' that's to get help locatin' my li'l burglar girl."

"How the hell…?"

"Because I ain't who you think I am, you *dick*. I got *resources*. I got connections can get me CCTV from places the cops need a warrant for. I got hackers can bust through your state-of-the-art firewalls in a couple a' hours, and I got people who'll fuck you up *prison*-style and dump you in the canal for fun—won't even want payin'. You think those minimum wage fuck-heads were all I gotta offer?"

"I suppose not."

"Now…" He calmed himself and steepled his fingers under his chin. "I could break you in half and leave your pieces in a park to traumatize some kids or dog-walker. That's what I *was* gonna do soon as Mikey clocked you comin' in the front door. Thing is, I like solutions. I'm a lateral thinker. *Businessman.* For real." He leaned forward on his desk, so his eyes looked out from under his brow. "So I got a proposal. My sources supplied me with pictures of my li'l burglar girl at Leeds-Bradford airport holdin' hands with that fuck of a bouncer. Headin' to Paris. Romantic fucks."

"And you're sharing this with me because…?"

For a moment I thought he was going to look away. For that same moment, I detected a weakness, a crack in his façade. He was taking a big risk with what came next.

He said, "We got a few internal issues right now, and since you in a shit-heap a' trouble … *you* are gonna work for *me*."

I forced a neutral expression.

He said, "I want Sarah found, I want Gareth found, I want my money, and—"

"I meant to ask, there's some speculation about the actual amount—"

He threw the iPad at the wall, smashing it to pieces. "DO NOT INTERRUPT ME AGAIN!"

I shut my mouth and sat completely still.

He continued as if the tantrum never occurred. "I want Sarah and Gareth found, I want my money found, and I want you to bring them all to me within one week of you leaving this office."

"You can't expect me to—"

"A week. That's seven days, and I'm bein' generous. Folk down in Paris with fingers in a lotta pastries, they can't find her. And I know these guys are thorough. Lord of the fuckin' underworld's helpin' me out."

"Lord of the—"

"I got the trains covered, I got the planes covered. Watchin' CCTV in both places for weeks. *Very* reliable. Car rental and police reports too. Can't cross the border on her fake passport, 'cause silly bitches used the same guy some of my less … official dancers." I thought he was going to chuckle like a proper villain but he didn't. "Now she's called Thandy Gallway. Gareth became Mark Gallway. So if they ain't in Paris, they're walkin' around France on foot."

"Or on coaches, or hitchhiking or maybe they slipped past your people."

"Nobody slips past my people."

"France is huge. You think I can—"

"It's what you *do*, detective-man. You track folks anywhere they go. Logic plus technology. Sherlock fuckin' Holmes in board shorts."

I needed time to think. Questions are always good. Questions that poke or stoke the ego are best. "You're well-connected enough to get into airport security…"

He nodded, satisfied.

"Why do you need some lowly investigator like me?"

After a pause, he said, "Our people're gettin' watched. Lotta chatter lately. Law closin' down a lotta places. Not mine, but friends a' mine."

"With the same side line in exploiting desperate women? Twenty-first century slavers?"

He pressed his lips together, holding in another outburst. "Those girls pay off their debt a lot quicker through me, through the wages I *pay* them, than the ugly hags pickin' fruit out in some farmer's field."

"You're doing a public service."

"Damn right," he said. "A service that's none of your fuckin' business."

"Gareth sourced his and Sarah's passports through *your* broker. They'd get new ones in Paris."

"No forger does work there without my guy knowin' who they are, and we got 'em all tapped."

I shook my head. "No one—especially some criminal—*no one* holds complete power over a city, no matter how much they think they do."

"Not complete," Benson admitted. "But the top dogs know the top freelancers. Forgers ain't common these days. It's a specialty. Understand? They ain't tapped up *no one* who can get 'em outta that country. You know I'm tellin' the truth. That's why I'm puttin' you on this case instead of that Gruffalo-lookin' guy."

I didn't know what a "Gruffalo" was, but I guessed it was big and hairy. I said, "They're guilty of a theft. Why get the police to blackout an investigation?"

"I told you already, we got law movin' in on some of our smaller operations. Somethin's leakin', and I ain't taking the chance it'll lead to me." Benson took an A4 envelope from his desk drawer and slid it to me. "And before you think of it, you go near the fuckin' Foreign Office, and bad things will happen."

I removed two photos. One was taken at Harry's house through a window while he and Jayne dined on a Chinese takeaway. The other was of me leaving my apartment on my way here.

"We been watchin' Harry, makin' sure he don't come back round here. Didn't want him stumblin' across Sarah and my money and doin' somethin' legit with it. Then you show up in town, so we gotta look into you too. Pretty tight with these old folks, huh?"

A couple of hours, maybe a couple of days if he intercepted Harry's planning with Caroline, but that's all it took him to acquire free reign inside Park Avenue Investigations, as well as digging up chunks of my personal history.

I said, "If your insurance paid out, how come you're so desperate to get Sarah back?"

"Look at me, Mr. Park. *Look* at me."

I looked at him. He clearly knew the silence made me want to speak, to fill the gap. An old interrogator's trick, neat and effective when your quarry isn't aware of it.

Finally, he said, "You're an investigator. Tell me. Am I the sort of prick who lets people get away with shit like that?" He didn't need an answer. "You gonna find Mr. and Mrs. Gallway, and you gonna find my money, and anythin' else in their possession, and you will bring it all to me by next Friday. Let's be all dramatic and say ... *midnight*."

"Anything else in their possession," I said.

The camera.

The SD card.

Benson and Gareth arguing.

If they even hung onto it.

I said, "Let's talk about that."

"No, let's not, you clever fuck. You still think you got a choice? Let's try somethin' else. *Mikey!*"

The steel door opened. Lily stood there, stiff and pale, her skin patchy, her physique now that of a sparrow. Red marks curled round both arms where she'd been held too firmly. Someone shoved her from behind. She stumbled in and fell to her knees, then crumpled onto her front, as if awaiting a further blow. After a beat, she sobbed. She was in her baby doll nightie, her underwear not yet replaced.

"Oh, come on," I said. "You're really doing this?"

Mikey closed the door and placed his hand on the top of her head. Made her look up at me through tear-streaked mascara.

Benson said, "We'll swap her for the money, and for Sarah and Gareth. You fail, she dies—badly—and your pal Harry will be implicated. And it *will* stick."

At some point, I'd got to my feet. Balled my fists too, some primitive hangover in the genes.

I said, "Let her go."

"Let who go?" Mikey swung his boot into her back and she yelped like a dog. "Her?"

A jolt of fiery sickness spiked through me. I threw a chair and followed it in, but Mikey stepped away from my kick at his knee. I feigned a throat-grab so he'd focus on that, but he shimmied aside, grabbed my wrist, and used my momentum to swing me onto my back.

He let me up and I switched disciplines and blazed into him with flurry of knees and elbows, most of which he blocked with ease, or shrugged off like I'd never even hit him.

"Mikey," Benson said. "This ain't a disco."

Mikey thrust a tight fist into the base of my sternum. It blew all the air out of my diaphragm and it felt like my heart had burst.

Unable to breathe, I dropped to the floor and readied myself for what would surely be a serious beating. But it didn't come.

Benson knelt next to Lily and helped her up into the chair I threw. "Sorry, Lily, but talk to fuckos like him and look what happens."

She sniffed and nodded.

Benson seemed almost tender as he stroked her knee. "Mr. Park here is forcing me to do things I don't wanna. But don't worry. We'll get you some clothes, patch you up. You go home, you wait. We'll come by, see how you are, we'll treat you good. Until next Friday. If Mr. Park don't come back with what I want, I'm sorry, but…" Benson's hand crept higher up Lily's leg, the inside of her thigh.

"Okay," I said, which hurt to say.

"Okay?" Benson said.

I managed, "I'll do it."

"You hear that, Lily? He'll do it. Now what do you say to Mr. Park?"

Her voice cracked, barely audible. "Th- thank you…"

Benson stood beside Mikey, both looking down on me. Benson pointed to the door. "Now get the fuck out, and go do your job."

Chapter Five

I'm not sure how I got out onto the street. There were corridors. There was the flesh-and-neon-orange blur of Blazing Seas and the curious faces of the dancers as a couple of new disposable security guys "encouraged" me toward the exit. I sat in a bus shelter a few meters up the road and tried to coax my breathing back to its regular rhythm.

When I did finally negotiate the winding streets past office buildings and coffee shops and fashion boutiques, and into the lobby of Park Avenue Investigations, it was like tension physically dissolving around me. We occupied the top floor of a ten-story office block five minutes' walk from my apartment, and as the lift doors clunked shut behind me, I was suddenly … *safe*. I hadn't registered feeling *un*safe before, but that trembling in my legs ended, and although my hands still shook, it was with less intensity, and all that remained was an ache in my stomach and chest.

When I last checked there were forty-two employees, eight board members—of which I was one—and a healthy bank balance. Now, the clinically-white lobby had seen an art-deco refurbishment and photo portraits adorned one wall displaying *ten* board members, but that was a little deceptive since I wasn't among them. Roger Gorman's photo was larger than the others by a good six inches and positioned above them, creating a swish-looking organizational chart.

My pass granted me access before the receptionist saw me, so I slinked off into the marble-laden gents and unbuttoned my shirt to examine my torso in the bathroom mirror. A bruise had already bloomed into a dirty purple smudge.

My training had been disciplined, and that supposedly made *me* disciplined, and it had made me the favorite in rare violent scenarios even when I was out-muscled. Mikey was utterly controlled, though. Never on the back foot. I went at him with Krav Maga, and with a Muay Thai assault furious enough to down a horse, and he waved me off like I was a snappy Yorkshire terrier. I'd pegged him as bodyguard to a small-time crook with big ambitions, and so underestimated both him and his boss.

Clearly, Gareth Delingpole had too.

I tidied myself up and returned to the lobby, but as I was about to announce myself to the receptionist, Roger Gorman blew in through a pair of frosted-glass doors. Although he appeared tanned in the photo, his skin color in real-life was close to mahogany, and when he grinned the falsest grin in the world, I wasn't sure whether it was a trick of the light or if his white teeth *actually* glowed.

"Adam!" He extended one hand and shook mine vigorously, while his other slapped my shoulder.

"Roger," I said. "Good to see you."

We stood in silence until Roger let out a short, nervous guff of laughter and swung his arm to the side. "Right this way."

The man trying to certify me mentally incompetent led me into the heart of my former empire, teeth front and center all the way. The corridors hadn't seen the extensive renovation of the outer shell, but they'd received a lick or two of paint, and some of the artwork had been upgraded from poncy to downright ugly.

Passing the accounts section, he said, "It's all in good hands, Adam. Thirteen percent spike on last year."

"Thirteen percent spike in what? Profit, or the number of people your clients' products have murdered?"

Another guff of laughter from Roger, then, "Always one with a joke, Adam."

"Always," I said.

Once we were past the gopher cubicles, his smile dropped. "And they're *our* clients. Mine *and* yours. They don't have to be, though."

When I didn't reply, Roger reinstated his lite-brite rigor smile and led me around a corner to where the carpets were deeper, and into a large room that could have been a conference space but, with the Rolls-Royce-sized desk and tall chair, I guessed it was Roger's new office. A rug featuring some oriental design spanned three-quarters of the floor, featuring dotted indentations to suggest the room was, indeed, occasionally used for meetings. The nearest wall doubled as a cupboard and grooves along the ceiling indicated something could slide out, most likely tables, with the chairs currently hidden alongside.

"Been a while," he said as he gestured to the slightly lower seat opposite his. When not entertaining a high-powered get-together, Gorman would enjoy an uninterrupted floor-to-ceiling view of Leeds, and for miles up the River Aire.

I took up position facing the window, hands clasped behind my back. "I need access to the Deep Detect System."

He joined me, talking to my reflection. "DDS? The software you called evil?"

"The software I designed and still own."

"Actually, Adam, the company owns it."

"Still keep it all on site?"

"I'm hardly going to trust possession of such a thing to an outside company, am I?"

When Gorman ousted me, one of the first things he did was dissolve all our cloud backup accounts to bring them in-house.

Separate servers, independent power and generator fail-safes, with a state-of-the-art CO_2 fire-extinguisher system in place of water. Nothing left to chance in the paranoia of a guilty man.

I said, "If it's on site, it shouldn't take too long to sign me in."

"You know our rates," he said. "If you have a client, sign them up."

"She can't afford your rates."

He turned from the reflection and faced me properly. "*Our* rates," he said.

"I'll send you the details when I have them." I concentrated on the view, dulled through the tinted glass. "I expect the results within—"

"No."

"No?"

"No," he said. "The software is the property of Park Avenue Investigations. Park Avenue Investigations has shareholders. DDS costs a lot of money to run." He leaned closer until I faced him. "If it's so important, how come *you* don't stump up the cash? Not given it all to some Oopma-Loompa tribe, have you?"

"Really?" I said. "Oopma-Loompas? That's a new low, Roger, even for you."

He shuffled uncomfortably. I expected my presence was keeping him from some meeting or phone call or eating another baby.

"Adam," he said, "do we have to go through this sermon again? It was pretentious hippie nonsense two years ago and it's pretentious hippie nonsense now. I don't force the world to be like this. I just happen to make money from *living* in that world." He gestured toward the door. "Now why don't you go back to Um-Bongo-Land or wherever you've been?"

I unclasped my hands and placed them in my pockets. "If I pay to use DDS, the money goes back into the company and it gets used for more death and more corruption and—"

"Damn it, Adam!" He strode to his desk and retrieved a thin

sheaf of papers, a prop he no doubt prepped when I announced my visit. "You are not running this company. I have the executive mandate. *I* control DDS."

"You have executive control," I said, "but I still know every pissy secret about this company. And you know my pretentious hippie nonsense doesn't prevent me from burning this place to the ground if I have to."

Gorman glared. "You couldn't do the jail-time. Way too pretty."

"I could be out of the country and in the wind an hour after leaving this building. Don't forget I'm also privy to the 'special services' you provided for the Collinson Armory Corporation. And don't get me started on conspiracy to bribe some dodgy psychiatrist."

He held himself as if about to assault me, but the pudgy old fart wasn't stupid.

"Yeah," I said, suddenly deeply grateful to the criminal forcing me to work for him. "I have evidence of your plans on that front. So don't even think about trying it."

He slowly paced back to his desk and dropped what he thought had been his trump card in a drawer. "When did you get to be so *bloody* sanctimonious?"

Better a sanctimonious know-it-all than a ... shit.

I argued frequently with friends about my views on various subjects. One minute I was a naïve, pompous lefty, the next an over-simplified blood-and-thunder rightist; I simply saw myself as a guy who liked to do the right thing.

I said, "I built this company as a means to find people who needed finding. DDS might be illegal, but when used correctly it—"

"And blackmail? Can you really not see your own hypocrisy?"

I finally took the seat and relaxed into it. "Blackmail's actually pretty cool when it's done for the right reasons."

As he settled into his own chair, his oddly-tuned brain worked behind that mahogany mask he called a face. "Fine, Adam. What's the deal?"

"I'll be treated like a freelancer, operating under the legal privilege which—I'm assuming here—but you being a lawyer and all, we still have that confidentiality clause?"

"You assume correctly."

"I'll work to PAI rules, which will ensure I'm not in breach of my non-compete clause, but will also furnish me with all the legal clout PAI commands. I'll feed DDS as soon as I have the details."

I stood and allowed the chair to slide back messily to the side. A little childish, but what the fuck. Who didn't enjoy messing with pricks like Roger Gorman?

After leaving the office, I wandered down to the Tech-Hive, a pocket of the building housing thousands of terabytes of data and software on banks of bespoke servers. Here, Jessica Denvers sat cross-legged on a tall stool, watching the door as I entered. Surrounded by the organized chaos of tablet computers, audio and video bugs, phones and assorted surveillance hardware that made up her lab, she was already holding out a smart-phone.

She said, "I figured if you blind-copied me in on an email to Roger Gorman that you'd be coming back to work. Here. You'll no-doubt need this." It was about five inches, far bigger than phones had been two years ago. "The latest operating system," she added in something of a monotone. "Syncs with the PAI mainframe. The 'Family Moments' tile is the link to DDS. Four-G network, naturally."

"Naturally," I said. "That's a lot of initials."

"Pay attention, Double-oh-Seven."

A hint of the humor I remembered.

"I always pay attention," I said. "You've changed your hair."

"About eight times since you last saw me."

She was currently rocking a platinum-blond look with a purple streak, held back in a glittery Alice-band. It shouldn't really have worked on her honey-colored skin, a mix of her white-British and Jamaican parentage, but her hair possessed more Caucasian genes than African, so it was easier to style.

She said, "The link takes you to a video website similar to You Tube or Vimeo. Tap on the 'About Us' option and hold for three seconds. This links to the DDS live section where you input your target's details. If you have something in front of you like a credit card, just snap a photo. It's a fifty mega-pixel camera."

"You've improved the interface."

"Even more times than my hair."

I played with the tiles, zipping them around, until I noticed Jess hadn't moved. "You okay?"

"Am I okay?" she said. "Am I okay with being dumped in this hole? Am I okay with Gormless Gorman firing three-quarters of my staff, doubling my workload and not giving me a pay rise for two years? Or am I okay with a guy I thought was my friend as well as my boss upping sticks and fucking off to God-knows-where without even a goodbye text?"

Harry often teased that Jess had something of a crush on me, but I didn't believe it. She was dedicated and brilliant and ten years my junior, which wouldn't be so bad, but she was the sort of person who alphabetized her CD collection, while I preferred to store them by color, starting with white at the left, building up through the spectrum to black on the right (yes, some of us still have CDs). Besides, a guy like me simply wouldn't be good for her.

Unwilling to reveal my gentlemanly thoughts, I tried glib again: "Are they my only options?"

"Do you need anything else?"

"Your number and twenty-four-seven access to your brain."

She took off her glasses and pointed with them. "You, sir, are pushing your bloody luck." She turned to her pile of junk and picked up what looked like an iPad but was nothing to do with Apple.

"It's a girl," I said. "Missing four weeks. An outside chance of kidnapping."

I recruited Jess straight out of uni, back when Park Avenue Investigations was still just me and a personal assistant. Her savant-like work with technology—both operating and developing it—was instrumental in expanding my business, and while we were doing "good" work she was happy. But, like me, she had misgivings about corporate espionage and supporting firms who exploited child soldiers. I convinced her to stay on with a promise that I'd get us away from those people.

I said, "The police aren't investigating and someone is covering up Sarah's movements." I stood closer to her. "I need your help, Jess." Then I ladled on some Hollywood cheese: "*She* needs your help."

Jess put down the not-an-iPad. "While I was waiting for you to come back and fight it out, Gorman made all us specialists sign non-compete clauses, like yours. I can't quit, and I blame you entirely."

"Sounds familiar." I nodded. "But alright. Help me with this case, and when it's over … you're fired."

"Thank you," she said.

Eager to get started, I hurried to the lobby and hit the elevator's down button. The receptionist said, "Mr. Park? There's a man here to see you. Says he's your dad?"

A man in rich-guy-casual clothes stood up from the sofa. "Step-dad," he said.

Stuart Fitzpatrick. Also known—by me, anyway—as "Sleazy Stu."

"Adam," he said. "I heard you were back in town."

"Well," I said, "you can fuck right off," and strode towards the stairs.

Chapter Six

My *actual* father had been a plumber of generous girth and massive heart, a heart my mother loved so much that even when Sleazy Stuart Fitzpatrick tempted her with an extra-marital affair, she still could not bring herself to leave him, or our terraced house in a street where we strung washing across the road to the home opposite, and where one family's Union flag spanned the length of their property, emblazoned with "Leeds Utd AFC." These patriots, though, not only did they refer to it incorrectly as a "Union Jack," but they rigged it upside-down, and no one dared correct them on either mistake. We lived without the trappings that made my school-friends' lives complete; no games-console or flashy sound system or holiday in Greece. Perhaps it is because of their marriage's near-miss that I never resented doing chores for pocket money. In fact, when it was time to clean the caravan, Dad and I laughed and splashed one another and generally treated it like a family excursion. Sometimes, I was even allowed to use the hose. He always promised we'd spend a whole summer in the caravan someday, not just here, but in France, maybe all the way to exotic Spain, if our fifteen-year-old Volvo would hold up.

However, a fortnight before my seventeenth birthday, while repairing the TV cabinet for the umpteenth time, Dad collapsed, having suffered a massive heart attack. He died before my mother even picked up the phone.

After a couple of months of scraping together enough money to eat and get me to school, Stuart Fitzpatrick came back a-calling. He swept my mother straight off her feet and into a four-bedroomed house in the sort of area where if you left a sofa in your front garden, the neighbors would call the police rather than waiting for a family of rats to move in, compelling the council to shift it on bin-day. My mother told me to be grateful.

"No more compromises," she said.

For her sake, I tried. I really did. In fact, the fortnight Stu took us sailing on Lake Como and taught the seventeen-year-old me how to pilot a powerboat, it gave me such a charge, I almost forgot to hate him. Almost. Our shared time behind the wheel of a throbbing water-bound rocket probably informed my only long-term love—adrenaline—but to this day, even as I fled his presence in the office I built from scratch, I could feel nothing around him, except the urge to turn my back and take myself somewhere else.

The two floors directly below Park Avenue Investigations had, for many years, been occupied by recruitment consultants, but these had now closed and the properties were being renovated. The constant drilling and banging would annoy the crap out of the other residents but you wouldn't hear anything on my floor due to the insulation that Roger Gorman insisted upon. Today, the only sounds emanating from the sites were the wind blowing through the empty space and the snapping of plastic sheeting used to protect the building's shell from the British weather.

I emerged into strong sunlight, stretched my arms to tease the bruise in a pleasantly-painful way, and I slowly became aware of something not quite right. This area attracted people with Porsches and Aston Martins, sometimes the odd Jag, but rarely did an old Ford Mondeo show up in the lot. From a couple of hundred yards away, the blue car's driver was indistinct, but I swear he was looking straight at me. I wondered about Benson's surveillance, about whether he would be so blatant.

Then I forgot about him, concerned only with the man who'd just caught up.

We walked, Stuart and I. The office complex was built in a crescent, backing onto the Leeds-Liverpool Canal, and we seemed to be heading that way. I knew exactly why, so I texted Harry to inform him of the change in venue for our chat.

We passed under the archway at the back of the crescent and over a small iron footbridge to the towpath, and we strolled some more until we entered a residential area, a gated community of barges with fun-tastic names like *Dun-Roamin-Gone-Boatin'*, *Home-from-Home*, and my personal tragi-favorite *Bat-Boat*, owned by a bachelor aged forty-four who lived there permanently and, yes, had painted it in the Adam West-era Batman colors, with added "Splash" and "Whoosh" decals.

After a while, Stuart said, "It's not even that valuable."

"So you keep telling me," I said.

"I'll do her up, get her back to the standard your mother maintained."

"I know."

"Would your mother really approve?"

"She didn't consult me when she married you."

Wow, could I sound any more like a stroppy teenager?

It was close to four years now since my mother was struck by a boat whilst swimming off Stuart's yacht on Lake Como, an accident no one could have avoided except, perhaps, the inexperienced helmsman who didn't see her, or even my mother herself if she'd heeded Stuart's warning to not venture out too far. I may have hated Stu's smarmy guts for taking advantage of a widow's grief, but I didn't blame him for her death ... even if *he* did.

We'd come upon the *Miss Piggywiggy*, named after my mother's favorite childhood toy, a canal barge she bought herself with the sale of our house. Once emerald green with red stripes and black trim, now the paint was peeling and crusted, the windows caked with grime, and the body shuddered when you sneezed too close. It now set me back a few hundred a month in mooring fees.

I said, "Make your offer."

He nodded. "I'm seeing someone. She's called—"

"I can't believe you haven't twigged to the fact that you actually mean nothing to me. Just make your offer. Then fuck off."

"A hundred and fifty thousand," he said. "Straight cash. No conditions."

One hundred and fifty thousand pounds for a barge worth more to the council on Bonfire Night than as a functioning vessel.

No more compromises, she'd told me. Damn right.

I said, "No deal."

"Fine," he said, and held out his hand for me.

I had never shaken it, but he always held it there for a few seconds longer than someone with real dignity ever would. He withdrew it and walked slowly away, leaving me alone with my mother's boat, and something of a headache, reminding me how early I rose that morning, of the lunchtime beer, and of how much caffeine I consumed to drag myself past two p.m. I wanted to get to work on finding Sarah Stiles, but now armed with the DDS software, I needed the information Harry was bringing me.

I boarded the *Miss Piggywiggy* and ducked into the galley. The barge creaked under my weight, and the air clawed, hot and musty. The whole furnished interior felt damp. I opened every window I could, and took a six-pack of mineral water from the deactivated fridge, only one of which was missing. The bottles were glass, so I had no worries about them being out of date. I downed one and felt marginally better, but with still no sign of Harry, I stepped into the bedroom where a mattress with no bedding waited.

The air was even more oppressive in this, the smaller space, much like a three-dollar-a-night room in a hot country. No window, no fan. You get used to it eventually; the humidity, the heat, the lack of breeze. Right there, lying down with my hands behind my head, the residue of Mikey's fist slowly lifting, I could have been back in Thailand or Columbia or perhaps some village in Senegal. Whatever I was thinking, whatever I was remembering, I floated down, gently, into a deep sleep.

Then I awoke almost immediately to a clattering noise. At least I thought it was immediately. I sat up. Assessed my surroundings. It was still light out. I checked the time: quarter to three. Just a power-nap. Whatever—I was on the barge and someone was banging about in the galley.

"Bloody hell, Adam. Where do you keep the milk?"

I opened the bedroom door.

Beard turning to grey and a rumpled manner that suggested he'd make a great tramp one day, Harry Riley had found the kettle and some cups and a jar of brown granules. He held up the jar, grinning like an idiot. "Coffee, sir?"

"Just water, thanks. That jar is at least four years old."

"You're such a bleedin' snob." Harry unscrewed the jar and sniffed. "Smells like coffee."

"Wow," I said. "The life of Riley. Glamorous. You should invite the queen for afternoon tea."

"If I'm havin' tea with the queen, she can stump up for a Starbucks." He held a mug under the tap, turned it on. A mass of brown sludge plopped out.

I picked up two of the glass bottles and handed one to Harry.

He opened his and sniffed it. "This ain't some expensive vintage is it? Cos I won't appreciate it."

I tossed my lid in the bin and downed half the bottle in one. When I breathed again, Harry had taken a sip and was now looking at me, fingers working around the bottle.

"Curtis Benson."

"Dodgy bloke," I said.

"I've done all the legwork as far as he's concerned. No need to go pokin' round there."

I rubbed my chest and when Harry clocked the movement I quickly dropped my hand.

He said, "Already been to see him then? Idiot."

This wasn't like Harry. I said, "They scared you, didn't they?"

"Not at first. But later, yeah. Got a phone call emphasizin' I weren't allowed in the club anymore, and blah blah blah, casually mention Jayne's name and where we live." He produced a Taser from his coat pocket, the sort you press against someone and hit a button, sending anywhere between one and ten-thousand volts through their body.

"Jayne know you have that?"

He put the weapon away. "Jayne's talkin' divorce just for sendin' Caroline to find you. Said I should let you stew 'til you're ready to come home, sort things out like a man."

"Is Jayne here?"

"You think she can't wait to welcome you home? Nah, she knows you're busy. Says if you need her help, ask. Otherwise, she'll see you when you bring Sarah back safe."

I dropped into an armchair. Dust erupted around me. I pretended I wasn't surprised. Harry lowered himself slowly into the one next to me.

I said, "She doesn't understand."

"No, and neither do I. Run into problems, so you abandon yer business and bugger off cowabunga-ing around the country. Very *cool, dude.*"

"Okay, fine, I'm a coward."

"You're anythin' but a coward, son." He pointed his bottle at my chest. "That's why you end up hurt more often than you would if you just bleedin' listened to me."

"The insurance," I said, hoping to change the subject. "Benson wouldn't talk about it. What isn't in the file?"

"Right." Harry sipped from the bottle like it was a wine sample. "I can't put me source in there in case it goes to court, but it's a solid mate. On the Monday morning, Curtis Benson filed an official complaint about one of his birds liftin' money from his safe. Crime number got issued. The investigation lasted one day, then got nixed from way up high. But no one interviewed Caroline. *No one*. The guy she spoke to was prob'ly one of Benson's goons. As for the actual police, the missing persons report on Sarah is a separate file. No one's lookin' into it. And no one's investigatin' the theft."

"Who can order a black-out like that?"

"My source ain't got clearance to probe deeper."

"But the insurance paid out."

"Because they got a *crime number*." Harry said this as if dealing with a remedial class. "Benson will have to repay any money he gets back, but stoppin' an investigation dead, it's heavy duty shit."

"That girl. Lily? I don't suppose you traced her home address? Surname? Anything?"

"Why? You already probed her didn't you?" He sipped his water with a "Carry-On" movie lift of the eyebrows.

"I got her in trouble."

"Jesus," Harry said. "I assume you don't mean you knocked her up already. How bad is it?"

"Provided I do as he says, Benson won't hurt her any further."

"Any further?"

"He'll kill her. Or he'll violate her." I drank from my bottle. Licked my lips. "Listen to me. *Violate*. Okay, I'll say the word: *rape*."

"Rape," Harry said.

Still a weapon in today's gang warfare, the tactic dated back to the beginning of conflict itself. The threat kept both men and women in line, and during the actual invasions, it was seen as a perk of the job. Sack a town, take what you want, do a bit of raping, drink some mead.

He said, "She's a stripper."

"So's Sarah. Is Lily worth any less?"

Harry ran a hand over his face. Rubbed his neck the way he did when he couldn't find the words, when he couldn't tell me what he thought I needed to hear.

"A man," I said. "He wants another man to do something for him. If the second man fails, the first man will take a young woman, hold her down, and force himself inside her. He will thrust and he will thrust. She will tear and she will bleed."

Harry closed his eyes, shook his head slowly. "You're gettin' into that zone again, Adam."

Yes, I was in "that zone." The zone where I latched onto some injustice in the world and could not rattle it free from my conscience. Some might call it a flaw.

"She could fight," I said, "but if she does they will hurt her even more. She will never, ever forget what happened to her. *That's* the reality."

"You're such a feminist."

I smiled, although it probably didn't look like a smile. Yes, I was one of "those" men. I'd heard us referred to by both sexist men and some hardline feminists as "white knights," a somewhat derogatory term to indicate that, while we were on the side of equality, we tended to dwell there out of guilt, or the sort of protective urge that came across as patronizing. Gorman labeled it "pretentious." Harry often called it "sanctimonious." I call it *commitment*. I didn't give such terminology a lot of thought, though.

"Don't take the piss, Harry. You're better than that. You know it's wrong that *date*-rape isn't straightforward *rape*. You know if a man punches his wife in the face and then hugs her and says, 'Oh, I'm so sorry, look what you made me do,' that's *domestic*-violence, while if I punch some random bloke in the pub, it's simply *violence* and carries a harsher sentence. This situation, here, now, it's a real girl. Under real threat from real blokes."

"I know. But you need to stay focused. Sarah is the priority. Bring her back, and Lily is fine."

"We don't know that."

"What you gonna do? Leap in like Batman? Disappear with her in a puff of bleedin' smoke? Maybe you could stash her in that idiot's *Bat-Boat* down the way."

And that was it. Sometimes it took a fella from another generation to show me how dumb I was being. I stood by the morality behind my case, though, despite the fact Lily's best chance was for me to locate Sarah.

I finished my water. "Okay, lecture over. But you have to tell me what's special about this case."

"Nothing," he said. "I need that magic computer tool thingy of yours to show us where she is."

"Bollocks."

He studied me a second. "Alright. It's a case you used to jump right into. Girl missing, people bullshittin' us. Plus…" He smiled as if he'd been caught out at something. "Maybe it'll do you good. Get back to yer roots. Put this corporate shit behind you. Rucksack on yer back, dirt under yer nails, cockroaches in yer sandwiches."

Of course. *That corporate shit.*

He said, "I feel bad for Lily. I do. But the best way to help her is keep yer eye on the prize. We'll make sure Benson keeps his word." He flashed me his Taser again.

"You have Sarah's financials? My magic computer tool thingy should snag a couple of leads you couldn't access."

"I assume I shouldn't ask how it works?"

"Doubt you'd understand it anyway, old fella."

He gave me a clip around the ear and passed me a small notebook with a spiral binding, a fresh one he'd obviously written up—or rather had Jayne write up—especially for me: bank account numbers, credit cards, phones.

"If I'd needed you sooner," he said, "would you have come?"

"Yes," I said. "Why didn't you ask me sooner?"

"Didn't need you sooner. I'm pretty good at this, if you remember."

"Yeah, I remember."

He held my eye a second and said, "If yer still in Leeds come Sunday, Jayne's ordered you round for a roast dinner. Beef."

"Thanks," I said, standing. "I'll find her."

Right after figuring out exactly who all the players were in this annoyingly opaque case.

Chapter Seven

I accessed the Deep Detect System via my phone and input the numbers associated with Sarah's life—financial data, phone numbers, email addresses—and waited. Over the years, Park Avenue Investigations had acquired backdoor access to many banks and financial institutions, which is where the "bot" would start, anchoring itself in the information I fed it. From there, the system would burrow through any matches linked to that data, first in Britain, and then around the world. If it came up against firewalls that could not be decoded, it would shoot spam at a random selection of employees with a virus hidden in a web link; no one opens uninvited attachments anymore. We did not tempt them with penis enhancement or miracle weight-loss, instead bestowing them with retail voucher codes. All they had to do was click the link to their preferred shop, and the redirect site first installed a bot on their computer, then sent them to the genuine retailer for the discount, thus avoiding suspicion. Once anchored within, DDS organizes transactions chronologically and links to any other people's data with whom the subject came into contact. When tracking complex financial fraud, this would instigate a spider's web of intel, branching out to nail the perpetrators *and* their accomplices or paymasters. In the case of a runaway girl, if she accessed any of her regular accounts, we would see which hotel she stayed in, who else stayed there at the same time, the last ATM she used, and any tickets to destinations either inside or outside the UK.

Of course, DDS has its limits. All it throws out is raw information. It's up to the user to interpret it. If the subject is clever about their crime, they will not touch any of their regular accounts or even use their own name if they can help it, and since I already knew Sarah procured a fake passport, it was better to back it up with good, old-fashioned detective work.

Back at my apartment, I called Caroline to let her know I had a little more information than Harry uncovered, and told her I was confident that Harry had been correct about Sarah absconding to Paris. I would be on the first flight out tomorrow. She thanked me and didn't ask me to elaborate, for which I was glad because there really was no reason I shouldn't be on a plane within a couple of hours. But I could not stop thinking about what may have been happening to Lily right now.

What was happening to Lily, *because of me.*

I had to *do* something.

Keep yer eye on the prize, Harry said. On the surface I agreed with him.

No more compromises, my mother told me. Beneath the surface, I agreed with her.

That's why, instead of catching the last flight of the day to Paris, I watched over Blazing Seas from a £5 parking spot two streets away in a Vauxhall Astra, the least conspicuous car I could hire at short notice. I used my time to call Harry via one of three brand new phones that Jess procured via PAI's Tech-Hive: one for this venture, a cloned duplicate and a nuts-and-bolts text-and-voice model whose battery would last over a week. I informed Harry of my plans for the night, and asked him for background on Gareth

Delingpole. I gave him a brief list of other items, some of them costly and, using the other smartphone, I transferred more cash than he'd need, just in case.

Following an hour of nothing suspicious, I moved to a bench beside Leeds Art Gallery, a hundred yards back from the road. I flicked through Empire Magazine and, between reading how cool the latest superhero movie was and saying hello to Jason Isaacs, I could see anyone entering or leaving Benson's club.

About eight-thirty, after the sky dimmed and the traffic calmed to a steady stream, Lily emerged alone in sweat-pants and a green coat, and hobbled into a white BMW that pulled up and flicked on its hazards.

As the car pulled away, the impressive lens on my phone zoomed in on its plates and snapped a photo, which fed into DDS. The system returned a name of Marley Holdings, based in the tax haven of Jersey. Marley Holdings was then cross-referenced with as many bank accounts as the system could find, whilst simultaneously whittling away at the company's charge card. I split the screen on the phone and saw the card purchases ping up on one half, with the suspected links to Marley Holdings on the other.

One thing that drew my attention was a regular shipping manifest leaving Liverpool docks on the second Monday of each month, dating back over a year. I could find no destination on DDS, but if there was a kink in Marley Holdings' security, I'd soon know exactly where those shipments were headed, and what they allegedly contained. Every link to the company, though, hit a dead-end right there, a combination of firewalls and fake account numbers. In the hope she could dig more deeply, I emailed Jess all the data so far, and switched off the illegal software. All I had were theories and more questions.

In a way, the supposed theft was good for Benson: I return the money, he bags it up, disappears the thieves, and the insurance has still paid out. Double-bubble on the cash *and* send a message to anyone else thinking of stealing from him.

Was his reputation that important? I doubted it. He'd tried to throw in a clause under the radar: *any other items in their possession.* Gareth's SD card was the obvious theory. Perhaps that linked to the shipments.

Let's talk about that.

No, let's not, you clever fuck.

If Benson employed people who could hack through PAI's firewalls, he had access to either high-level politics or law-enforcement, or even interested foreign parties. Whatever Benson's source, Roger Gorman was taking extraordinary steps to oust me from a controlling position, skirting closer to the legal line than I'd ever seen. He avoided tax without an ounce of guilt, and circumvented international sanctions through a network of companies more complex than the human nervous system, yet here he was, willing to bribe a dodgy psychiatrist to certify me unfit to make decisions at an executive level.

But, with Sarah missing, and Lily under threat, I had no time to address Gorman's plot.

Yesterday's storm was creeping north, almost blown out, but carrying a fair amount of drizzle. For no other reason than I didn't particularly want to get soaked, I decided it was time to do my thing. I stood up sharply, and ran as fast as I could around the corner, waving my arms like a madman.

Chapter Eight

Okay, it's a bit of a hack trick. I mean, like, first year spy-school stuff. Or PI school. Harry actually taught me this in my second week after agreeing to work with him. Move quickly, move suspiciously, but do it unexpectedly. Take in as many reactions as possible, and if you have a tail, you'll get the reaction you want. I got that two seconds into my sprint.

The guy was in his forties, sat at a table outside a coffee-shop with a near-full cappuccino. While everyone else gawped at the crazy dude who suddenly took off running, this guy, in his cheap grey suit and blue shirt, kept his gaze firmly on the book he was pretending to read.

The second tail was walking towards me. Others heading the same way rubber-necked as I passed them but, like his colleague, this slightly-overweight chap in a way-too-tight white t-shirt gave zero reaction.

Around the next corner, I slowed to a walk. I donned a baseball cap and allowed a smooth wooden cosh to slide out of my sleeve and sit discreetly in my hand. The object had been a gift from a Japanese Catholic priest, presented to me upon my departure from the Tokyo soup kitchen in which I was volunteering. It was inscribed with Japanese *kana* meaning, "Love, peace and happiness."

The reflection in a bank's window confirmed one half of the tailing pair followed. I continued down a commercial street called The Headrow, noting new stores had opened since my departure, then turned right onto Briggate, once a major city-center thoroughfare clogged with diesel fumes, now a sand-blasted precinct of a shoppers' paradise. It still had its narrow, enclosed alleyways branching off, though. Up one of these lurks the Angel Inn, which may have seen a number of renovations over the years but it is still, at its heart, a pub for drinkers. Compact and narrow, I passed by the entrance and slipped round a corner into what regulars call "the courtyard"—basically a scattering of bolted-down tables and chairs to one side of the narrow passage. It was empty at the moment. I used the cosh to nudge the three floodlights upward, and within seconds the motion sensors got confused and extinguished the bulbs, darkening the alley. Not completely, but enough to conceal my movements as I backed into a recess that used to house a drainpipe.

Seconds later, Cheap-Suit and Tighty-Whitey came in from separate ends. Tighty-Whitey stopped a few feet away as a third man approached from Cheap-Suit's direction. Seemingly immune to the fine rain, he sat at a table and lit a cigarette. He wore a blue suit and had greasy hair and a square-ish head, like a doughy Frankenstein's monster.

The third man said, "Alright, let's be all civil then."

I stepped out of my hiding place and approached the trio, stopping an arm's length away from Cheap-Suit. I said, "Not so covert any more then?"

Cheap-Suit said, "Want a word is all."

"Okay. Go for it."

"Back off."

"That's two words," I said.

Cheap-Suit came a step closer.

The cosh sat conspicuously in my hand.

Cheap-Suit said, "We don't want you in the way. Don't want you getting hurt."

"Right," Tighty-Whitey added. "None of your business."

The third man said, "Hey guys, this gonna get violent?"

"It might," I said.

"Okay." He shifted away from us, and positioned himself for a better view.

Cheap-Suit said, "It doesn't have to get violent."

"Then fuck off," I said.

Cheap-Suit reached in his pocket. Before he could remove whatever was in there, I kneed him in the balls and he doubled over. As Tighty-Whitey moved forward, I swung the cosh in an arc—a foot-and-a-half of wood, infused at the business end with a couple of pounds of lead—and slammed it down on Cheap-Suit's thigh. The third man laughed throatily.

"Hey." Still unable to stand fully-erect, Cheap-Suit held up an item.

I stepped back to improve the angle, Tighty-Whitey gearing up for another shot at me. But Cheap-Suit flipped out a warrant card: *West Yorkshire Police*. Detective Inspector.

I said, "Oops."

Cheap-Suit said, "Yer under arrest, smart-arse."

The third guy ceased laughing. "Nah, don't worry about it."

Cheap-Suit deferred to him. In turn, the doughy monster-guy came round this side of the table and perched himself casually on the edge.

He said, "I'm Frank," and held out his hand.

I still held the cosh on my shoulder, ready to strike, the pose usually associated with coppers fending off a mob of protesters. I said, "What the fuck is this?"

Frank lowered his hand. "Rich, grab four pints, hey?"

Tighty-Whitey frowned.

Frank said, "*Now* would be *great*."

Tighty-Whitey limped off. My guess was he was a copper too, not used to being ordered to bring refreshments to someone they were tailing. For whatever reason.

Frank said, "My investigation has no room for civilians, Adam. Go back to your surf-school."

I said, "What if I don't want to?"

"If you bugger off now, we won't requisition the CCTV of you assaulting a couple of police officers."

"Let's see some ID."

Frank shook his square head. "I'm not the sort of guy who carries ID."

"But you get to order around local cops who do carry it."

"I know it may not be obvious right now, but you and I, Adam, we're on the same side." He was using my name too much, like he'd been on a "building empathy" course. He said, "I want to locate Sarah too. But I have to tread carefully."

I lowered the cosh so it rested by my leg. Non-threatening, but visible. "What are you, Benson's money-man? His accountant?"

Frank wasn't built like a fighter. That didn't always mean a lot, though. The guy under whom I first studied Muay Thai was as round as a beach-ball.

Frank said, "I don't work for Curtis Benson."

"What sort of police don't carry ID?"

Tighty-Whitey returned with four pints of Black Sheep bitter and set them down. "Not police, you idiot."

Black Sheep is a beautiful drink. Doesn't travel well, though. Brewed a few miles from Leeds in North Yorkshire, I'd tried it down south, but it just didn't taste the same as it did back home. Although I was tempted to gulp down a half-pint in one go, I kept my focus on this "Frank" character.

He said, "I work for a special unit. Organized crime division. I won't bore you with the initials."

"MI5," I said, and a few things fell into place. "You managed to shut down the police investigation. How? Terrorism threat?"

Frank smiled. *Agent* Frank, I should say.

"And why?" I asked. "Why would you do that?"

He said, "Phil, take a walk. You too, Rich."

Cheap-Suit looked kind of insulted. Tighty-Whitey just shook his head and trudged off with his pint. Cheap-Suit followed with his own.

Frank plucked up one of the two remaining beers and took a good gulp. His tone darkened. "It's not just a missing girl or a missing guy. It's not just some cash."

"You're a bit behind on my progress, Frank." I secured the cosh in the back of my trousers. "I already know it isn't about a robbery. Benson wants me to work for him now."

A tiny shift in his features told me it was new information. "Why?"

"Same reason you want me to back off. Other items in the safe."

"Go on."

"Okay. Benson requests the police don't investigate the theft too much, and the guys he has in his wallet, they tell him 'no problem'. But really, it's *you* who stopped it because you didn't want to spook Benson or his smuggling friends. Likewise, you blocked the missing persons report because you don't want Sarah and Gareth to see the cops closing in, and dump whatever they took." I realized I was talking too much. "Sharing time means it's your turn. How did you get the police to mothball the miss-per report?"

He considered it a second. "Okay, sharing. Gareth's known associates are linked to some far-right protests that attacked mosques in the past. As far as West Yorkshire Police are concerned, Gareth and Sarah haven't disappeared. We say we're watching them, and we don't want local plod scaring them off."

"But you're not watching them."

"No." He fiddled with a cigarette, lit it, and blew smoke away from me. "So why does Curtis Benson want a private eye to do his legwork for him?"

"You've been making in-roads lately. Arresting smaller operators in the human trafficking racket. He doesn't know who to trust." I thought some more. "What is it that Gareth took?"

"In all honesty? I don't know. It's got Benson worried though. Accounts probably, or details of other gangs, maybe politicians and police on their payroll. Who knows?"

"Accounts?" I said, thinking about the shipments every second Monday and their hidden destination. "They really keep those things in safes?"

"It's called *organized* crime for a reason." This time he blew smoke in my face. "So, Benson and his partners, they're all too paranoid to mount a visible operation? Sounds about right. We're at a pivotal phase. We need to play it right."

"Still want me to back off?"

"I let you go about your business, I risk exposing my guys. You get in trouble, they're good people. Some of them might even blow the case to help a dumb amateur." He cocked his head with a wry grin. "They'll kick your head in afterwards for fucking up years of work, but they'll save your life."

I had little to come back at him with. He was right. "You're not looking for Sarah, though."

"We need what her and Gareth are carrying. If we need to help her, we will."

"But if Gareth is threatening her—"

"Domestics aren't our department."

"You want whatever they took from the safe, but I'm concerned with *her*. Nothing else."

Agent Frank stood and faced me, lager-breath mingling with cigarettes. "Then we're gonna have a problem."

"Need me to sign a disclaimer?"

"What? Exonerate my people if you die?"

"Sure," I said. "Whatever you need. And consider this: you can't *actually* stop me going after them. Unless you have time to manufacture some evidence of my terrorist intentions."

Agent Frank rubbed his face, thinking. "You are one dumb guy, Adam. But you're right. I can't stop you." He stubbed out the cigarette. "But I can give you this warning. If I hear even a hint of you breaking *one* law, endangering *one* of my people, or if I get the slightest inkling you're thinking of returning Curtis Benson's property to him, there'll be a European arrest warrant with your name on it before you can say 'human rights abuse'. You get that?"

I should have been insulted, but it actually felt like progress. I now knew who, in addition to Benson, was following me, and I knew why the police investigation got nixed.

"No backup, no help," he said.

"Yeah. I get it. You mind if I crack on now?"

He did not reply. Instead, he picked up his pint and the one intended for me, and headed inside the Angel Inn, leaving me with just one loose end to tie up before heading to France.

Chapter Nine

I arrived back at my apartment around ten p.m. Harry handed me a beer and, in my kitchen, the breakfast bar greeted us full of various foodstuff: pizza from a local takeaway, finger-foods from the frozen section of Sainsbury's, and drinks both alcoholic and soft. Nibbling at this, sat on my tall chairs, were Caroline Stiles and Jayne Riley, Harry's wife. I hadn't been expecting all this company, but Harry explained they both insisted they see me before I left.

As soon as Jayne saw me, the first time in nearly two years, she came over and hugged me. She looked at me properly and tutted. Didn't ask questions, just embraced me again. She smelled strongly of coffee; ten p.m. was roughly two hours past the sixty-four-year-old woman's bedtime. She finally let me go and opened my laptop computer to the side of the food; she clearly still remembered my passwords. Jessica Denvers' face appeared, looking off to the side. Jayne smiled proudly.

I said, "Looks like someone's been keeping up with technology."

Jayne patted me on the arm. "You know what Harry's like."

Harry heard but pretended he didn't. "Are we all here now?"

We sat around the table, with Jess a disembodied face in one corner.

I said, "The money is no longer the key focus. Curtis Benson has added to the problem in a big way, along with his Odd-Job-wannabe henchman."

"What's an Odd-Job?" Jayne asked.

"James Bond villain," Harry said. "Little chinky guy with the hat."

Jayne said, "You can't say 'chinky' anymore. It's racist."

"Is it? Thought it was like saying 'Brit' or 'Yank'."

I coughed and they turned their attention back to me. I then outlined everything I learned since dropping Caroline at home, highlighting that Benson believed Sarah was still in France with Gareth.

Caroline said, "Who's Gareth?"

Harry opened a file on the table and took out two photos. The first was a CCTV still taken from above while Gareth worked the door, showing him to be of rangy build and with short-cropped hair. The second was snapped upon Gareth's arrest. He had a round face and full mouth, yet his eyes gave off a rodent-like quality. Too small, too close together. He was thirty-three.

"Sarah's boyfriend," Harry said. "Two wives behind him, suspicion of four assaults. All on women. Two convictions."

Another glance to Caroline, who looked away.

I said, "Men like Gareth are extremely clever. They lavish affection, create dependency, isolate their victim from friends and family. And then the fear starts. The threats. The violence."

"Lower than whale shit," Harry said.

"What?" Caroline said.

"Bottom of the ocean, dear," Jayne replied.

Harry continued. "After his second divorce, his next girlfriend we know of was a more headstrong sort. She fought back, and he didn't like it. Details are sketchy, but essentially a bunch of her friends missed her for five days and called the police. Found her in the cellar, on a mattress in her own filth. Forced imprisonment, assault, it all cost him five years. He's been out eighteen months, but was still on license until a month ago. Fancies himself as a landlord now. Bought a new house out in Birstall, bringing in a couple of lodgers. Sarah's the latest."

"Property," Jayne said. "Perhaps he's behind? Needs the money?"

"No," Harry said. "He pockets a wedge of inflated rent from the tax-payer. Unemployed family living in his Chapeltown property. It's enough to cover the mortgages on both houses." He fished out copies of letters from an energy company. "But he cut off the utilities to his Birstall property the day after Mr. and Mrs. Gallway flew to gay Par-ee."

"What does 'on license' mean?" Caroline asked, voice a little high.

"Parole," I said. "He served his time, then persuaded Sarah to help rip-off a load of cash and run away with him."

"But … she told me she was coming *home*."

"If she's in love," I said, "if she's worried he won't love her anymore, wouldn't she take direct action? Mission mode?"

I expected Caroline to break into tears, but crying didn't seem to be something she did. Not unless she chose to.

Jayne said, "Perhaps we can move on to another subject for now? Like this 'Mikey' chap?"

Harry switched to another file. "We think he's Michael Durant, former Captain of the North Yorkshire Fusiliers, who saw action in the first Gulf War. Most of his unit were killed during an ambush. Left the service right after his tour, and disappeared. Late-nineties-early-noughties, Michael Durant surfaces as a private contractor, leadin' raids into Bosnia, escortin' vulnerable people outta war-zones."

"Sounds pretty honorable," I said. "Okay, we've nothing on Sarah's phone or bank cards, so we need to get dirtier. We know they got *fake* cards when they bought the passports but we don't know the numbers."

Jess took over. "I've hacked the retail arm of BAA—the firm that owns Leeds-Bradford Airport—and we got a few hits on new credit cards."

To Caroline, I said, "Plenty of people take out a new credit card for holidays. Offers protection against cancelled flights and suchlike."

"Thank you, Mr. Trivia," Jess said. "I got a list of all cards taken out in the past month paying for goods both in the airport *and* in Paris, then used DDS to eliminate all those that couldn't be Sarah or Gareth."

"That's extraordinary," Caroline said. "Who *are* you people?"

Jess continued. "A couple of cards went on to Spain, one to Belgium, half a dozen to the US, one to Vietnam, some Middle East countries too. But we're sure she hasn't left France, right? So we can scratch those spending in onward destinations. Only *five* cards were all taken out less than a week before Sarah left, only *five* ceased spending in Paris. No hotels, but one did buy something at an internet café situated in *l'Hostel Centrale*. The same day Sarah sent her last email. That was the final transaction."

Jess didn't say any more. She didn't have to.

Caroline was the first to speak. "So she's laying low or she's … dead."

Harry said, "We'll find her, love."

Caroline hugged her legs. Jayne Riley's first instinct was to comfort. Caroline's first instinct was to pull away. "Illegal hacking, gangsters … it's all so … surreal. It all sounds so dangerous. I don't know if I want to go this way. I could try the press again, the foreign office—"

"That isn't possible," I said. "You know that."

Jayne refused to pull away. Rubbed Caroline's shoulders. She said, "What Adam has put himself through in the past so he can help strangers, if I needed someone to find my sister or my daughter, or my niece … I wouldn't want the police. Nor MI5 or He-

Man or James Bond. But *Adam*. He's who I'd want looking for her."

"Thanks a bunch," Harry said.

Caroline levelled a stone-cold stare my way. "You've done this before? With this much danger?"

Harry said, "Tell her about Thailand."

"I don't think that's relevant," I said.

Harry and Jayne often tried to get me to talk, and Harry even proffered some dumb amateur psychology lesson that maybe it made me more willing to face physical problems than emotional ones. I thought it was bollocks.

"Adam," Harry said. "This lass needs to believe you can bring her sister home. If you can offer her some hope that you're actually hot shit at this travelin' malarkey, maybe she'll sleep tonight."

I stuffed another chicken pakora in my mouth and chewed slowly. All eyes remained on me until I swallowed.

I said, "Give me another beer."

I had lived in Thailand a little under four months when a third local case pinged into my email account. According to John Baldwin, his wife, Sheila, had disappeared from their Bangkok hotel room two days earlier. John told me Sheila used to have a gambling problem and suggested she might've got involved with that sort of crowd. I had tracked maybe fifty people, and studied martial arts on three continents, so I knew I could handle anything.

I didn't even think to check out his version of events, just blundered head-long into the Bangkok nightlife. I was pulled beyond the cigar-fog of backroom poker sessions and into the world of high-stakes hold 'em, where a hand could lose or win you a Mercedes, and a bluff without the finance to back it up could cost you a lot more. I flashed Sheila's picture, asked questions with no re-

plies, bribed barmen and waitresses and even a policeman to provide the flimsiest of rumors about possible games. Eventually, as I
was about to give up, they came for me.

I awoke on the floor of a wooden construction far from any traffic noise; a room, ten-foot square, heat radiating off each wall. I
was covered in sweat and grime and a sticky patch of blood from
where they'd knocked me out, though I had no idea how long I'd
been unconscious. I insisted it was all a misunderstanding, but the
four heavily-tattooed Thai men who guarded me did not want to
talk, so I soon gave up trying and threw up on the dusty concrete.

The four men stepped back and one of them spat on me. They
dragged me out of the room by my legs, and down a short passageway and out into a yard with two mongrel fighting dogs
slamming against their chains and yowling to get at me. The dogs'
jaws chomped down inches from my feet and the men would not
let me back up. Not that I could go far.

The street beyond the hip-high wall was deserted, lined with
small square houses whose paint had peeled off long ago. The road
was once tarmac but a combination of human neglect and the
willpower of nature had other ideas, and the humid night air made
the stench of open sewer even meatier in the back of my throat.

Two of the men moved to position next to the poles to which the
fighting dogs were attached, while another watched the street. The
fourth sat beside me and observed in silence.

About half an hour later, the man in the suit arrived.

He climbed out of a 4x4 that I could not focus on, and pushed
open the gate. The dogs shut up immediately. He came straight up
to me, crouched, and spoke in accented but precise English.

"Stop looking for the woman."

Then he stood and turned. Evidently he thought this would be
sufficient.

I said, "No."

The man in the suit waved a hand and the thugs reached to release the dogs.

"How much did he owe?" I asked.

"Who?" An open palm halted the dog handlers.

"Sheila's husband."

By then, I'd heard enough about John. *He* was the gambler, not her. I checked up on him quietly and learned he ran an online poker school back in Britain, but further research revealed these places were about as useful as those books "guaranteed" to power you to a career writing Hollywood movies.

The man in the suit gave me an oddly-camp look. "You think he owes us money? His debt is paid." He then spelled it out like I was four years old. "He wagered his wife against my apartment in central Bangkok. He lost."

If I hadn't been so woozy I'd have gasped or showed some level of shock. "I could buy her back," I said. "Forty thousand US dollars." It was the sum total of my savings. "Cash," I added.

"It is too late for that." To his men he said, "This person is no threat to us. Make sure he knows it."

The man in the suit sauntered out of the yard, and my four jailers closed in and dragged me back inside.

When they had finished punishing me, I felt like everything in my body was broken. My lips were swollen and bloody, one eye closed entirely. I don't know how long we drove for in their stifling van, but I eventually found myself being dragged yet again. This time I landed with a soft *whumpf.* I heard the van drive away, and I lay there. Hurting.

I slowly became aware of a texture. I moved an arm. Pain shot through my shoulder. My hand touched the ground. Sand.

Through the blood pounding around my head, I heard the ocean. I was on a beach.

Voices. Kids, adults.

Someone expressed concern. Then shock. Then revulsion. A man told a woman to keep the kids away. A shadow fell over me. A British voice asked if someone could hear him. *Me.* He was asking if *I* could hear him.

The man told me he'd get help. And he did.

Caroline asked, "What happened to Sheila?"

"Shallow grave," I said. "She'd been dead about a week before I even started looking for her. Her husband stuck with his story. Said she went out and never came back."

"Someone should do something about him."

"The man in the suit already took care of the husband," I said. "Couldn't resist going back for more, and this time he didn't have a wife to use as collateral." I slapped the table and painted a grin on my face. "So come on, Caroline. What's it to be? Do I go find Sarah or what?"

This time, the single tear rolling down her cheek seemed to be in spite of her willpower rather than because of it. Harry and Jayne were the only ones present who knew the story as I told it. Jess knew the abridged version. No one knew the full details. It still hurt too much to give it voice.

I was forever grateful that it was over.

Chapter Ten

Jess's research into Marley Holdings dug up the same dead ends as mine, but the Beamer itself had been easier to trace. The car's alarm company was one in which PAI had contacts and was able to extrapolate the GPS movements for the past twenty-four hours. It took Lily to an area of Leeds called Seacroft. Jess pinpointed the final stop, then checked council records for the first name "Lily" and identified only one address on that street: a studio apartment occupied by one Lily Blake.

I collected the thick packet Harry brought for me and we drove the Astra out to Lily's address. By midnight, the street was silent but for the buzz of streetlights and the occasional distant engine. Harry and I negotiated the washing machine and sofa strewn on the grass, and climbed the stairs to the first floor. The flats' windows opened onto the passageway, and all but one was in darkness. Our feet crunched over a slew of broken glass and number eight's net curtain twitched.

A muffled, "What the fuck do you want?" came from within.

"Are you alone?" I asked.

"Course I am. I try to go anywhere, he'll find me."

"I have something that can help with that."

"Unless it's Curtis Benson's head, I don't want it."

I knocked on the door and felt stupid for doing so. "Please hear me out. It's a good thing."

A pause, then, "How good?"

Harry said, "Love, I'd take this offer even if I didn't have some knob-head threatening me."

"Oh," she said. "You again."

Movement within. The door opened a crack. Lily's face appeared. Boyish hair. Wide brown eyes, a bruise to one cheek, her lip swollen. I hadn't noticed her eye-color before.

She said, "If I let you in, you leave when I say you leave. Okay?"

"Deal," I said.

She unchained the door and we entered a warm room that smelled of Chinese food, a couple of cartons stacked in the kitchenette's sink. The lounge contained a sofa-bed pulled out into bed-mode and a TV tuned to a 24-hour news channel.

While Harry kept watch by the window, I placed his packet on the side of the kitchenette.

"That for me?" Lily said.

"What do you think?"

She emptied the contents onto the worktop. The first thing she picked up was one of two passports.

"It's me," she said. "Paula Grainger. I don't look like a Paula."

"You will," I said. "Harry is going to drive you somewhere. Nowhere I know about, but some sea port. Hull, Portsmouth, somewhere like that. When you get to wherever you want to go, buy yourself a rail ticket and keep on going until you choose to stop."

"He found Sarah at the airport easy—"

"That's why there's two IDs."

She opened the second passport to meet Lilith Hughes.

"Lilith?" she said with disgust.

"It's close to Lily. Easier to remember. The cards are in Lilith's name too."

She examined the two credit cards. A standard silver one and a gold one.

I said, "Use Paula Grainger to leave the UK. Then burn the passport. Literally burn it, so no one can see who it was. Harry bought that one from the club forger, so when Benson finds out, he'll think he knows your identity. Then you use Lilith Hughes to get around. She's been created by my own contact, a rush-job couriered up from Birmingham. No association with Blazing Sleaze."

I paused in case she had questions. She didn't.

"The silver credit card is for small purchases—food, clothes, drinks. You need cash, keep it to a hundred euros a day. It's connected to my own account, so it's all my money. Do not go wild on it. It's not for buying fifty people champagne. If you do that, the card will cease working."

That was a lie, but I wanted some limits in place.

"The gold one is for more expensive purchases. Travel, accommodation, that sort of thing. Plus instructions on how to get them replaced if you lose them."

She stared at the documents. "Your plan is to send me on a *holiday?*"

"You said you'd hear me out. Listen for two more minutes and—"

"You can stop talking." She bit her lip, her bruising a nasty blue. "I'm actually okay with that."

"You are?"

"Shit yeah. I've never been abroad before. You wanna pay, I'll take that."

"Great," I said. "I'll get in touch with you once this is all over. Until then, you cannot contact your family—"

"No problem. They're all dicks anyhow."

"Or your friends. No Facebook or Twitter or Instagram. Leave your phone, buy a pay-as-you-go outside of Britain. Move cities a lot, stick around somewhere if you like it, but do not get sloppy. Do not reveal your real name. Okay?" I waited for her to respond, but she poked around at the health insurance certificate and the driving license. Her photo came from the DVLA servers, where— yep, you guessed it—PAI had a contact who let us in the backdoor. I said, "Lily, focus."

She snapped out of it. "So I can go anywhere, right?"

"Anywhere except Paris."

So Lily was out of the equation, making that one complication taken care of. I left her packing minimal items into a gym-bag, advising her to pick up a rucksack at the earliest opportunity. I left her with Harry, gave him the car key, and called a cab.

Back home, I packed my usual equipment: binoculars, digital SLR camera, gaffer tape, a folding tool kit smaller than my phone, and an iPad with a company SIM card. Then I dug out a razor, but figured I would shave in the morning rather than pack it. Hopefully I would be back in a couple of days. Finally, I weighed the wooden cosh in my hand. Easier to use than a knife, infinitely less messy, and far more legal to transport between countries. I tucked it into the middle of my bag, surrounded by items of clothing. With everything ready to grab and go first thing, I hit the sack for what I hoped would be a decent night's sleep.

However, four hours later, at six a.m., I awoke to my phone ringing. I hadn't dreamed, so it took me a while to realize where I was. I answered it, still groggy.

Curtis Benson said, "Are you fuckin' shittin' me? You think I don't know it was you and that Gruffalo motherfucker who took her?"

"You'll get what you asked for," I said. "But I can't work with that hanging over me. You'll get your other items, you might even get Gareth, but you leave Sarah to me. That's the deal now. I don't care about your business. Just give me some space, and leave me to it."

"Space? I'll give you *space*—"

"If you were really going to do something you'd have kicked down the door already. You want what they took, and if it means I get your cooperation in finding Sarah, I'll bring it to you. Whatever it is."

A shuffling sounded on the other end. "You got a pen?"

I picked up one of the other phones and told him I was ready. He gave me a number with a French prefix, which I typed into the phone's memory.

Benson said, "You gonna be on a short leash, *fucker*. You get to Paris, you call that number. You don't call, we'll come lookin' for you and whoever you care about."

"Who is it?"

"Name is Vila Fanuco." He spelled the name for me. "My contact over there. He runs everythin' worth runnin'. Remember? *Lord of the fuckin' underworld.* Play any fuckin' games, show any reason I can't trust you, and I'll know. Got it?"

"Sure," I said, and hung up.

It was pointless going back to sleep, so I caught a cab to Leeds-Bradford airport and booked myself on the ten-thirty flight to Paris. I was wearing beige combats and a loose cotton t-shirt, carrying a rucksack. I looked like anyone else embarking on a trip abroad, and I felt that tingle I always get when I'm about to cross another border.

I was finally on my way.

EUROPE

FRANCE

Chapter Eleven

When I was eighteen years old, I fulfilled my father's exotic promise for him, and entered France for the first time in my life; my first time outside of Britain. Armed only with an Inter-Rail ticket and a desperate need to flee as far as possible, I yearned to simply turn up in random places and find a room, perhaps some remote village smack-bang in the middle of their Festival of Welcoming Foreigners or something. But that evening, as I rocked up in Paris with wide eyes and a fast pace, a major car convention had hit town, and there was not a single vacant hotel, hostel or guest room. My pace slowed and I wandered the streets all night, sampling one late night cafe's wares after the next, alternating my intake between the sweet aniseed liqueur called *pastis* and strong black coffee. Unlike the UK, there was no hurried last-orders, no groups of lads downing several pints to beat the bell. There were just people, enjoying the coffee, the alcohol, the food; a young family dined at eleven p.m., lovers ignored their drinks in favor of one another's mouths, and elderly men sat on pavement tables, their legs spread wide as they sorted out the world's problems in a fog of aniseed. I did not sleep, and I hardly noticed the fatigue. In the morning, when *Gare du Sud* opened for business, I used my Inter-Rail ticket on the first train south, and by mid-afternoon I was in Marseille, paddling in the Mediterranean.

Today, the rail link from *Charles de Gaulle* Airport into the heart of Paris was as clean and efficient as I remembered. It deposited me not far from a Metro station, but the first thing I did was pop into a narrow café where a full-bosomed *madame* greeted with me an enthusiastic, "Bonjour!" I returned her greeting in my school-boy French and purchased *un café-noir*. I fought off sleep most of the short flight, instead reading through the DDS info on Benson again, so I needed this boost.

> *Adam's Smug Travel Tips #15: To get oneself into the mental space necessary to acclimatize to a foreign country, fine coffee in a tiny café (or whatever the local specialty beverage happens to be) is a great place to start.*

I left the cafe with a clear head and went straight to a tourist information booth.

Due to the ease with which Benson had monitored my other activities, I did not book accommodation in advance, and I was concerned that staying at Sarah's last known location could have tipped off the pair, or—more pertinently—whoever caused harm to befall them. I chose a three-star option called *Le Grecian,* paid her in advance, and descended into the bowels of the Metro, Paris's underground rail network. I took the pink line to the Opera station, where I emerged into the afternoon sun.

Four hours after leaving Leeds, this was my first proper glimpse of Paris in years: a wide, busy road, lined with three and four-story buildings. The windows all bore wooden shutters, with iron railings for residents to lean upon, as many were now doing. Scooters whined by, some honking, although not bad-temperedly; more of a "Hi, pleased to see you" honk. Every street corner boasted a zebra-crossing, with red and green traffic lights, along with a red and green-man guide.

I made it inside the Hotel Grecian and tried my French on the receptionist. I didn't get far, but she seemed happy I at least tried. My room had a soft bed and a fifty-year-old dresser, and the bathroom came furnished with a four-foot bath with a shower over it, and a sit-on toilet. The whole space smelled a bit like the *Miss Piggywiggy*.

I pushed the net curtain aside, opened my window, and leaned on the railings. Sounds of the city floated by: engines, car horns, the occasional argumentative shout. Tobacco swam through the air, blending with Mediterranean dishes sizzling a couple of buildings away. It was three-thirty now and the sun was lower than back home, filtered orange through the mild smog, hanging between the old white buildings. It's a scene, an *atmosphere*, no other place can provide: Paris in the afternoon, preparing for evening.

I had to venture out into that evening pretty soon.

Back inside, I left the window ajar, and dug out the number Benson had given me. Figured I was better off calling than not. No need to antagonize these people further.

A gruff, "Allo?" greeted me.

"Vila Fanuco?" I said.

"Adam Park," the man said.

"I'm supposed to check in with you."

"Yes."

I couldn't place his accent. Certainly not French. Eastern European? Russian? The name *Fanuco* was Spanish in origin but his lilt was a million miles away from Spanish. I wouldn't expect *Vila* or *Fanuco* to be genuine anyway.

"I can assume you will start your assignment straight away?" His English was near-flawless.

"I'm planning on a visit to the police first."

"Oh? To what end?"

"I'm looking for a missing girl travelling with a violent thug. It's a courtesy to check in with local police to let them know I'm

A. D. Davies

snooping around their city. Things might get tricky if I annoy a *gendarme*."

Fanuco laughed. "Okay, Mr. Park. Very well put. Logical. You sound like the sort of man I would like."

"Cool. Let's have a beer sometime." *Why the fuck did I say that?* Mr. Glib returns.

"Mr. Park, you should take this situation more seriously. Your stay in my city will be far more comfortable if you behave."

"I'll be good as gold."

The man breathed for a couple of seconds. He said, "Enjoy the Grecian," and hung up.

I sat on the bed, listening to the sounds of Paris through my window. It took me a moment to realize I had not mentioned the name of my hotel, and that I had used my mobile to call him, so any caller-ID would have been irrelevant. I'd taken the usual precautions, but still they'd learned where I was staying as simply as flipping on a light.

Unlike I had with Benson, I could not chance underestimating this man.

Chapter Twelve

The *Préfecture de Police* was located in the *Île de la Cité,* one of two natural islands in the River Seine. It was more of a castle than a police station, and when I found the public entrance I felt I was about to be picked off by an archer. The reception area alone was the size of most British cop shops, and shone with pristine marble and artistic coving. I communicated with the woman on the desk in broken French. She thanked me for having called ahead and *oui*, there was still someone here who might see me. She warned they were still working a high-profile case, though, so there might be some delay. I said that was fine, and she directed me through a huge art-lined corridor, up to the third floor to wait beside Pierre Bertrand's office. She told me he was a *gardien de la paix*—keeper of the peace—which sounded grand, but as I waited, I looked it up and learned it was only a rank or two above a *gendarme* on the beat.

Gardien Bertrand himself was a liaison for the Criminal Investigation Division, employed predominantly to deal with the foreign and domestic press, so I expected he would speak English pretty damn well. Before I could look any deeper into the man himself, he appeared beside me, a fifty-something chap with older eyes and a trim brown beard going grey at the edges.

"Excuse me, Mr. Park," he said, juggling his coat and briefcase to shake my hand, "but it is after seven and I am on my way home. Perhaps we could walk as well as talk?"

"Of course."

He limped on his left leg, but at a regular walking pace, so he'd obviously had the ailment for many years. No cane, either. His accent was only mildly inflected by French, so he probably spent time in England or the States. "We have a girl who is missing—Henrietta Dupree, just twelve years old—and we are not close to finding her. Our investigators think she may no longer be in France. Interpol is taking things over now and I have to field a million questions to the press. How come the *Ministère* failed? How come we cannot find her? Why are the police such idiots? You know these sorts of things."

"Actually, I'm not a police officer."

He stopped. "But I thought…"

"I'm sorry, I told the secretary I was an 'officer of the law' because my French is rusty. I couldn't remember how to say 'private investigator'."

"*C'est un enquêteur privé,*" he said.

"*Enquêteur privé.*"

We started walking again.

"Gardien Bertrand," I said. "I'm looking for a missing girl too. She's eighteen. Older than yours, I know, but still young."

"Ah, yes, still a girl in England. In France, she is an adult."

"I understand."

"Then you will understand, too, our budgets are very thin. All our money, these days, is in counter-terrorism, community relations, and … well, there is never enough to go around, is there?"

"I really don't need anything specific from you. Certainly nothing that will take you away from your business. I just—"

He limped a little faster, swinging the left out in a wider arc. "Why are you here, then?"

"I'm going to be around the Opera district, probably the Latin or Gothic Quarters too, might have to ask a few questions. I wanted

to let you know in case the *gendarmes* thought me … suspicious."
As long as I wasn't planning on running around like Liam Neeson
displaying my "specific set of skills" on swarthy locals, I guessed
this was the right way to go about things.

He stopped by a lift and pressed the call button. "Forgive my
brusque manner. Madame Bertrand understood my hours when
poor Henrietta was our case, but now…" He shrugged in a way I
can only describe as "Gallic."

"Well, I won't keep you," I said.

The lift arrived and we got on, and he pressed for the ground
floor.

Bertrand said, "It is a tragedy when girls are missing. More so
even than boys. Vulnerable, exposed. Don't you think? It must be
difficult for her family to accept she may be happily bouncing, as
we speak, on a young man's bed. You understand?"

"It's actually what I'm *hoping* for." But wasn't expecting. "Certainly better than the alternative."

"Ah." He stopped in the foyer, signed his name in a book. "So
you are a realist. As well as an optimist."

I smiled, unsure exactly what he meant. Suspected a little was
lost in translation. I said, "Something like that."

I followed Pierre Bertrand out of the building to the parking lot.
Each row contained twenty cars. I struggled to keep up as he hobbled with that odd gait.

He said, "This girl, what is her name?"

"Sarah Stiles. I think she's travelling with a Gareth Delingpole,
but their passports may be in the names of Gallway."

"I will look out for her in the police reports. You have a descrip-
tion?"

I passed him copies of the photos of Sarah and Gareth. "Their
last known location was *L'Hostel Centrale*. Low budget, backpacker place."

"I know of it. On the edge of the nice area for tourists, on the edge of the less nice area too … even for Parisians. Our home city gangs operate here. Prostitution, drugs. And Asians are close to moving in, I believe. You should be careful." He studied Sarah's picture, then stopped beside a Renault and placed his briefcase on it, popped the locks. He put the photo inside and handed me a business card. "These are my numbers. If I can help, please call me."

"Asians?"

"South East Asia. Many migrants. Like the Arabs and Africans, most are okay, but there are always criminals in any people. As far as I am aware, they do not yet have a solid hold in a particular district. But then I am not as connected to the street as I used to be."

"Thank you," I said, and shook his hand.

"You are welcome," he said, climbing into his car.

"One more thing." He wound down the window and I asked, "Do you know anything about a guy called Vila Fanuco?"

The friendly perma-smile faded beneath his beard. "Why do you wish to know about such a man?"

"Curiosity."

"Get in," he said.

And Gardien Bertrand proceeded to scare me half to death with his driving.

Chapter Thirteen

Gardien Bertrand pulled into traffic at a pace I thought unsafe even on clear roads. He zipped in and out of cars and mopeds, my foot pressing an imaginary brake pedal in the passenger foot-well.

"You are staying in the Opera district?" Bertrand said.

"No," I said, gripping the seat. "The Grecian, in the Gothic Quarter."

"I will take you there. But you must tell me: how do you know Vila Fanuco?"

"I don't know him."

He looked so pissed off at this that I think he genuinely tried to knock a young couple from their moped as he cut them up. "Then why ask of him?"

"I heard his name."

"In associate… Apologies. In *association* with your missing girl?"

"Not exactly. Overheard a conversation."

"I do not believe you."

He yanked the wheel to the right. We pulled off the main road and onto a dirt path. The car slowed a little but we continued to skid until the driveway opened up into a car park with a dozen spaces. Gravel crunched under the wheels and he finally came to a halt beside a small manmade lake, facing the south side of the water.

Bertrand killed the engine. It ticked slowly and the policeman's breathing grew longer and quieter. His eyes settled on the lake. I watched in silence. He focused on the water, the setting sun rippling gently across its surface. Geese swam. A mum and dad and two toddlers threw bread into the water on the opposite side, and the geese took flight, chased away the approaching ducks, wings batting at them, hoarding the bread for themselves. Night would soon fall, but the family carried on, widening the spread of their throws, allowing more birds to feed.

"This lake," Bertrand said, "was donated to the city by Jaques Poulet. A businessman with holdings here and eight other European countries. His wife was kidnapped one day, but there was no ransom. We found her here, face down, shot three times through the back."

Hard to imagine such a scene in this pretty corner of Paris, a corner I'd never seen before. It seemed doubtful many tourists would have either. A garden, private; exclusive to Paris's own citizens.

"After the funeral," Bertrand said, "a man contacted Monsieur Poulet to say that his shipping corporation was perfect for moving goods between countries, and this man was going into business with him. Monsieur Poulet refused, but the threat was implicit: 'You do not want your children to end up like your wife, do you?' A proud man, a father of three teenagers, he called us in."

"You were involved?"

With a pained expression, he said, "I was not always a little press monkey." He looked ahead. "We traced the interest back to Vila Fanuco, a smuggler with a growing reputation among our informants, and we gathered much evidence."

Bertrand fished in his pocket for a pack of cigarettes. He stepped outside the car and I followed him. He took his time to light-up, and when it got going he limped to the water's edge. I matched his pace, but his expression suggested I wasn't even there.

"When he realizes we are coming for him, one of the policemen on the task force is beaten up in his home. His wife and mother are killed, his children ... threatened. And a videotape of the whole thing is sent to the Ministère. Everyone on the case watched this video. Some of us were ... angry. We wanted to catch him even more badly. We smashed every door, used every lead, and finally we brought him in. But some in the Ministère... some were scared. Others were contacted directly. Phone calls, notes in their children's schoolbags, that sort of thing. His reach was far bigger than we first guessed."

"A regular Keyser Söze," I said.

"Who?"

"A ... fictional villain. Famous in Britain. And America."

"Oh, a film," Bertrand said.

"He got off?" I asked.

"A scapegoat was needed, someone to fuck up the operation."

"You?"

"Me. I used excessive force, I failed to read his rights, I did many things."

"Were they true?"

"Partly. But I had done those things before. Excessive force is what keeps us on top." He lowered himself to the floor, his straight leg a hindrance, but I got the idea an offer of help would be insulting to this man. "There are bad people out there who keep the streets stable. Some of them, they have trouble, they call our criminal investigation division and we take care of it. The bad people who keep their business to themselves and to others like them, the public does not care what they do. Even the Asians ... when we investigated Henrietta's disappearance, even they were cooperative to a point, although they probably did not want us poking deeper into their business. But Fanuco does not respect the police. He does not care how we keep the peace. He only craves power. And now he has achieved that power, he will do whatever it takes to hold onto it."

Bertrand finished his cigarette and crushed it out on the grass. Pocketed the butt. He turned to me, as serious as I'd ever seen another human being. He said, "Vila Fanuco … he does not *fear* us. He does not fear anything."

Chapter Fourteen

It was almost nine, but I was not yet willing to turn in. There was still one lead I could follow-up at this time of night: the hotel with the internet café, where someone bought items on one of the fake credit cards. I didn't fully understand why their spending was mostly on credit, though. Perhaps they knew the card only had a limited shelf-life and were saving the stolen cash until they needed it. If the hotel didn't pan out, tomorrow I would hit the shops and restaurants in which they'd also used the card, and then start flashing their photos at the bus stations and travel agents. This work takes a toll on the feet, but it's how these things start. Slowly.

L'Hostel Centrale's Formica-clad lobby was painted magnolia, with cheap printed artwork in cheaper frames, like something from a council office, and a man in an off-white shirt slouched behind a reception desk that might have been new around the same time as the Eiffel Tower. The "internet café" from which Sarah sent her final email more than three weeks earlier was actually an espresso machine beside a bank of four computers that ate two euros per minute. Next to that was a reading area equipped with a book exchange where backpackers and other budget travelers swap their done-with novels for one on the shelves. In theory, this meant a lasting supply of decent literature. You get these in most hostels and budget hotels, and I used to take advantage of them wherever I went. It's not about the expense, either. It's being able to obtain English language novels whilst on the road. But in the age of the Kindle and other e-readers, many folk on lengthy jaunts simply no longer possess the literature to swap. A shame, but hey, convenience and progress always trump romantic notions and nostalgia.

The man behind the desk didn't speak fluent English but between his basic knowledge and my high school GCSE we managed to ascertain that I was a private investigator looking for the girl and man in the photos I showed him, and that no, sorry, he could not remember either. He ran through the register and found nothing under their real names or under Gallway. If they were ever here, they definitely weren't now. I did manage to establish, however, that I could pay in cash and a little bonus would mean my ID would not be retained.

At first, he was reluctant to allow me to ask around, but when I offered him a hundred euros, he set me a boundary of the public space, the internet station, and reading area. He sold me a nice coffee and a stale croissant, and I logged onto a computer to kill some time. In a budget place like this, people would stay for a month or more, so it was conceivable, albeit not very likely, that someone could have been here at the same time as Sarah.

I read about the weather for the next few days—rain was due tomorrow evening and all day Monday—and I logged onto the PAI network. Or, rather, I tried to. An aggressively red-colored box flashed up to inform me my sign-on was suspended and suggested I contact the system administrator. I called Jessica Denvers.

"They've locked you out," she said. "From what I can see it happened in the last hour."

"How can they do that? There's been no court order, no notice."

"They don't have to. They just need reasonable suspicion of wrong-doing, and you accessing the database using company equipment via a foreign server … it kind of gave them enough."

I was on an official PAI case, and I agreed to abide by PAI's operational rules. There were procedures to follow if I wanted to use company equipment abroad. And since I had instigated those rules myself to prevent Roger Gorman and his dodgy subcontractors from operating in vulnerable areas, I could hardly complain. I should have known they'd be monitoring my activity.

I asked, "Can you get me a backdoor in?"

"It'll take time. I'll need to do it via a backdoor myself, so they don't know it's me."

"Thanks, Jess."

As I hung up, a woman of about thirty with curly blonde hair struggled down the spiral staircase with a backpack twice her size. I figured her for the type of traveler who jams every home comfort into her pack, then slowly loses all that vanity when kit such as waterproofs and food become more important than curling tongs and hairdryers. Unless she was only here for the weekend.

"Here for the weekend?" I asked, helping her with the rucksack.

She laughed. "No. The opposite." She had a Geordie accent. "Hittin' the road." She pronounced it "roord." "Five years in a call center—need a break."

The pack weighed more than me, but I managed to get it into the lobby without fracturing my spine. Somehow, she lifted the enormous rucksack onto her back and tied the straps at the front.

"Ta," she said. "You stayin'?"

"No. I'm looking for someone." I showed her the photo of Sarah. "Might have been here a couple of weeks ago."

"Sorry," the girl said. "Was only here three days. On me way to *Gare de l'Est*. Zurich next." *Gare de l'Est* in a Geordie accent ... I could talk to her all day.

"Zurich's expensive," I said. "Take care."

She waved goodbye and struggled through the door and out into the street. I'd give the hairdryer a week.

Already planning what time to set my alarm for the morning, I promised myself another ten minutes, and took a seat in the reading corner, Sarah Stiles' face looking back at me from my phone. This wasn't a girl to run off and keep going without any contact. She was troubled, sure, but she was also easily influenced. She followed her feelings, her instincts. Unlike me.

For me, teen angst had been a delayed reaction. Between the ages of twelve and fifteen, I suffered bullying. Not the physical kind, nothing I could fight back against, but the relentless, psychological warfare at which teenagers seem to excel. My shirts were not the trendiest, my trainers had no swoosh or other branded symbol, and I often wore the same pair of trousers two days in a row. My hair would grow to unmanageable lengths, drawing taunts of "hippie" and "tramp." Home was sanctuary for me. Home was safe. Until Dad died, and my mother fell through the depths of clinical depression and into the life of Stuart Fitzpatrick, dragging me with her. When I objected, she repeated her new mantra yet again: "No more compromises."

I took that advice to heart and—some time later—spent the night of my nineteenth birthday on a Moroccan beach in a fog of hashish with a bunch of people who spoke no English.

That was me, though. That was *my* vanishing act. Not—

"Sarah?" said a female voice.

A young woman in her early twenties stared at the photo of Sarah on the table before me.

"You know her?" I asked.

"Yes, she was here." Light Midlands accent, British.

I sat up sharply. "Have a seat."

"I'm meeting some people." She headed for the door. "It's my night off."

I said, "Sarah might be in trouble."

The girl stopped, let her head drop. Turned. "Damn. I knew there was something off about that guy."

Patricia Norman was a receptionist here at *L' Hostel Centrale*, preparing to start her first year in the Paris College of Art. Sarah supposedly checked in alone. She asked Patricia one thing straight away: how to locate the Shakespeare Bookshop. I hadn't known Sarah was interested in books, but it made sense. She liked to concentrate, she liked order, so that was the sort of place she'd gravitate toward. And find it she did, with Patricia happy to have met someone who shared her passion. She had originally hoped to stay in one of the rooms that the proprietor offers to travelers in exchange for chores around the shop, but, alas, they were full, as they were when I tried over a decade earlier.

The two girls continued to hit it off that night when they toured the Latin Quarter, sinking a bottle of wine between them over dinner and then allowing a couple of Irishmen to throw a few cocktails their way. Neither girl "pulled," but it was fun.

"I'm not her father," I said. "No need to sugar-coat. Did anything happen with those guys?"

Patricia tightened her mouth and shrugged her shoulders, sighed and said, "Fine, I might have snogged one of them, but Sarah wasn't interested. She was almost too pissed to talk, but she knew how to say 'no'."

Still no mention of Gareth.

Patricia said, "That was a Friday night about two or three weeks ago. Saturday, she was still hung-over. Said she'd have an early night. Sunday morning, I didn't see her, but in the evening, there's some guy taking her bags. He's got this uniform on, and my boss, the owner—*that* guy—lets him do it."

We both looked over at the surly receptionist. He didn't care.

"What was it?" I asked. "A police uniform?"

"No. One of those posh hotel things. Red, with frilly shoulder pads."

I jotted that down. "Anything else about him?"

"Just that he was Chinese. Or Japanese. Heck, I sound like such a racist. I don't know."

"Humans are a tribal race," I said. "We recognize members of our own tribe far more easily than those from elsewhere. Westerners sometimes *do* have trouble identifying different racial groups from linked parts of the world. India, Pakistan and Bangladesh, or China, Japan and Korea. It isn't racist. It's just the way we take in faces."

While I reassured her, Pierre Bertrand's words came back to me, his assertion that South East Asian gangs were stepping up their game. I asked Patricia to elaborate on the guy's appearance, but beyond saying he was about six inches shorter than me and broad-shouldered, he was just "average."

I said, "Did you ask the manager what was happening?"

"He said that Sarah had met a friend—he said it in that saucy way, you know, nudge-nudge, wink-wink—he said she was moving hotels and the concierge was shifting her things. He'd had a phone call from Sarah, so it was all above board. There was a fella waiting down here for this Chinesey guy too. I think I'd seen him around here. Older, like about your age."

Thanks, I thought. I also noted Patricia was using the name "Sarah," not "Thandy" as per the passport.

I flashed up a photo of Gareth. "This him?"

"I think so, yes. He was staying here, always paid cash, but I never saw him and Sarah together."

Sarah and Gareth were pretending to be alone. One going about things like any other tourist, using her forged credit card to pay for things, while the other was a cash-only guy. If the card got flagged, it would be Sarah who found herself being questioned through an interpreter in a stale room with a two-way mirror.

I said, "You tipped off the sister on Facebook."

She nodded. "Anonymously. There was a thing about her having stolen some cash, and I didn't want to bring any trouble, but … she seemed nice. They didn't reply, and then all these trolls started attacking me, so I closed the account before some nutter worked out my address or something."

I wrote as fast as I could, hoping to decipher my handwriting back at the Grecian. "Did you speak to the other Brit at all?"

"Only to tell him to piss-off earlier that week. He wanted to know where someone might obtain what he called 'no-questions-asked' documents."

"A passport?"

"I guessed that was it. But I didn't want any part of it."

"You couldn't give him a name?"

"No. But Domi might have." She nodded again at the owner-cum-receptionist. She called, "Domi!" and took him my photo of Gareth. "This guy. He asked you about…" She caught herself and reverted to French, asking—as far as I could tell—about a name and a time.

He replied, "Non."

To me, Patricia said, "You'll have to pay him."

This man had information about a missing girl, and he'd lied to me earlier. I should've dragged him in the back room and hit him until he told me the truth, but I'd supposedly grown out of that sort of thing.

I opened my wallet, revealing another hundred euros. I asked Patricia to explain it was all I had.

He took it and said, "Sammy LeHavre."

"Sammy LeHavre," I said. "Where do I find him?"

Patricia translated, "He doesn't have Sammy's number, but he sent Gareth to a place called Suzie's Tabac. Sammy takes breakfast there every morning."

"And this Sammy, he provides passports for people?"

"Non," Dom said. "He know people who make passport for people."

"Thanks." I moved out of earshot of the man who knew more English than he'd let on. "Is there anything else you can think of? Anything about where she might have gone?"

"No." She slung her handbag over her shoulder. "Oh, yes. One thing. I tried calling her phone. It rang and rang. On my third try, this guy answered, so I asked if Sarah was there."

"What happened?"

"The guy laughed for about five seconds and hung up."

Chapter Fifteen

The next morning, I showered first thing, but in my haste to leave the UK I'd forgotten that damn razor, and my chin was already rough, my neck itchy. I made a mental note to buy one later, although I thought I was beginning to look stereotypically French, so maybe it would help for a while. I was on the Metro by seven, joining Parisian commuters for their daily crush, ascending into a smog-tinged street by half-past. Unlike the sculpted stone and pointed roofs in the Latin or Gothic Quarters, it seemed like every other building in the east of the Opera district was a garage operating from gaping segments of larger properties. The banging of hammers and screech of power tools dominated the air. Traffic was light and the longer I walked the sparsely-populated streets, the more the cosh in my waistband served as a comfort.

Suzie's Tabac was a cramped affair with enough space for three booths along one side and half a dozen tables packed so close that, once it was full, you'd have to dislodge the patrons from the outside ones, in. The barista was tall and hairy and wore a clean white vest. He didn't look like someone who'd be named "Suzie," but I wasn't there to judge. Today saw only one customer.

Sat in the far corner by the fire door, filling in a crossword, the man I assumed was Sammy LeHavre could have been any Frenchman on any normal day, except for one thing. Like England, France had years ago instigated a smoking ban, yet Sammy puffed away on a truly pungent cigarette.

Two broad-shouldered, broader-stomached men, who hadn't been visible from the street, ate nothing a couple of tables down. They looked soft and overweight, but I knew the baddest of the bad men were not necessarily muscular. This Michelin Man and Butterball pairing watched me all the way down the narrow aisle. They stirred as I asked Sammy, "*Parlez-vous Anglais?*"

Without looking up from his paper, he signaled the men to settle. Like he'd been expecting me. A skinny white man in his twenties, with his slicked-back dark hair, tan skin, and dressed casually in black, it was like he'd crafted his whole image to scream "pimp." He even sported a gold ring in one ear.

I squeezed into his booth across from him and he exhibited one of those droopy, faux-bored expressions. I said, "Sammy Le-Harve?"

He scribbled on his crossword before looking up. "Is polite to say '*excusé moi*' before interrupting."

"Your English is excellent."

"In my business, it pays to speak the language of the tourist. *Ich habe auch Deutsch zu sprechen.*"

"German, too? Jolly good."

He dragged on the cigarette. "I hope you are here to either make me slightly richer. Otherwise, I may get grumpy."

"I was told you may be able to provide documents to people wishing to leave France without detection."

"You think I am a criminal?"

"I could check with Gardien Bertrand."

Michelin Man and Butterball shifted, but Sammy smiled, which seemed to calm them.

He said, "Ah, our fallen hero. Such a shame about him." He

stubbed out the cigarette. "You think he has anything over me? He is just some bitch for the press."

"Okay." I slid out of the booth. "Bet he can still make trouble for you though."

"Hold on, mister," Sammy said, and the two large men stood and allowed their bellies to flop over their belts. "How you know Pierre Bertrand?"

"I'm not police. I'm looking for someone. And I believe most of you know Vila Fanuco. I'm pretty sure he'll be annoyed if you don't speak to me when he's so eager for me to do my job."

Sammy sighed. "Sit."

I slinked back onto the booth, the cosh resting hard in my back. "So can you help or not?"

Sammy lit another cigarette. "What help you needing?"

I brought up a photo of Sarah on my phone and laid it on the racing paper. "English girl. About three weeks ago. She was staying in the Opera district. You'd hear if she got herself in trouble. Or someone like him." I flicked to the next photo: Gareth's rodent smile.

"And why would I know this?"

"You can tell me or speak to Mr. Fanuco."

Sammy narrowed his eyes. "Why?"

"I told you, I'm working with *his* permission around here."

"What business do you think I am in?"

Over the next five seconds I considered about thirty of the more polite euphemisms. In the end I settled with, "You're a lowlife who exploits desperate women."

Sammy's smile through the smoke was wide but humorless. "And if I do know something, what is it you will want?"

I held his eye. Watched as his smile flickered slightly. "You're no poker player, are you, Sammy?"

"I make sure I am *always* the house. That way, the odds are always in my favor. I only ever back winners."

"That why you're loyal to Vila Fanuco? Because he's the power here?"

"I am a survivor. Remember that … if he ever commands me to hurt you."

Okay, time to change tactics. Go on the offensive. "Your English is virtually perfect, Sammy, as good as Gardien Bertrand. Which means you're educated."

"I was not always."

"But you are now. Thanks to Fanuco, I'd bet. But guess what? I know, Sammy. I know you're taking money on the side, money you don't declare to your boss."

He sucked on the cigarette and extinguished the near-stub in his empty cup.

I said, "You see, what these two people are carrying is valuable to Mr. Fanuco, and to folk back in England. They told me all Fanuco's people are on the lookout for Sarah and Gareth, which means you must have sold them something. But that was before this kicked off. Before you knew Fanuco needed them. Am I right?"

"Keep talking, Englishman."

"Thank you, I will." I switched tactics again. I'd done the accusations; now I needed empathy. "You found someone to make the passports, you took your profit, but you didn't include Vila Fanuco's cut. So when he comes along saying he needs you to be on the lookout, you can't risk him finding out you short-changed him."

Sammy's face drained of color in small increments until his skin developed an off-white shade close to grey. I could virtually see the brain-cogs turning, each facial tic charting my progress. He lit yet another cigarette and forced a grin.

I said, "You have that 'street' swagger, Sammy, and you have that look, and you pretend to be this vile piece of crap who uses women for his own ends. Really, though, you *are* running a business, no matter how disgusting it is. And you need to squeeze every ounce of profit you can."

He nodded. Empathizing with his wrong-doing, becoming his confidante, inviting myself into his secret and promising to keep it, sometimes this is more effective than direct threats.

Third class psychology degree, my arse. I deserved at least a 2:1. Or a B-grade.

I said, "I don't care about Fanuco, or your internal politics, but if I have to go directly to the big man, it could get you in a ton of shit. I don't want to place you in danger. I don't want to get you hurt. So if Sarah got in trouble, you either tell me right now, or give me the name of the damn forger. Because I'm sorry, but if you don't, you'll force me to go to Mr. Fanuco directly."

Even though I framed it as an apology, Sammy's face progressed from grey to slightly pink, and one of the two giant men might even have *growled*. Also English-speakers?

"Okay." I locked my phone screen and tucked it back in my pocket. "That's no problem. No hard feelings. Gonna see if Mr. Fanuco fancies splitting a croissant down by the Seine."

I stood and, for some instinctive macho reason, I winked at Michelin Man before making for the door. Sammy's twins eye-balled me as I went and I readied myself to whip out the cosh at the first quiver of the first lump of flab.

"Wait," Sammy called.

I stopped, turned, but did not approach.

Sammy said, "Okay. I *am* a businessman. Times are not good, and sometimes yes, I must act outside the rules. I do not wish for anyone to think I am betraying them." He placed his hands flat on the table. "What is the deal?"

"The forger," I said. "I want him."

Sammy shook his head. "My forger has no fear of Vila. A forger is just a tool. A valuable tool. If I requested the passports—*if* I saw your man here—Vila will punish *me*, no one else."

"If I can meet him, Vila won't find out."

"You must be more persuasive."

Roger Gorman wasn't good for much, but he taught me the best possible conclusion to any negotiation was both sides walking away having achieved something, even if one of you ultimately gained more than the other. I thought about why I was here. What I could realistically take away. If Benson tracked down the forger Gareth had used, he and Sarah would be caught quickly, so they had to obtain new documents. The lack of recent activity on their card suggested they were both probably dead, but if they procured new passports, new cloned cards, there was a good chance they did indeed leave France. To learn one way or another, I needed a deal that benefited both me and Sammy, *and* would endear me to this unnamed forger.

"I want documents," I said. "Good ones. Passport, credit card."

"A transaction?"

"I will pay your forger for them, he gives you your usual cut. In exchange, you tell me what you know about Sarah and the man she's travelling with. That way, you don't force me to mention your dishonesty to Mr. Fanuco."

He shook out another cigarette, his third since I arrived, but did not light it.

I said, "You know him better than me. Maybe he'll be chilled about it—"

"*Okay.* But I did not meet the girl. The same person at *L'Hostel Centrale* who sent you to me, he sent the man to me too, the picture on your phone."

"Gareth."

"I did not ask a name."

"How many?" I asked.

"I am sorry?"

"How many *passports*?"

Gareth. Alone. If it was only him, it could mean the worst had happened. Sarah had gone out drinking with a girl who snogged a random Irishman, so if he learned this it may have been too much.

Sammy waved his unlit cigarette toward my phone. "Two, of course."

I quickly agreed to Sammy's terms and instructed him to send the so-called "craftsman" to my hotel at two p.m. *If* the forger was willing, of course. He tried to negotiate the appointment time, but I didn't even acknowledge his effort. I had to get moving again, the notion that Sarah might still be alive supplanting the pessimism I'd harbored since I first read her file. I could not afford to let anything dampen that.

Chapter Sixteen

I left the cafe knowing there was something else I should have asked. Something important. It slipped around the outskirts of my brain, just out of reach, so I took a cab to the Grecian, skipping the Metro so I could call Jess en route to update her on my progress.

She said, "Be careful, Adam. These aren't the everyday thugs you're used to, and they sure as hell aren't greedy accountants in suits."

I knew this, of course, but I had little choice. They were bad people, hurting good people, mostly women and girls, as men had hurt women since what felt like the dawn of time.

"Jess," I said. "Be honest with me."

"Always."

"Am I reading too much into this? Do I make women into victims too easily?"

"Do you see me as a victim?"

"No. I see you as essential."

"Then there's your answer. I'm a woman, and mixed-race. If I was a disabled lesbian, I'd tick all the liberal guilt boxes that you agonize over. But you're not one of those guys. If I had a problem, you'd kick my backside to solve it, because you know I can handle it. Right now, you're looking for real victims. Just because you want to help them and punish those responsible, it's not liberal guilt. You're a decent human being, and I know if you get the chance, the action you take will make the US military look like an Oprah love-in."

I couldn't reply, as I was actually welling up. Like a teenage boy, I heard a mantra rocking through my head: *She gets me. She really gets me.*

She said, "Just be realistic, Adam. These people will hurt you first if you let them. Heck, they'll do more than hurt you."

"I know," I said with a cough. "It's actually a greedy accountant in a suit I'm calling about. Did you get me back onto the PAI mainframe?"

A pause, then, "No. I did get a backdoor in, but all you can do is watch my screen. Here, I'll sync you up."

"Not necessary. I've got a whole morning to kill until I get to the forger. Is there anything else? Any activity I can look into?"

"I'm sending you some links about that guy Benson made you call. It's not much. Background on his name, rumors, and I think he pops up a lot on the dark web."

"You think?"

"He's well-hidden, and it takes a lot of digging but he's there. Information-gathering, provision of services, covert access to countries."

"Covert access to countries," I said. "*Smuggling*, in other words." And if he was operating down in the bowels of cyberspace where shiny happy Google and Microsoft and Apple feared to tread, he clearly had a reason to dwell there.

Jess said, "Nothing concrete, but yes, smuggling is an option. Weapons are mentioned, people too. But I haven't managed to find a way into his network. It's all recommendations, warnings, praise—depends who's encountered him."

"Still, it's something. Be careful in the servers at PAI. Especially on a Sunday."

"I've come in on the pretext of diligence," she said. "I'll complain and moan about my extra hours so no one's suspicious. What's next for you?"

"Lunch, I suppose."

"Need company? Want me to pop over?"

"Nah, I don't think you want to be hanging around these people. Or me."

"Hey, I can play Felicity Smoak all day, but a bit of excitement never did a girl any harm."

Although I didn't feel like it, I laughed, assuming Smoak was some comic book sidekick—did I mention she was a nerd?

I said, "Thanks, Jess. I'll be in touch," and hung up the phone, collected the iPad from my room and strolled down the street to the Metro.

In my backpacking days, I was one of those oddities. I planned to steer clear of tourists as often as possible, but for the first couple of years I lacked the skills and confidence to neglect the guidebooks' must-sees. Then, one day, all that changed. I don't know what day that was precisely, and in truth it must have happened over several months, but one day, suddenly, I was simply there—shopping in a souk, living in a spare room above a cycle shop, taking my meals amongst brown-skinned turban-wearing locals, and growing a tad jealous whenever a fellow Brit or a Yank discovered my private corner of the world. It was somewhere in Turkey, I seem to recall. From that day on, I viewed wandering the most obvious places as tantamount to failure. The major attractions, of course, were still required viewing, but I comforted myself that the native people also frequented those sites. Thinking that way, touring Ankor Wat and the Great Wall of China and Tabletop Mountain, I wasn't a tourist in those places; I was a *traveler*.

Now, I figured, getting around Paris would be a doddle, and although a trail of credit card transactions detailed Sarah's movements around the city's retailers, I started in the place that, just maybe, could have been her most impressive stop. Before I dared step into the Shakespeare Bookshop, though, I headed down the embankment a way, hoping to pick up on any tails that may have latched on—either Sammy's people or those who located me in the Grecian. Spotting nothing suspicious, I headed for the ramshackle bookstore down its narrow street.

Outside, cartons of novels lay spine-up, a simple maze where people mooched about in search of that perfect literary experience. Inside, its shelves heaved under the sheer volume and the musty smell cast me back to that first time I turned up here, got rejected for accommodation, and spent two hours choosing a Stephen King paperback. I requested a moment of the owner's time, and of the people who worked here, and showed them Sarah's photo, but they only told me what I already knew: one girl sort-of thought she saw Sarah around, but no Gareth. No additional info or overheard conversation. I thanked them and wandered the shelves for a few more minutes.

I'm not sure what I'd been expecting. Some sort of psychic infusion with the ghost of Sarah's presence? I got nothing from the ether. No epiphany. No irrational tingle.

I left without buying anything, and checked my mapping app, set it to estimate how long it would take to walk back to the Grecian for my meeting. It said ninety minutes. That would do me good. Trek the streets, gazing at the pretty buildings, maybe stop for a coffee and a *croque-monsieur*. Figured it might dislodge that question I should have asked Sammy.

I crossed a bridge and rounded a corner into an expansive square with the Cathedral known worldwide as Notre Dame lumped there like a sheer rock face infused with gargoyles and spires and crevices, its massive wheel of stained glass dominating the wall above the entrance. As with all famous monuments, blokes played

David Bailey with their swish cameras, less well-prepared types angled iPads and phones, and the craze for selfie-sticks showed no sign of abating. I guessed they were here to stay.

I sat on a bench, and after reading the scant research from Jess I tried to arrange my thoughts. If Sarah obtained a second passport, it was likely she was out of the country by now and I really was chasing her ghost.

I was about to call Jess and ask her to start whittling away at all those credit cards that continued spending in onward destinations, when a man stepped in front of me, casting a shadow. I waited for his gaze to wander back to Notre Dame, but it remained fixed on me.

"*Bonjour*," I said.

"You lost us for a short while." The forty-ish man sat on the bench beside me. "But this was the correct direction. I am surprised you took time out for sightseeing."

His French-cum-Eastern-European accent marked him as Vila Fanuco himself.

I said, "I'm waiting for my next lead to call."

"What is this lead?" he asked politely.

"Confidential."

"You met with Sammy LeHavre this morning. Why?"

I shook my head. "Come on. You don't need to know that. I'm doing what I've been instructed to do."

"You found a forger." Fanuco possessed a full head of black hair, but his face had a sheen to it, a plainness that robbed him of any real expression, Botox-like in its rubberiness. "What did Sammy tell you?"

"Very little."

Fanuco nodded, his eyes on me. "Ambitious boy, Sammy is. Clever. Sometimes, not as clever as he thinks, though, eh? This would not be the first time he made a deal independent of me, but it is disappointing that he lied."

If Fanuco had already worked out Sammy's secret I saw no reason to protect him. I said, "He was scared."

"Still, I perhaps did not emphasize the severity of the situation when I made my inquiries." A friendly smile creaked onto his face. "How did you find him?"

"I'm clever."

"No tips from Pierre Bertrand?"

"No," I said. "The old fashioned way. Bribery. Your old pal didn't offer anything."

"My 'old pal'." Fanuco chuckled. "Of course. How is dear Pierre?"

"His knee is still stiff, and his wife likes him home on time now Henrietta Dupree is about to move to Interpol."

"Henrietta Dupree. Young. Pretty." Fanuco leaned forward. "Like the girl you took from my colleague in England."

"Yes. And you won't find her."

"No, you have done well. But then, we are not actually *looking* for her." With the lack of movement on his face, the grin took on a rictus quality, lizard-like, an illusion giving him too many teeth. "Do you know how we maintain such a grasp on our people here?"

"I'd say by making your operation look bigger than it really is. It gives you a god-like presence. You employ teams of private security personnel who have no idea who they're working for, like your surveillance of me. There are still some small-time operators who fall beneath your radar, but it's hardly worth pursuing them, so the big guys, the skilled criminals—like the forger—they fall in line. Something like that?"

"Again, I am impressed. First you relieve Mr. Benson of his lovely dancing girl, and then you identify one of my street people without my help, all after making nice with a policeman who would kill me on sight."

"Why are we talking?" I asked.

"I wanted to look at you. I mean really *look* at you. Not through a camera or a lens."

"Who are you? Vila Fanuco? There's no record of anyone by that name, just rumors, veiled mentions." As evidenced by the lack of data from Jess.

"Do you really think I'm going to answer that?"

"It doesn't matter anyway. You're probably ex-military, *maybe* Middle Eastern, but with the tinge in your accent I'm going with Eastern Europe. Balkans. You set up your trafficking routes using other military types in the countries whose officials are easiest to bribe. And you rule through fear. Your reputation, as much as actual events. Like murdering a man's wife to force him to do your bidding."

Fanuco's posture shifted so his shoulders aimed squarely toward me. "Recover the things you need to recover, and we will not seek out your dancing girl prize from wherever she is hiding, and return her to Curtis Benson in a bag."

"Mr. Benson isn't too high in your organization, then? Otherwise you'd be making *absolutely sure* she got sent back."

He sighed. "Mr. Park—Adam—I know this will surprise you. But there *is* no organization."

"Right. Okay."

"No, really." He sounded amused, but it was a hard to tell. "We are not some international gang, like Spectre in James Bond. We are not an evil corporation with a ladder to climb. We are not even like Al Qaeda with firewalls between different cells. We are *not* an organization."

I tried the silence trick and stared ahead. It worked.

He said, "We are just businesses. Even to call it 'we' is an exaggeration. People in similar lines of work. We agree boundaries, and we agree to help each other when we can. Unite against common obstacles, like border agencies, Interpol, the CIA. But we do not take risks, as one would for a friend."

"I have to meet my guy in an hour," I said. "Can I go now? Unless you want to detail your own corner of this ... *network*, or whatever it is."

Fanuco took a moment. "I would not like to detail it, no. You are free to go."

I was about to leave, but I had to ask, "What makes a guy of your obvious intelligence get into this game? If it's money, you'd make a fortune legitimately."

"It is not just about money."

"Power, then? You submit women to the most degrading life—"

"I perform a service."

"I've heard that somewhere before. Do all you people justify your actions this way?" I felt Harry in my not-so-distant past telling me to quit, to stop talking, to *shut fuck up, son.* I said, "Come on. Why are you different?"

"Sometimes they suffer, yes," he said. "But far less than if they remained in whatever hellish country they are running from."

Considering what little I knew of his background, I took an absolute punt. "The genocide in Bosnia? Or did the Russians do something?"

Fanuco lowered his voice to a gravelly monotone. "You are not here to investigate me. You are here to do as you are told, and nothing more."

"A daughter?"

His jaw tightened. "Two, actually."

"And you'd be happy for them to be forced to strip nightly for drunk men? To suck their dicks for fifty quid a pop?"

I thought he was going to hit me, but instead he said, simply, "It is better than what they endured at the hands of Mladić's kill squads. I know it is better ... because they forced me to watch."

We are the sum of our experiences. Whether in business or potentially physical confrontations, I try not to involve myself in situations without a clear exit strategy. That had been my mistake in Thailand, and it's why I trained so much, why I over-thought every plan, every move, to the point I frequently made the wrong decision whenever I had to act on instinct. Vila Fanuco must have followed similar rules, but had been better than me at making those decisions, otherwise he never would have risen this high. Whatever those soldiers did to his family, it had closed off a part of his brain. Anything less sadistic than what his daughters experienced stirred nothing in him now.

"Okay," I said. "I'm sorry to hear that. Really."

I moved to stand, but Fanuco rested a hand on my leg, implying I should remain seated.

He said, "You are investigating the background to this case instead of focusing on your goal. Including unnecessary curiosity about *me*. Do not do that."

His right hand smoothed over my thigh. I heard nothing but his voice, the background noise muffled.

"I will provide whatever support you need to accomplish this goal. You must only ask."

His fingers touched my left hand.

"You have shown much intelligence and courage. I even think you would do well working for me."

His hand closed tenderly over mine.

"But do not for one moment think that I will tolerate any interruption to my affairs. Do not scream. This is going to hurt."

I said, "What is?"

With a subtle but firm movement, he jerked his fist sideways and a wet snap sounded as my little finger broke in half. I obeyed the man and did not scream. Just cradled my hand, not touching the digit that now sat at a forty-five degree angle to the knuckle.

I managed to ask, "W-why?"

"A reminder. Whenever you feel this injury, think about me. Think about what I said. Remain focused."

He reached again, this time with two hands. He held my wrist with one, and with the other he pulled, twisted the digit back into position. I felt the broken ends touch. When the two halves settled in place, he let go. He'd reset it. Sort of. It throbbed. When I tried to move it, the swelling grated beneath my skin.

"It will hurt for some time," Fanuco said. "Strap it to your ring-finger and it will mend itself. Take painkillers." Then he stood, fastened his jacket, and added, "Unlike Sammy, the forger asked my permission to speak with you, and of course I said yes. This is not a person who will volunteer information that might incriminate, but your questions will be answered."

Finally, he walked away without a care in the world, and I—hurt in the most random of ways—planned how to handle a meeting that could send me in a new direction entirely.

Chapter Seventeen

The Grecian Hotel's bar was furnished with a couple of leather sofas in one corner, on which a man in a leather jacket leafed through a book, while on a plastic-covered table, a ginger-haired woman with pale skin browsed her laptop, but that was the extent of the Grecian's custom. Once the older barmaid saw fit to put down her magazine, I ordered a coffee and approached the chap in the leather jacket and asked if he was here from Sammy. He looked at me like I offered him a turd, and in an American accent told me to go fuck myself, then got up and headed for the lobby.

A cough drew me toward the ginger woman, who was on her feet, looking over a pair of thick-rimmed glasses. "You are late."

"I'm sorry." I downed the café-noir. Showed her my bandaged hand. "Minor mishap."

Once I found a pharmacy open on a Sunday—and very little is open on a Sunday in France—the elderly Persian woman sold me three bandages and strapped me up there and then, recommended some stronger-than-usual ibuprofen, and instructed me to visit an emergency room.

The red-haired woman said, "You want to ask me things that I should not tell. Not in my work."

"Vila Fanuco has given permission."

"He has *ordered* me to," she said, with clear distaste. "If I had known Sammy LeHavre was acting in a way to harm Monsieur Fanuco, I would not have worked with him."

"I know. And Mr. Fanuco knows that. I don't think he blames you."

I ordered two more coffees and asked the woman her name, but she just sat heavily on the recently-vacated leather couch. I handed her the envelope containing passport-sized photos of myself and a wedge of money.

She checked the pictures over, considered them, and said, "Are you sure this is correct?"

"Yes," I said. "They're fine."

She placed the envelope in a soft, finely-stitched handbag and said, "Go."

"Go?"

"What is it that I must tell you?"

I took out a notepad and a pen that I'd all-but forgotten about. "Tell me the new identities you supplied for Sarah and Gareth."

"I do not know those names."

"They were calling themselves Mister and Missus Gallway."

"Show me."

I presented my phone and flicked between the two photos.

She said, "Yes. I made for them two perfect passports. And this man, the photo on your phone, he was willing to pay me five thousand euros extra for a fast result. They became Isabella Laurent and Joseph Coulet."

I noted the names. "French passports."

"You are in France, monsieur detective. What else would I make?"

"Right. But they don't speak French. Or do they?"

"*Non*, they do not. Creating these passports, it is no longer enough to have artistic talent."

At the mention of "artistic talent," I saw Sarah's pictures in Sanjay's Bar, how Caroline treated them with such affection. If I failed to bring her home, that's all that would remain of her impressions on sheets of paper.

"It is no longer just a reproduction," the woman went on. "Thanks to jihad, thanks to America, we all must have bio-chips. We must have … what are those…?" She drew a shape with her finger in the air.

"Watermarks," I said.

"Yes. This. Watermarks. Very inconvenient for me. Two white people is easier than two Africans or Asians, but I still must match person and data on the chips."

In relation to what Patricia told me in the hotel, it all fit. I asked the forger how I would go about obtaining a passport at short notice.

"If I own a chip in my workshop that matches to your details, I could do it in a few hours. You are easy. Six foot, slim build, dark hair, blue eyes. I have twenty of these."

I asked her to wait, then checked my phone. The actual telephone functions no longer worked, meaning the SIM card had been disabled, which I had been expecting. *Thank you, Mr. Gorman.* But as a handheld computer it could still connect to Wi-Fi, so I emailed Jess the names "Isabella Laurent" and "Joseph Coulet." It took longer than usual; I hadn't noticed how much I used my little finger before a sociopath broke it in half.

I said, "If I wanted you to do something for me, would you report it to Vila Fanuco?"

She frowned. "You are not going to ask me if I can break into a password are you?"

"No. Why would I do that?"

"No reason." She looked away.

She was willing to tell me something important but felt she had to play this game. She wouldn't betray the conditions we'd laid out at the start.

I said, "What did they ask you to do?"

"Ask better than that."

Back at the Angel Inn, Agent Frank claimed to work for MI5, and was more interested in the "other items" Sarah and Gareth might be carrying. Even Benson implied they had taken more than money.

It's called "organized" crime for a reason.

So maybe Gareth's photography really was just a distraction.

I said, "Did either of them ask you to help access a computer or hard drive?"

"A what?"

"Or maybe a pen drive. With information—"

"The man. He asked if I knew anyone capable of cracking codes. He used a word. De ... something."

"'Decrypt'?"

"Yes, 'decrypt'."

I was so close to it. Returning this item to Benson could set me free to concentrate on finding Sarah without interference from interested parties like Fanuco.

"And?" I said. "Where did you send him?"

The forger said, "I do not know anyone like that. I could not help."

I closed my eyes, a moment of optimism dashed on cruel rocks. "So, would you have to report anything I requested to Vila Fanuco?"

"I am independent. I do not work for anyone, and Monsieur Fanuco does not try to keep me for himself. But he is someone I must respect. I do not have to tell him, but if he asks ... I dare not lie."

"I understand," I said.

I told her I wanted the same service that Gareth had paid for, the quick turnaround. This case was rapidly descending into the sort of story that does not end well. The ability to run from a seriously psychotic criminal would be essential, if I felt the need to betray him.

She quoted an additional three thousand euros to the two I already handed over, and I asked her to wait ten minutes, popped out to a money union exchange a couple of streets away, and withdrew five thousand euros from my personal cash reserves. I returned and paid the ginger woman, keeping the other two grand for my back pocket. Just in case. She asked again if I was sure I wanted to use those passport photos, and again I assured her it was fine. After she left, I spent the next half-hour on the hotel's Wi-Fi, giving Jess as much information as I could relating to Sarah's and Gareth's new documents, but Jess would have to confirm where in the whole world their new identities had fled.

Still, I needed more traction, more intelligence. I needed someone to point me the right way, and I only knew one good person in this city who might help. I called Pierre Bertrand and requested he meet me … yes, I told him, on a Sunday.

Chapter Eighteen

I caught the Metro west, locating on a paper map the quaint park where Fanuco dumped the body of an innocent woman in order to make a point. I arrived fifteen minutes early and paced the bank where the water reflecting the greying sky, wishing I smoked. I thought about the pen drive and what it might contain. Blackmail documents? Photos? Accounts? As Agent Frank said, it's what organized crime did. They needed records in order to launder money and to keep track of employees and ensure not one penny ended up in someone's pocket who hadn't earned it. I'd heard of entire payroll databases before, although I didn't know how much was true and what was urban legend.

Someone handed me a coffee.

"Thank you for coming." I accepted the steaming drink.

"What happened to your hand?" Pierre Bertrand asked.

"Trapped it in … oh, it doesn't matter." I sipped from the paper cup. It tasted deeper and thicker than anything back home. I said, "I met a man called Sammy LeHavre today. He was helpful."

"Then what do you want from me?"

"I know the names of my subjects' new identities. I was hoping you could check, see whether they left the country already."

"Of course, no problem."

"If you can see where they went, maybe you could get me the CCTV footage."

He nodded. Smoked. Sipped. "Easily obtained."

"If they are travelling with anyone else, would you be able to trace them? Get a name, maybe an address?"

"In today's world? Of course. We can do this with one phone call."

"The names are Isabella Laurent and Joseph Coulet. They will have travelled somewhere between—"

"Why don't you come to the station, Mr. Park?"

"The station?"

"*Oui.*" He took a drag on the cigarette. Exhaled in my face. "Perhaps I can give you a pass and my access codes so you do not need to keep calling me."

"I'm sorry, I don't understand. You want to give me your codes?"

"Yes! And I will cook for you too. How about a nice chicken?"

"Right," I said, finally realizing what he was doing.

"And your cock, Mr. Park. Perhaps I could find a nice lady to service you. Or why not do it myself, hm? Yes, I cook for you and while you eat, I—"

"I get it," I said. "Look, I really need this. These people have stolen money and important information that I need to retrieve or—"

"Or what? You have some personal stake in this? Something you cannot explain?"

I wondered then, what *did* I have riding on this? I sent Lily away, so Benson's main leverage over me was gone. I still had to find Sarah, of course, especially now I had no doubt she was in trouble. Whether that was with a highly-manipulative abuser or some wider crime, I couldn't say. If she was even alive.

He said, "As much as I would like to be your personal informant in the police, I am afraid I have a little pride left. *Au revoir*, Mr. Park."

Before he could move, I said, "Tell me again about the criminals moving into Paris. You mentioned them getting bigger, more successful. Asian origin, you said. Chinese, Korean?"

He deliberated with himself. Finished his coffee. "Bad people. They keep mostly to their own territory, but their trade is similar to Fanuco, so they fight sometimes. People is big business."

"White slave trade?"

"Yes." He lit another cigarette. I hadn't realized he finished his first. "But not just white. We have a high African population here. Easy targets. These gangs, they bring girls in, they take girls out, bring boys, take them away. I do not know all the details. As I said, I am only a press monkey these days."

"What do they do, these girls and boys? Sex workers?"

We were alone here. No Parisians, no tourists.

He said, "Sometimes sex, sometimes domestic people who work in houses for food and a bed. There is a culture of this in many parts of the world."

"Do you think Sarah might have been taken somewhere else?"

"I think nothing. If there is no sign of her, no clue—"

"I have clues," I said. I told him about the man taking Sarah's luggage, about Gareth possibly being "with them" and of the documents they'd had made. "So who is most likely? The Koreans? The Chinese?"

Bertrand shook his head dismissively. "Mr. Park, I think it is time you filed an official statement. Go to your embassy, they will help you complete the paperwork. If not, you should leave Paris." He started to walk away.

"I'm touched. Do you think these Chinese or Korean guys might hurt me?"

"Okay, you win," Bertrand said. "Not Chinese. Not Korean. Vila Fanuco's main enemy now, the fastest growing gang… they are Vietnamese."

Now that rang a round, fat bell. Clanged loudly but, like the niggling question, I couldn't quite grasp it.

He said, "If the *gendarmes* catch you making trouble, I will not protect you. If you are caught in a place you should not be, there will be no police to back you up. You will be arrested or hurt, or worse. And if these people have your girl, or your man, they will not give them up easily."

After that, he stubbed out his cigarette and walked calmly away. I did not try to stop him. I had to go do something Harry would term "stupidly-dangerous."

Chapter Nineteen

Without Wi-Fi, my phone was a shiny brick with a pretty interface, so I picked up a pay-as-you-go 4G SIM and, to prevent getting cut off through over-use, I paid two-hundred euros onto it. I Googled the Vietnamese district in Paris, and learned there was not a "district" as such, just a growing number of people emigrating from the former French colony to settle in this corner of Europe, working low-paying jobs, raising families, opening businesses, a few such businesses bunched together over a five-mile area. While this was still too multicultural to be deemed a ghetto, it was certainly viewed by various race-hate groups as a "Vietnamese stronghold" albeit one more palatable than the Muslim and African suburbs.

I called Jess from the back of a cab. She answered cautiously, not recognizing the caller ID, but after briefly explaining the change in numbers, I said, "When you were going through that cross-check of credit cards, you discounted all those with onward journeys, right?"

"Working under the assumption that Sarah and Gareth are still in France. I'm fine, by the way, thanks for asking."

"Sorry." I rubbed my eyes. "Just … please can you remember? Things have changed. Didn't you say there was a hit in Vietnam?"

I heard a keyboard tapping. "Only one that fits the timeline. Five days in Paris, then active in Ho Chi Minh City. We originally assumed it couldn't be them because we nailed that card in the internet café."

"They must have two cards."

"Want me to send you the data?"

"Yes please. And can you look up Isabella Laurent and Joseph Coulet, see if they left France?"

"I'll unpack my wand."

I forget sometimes that hacking isn't as simple as it looks on TV. The DDS software was invisible to the company being scanned so to the user it felt like an automated process, but the skill and guile it had taken to create was almost unfathomable. Genuine talent makes stuff like that look easy. And Jess made it all look *very* easy.

"Sorry," I said again. "Can you try? DDS might work. They're real people somewhere in France. They had their identities stolen and used for the passports. See if they cross with that credit card."

"I'll do what I can," she said. "Might take a while, though. And Adam?"

"Yes?"

"I won't be able to build a backdoor for you into the PAI mainframe, no matter how much time I have. Everything outside the UK is completely locked down. Unless you know how to clone a UK server IP address from your end?"

"I don't."

"Well, I have an undetected entry-point here. If you need access, you'll have to call."

I thanked her as much as I could, and promised I'd look after her when I got home.

"I know," she said. "I know you will."

Rain loomed over the edges of the city, meaning taxis would soon be at a premium. With movement in the case, I would have to be more mobile than this, so I had my current cab drop me at a Hertz. I managed to snag a small Fiat before they closed and drove out into the muggy evening.

Beyond American war movies, I knew nothing about Vietnam. It wasn't somewhere I visited when I lived Out There in the World, Vietnam being—back then—a repressive communist country that did not cater well to travelers. Events, though, led to one obvious question: what involvement could the Vietnamese gangs have with Sarah and Gareth? Fanuco and Sammy were on the opposite side, so there was no reason to think the passport acquisition led directly to the Vietnamese. More importantly, I needed to ascertain whether they were still here, or if I should be booking a flight.

My remaining lead was Sarah's phone. Harry had thoroughly checked her known number and it had been switched off, but I knew she was using a phone in Paris. Someone had told me that.

I followed the sat-nav to *L'Hostel Centrale*, and found Patricia Norman in the reading area, enjoying the damp remnants of her weekend off with a copy of *At the Mountains of Madness*. I asked her outright for Sarah's number, the one she dialed a few days ago and heard only a laughing man. As I suspected, it was different from the one Harry had attempted to trace.

A new phone for her new life.

Back in the car, I called Jess, and no, she hadn't been able to check those names against airport departures. I told her not to worry and asked her to see if Sarah's new phone number was still active. I expected more bad news. But it *was* active.

"And, wow," she said. "Will wonders never cease? It's transmitting as we speak."

I punched the air and asked her to text me the GPS location. She went one better, syncing my phone with her laptop so I could see the DDS data in real time. I used the text to load my sat-nav and drove toward *15, Rue Marie-Gauche*. The drizzle started about twenty minutes in and continued to wisp around the car as the wind picked up. Twenty minutes later, I reached my destination.

Number fifteen was a narrow three-story townhouse. The railings surrounding a lower floor were black iron and the door was red and looked sturdier than 10 Downing Street. Paint peeled from the doors and windows on the houses either side, so the pristine number fifteen seemed embarrassed by its neighbors.

In my haste to ask Patricia about the phone, I left my binoculars in the hotel along with my Nikon and its lovely zoom, so I had to get closer than I'd like. I trundled past the house and parked two doors down, my rear-view mirror trained on the door, and wing-mirrors angled to see the road and pavement. And there I sat. For over an hour.

No distractions.

Just watching. And waiting.

Theorizing.

I fought off the sting of sleep by utilizing an exercise taught to me by a yoga instructor a couple of miles north of Bondi Beach: I held my nose, pursed my lips as tight as possible to form the tiniest hole, and blew with as much force as I could muster. It channeled air out of the pinhole gap, and the pressure building inside me refreshed my brain. On the third repetition of this exercise, I finally identified that question I should have asked hours earlier.

As I predicted, it was so obvious Harry would have barked the word "amateur" at me for not snagging it hours ago. I made a bet with myself to see if I was right about the answer. Childish, yes, but hey—I was *really* bored.

Eventually, I saw movement in my rear-view.

And I won my bet.

Sammy LeHarve emerged from the red door, flanked by Butterball and Michelin Man. They hurried down the stairs and into an old American car, a Mustang by the looks of it. The engine roared and they took off down the street in a cloud of fumes and revs. I checked Jess's synced GPS data and, indeed, Sammy LeHavre's car was giving Sarah's phone a ride somewhere. I pulled the Fiat out, executed a one-eighty turn, and followed.

If Vila Fanuco, "Lord of the Parisian Underworld," had been looking for Sarah and Gareth on behalf of Curtis Benson, why would Sammy not have told Fanuco, "A girl and a guy? Mais-oui, I 'ad zeez documents made"?

That's what I should have asked. The niggling question. Obvious now. Sammy had made out his boss would be dangerously upset with him, but Fanuco himself acted fairly chilled when he learned about it; a minor indiscretion by a protégé whose ego swelled larger than his ability. Nothing more.

So there was my question: *Why didn't Sammy tell Fanuco he'd had passports made for Sarah and Gareth? Why was he so scared?*

I knew the answer now, of course. There really was only one.

Nearing the city, traffic all-but disappeared, making the tail harder, but the darkening streets and the steady rain made it doable. Plus, it was a fucking *Mustang*. In Paris. If I wanted, I could hang two streets back, stick my head out the window, and listen for the engine. And we had the phone's GPS, but the prospect of taking my eyes off that vehicle even for a second made my hands grip the wheel even tighter, and my foot grew heavier over the accelerator.

They eventually pulled into a multi-story parking lot and I was forced to make an illegal U-turn a hundred meters further on. I reversed into a disabled zone and turned off the engine. It ticked loudly in time with the rain on the roof, which meant more waiting.

Jess's DDS data streamed through the phone. The purchasing history for the card currently in Vietnam was listed chronologically. The spending pattern indicated two cards on the same account, like a husband and wife may have, showing they spent in Paris and, later, in Ho Chi Minh City. There remained the possibility that the cards were, like the phone, taken away from Sarah and Gareth. If the cards alone were shipped out to Vietnam, it meant the pair had not left Europe, and if the cards were taken from them they'd have lost the cash too, and I would be searching only for their corpses' resting place.

I couldn't read any further, though, as Sammy and his two fat guards exited the car park, collars folded up against the drizzle. They hustled down the street and entered a bar. The establishment had no name that I could see, and the wicker chairs outside were too wet to sit on. I watched for five dead minutes, until Sammy dragged a tall, scantily-clad black woman out by her arm, her long legs gangling. Butterball and Michelin Man followed.

Under other circumstances I'd happily have driven my car into the two enforcers and battered Sammy with the cosh until he could no longer plead for me to stop—the heroic knight Sir Adam yet again saves the damsel. But there was a bigger picture to consider.

I lost sight of them around the next corner. I started the engine and pulled out, halting at the junction. The party turned into a building and I swung right into the narrow one-way street.

The window to the second bar Sammy entered was almost fully steamed-up. Vague shapes swayed behind the glass. This time a name was displayed above the door in peeling gold letters. I had to read it more than once: *The Golden Lion*. In English. I pictured a gaudy theme pub with union flags, Winston Churchill portraits, and faux beer pumps.

A honk sounded from behind. A white Mercedes revved, trying to get past. I found an empty stretch of pavement and bumped the small car onto it. The Merc glided past and stopped outside The Golden Lion. A leather-jacketed man got out, flicked open an umbrella, and opened the Merc's back door. A second man stepped into the wet road, the umbrella held over him by the first. This second man was expertly-quaffed and wore a tailored tan suit and professorial spectacles. I was close enough to see both were oriental, although their skin was darker than the average Chinese. They could easily have been Vietnamese. I doubted that the Man in Tan was the same one who collected Sarah's things, but I'd bet another broken finger he'd know who it was. Umbrella Man, perhaps.

They walked briskly into the bar.

I had Pierre Bertrand on the phone before the door closed. I briefly explained how I tailed Sammy, and recapped how Patricia had seen the oriental man taking Sarah's luggage, that Sammy Le-Harve himself was in possession of Sarah's phone right now.

"And this concerns me how?" Bertrand said in a bored voice. "I told you, I have no interest in your activities."

"Sammy is one of Fanuco's guys, right? Fanuco controls Sammy's operations, 'lets' him work his corner of Paris. The phone is *evidence*."

"Yes. This is true."

"So …" I knew he understood. He had to.

"Illegal evidence that will send me even further down the ranks of the *Prefecture*. Again, unless you are about to reveal how I may arrest or kill Vila Fanuco, I ask how this concerns me." This was not the same man I met yesterday. Heck, this wasn't the same man I saw this afternoon.

"He got to you," I said. "Didn't he?"

"No," he said. "That is not why I cannot help you."

"Then why?"

"Because, Monsieur Park … this Vietnamese gang has been moving into Paris for six months now. At first, Fanuco wanted to be partners, but they refused."

"That makes no sense. If you want—"

"The Vietnamese are organized, my friend. After decades of communist rule, they are *disciplined*. They are also ruthless and lack any concept of remorse. But they have rules. A code. Fanuco has none of this. Sammy LeHavre, he is a rat. A cockroach."

"A survivor." I understood now where Bertrand was going with this.

"Correct. If he is working with the Vietnamese gangs then he believes they are his key to staying in business. He is useful to those bigger men, but they are not useful to him unless they are running the city."

I am always the house, Sammy told me. *I only ever back winners.*

I said, "You're hoping the Vietnamese will rub Fanuco out."

"*Rub him out.* Ha! A good phrase, yes." He paused and let out a sigh. "Mr. Park, I am sorry. Your girl is dead. She must be. She is dead, or in Vietnam, or the Middle East, or some place they desire young flesh. But it is no concern of mine."

"Don't you care that more people will die?"

"If the Vietnamese take Fanuco down, hundreds more will be saved."

"And you're going to let the Vietnamese do it."

"No, Monsieur Park. My *colleagues* are going to let them do it. I am only a press monkey."

He hung up. The man had wanted so badly to nail Fanuco, but he was tired now; he just wanted Fanuco gone, destroyed. I could call one of his colleagues, I thought, or I could take a chance and phone the embassy.

But I made a different call instead.

Chapter Twenty

I had to question if I could really do this without compromising my safety. My life. Even Sarah's. Entering a bar in which a pimp, two big men and two potential people-smugglers now met, men who would be less than comfortable with my activities, was it the smartest move I could make?

No more compromises.

I stepped inside.

A heavily-mustachioed man served drinks from behind a plain bar surrounded by cheap MDF walls. It was the sort of place a couple of dozen soccer hooligans might congregate to yell at the screen, and throw beer bottles at the window. A smattering of Vietnamese men—young and old—sat drinking *pastis* and, despite the ban, each held a real cigarette, smoke coiling up to the ceiling. Most of the occupants looked surprised but not particularly bothered by my presence.

Sammy LeHavre and his associates were not among them.

At the bar, I ordered a *pastis* but the jowly barman just rubbed his nose and flicked something on the floor. Waved a dismissive hand.

He said, "*Allez.*" Meaning "go." In this context, I think it meant, "Get out, dickhead."

His hands gripping a glass, a damp rag motionless within. The door behind him opened a crack. Nobody exited. The man allowed a sideways glance, during which he positioned the glass on a shelf, nearly dropping it in the process.

"Who's in there?" I asked.

He wouldn't look at me. "*Mon chien.*"

"A dog? *Un chien* is your dog?" I whistled a *come-here* whistle. "Here boy! *Allez!*"

The door squeaked slowly open.

Sammy LeHavre stood in the metal frame with Butterball and Michelin Man behind, both expressing that bored look known the world over as *"I'm-a-tough-guy-no-one-can-touch-me."* Sammy shook his head as if amused, but his eyes were dark, his hands fidgety.

The barman looked at the customers. Nodded. Like some 60's or 70's western, the older fellas exited without finishing their drinks, followed by all but the two youngest Vietnamese men. The barman then relocated further away from Sammy, and busied himself in the corner wiping down the clean surface.

The two Vietnamese lads sipped their drinks. Looking my way.

"You must leave now," Sammy said. "You get one chance. Go."

"You have her phone," I said. "You met her, you know what happened."

Sammy risked a glance back at the room into which I could not see. Breathed out loudly through his nose. He said, "I am sorry I did not tell you earlier. But she is dead. The man too. They flashed too much cash, and they died. End of story. You can go now."

"Where?"

"In the sewer. A hole in the ground. I do not know. They are dead. You stop looking, and you go home, or you end up in this same place."

Okay, I still had the option to walk away. Tell Caroline her sister was dead, and get the Foreign Office to instigate a search. But the police here had their hands full looking for one of their own. I still remembered Henrietta Dupree, and how the pain of her disappearance clearly haunted Bertrand when he told me they had failed her. And what were the chances that Caroline would accept the word of a loyalty-deficient scumbag like Sammy LeHavre?

I said, "And how does Vila Fanuco feel about you playing nice with the opposition?"

Sammy dead-eyed me. With a flick of his fingers, Butterball and Michelin Man advanced from the doorway. As they flipped up a section of the bar on its hinge I caught a glimpse of three Vietnamese men inside the room: the Man in Tan and Umbrella Man, both staring out at me, plus a third in a slick suit and wraparound sunglasses and built like a rugby back-liner, holding hands with the terrified black girl Sammy had pulled out of Bar Nameless.

"Okay," I said, backing toward the exit. "I'm leaving."

"Too late," Sammy said.

Slightly in front of his colleague, Butterball reached for me. I whipped out the cosh with my right hand and cracked it into the bony part of his wrist. He yelped and pulled back. Michelin Man pushed by and I tried the same, but he blocked my arm and twisted my elbow in a rigid grip.

He'd had some training.

I kicked at his knee, but didn't have the angle to be effective. Cradling his wrist by his body, Butterball punched me in the stomach with his good hand. I doubled over, pretended it hurt more than it did, and dropped the cosh. As I hoped, Michelin Man released my arm.

I crouched on the floor and Sammy gave commands in quick-fire French. I picked up words for "hurt" and "hotel," which I assumed meant they would hurt me and dump me back at the Grecian.

But no. I will not be hurt like that again.

Michelin Man grabbed me by the hair, letting me in close. I used my heel, brought it down into his knee, this time at the correct angle. A series of wet snaps followed as tendons and bone came apart. He tipped over toward me, screaming. I brought my elbow upward into his jaw. His head flipped sideways and his jawbone kept going the other way. He crashed to the floor.

He would never walk right again.

Butterball grabbed a heavy stool and rammed it toward me one-handed. I ducked and snatched up my cosh. With the bigger man off-balance I kicked at the hand holding the stool and brought the cosh into his groin. The noise he made would have been comical under other circumstances, a high-pitched "Ooof." As he folded, I drove my foot through the side of his head—his temple to be exact. His eyes had already rolled back before he hit the floor.

A concussion at best. Permanent damage at worst.

I spun to meet Sammy and dole out the same to him, but he was aiming a gun at my chest. A large-caliber auto. Way beyond my reach.

"Put it down," I said, on my toes, fists clenched. "Come on, you and me."

"You crazy," he said.

A hand on his shoulder urged him to move aside. Umbrella Man made his way out of the room, followed by the Man in Tan. The first was taller than what I took to be his boss, and well built.

The short time that had passed between noticing the gun and that moment gave me time to think, and now I heard sobbing in the back room and remembered the woman. She, and the guy holding onto her, had barely moved. The guy watched me through sunglasses, and his bald pate and sharp suit made him look like a mafia goon in a cheap TV show. I tried to put them out of my mind, both the Goon and the girl. Told myself it was none of my business.

A quiet corner of my mind asked, *Doesn't she deserve the same attention as Sarah?*

The two younger Vietnamese customers had found their feet, unsure what to do. They were scrawny and they had no weapons. The barman watched.

"You know what happened to Sarah Stiles," I said to the Man in Tan.

"Indeed," said the man. "Who are you? And how did you find this place? Was it the Giang problem again?"

I said, "Where. Is. Sarah?"

"So you are one of Vila Fanuco's men?"

His English was good, better than Sammy's. Spoken with a somewhat upper-crust accent, the Queen's English rather than American. And what the hell was *Giang*? A person? A place?

"Yes, he is with Fanuco," Sammy said.

"Wait, I'm not," I said.

"He is. You heard him talking to me. He is here to kill me."

The bastard weasely fuck.

I said, "No, mister, I am not with Vila Fanuco. Sammy is playing both sides. Sir, I don't wish you any harm, and I don't want to hurt your business. I don't even really give a shit about Gareth. I just need to know what happened to Sarah."

"She is dead," Sammy said again. To the Man in Tan he added, "I told him she was dead. He should go home."

The Man in Tan adjusted his tie. "Perhaps we should show him."

Umbrella Man stepped forward and, lightning-quick, jabbed at my windpipe. I gagged at the blow, readied my cosh, but the man was too damn quick. He swept my foot and I landed hard, gasping for breath. In seconds, the two young customers were on me and a piercing chemical smell filled my mouth and nose.

A cloth.

Smothering me.

Umbrella Man kneeling on my chest.

I had no option but to breathe it in. The clagging fumes filled my lungs. I tried to cough, tried to buck, anything to stop these people from doing as they wished.

And, as if a bag was being lowered over my face, my world faded to black.

Chapter Twenty-One

I drifted slowly on a rolling sea. My subconscious swayed me and my surfboard into deep troughs of blue, then I would rise and crest a swell to witness the ocean all around. The sun shone in a cloudless sky, but I was cold and rain fell upon my face. Slowly, the sun darkened, a grey-blue ball, misty and indistinct. Then it fell toward the horizon, dipping beneath it as my body shivered and the moon spread over the water like a hand. The wind blew harder. I breathed in, and water snorted up my nose, and I—

Opened my eyes.

Woodland. Trees. Night.

A rumble of thunder ground itself out overhead. Footsteps squelched. Rain pitter-pattered on every surface—the canopy of bushes and trees, the soggy ground, clothing. I shook water from my eyes. I heard someone say in accented English, "He is awake."

A mass surged in my throat. I could not stop the vomiting. My head automatically lolled to the side, but chunks remained on my face and neck and chest. I knew, then, that I was being carried, hands and legs gripped by persons unseen.

My focus swirled with browns and blacks and a ghostly apparition that I thought may be the moon, but with the force of the rain I doubted it would be visible. Umbrella Man held my hands, my weight no problem. His leather jacket offered no protection from the elements but he didn't seem to care. My cosh sat snug in his waistband. He wasn't taking care of my finger either, so it felt like a rodent gnawing at the bone. Sammy hefted my legs. The Man in Tan strode alongside, his superb hair and tailored suit sheltered by the wide umbrella. He sensibly wore wellington boots. If the younger Vietnamese guys were present I could not see them.

I tried to find my voice but my brain could not yet form words, and I drifted again. The rain faded, and what sparse light there was, died.

I stood in the shallows of the beach. The blue twilight pressed in from all sides. Left and right, the sand stretched into the distance. No cliffs, no promenade, no cafe. I was so alone, I longed for the call of a hawker trying to flog me a piece of local art. I'd watched the moon before, splayed on the ripples, but now nothing shone, and I could not understand how I could still see so much.

I'd been here so many times, thinking—just thinking. About Roger Gorman, about my life, my death, about my father and my mother, and what the hell I was doing about all the things I wanted to change.

This was my thinking zone, my pondering place. I'd never once found an answer here. It was unlikely I ever would.

A slap woke me. Umbrella Man still held my arms, but Sammy had dropped my legs into a muddy recess. A torch shone in my eyes, flashing through my brain like cheese-wire. *Was that the white glow I'd seen earlier?* Probably. There was no sign of the moon now. Just the ground before me, and a dark expanse of absolutely nothing immediately ahead.

The Man in Tan formed a silhouette behind the powerful beam. "You were sent to kill my colleague here, correct?"

"No," I said, the word bloated on my tongue.

Sammy tramped toward me. "YOU LIE!"

I was expecting a slap or a kick, but maybe the Man in Tan realized it was pointless.

He said, "Mr. Park, you come to my place of business just as I am selling one of Mr. Fanuco's whores to an important client. You do not think this looks suspicious?"

"I'm looking," I said, but struggled to finish the sentence. I managed, "For a girl."

"You should kill him," Sammy said.

My vision had virtually cleared and I allowed the rain to wash down my face. Trees lined one half of my peripheral vision, but a deep, black hole seemed to span the other.

I said, "I want to find Sarah Stiles. She's just a kid—"

"I have no interest in what you want," the Man in Tan said. "Did Mr. Fanuco promise he would help if you took care of his problem here?"

Umbrella Man hoisted me up so I was on my knees, holding my arms above my head.

I said, "I don't know anything about any problem."

The Man in Tan nodded. "Very brave. Sammy?"

Sammy crouched right in front of me. Kneeling there returned blood flow to the muscles in my legs, but I couldn't summon a kick.

The Man in Tan said, "Kill him."

Sammy looked at him sharply. "Me?"

"You."

The big man shifted his grip. Now only one hand held me up so he could stand to one side.

"Come on," I said. "Police know I was following you, Sammy."

Sammy drew his gun.

I said, "They will come to you first."

The Man in Tan turned his back, facing the dark hole that spanned further than I could see, like we were at the edge of a cliff, but I could hear no ocean.

He said, "Hurry up."

I remembered one glimmer of hope, one tiny chance. A delay, at least. I said, "Giang," and hoped I pronounced it right.

The Man in Tan bent so we were at the same eye-level. "Yes?"

I said, "I identified you through *Giang*. Sammy is lying to you."

The man did not blink, just tilted his head. Allowed an almost inaudible, "Hmm." If I could get him to expand a little, tell me what it meant, some hint … He was about to speak when I must have given something away. He blinked, stood upright, and said, "A word. Nothing more. You do not know if 'Giang' is a bar or a restaurant or the name of a song. Good try, Mr. Detective."

My jaw clenched.

The Man in Tan laughed as he returned to that black, featureless view.

Sammy's boots sucked mud behind me.

"I can pay you all," I said. "I have money. A lot of money."

Sammy paused. The Man in Tan nodded to Sammy, then looked back out into the dark.

Tears escaped my eyes and merged with the rain. I had no strength. "Don't … Please…"

The hammer clicked back and the muzzle pressed in the back of my skull. I writhed hard, bucked with all the energy I could summon, but Umbrella Man's grip merely tightened and held me a little higher. I was nothing but a hunk of meat in a butcher's window.

Sammy took a step back to avoid the splatter.

Umbrella Man angled his face away.

The Man in Tan stared across the void.

The gunshot rang out.

But nothing happened. Nothing, that is, except Umbrella Man spoke for the first time. In Vietnamese. Panicking.

More gunshots cracked all around and Umbrella Man released me and I flopped into the sludge. My captor tackled the Man in Tan, and both appeared to sink into the floor. I scrambled around, looking for Sammy, unsure why I was still alive. He lay, gurgling against a rock, gun in-hand. His chest pumped blood from a hole the size of a £2 coin.

Then it hit me like a fist in the chest—the phone call I made after the brush-off from Bertrand had paid off. Vila Fanuco was upset but grateful for my tip about Sammy. I told him my location, if he needed it, and also about the Man in Tan. He sounded even more pleased about that, and basically told me to hold tight outside the British-named bar. As usual, I hadn't listened.

Still dazed, rain obscuring my line of sight, I relieved Sammy of the gun and made my way on all-fours in the direction of the two Vietnamese men, even though I had never fired a gun in my life. I stopped crawling at the lip of what I at first thought was a cliff, but now my vision had all-but adjusted to the dark I saw a regular shape about a thousand yards across and a hundred feet deep.

It was a *quarry*.

An old one, judging by the vegetation sprouting around the sides and down inside the bowl.

So here I was again. A more experienced man instructed me to wait for help but I blundered in anyway with no real plan, despite knowing full well I needed an escape route. No, Adam Park doesn't need to *think*. Doesn't need to *plan*. And without that fore-thought, some bad men had transported me to a quarry to execute me.

The fuckers.

Now, presumably, my saviors were descending. Skilled fighters, well-armed, snipers. Highly-motivated individuals with a grudge to bear out. *Soldiers*. Street-soldiers, but soldiers nonetheless.

I could lie here and wait for them to do their thing, and the crackle of automatic gunfire over the next ridge suggested they were doing just that. And yet...

If the Man in Tan was still alive—and his lack of a body and quick reactions from Umbrella Man indicated a good chance of that—he knew what happened to Sarah and Gareth. If I allowed events to play out organically, the pair could well end up dead, and my only advantage would turn to stone beneath my feet.

I checked Sammy's gun, raindrops bouncing off the matt-black automatic. The turncoat pimp had already cocked it, so I did not mess around with the mechanism. I held it away from my body in a one-handed grip, so much heavier than I expected, a solid mass of metal. Then I slid down over the edge on my belly, searching for answers.

Chapter Twenty-Two

I barely noticed the rain easing to drizzle as the ground leveled out and I found a thick shrub to hide behind. Since the gunfire ended, all was silent except for distant rumbles of receding thunder. I listened for the two men.

Then movement flashed to my right. I whipped the gun around, but it behaved like a pendulum. For a tenth of a second I acknowledged I was the world's worst person to be in possession of a firearm, but caught sight of Umbrella Man dashing behind a mound with the Man in Tan now caked in mud. I ran from the shrub and dived behind another heap of earth about thirty yards from the two men. I held the gun in my good hand and rested it on the shallow muddy dune.

Aimed as best I could.

Braced for the recoil.

I saw movement again and pulled the trigger. The gun bucked, the barrel roared, and smoke belched. The stench of burning powder rushed up my nose. My ears rang. I had no idea if I hit anything.

Four shots replied.

I lay flat, the bullets gouging out lumps of wet muck. I remained stock-still, on my back, looking up at fast-moving clouds. Until that point, I'd been acting on sluggish instinct. Stay alive. Fight. Do whatever it takes. Even shoot a fellow human being. But the barrage I narrowly avoided slammed my brain into a place that concentrated my thoughts, and strength surged through my limbs. I perceived not only the clouds roiling high above, but the mound I was using as cover, and its size and shape suddenly struck me as dreadfully coffin-like. I risked a peek toward Umbrella Man and ducked back as he squeezed off two more shots, but not before I confirmed my horrible suspicion.

The dirt they were using as cover was shaped almost identically to mine. Another loomed behind me, and as my eyes adjusted, I saw deeper into the quarry. More mounds became clear. I counted another five before a report rang out and I flattened myself on the ground.

I pointed the gun in their direction without aiming and fired. Again. Again.

There was no return fire. I told myself I'd count to ten and then risk another visual check.

One … two … three …

I gripped the gun.

Six … seven … eight …

I readied myself and—

Fast moving *sloshing* sounded. I looked over the mound.

Having cleared the distance, Umbrella Man dived forward and tackled me with his massive arms. The gun went flying and we both splashed into the soft ground. I tried to roll with the momentum but he had me in a bear hug. I struck with my elbows and knees at every part of his body I could reach, but it was like battering clay. He pummeled a fist into my ribs and blew the wind out of me. Unable to take a breath, I head-butted him. His nose crunched and he reared back. It made him madder. He gripped my neck, thrust me deeper into the mud. Blood gushed from his nostrils, teeth bared and bloodied. His free arm prepared a huge punch that I knew would end me in this fight.

Last chance. So small. Probably wouldn't do anything.

I had to try.

In that split-second, I reached for the man's waistband. Grasped my cosh. I pulled it out and held it two-handed in the path of his fist. The wood splintered but, due to the lead lining, it did not break completely. His knuckles shredded and the diversion sent the blow past my face. It was enough. As he cried out again, I twisted in the mud and he tipped over.

Then I hit him. I used what remained of my cosh at first, one blow after another—his face, his legs, his body—and when the wood finally gave up and crumbled off the lead inner, I hit him with my fist. It hurt, even in my frenzied state, but I did it anyway. Over and over, I pummeled his head and I pummeled his body, the soft spots that drop the strongest of men if you strike just right. I kept going, even when he ceased moving.

A hand on my shoulder squeezed gently.

"I think you have slain him," Vila Fanuco said.

I sat back on my haunches. Umbrella Man's nose was obliterated and both eyes had already swollen, one of them shut completely, and there were gaps in his blood-filled mouth. No telling what was going on under the bone, beyond the muscle where his organs lay.

Fanuco was all in black, boasting a flak-jacket accessory, with night-vis goggles raised to the sky. He wielded a shotgun, with a knife and automatic handgun holstered on his hip. He carried it all off as naturally as I did a Hugo Boss suit.

I breathed there for a while, listening to feet on mud, to people dragging others around and barking orders in French and in English. Wide, powerful beams of light swung into play and my fatigue lifted some. I used my hands to heave myself to my feet, then straightened slowly, unsteady but upright.

Off-roaders guarded the lip of the quarry, shining massive torches to illuminate the basin. Shrubbery had taken over much of the land but it was clear that more of those mounds dotted the floor. The level we were on was flat, but further out it sloped sharply down again, into places I could not see.

Fanuco stood over the Man in Tan, who knelt at his feet, shotgun at his head. His hands were bound by electrical ties. To one side, a man I'd never seen before, in a bomber-jacket and carrying a rifle on his back, dragged a body down the incline by its foot.

I pushed through the drizzle toward Fanuco, the ground sucking at my feet. "Who is he?"

"This is Dac Kien Anh," Fanuco said. "He is in charge of the men on the street in Paris. A 'gang-master', you call him in Britain."

Anh whimpered. A bullet-wound oozed from his shoulder, a souvenir from the initial foray atop the quarry. Now I'd calmed some, I almost felt sorry for him. Almost.

I gripped his chin and forced him to look at me. "What happened to the girl I'm looking for?"

He said, "I ... cannot..."

Fanuco racked the shotgun as punctuation, and the gang-master tried to pull away. I held firm and asked through gritted teeth, "What happened?"

Bomber Jacket arrived, his manner gruff and to-the-point as he awaited instructions from Fanuco. He dumped what I'd taken to be a corpse in the mud, but it had actually been patched up with a field dressing and was breathing fitfully.

Sammy LeHavre.

Fanuco knelt beside him, seemingly forgetting Dac Kien Anh. He said, "Sammy, Sammy," and shook his head, truly disappointed. "I was ready to give you your own team."

Sammy could barely speak. "Vila..." His breath caught, coughed speckles of blood onto Fanuco's face. "S-sorry."

Fanuco wiped himself. "You thought these people were growing strong?"

Sammy nodded.

Fanuco said, "You thought they would beat me."

Sammy nodded again, fast, panicked. "Sorry … I will help—"

I was still holding Anh's chin when Fanuco rose slowly and deliberately, and aimed the shotgun. He pulled the trigger and blew a hole the size of a grapefruit in Anh's back. The exit wound was even bigger, blood and bone and shredded organs exploding over my legs. I jumped back, letting out a brief scream.

Fanuco pointed the shotgun at Sammy. The hot barrel hissed in the light rain as Anh's body tipped forward. Fanuco beckoned me toward Sammy.

He said, "You would not have made him talk. They are conditioned well in their country. But this … worm … *he* will talk."

Sammy cringed. "Please…"

"It was me," I said.

"You?" Sammy said. "What you mean, you?"

"*I* called Mr. Fanuco. When I knew it was you who had Sarah's phone. I knew what he'd do to you, and I knew I'd lose sleep about it. But if you'd just told me what I needed to know … you are responsible for what he does to you now."

Fanuco placed the barrel on Sammy's forehead. His skin reddened immediately.

Sammy shut his eyes tight. "Okay, okay, I'll tell you."

I tried to convince myself that he'd left me no choice, but when I faced the stricken body of Umbrella Man, I wondered if that were true. I could have gone another direction. I could have done it right. That the man was still breathing was of limited consequence.

"I thought they were more disciplined," Sammy said. "They don't take big chances like hurting police. They are not as … brutal."

I said, "So you agreed to join them instead."

"To pass information, nothing else. At first. Then they wanted to damage Mr. Fanuco."

Fanuco said, "Is this why you gave Marie to them?"

I assumed he meant the black woman I'd seen with the Goon.

Sammy nodded, still struggling to speak fluently. "They wanted your favorite."

"And what of the other girls? Why take them?"

I didn't know what they were talking about. "Girls" plural?

"They have demand," Sammy said. "They order for demand."

I said, "Like shoes or a car."

"Yes. Like that."

I couldn't tell if it was his failing health or if he really felt no shame. I said, "Sarah. What about her?"

"She …" he said. "The man … the British man … he came to me. He wanted documents. Said his were … not good anymore."

So Gareth *had* learned a bit in prison.

He continued, "I sent them to Madame Rouge …" *the Red Woman* … "And she made their documents … but … the man, he wanted more."

"More?"

"Computer. A computer expert. To crack a code."

"The pen drive," I said.

Fanuco perked up at this.

Sammy nodded rapidly. "He said it was better than gold."

"This drive," Fanuco said. "What was on it?"

"They did not find out. Because I put them in touch with the Viets. They might help, I think. But they see Sarah and they want her, and—"

A loud *WHOOP* shattered the air, followed by gunshots. Fanuco whipped around and Bomber Jacket pushed his boss into a crouch, gun ready. Loud speakers blasted quick-fire French into the quarry. I picked out words like "mort" meaning *dead,* and phrases giving orders.

"*You?*" Fanuco growled.

"No," I said. "I swear."

A helicopter searchlight crashed on overhead, and swung onto our small gathering, casting all of us in a moon-bright spot. A voice I recognized boomed over the speaker.

In English, Pierre Bertrand said, "You are surrounded. Put your hands on your head and you will not be killed."

Police swarmed down into the quarry, armored like SWAT officers emblazoned with "GIPN," Paris's equivalent paramilitary response unit. Others hustled handcuffed prisoners into view and made them lie on their faces high above us. Fanuco's other men, I assumed.

A second chopper reverberated from the top end and circled as the operation closed in.

Bomber Jacket and Fanuco dropped their weapons and knelt in the dirt, hands on their heads. I leapt at Sammy, grabbed his neck and applied pressure. My face right in his, I said, "What happened? Tell me!"

He grinned. "Look around you, Mr. Detective. Pick one. No, pick two."

The mounds were spread out over the terrain, dotted seemingly at random, not hidden, no one caring about the state of them. I had no doubt about what they contained.

"*Which one?*" I yelled over the rotor-wash, now growing in intensity as the helicopter set down.

Sammy kept on grinning. Started to laugh. "Any of them!" he said. "Pick! I do not know. But be happy your search is at an end!"

And he laughed harder and harder, like some villain in a kids' cartoon. I was about to launch into yet another physical assault, when the clack-clack of a gun being cocked sounded right next to my ear.

"That man is a prisoner," Gardien Bertrand said. "And you, Mr. Park, if you do not let that man go, will be shot. Choose. Now."

Chapter Twenty-Three

Bertrand could not stop grinning as he handcuffed Vila Fanuco. A smidge too tightly, I might add. A second GIPN officer secured Bomber Jacket, who went with him quietly, like a good soldier should. As soon as Bertrand had aimed his weapon at me, my fists had unclenched and the urge to smash them into someone drained away so fast that I knew I blanched. When I raised my hands and assured him I wasn't going anywhere, and showed him that I was injured, he reluctantly agreed not to restrain me.

The second helicopter, it turned out, was a medevac unit, which landed at the far end of the quarry on flatter ground. The medics treated Umbrella Man first, ascertained he was in bad but not critical condition, then triaged Sammy.

I'd pounded Umbrella Man with all the rage I could muster, but in my weakened state it had not been enough to kill him. Since Harry's calming influence, I wished my rage-filled revenge-fantasies belonged to another person. Yes, I wanted to hurt those men in Bangkok, and had intended to do so one day, but I am a different person now. Someone who can resist the desire to break those people whom I hate, just because I can. Having reduced Umbrella Man to a mangled lump, I had to ask myself if I had really changed so much. Was it simply a veneer that had slipped?

As more than a dozen GIPN troops roamed the scene, Bertrand cheerfully read Fanuco his French rights, while another chap in a suit and trench coat filmed the entire operation with a camcorder.

To me, Bertrand said, "There will be no hint of improper conduct this time. Fanuco will not even hurt his head getting into a car." He looked ten years younger than when I first met him. "*Merci*, Mr. Park. Thank you so much."

Fanuco's eyes met mine. *It wasn't me*, I wanted to cry.

"What is this?" I asked, as a bearded officer examined me. "How did you—"

"I tracked your phone, Mr. Park. We followed you to *L'Hostel Centrale* and bugged your car. When our unit picked up that your phone was moving but the car was not … well, we followed you. We are not *amateurs* at this."

The medics had secured Sammy to a bright orange stretcher and now ran him to their helicopter.

Over the noise, Bertrand laughed at the sky. "Oh, Mr. Park! When I was married, when I had my first child, my second, my third, when I lost my virginity years earlier, my promotion to become the youngest *commissionaire* ever in Paris … none of it compares to this. When I die, this … right here … today…" He jabbed a finger toward Fanuco. "This is the part of my life I will remember most fondly."

I said, "You would have waited until I was dead, wouldn't you? As long as you got him?"

Bertrand came in close, out of range of the camera's mic. "I gambled my pension on you. Called in every favor. I knew you had called someone. I guessed it was your friend Vila. And look at you. Dead people everywhere. If even one was killed by you, I will find out."

My head throbbed from whatever chemical the young men used on that rag, my broken finger ached, and my ribs were certainly bruised, maybe worse.

I said, "All these mounds." I let him look around. "I think they're graves. It's where the Vietnamese gangs took people they killed."

"Indeed." Bertrand concentrated on the nearest. "Shallow graves. They start out flat, but gases in the body push up the dirt, then animals burrow in to make them bigger. Eventually, as you see, things grow, and cover them."

Through the vegetation, the new grass and shrubs and weeds, the medics returned from securing Sammy in the medevac unit. They carried another stretcher for Umbrella Man.

Bertrand nodded grimly. "This is private land. An old farm. This quarry, a company exploring the ground for minerals, they found nothing and sold the land cheap to a man based in Vietnam."

"Which man?"

"A shell company. We researched it when your triangulation halted here. Over there," he said, pointing, "is a house with a basement. There are eight dead Vietnamese, courtesy of your partner."

Fanuco said, "You will not prove this."

"Oh, I will," Bertrand said calmly. "And I will find the people who were held captive in those cells."

"Cells?" I said.

"In the basement. Blown open with small charges. The prisoners are gone."

"He saved them."

"He *stole* them." Bertrand gestured to Fanuco. "This man, your savior, he is in *competition* with the Vietnamese. He does not do this rescue to help. He does it for *profit*. He takes the people his competition has obtained and *sells*. Same way this Vietnamese gang would have. He is pure evil, Mr. Park. You should not forget this."

He seemed satisfied at my stony expression.

Fanuco said, "Adam. Check your phone."

I waved the bearded officer away and checked my pockets. My

phone was still there. Now waterlogged and the glass cracked, it had died, likely on the slide down the quarry.

"Find one that works," Fanuco said.

"Why?"

Bertrand said, "Stop talking."

The helicopter's blades still whipped through the air but the engine whined down.

"No," I said. "I want to know what he means."

Fanuco bowed his head, water dribbling off him and forming a puddle on the ground. "Call Harry."

I held out my hand to Bertrand. "You nearly let me die in order to catch this man. The least you can do is give me your fucking phone."

He handed over an old-fashioned Samsung. I dialed the 0044 number for the UK plus Harry's landline, which I memorized many years ago.

Someone picked up after a single ring. "*Yes?*"

I said, "Jayne?"

"Adam. What's going on? Where's Harry?"

"I'm still in France. Is Harry not there?"

"It's one a.m. and he never came back from his swimming. He's usually home by eight. He isn't answering his phone."

I lowered the Samsung. I could hear Jayne calling my name from the earpiece. The rain had stopped completely now. The helicopter engine no longer whined. Boots shuffled. Clothes rubbed together. But it was Jayne's crackled plea of, "*Talk to me, Adam!*" that fired the images to life.

Jayne and Harry, standing beside me at my mother's funeral.

Jayne, at my first PI office, bringing me coffee, water, and Alka-Seltzer.

Harry, introducing me to fine single malt.

Jayne, insisting I remove my shirt in the office so she could iron it properly.

"It was not me," Fanuco said, his head still bowed. "Curtis Benson took action when he discovered your phone was not working."

He couldn't get hold of me. Add that to my smuggling Lily out of the country...

Fanuco added, "I am sorry for your friend. But all I care about is the information stolen from Mr. Benson."

"It can hurt you." My grip tightened around the phone. "The pen drive."

"Yes."

Bertrand made grab for his phone. I pulled it away and raised it shakily to my ear.

Harry, making crude innuendos about his love life.

Jayne, cracking more subtle sex jokes.

Harry, face-to-face with Sleazy Stu, telling him to leave me the fuck alone.

They went on and on. I mopped my forehead, images of the past blurring with possible futures—

Me, at a graveside next to Jayne as they bury her husband.

Me, telling Jayne it was my fault, all my fault.

"Jayne?" I said.

"I'm still here."

"Curtis Benson took him."

She went silent on the other end. I was aware of eyes on me. Not all of the dozen men and women in uniform would speak English, but they all knew something was wrong. Gardien Bertrand, who had been willing to risk my life a short time ago, watched me with an expression that showed he did have some semblance of a heart after all.

"Lovey?" Jayne said.

I turned from Bertrand and strode toward Fanuco, my feet sinking a couple of centimeters with each measured step. I said, "Yeah."

With a shake in her voice, she asked, "What have you done?"

"I don't know."

"You rescued that young girl. The stripper." Her tone was calmer, but I could tell it was taking real effort. "They took Harry instead."

"Yes," I said.

"You will listen to their instructions, Adam. You will do everything they say. Everything."

"Yes, of course."

"I mean it. Do not deviate, do not go off on some flight of fancy or try to improvise. *You'll get him back for me.*"

"I will." I steadied my own tone to match hers. "I'll do whatever I have to." I hung up.

Fanuco raised his head at last. "Report in." He reeled off a phone number. Bertrand tried to stop him, but I held up one hand, the phone at arm's length. Two GIPN guys hurried my way, hands on the butts of their guns, but I dialed the number before they reached me. Bertrand gave the approaching officers a look that stopped them.

Benson answered. "You in a lot a' trouble."

"I'm doing what you asked," I said. "I still have five more days."

"You gonna get my burglar girl an' her dumbass fuck-up of a boyfriend back here—"

"This isn't about revenge." I switched the phone to my other hand. "I know you want me to bring them to you so you can extract the information about what they'd done with the pen drive. Right?" Pause. Silence. "Am I *right?*"

He theatrically sucked his teeth on the other end. "You want the old bastard back unharmed? You bring everything to me."

"You only need the encrypted drive."

"I need what I tell you I need, motherfucker. You thought my leverage over your ass was gone soon as you got the stripper hid, but now the deal is the same as before. You bring those two *to me*, and the Gruffalo lives. You don't, I kill him. I hunt you down and I fuck you up, and I will find that whore you took from me and I'll feed her to biggest, baddest sadistic fuck I can find. And I know a lot of sadistic fucks, boy. A *lot*."

I forced my breathing to regulate. My injuries seemed so superficial now. I said, "I will bring you the drives and whatever money is left. You're welcome to do what you want to Gareth Delingpole, but I will not endanger Sarah. That is the deal. The drive for Harry. Anything else is gravy."

"Gravy, huh?" He was silent for a moment. "I hate gravy. But you want your lady? You want a pass on the retard? Then you gotta earn that pass. One last thing you gotta do."

"Name it," I said.

"My buddy you got there. Vila Fanuco? Free him."

"I can't! He's in handcuffs—"

"I wanna hear from him in thirty minutes or I cut the old fucker's thumbs off." Benson hung up.

Fanuco nodded like he expected that. "Good deal?"

I handed the phone back to Bertrand.

"More problems for you?" he asked.

"Yes," I said.

"I am sorry, but I must take you for interrogation. You are not yet under arrest but I must cuff you. Precaution."

The medics hefted Umbrella Man, now strapped to the stretcher, and dashed toward their chopper.

I was sure Benson would carry out his threat to mutilate a man who literally meant more to me than my own life. To stop it, all I had to do was get Fanuco past a dozen highly-trained GIPN officers.

Bertrand took my arm and dangled the cuffs toward me.

"Wait." I shook him off and threw myself on one of the graves. "I have to find her." I pawed desperately at the mud. "I can't go home without knowing. She's dead, I know she's dead."

Two GIPN officers grabbed my arms, one saying, "*Non, non, c'est evidence.*"

Bertrand gave firm orders and they relinquished me, and I threw myself on the mound again, scraping handful after handful, digging deeper and deeper. Bertrand placed one hand on my back, his cuffs dangling from the other. He said, "Mr. Park, I do not want to hurt you. But if I cannot bind your wrists I will order my men to do it."

I barely noticed the medevac unit taking off. I kept on going, broken finger screaming at me to stop. "She's in one of these graves. She's under this dirt."

"If your girl is here we will find her. I promise."

My hand scraped something hard and smooth, and soon I was looking at a brown-stained face, not a skeleton, but a person, skin leathery and taut over their skull, chewed in places.

"Look!" I cried. "It's *her!*"

Bertrand finally lost patience. He took me by the shoulders and heaved me to my feet. I spun, grabbed his cuffs, and attached one bracelet to his wrist, the other to mine. I snatched his gun from its holster and dragged his cuffed hand across his body away from the weapon. Every cop drew a firearm, but I was already moving us up against the police helicopter. I gave the pilot a "don't do it" look and he raised his hands to say "take it easy."

Bertrand said, "What are you doing, you fool?"

"No one's called me a fool before," I said. "I can tick that off my bucket list. Keep them back."

I had no idea where I learned to be so glib in such a position. Occasions like an Aussie biker gang descending upon the quiet bar in which I was enjoying a cool glass of VB and trying to tempt a local farmer's girl into inappropriate relations—sure, glib is fine. But not where I could go to jail or die in a slow-motion hail of bullets.

That's right, I was actually picturing my death in slo-mo. How fucked up is that?

Fanuco struggled to his feet, hands still cuffed behind him. "A new mission?"

"Get in," I told him.

I helped him into the helicopter with my gun-hand—"Careful with that," he said—and then struggled inside with Bertrand. The *gardien de la paix* resisted minimally, and as the engines whined to life again the cops outside ran back and forth, torn between securing their prisoners and aiding one of their own.

The rotor reached its optimum speed and we lifted off, and swept over trees, over fields and other holes like the one hiding dozens of bodies. I rummaged in Bertrand's pocket, found his handcuff key, and freed Fanuco, who put on a headset and gave the pilot orders in French. The helicopter banked sharply, the nose dipped, and we sped toward a blanket of lights that I took to be the metropolitan city of Paris.

Chapter Twenty-Four

The chopper touched down on a helipad atop a building at least fifty stories high, from which I could see the Eiffel Tower illuminated about a mile away. I backed out, keeping Bertrand wrapped up in his own arm so he couldn't make a move on the gun, and as I awaited instructions from Fanuco, who was cuffing the pilot to the skids, I noted other landmarks—the *Musée d'Orsay*, the glittering Seine—and concluded we were south of the river. I couldn't name a structure with a heli-pad in Paris, but apparently Fanuco was able to land on a fifty-story building with next to no warning.

Battered by the downdraft, he ushered me and Bertrand to a doorway held by a man in overalls to whom Fanuco handed a wad of damp cash. In French, I heard him say, "More later," and we pushed inside onto a metal staircase that wound down past machines, clunking and whirring—an elevator pulley and cable. Bertrand remained compliant throughout. We hurried out of the maintenance area into a plush, blue-carpeted corridor and left a trail of filth in our wake. The mud and grime from the quarry would probably get some cleaner fired tomorrow.

Fanuco called the elevator.

Bertrand said, "What do you plan to do, Monsieur Park?"

I watched the numbers illuminate in turn. We were on the fifty-seventh floor.

I said, "I don't know."

"You will go to jail here," Bertrand said. "No doubt."

"I'm sorry. But someone I care for is … has been taken…"

"In exchange for freeing me?" Fanuco said. "How sweet."

"I have to finish the job," I told him. "Freeing you was just a clause he seemed to enjoy."

"So you would have let Gardien Bertrand take me?"

The doors opened. "Of course." I followed him in.

He smiled that lizard-grin of his. "So what will you have me do with him? My old pal Pierre?"

"Let him go as soon as we're clear."

"Let him go, yes. Yes." He thought about it, a pantomime pause. "*Or* … we kill him. Only *he* saw us close up. Apart from the man who checked your good health and the pilot, and they can be bought or … otherwise persuaded."

Bertrand watched him constantly.

Fanuco gripped Bertrand by the jaw and pursed his lips into a comedy-kiss. "If it were the other way around? Me and you alone? What would you do, Pierre?"

"Kill you," Bertrand said, although the words were distorted.

Fanuco let go. "Mr. Park, you show excellent instincts for this. You could be a valuable asset."

"No thanks," I said. "I'm already going to jail. I hope it isn't for nothing."

"Oh, it won't be for nothing, I promise you that."

Fanuco had pressed for the fourth floor, and we came out into a corridor with no carpet. Decorators' ladders and tarpaulins lay along the walls. Inside the end room, we were greeted by a wall of pane-glass windows looking out over the city. A mere four floors up, and we could still see the Eiffel Tower illuminated a mile north. This room was also bare but for girders and an array of building tools and machinery.

Fanuco relieved me of the gun and said, "Uncuff yourself."

I obeyed. I rubbed my own wrist as it came free, but left one bracelet on Bertrand's.

Fanuco aimed the weapon at him. "I kill you here, I get away. Easy."

"Someone will find you," Bertrand said.

"You gambled your career, did you not?"

Bertrand averted his eyes.

"When I escape," Fanuco said. "Sorry, when *we* escape, Mr. Park and I, you will be retired. On a reduced pension, perhaps?"

Bertrand nodded.

Fanuco took a couple of steps back. "It was never personal. That man, his family, they happened when I was an angry person. Emotionally unstable. My country had just come out of a war. My skills were no longer required."

"Skills?" The word spat in contempt from Bertrand's mouth. "You murdered your competitors and took their business."

"I murdered my bosses too," he said with the air of a teacher correcting a student. "But I am not that person any more. I regret loss of life. I kill now only when it is necessary. Sammy LeHavre was correct when he said I take too many chances. But it was the Vietnamese who taught me that. Their discipline, their tactics."

"This is why you wear a new face now? Why we have heard little from you for a year or more?"

"Partly. Yes."

"Why are you telling me this?"

Fanuco said, "Why am I telling him this, Mr. Park?"

I took Bertrand's cuffed wrist and attached it to a sturdy-looking pipe. Fanuco lowered the gun but kept his distance.

I said, "He wants you to understand why he's letting you live."

"Indeed, Adam," Fanuco said. "You may even live yourself."

Bertrand looked us both up and down. "You two seem friendly."

"I need him," I said. "That's all." I placed Bertrand's mobile well out of reach. "Leave it on. They're tracking it already. Or the chopper."

I moved for the door, but Fanuco had one last thing to tell Bertrand. "If you wish to have a small chance of saving your career, be at your finest monument at sunrise. *If* your people have freed you by then."

I didn't care what Fanuco was talking about. We didn't speak as the elevator descended to the ground floor, or when we exited the lobby with no guards. We passed CCTV cameras whose red lights did not glow or blink and glided straight into a waiting limousine. Fanuco talked on the phone in an Eastern-European language of which I had no knowledge, while the city zipped by outside. If Bertrand's threats were achievable, I'd be living here for many years to come, albeit in far less luxury than a stretch limousine.

We soon merged with the night-time traffic, and the city swallowed us up.

Chapter Twenty-Five

It was about three a.m., and the *tabacs* and bars were still open. ld people still sat inside, younger more wrapped-up folk sipping alfresco beer and liqueurs. Laughter. Arm-waving discussion and debate. Kissing, hand-holding, eye-gazing. If they knew what had passed them by, would they be so calm, so serene?

"Bosnia," I said. "You're from Bosnia."

He cracked a window and street noises filled the car. Even a passing argument outside an XXX club made its way through the glass.

"Yes," Fanuco finally said. "A year before I lost my wife and daughters, my mother and father were killed. I was away, training with British and American Special Forces."

"Special Forces," I said. Coincidences happen from time-to-time, but this meant something. "You know a short-arse with a bad temper, hangs out with Benson? Good with his fists."

"I have met many people. Our paths may have crossed."

The limo veered sharply off the road and down a steep incline into a parking garage. A barrier swung up and we advanced past high-value cars and 4x4s all gleaming in the fluorescent light, until we reached a service elevator. We both exited the limo, entered the elevator, and the doors closed.

He said, "You wish to find the girl. I want you to trace the pen-drive. I have something here that will aid you greatly in this."

"Giang?" I said.

"Giang?"

"Yes. The man you murdered back there, that gang master. He asked if that was how I found him."

"Giang … I do not know what that is. I have heard it mentioned, I think. A place, a route, a person, I do not know. It may be one reason the authorities have made many arrests recently."

"And the reason I'm being employed to do your work for you." I thought back to Agent Frank telling me to stay out of his business. I said, "The data stick is too valuable to risk getting into the right hands. Co-operation between organizations."

The elevator hummed.

I said, "You think Giang is the source? The Vietnamese using whatever it is to eliminate competition?"

"It is not connected to us. The Vietnamese have their own losses. We have a leak, or several leaks. But yes, this is why you are looking for our data. If you are caught, you only mention the girl. Understand?"

We stepped out into a corridor adorned with flowers and solid oak furnishings. Fanuco turned a corner and swept toward a dreadlocked black man dressed in a grey Armani suit. He could've been a stock broker but for the sub-machinegun across his chest.

With Mr. Dreadlocks now accompanying us, we came to a lobby of sorts. A *reception*. A well-dressed young woman awaited orders behind a low, half-moon-shaped desk, overtly antique, as if it belonged to a lost age, or even a museum.

The receptionist said, "*Bonsoir*," to Mr. Dreadlocks, nodded—virtually bowed—to Fanuco, then went back to smiling sweetly at nothing. I didn't merit a greeting of any kind. Or perhaps my appearance put her off: caked in mud and sweat, hobbling with exhaustion, cradling a deformed left hand. Which, by the way, had begun to jab into my wrist.

A click released double oak doors. I entered the room after Fanuco, Mr. Dreadlocks a couple of steps behind me.

Fanuco held my good hand tenderly, and led me through into
the suite. "Mr. Park ... Adam ... I cannot ever be accused of being
a man of my word. Lying is the staple of any successful businessman. But in this case..."

A chandelier hung in what I assumed was the living room. An
open door revealed a bathroom with terracotta tiles and stone-
effect bath. We passed through into a dim bedroom boasting a
four-poster bed, on which lay a scruffy pile of thick white bathrobes. I was so exhausted I thought I might drop on my arse, so
the strange hand-holding gesture was actually welcome.

"She is not with them," Fanuco said. "Your girl, Sarah."

We stopped beside the bed. Blinked away a speck of dried mud.

What I thought were bathrobes in my hazy state were actually
women *wearing* bathrobes. No older than eighteen, any of them.
Some far younger. Unconscious rather than asleep.

I said, "What did you do to them?"

Fanuco sat on the bed, stroked the youngest one's blond hair
from her face. The girl, maybe twelve years old, did not stir.

He said, "My people cleaned them, disposed of their clothing.
Provided these robes. Someone will bring suitable attire, and then
they will be revived."

"I mean, what's happened to them?"

It may have been my depleted mental reserves, but right at that
moment, I thought I saw a tear in the Botox-ridden man's eye. His
nostrils flared with every loud intake of breath, his lips pushed
together. He leaned down and kissed the girl's forehead, before
wiping it away with his thumb, as if he might transfer something
of himself to her.

"I have never harmed a child," he said. "That place they took
you, the quarry, my men observed it from afar. A building in the

middle of those holes, beside a field that once grew maize. Before the land was sold."

"A farmhouse," I said.

He nodded. "With a cellar. A dungeon, really. My men met with little resistance. It served as a halfway-house, ready to ship people back to Mr. Anh's homeland, or to his partners … elsewhere. Girls, taken from streets all over France. Some are like Marie, the one Sammy gave away, people who would not be missed by family. But others … these I do not recognize. Not all are working girls. Especially this tiny angel. They must have paid Mr. Anh a fortune for her. Millions."

He picked more loose strands of hair gently out of her face, smoothing each perfectly in place. Those that did not settle, he curled behind her ears.

"She is called Henrietta."

"Henrietta Dupree," I said.

"She is missing for a month. The Police believe she is dead or taken out of the country. They are about to pass the case to Interpol. And so I have a dilemma."

He lay Henrietta's head on the bed, slid out his hand so very slowly, then stepped over to the window. Opened it to the sound of the odd moped, and the squeal of high-pitched police sirens in the distance.

"I cannot hand her over," he said, "or I will be seen as a conspirator of the *gendarmes*. But despite what Bertrand believes, I am not an evil man."

"Tell that to your old business partners. Tell that to Sammy."

His glare would have melted iron. "That is *business*. And none of yours."

"Violence is all you bastards understand." I held up my left hand for emphasis.

"Violence is what freed these girls." He stood over them again, gazing down, his eyes hooded in shadow. "Mr. Park, you claim to be one of the good guys? Yet you strike without hesitation. I heard what you did to Sammy's men in Anh's bar."

"I had no choice."

"You are not afraid of falling into the same darkness as the rest of us?"

"No," I said. "Your goals are selfish—power, money, whatever—I'm trying to help others."

The window filtered the first light of dawn, casting a cirrhosis hue on Fanuco's skin.

"You are like a reflection," he said. "The sun shining on a street, half in shadow. But the light bounces off a pane of glass, and this throws a glow onto the pavement." He faced the window. "You may be from light originally, Adam, but you are reflected in my shadow."

"Was Sarah there?" I asked. "At the house? Before you got there?"

"She was not in any of the buildings we searched. The police will dig up the land. I think she is not in France, though. They may have taken her, or she may have left with the man you look for. But that is for tomorrow." He turned himself fully toward me. "Today, now, you will take Henrietta. You will proceed south, across the Seine, and wait beside the Eiffel Tower—"

"Bertrand's 'greatest monument.' Why the theatrics?"

"The Vietnamese presence in this city is all-but gone. I hold their territory now. Bertrand will be made to look a fool with my escape, and again when you, my accomplice, delivers the girl his unit were unable to locate." He placed both his hands on my shoulders. "Adam … if you had not come looking for Sarah, I would still think Sammy is loyal, and Henrietta would be … I do not know what would have happened to her. I thank you."

I tried to find it in me to be insulted, *angry* at his thanks. But it stayed within me, smoldering, lacking the energy to ignite. Perhaps I was too tired. Perhaps it was something else.

I took a few seconds to make sure I wouldn't collapse from exhaustion. When I was certain, I took hold of Henrietta in both my arms, supporting her head like a baby's. She was so light, I was surprised gravity didn't let her go, float her off into the atmosphere.

"You will get out of Paris unharmed by me," Fanuco said. "But do not think this will save you if you cross me. Find the girl and her boyfriend. Find the data stick. Think of your friend in England. And remember, my reach is greater than just Paris. Now go."

I stepped out into the landscaped gardens of what turned out to be the *Fierté en France* hotel. Sneaking low, I hurried out the back gate and searched the skyline for the Eiffel Tower. Pedestrians dotted my route, but nothing compared to the bustling metropolis this would, within a couple of hours, become. No one interfered with me.

Don't mess with a beaten-up guy coated in drying mud and carrying a young girl through the streets.

Soon, the lightest girl in the world began to weigh down on me and I was drenched in sweat. The grand form of the *Palais de Challiot* loomed behind me, and the bridge guarded by golden cherubs and a couple of knights, *Pont d'Iéna*, stretched toward *la Tour Eiffel*—the Eiffel Tower. There was no sweeter vision in my recent memory.

I crossed the bridge to the sight of a squad of police cars—the *Police Urbane*—set up beneath the monument I had snobbishly avoided on all my travels. More than halfway over, I knelt on the rough pavement, my legs and lungs unwilling to function.

One of the gendarmes called, "*Regardez!*"

Here's where everything stuttered into slow motion. Like I was watching a replay on television.

Me, holding Henrietta to my chest, cradling her as if the police unit arrowing my way would harm her ... its blue lights flashing, doors shutting.

Two men, all jumpsuits and guns, stern and threatening, calling French things I don't even try to understand as they jog toward me.

My nerves, frayed, some sense of justice steeling me against surrendering.

They are the law. I am the good guy. I am trying to help an innocent.

I look past them to the Tower. A blue van parks beside a closed souvenir stall.

One occupant that I can see.

Pierre Bertrand drops his cigarette and crushes it underfoot.

The first *gendarme* stands beside me, both hands gripping his gun...

Me, still on my knees...

A tear, cutting a path through the grime on my cheek.

"Please..." I say. "I'm so close."

More French assaulting my ears, but I can't concentrate, can't even get the gist.

Me, pulling Henrietta closer.

"Monsieur Park?" Pierre Bertrand, urging the officer to holster his sidearm, crouching to my eye-level. "Are you there?"

Me, nodding, rocking back and forth, the pavement hard, so hard. But not wet. Not even damp. Odd, after so much rain.

Bertrand touches the top of Henrietta's head. I snatch her back.

Me, flush against the wall now, the golden cherub high above me on its pedestal, and I have the urge to climb it, get away.

"*Monsieur,*" the other *gendarme* is saying. "*La fille…*" Reaching for her …

And then, with a jolt, I was back. I relinquished Henrietta like a doll into Bertrand's arms. Blue flashes filled the night, tears blurring. All Bertrand seemed interested in was her, the girl. He felt for her pulse and his smile was so wide that it stretched beyond his wild beard. There was more grey in there than when I first met him.

The two *gendarmes* helped me up, my legs barely able to hold my weight. I should have been happy, overjoyed at having delivered this girl safely. But I had other things to worry about. Other destinations.

Bertrand ushered me aside, away from the others, still holding Henrietta, his colleagues straining to see what had filled the press monkey with such glee.

"Fanuco," he said.

I leaned on the wall, ready for the cuffs. "Gone," I said.

Bertrand's glare drilled through me before gazing back toward Henrietta. "You think this will make me forgive you?"

"No."

Every cop, to a man and woman, wanted to see Henrietta, the girl they failed, the one rescued by a psychopath and a British *enquêteur privé.*

Chapter Twenty-Six

After cleaning me up and furnishing me with a musty-smelling red tracksuit, the origin of which I did not probe too deeply, the police administered professional medical attention, my little finger injected with painkiller, then re-set and strapped with fresh bandages. My other injuries, including my ribs, were deemed non-urgent and I was allowed to sleep for two hours. Those two hours was how long it took to get Henrietta to a hospital and to contact her parents, and for whatever red-tape the French police endured when arresting a foreigner. I was then shaken awake and questioned for a further two hours in a sterile room with a fixed table, two molded chairs and a mirrored wall. The first hour of my stay was consumed by a black-eyed, fire-breathing Pierre Bertrand and, when I refused to even acknowledge his presence, the second was hosted by someone I hoped was on my side.

Terrance Potter was a fiftyish man standing five-ten and weighed around two-hundred-and-eighty pounds. It was nine a.m. when he entered but he looked like he'd done a full day's work already. When he took off his cheap suit jacket and slung it over the back of a plastic chair, his pits were stained with sweat—what we used to call "disco rings" back in my youth. After identifying himself and presenting Foreign Office ID, he spoke in a language I did not grasp much more than I did French.

Politician-ese.

The gist of it was that I had created an international incident. It was being handled by various ministries, but even intervention by the prime minister himself might not prevent me doing time in a French jail.

"So what happens next?" I asked when a lull appeared in Potter's dialogue.

He said, "You might get lucky."

When I registered nothing, he sighed and laid a copy of *le Monde* on the table. A photo of Pierre Bertrand carrying Henrietta into the station filled half the page. In the background, there was me, being led by a mustachioed *gendarme* into the building, the cop's hand on my back like a congratulatory gesture. The man's body obscured my cuffed hands. Potter translated the headline: "*Hero brings Henrietta home.*"

"Yeah," I said. "Your friendly neighborhood Adam Park."

Potter slammed his hand on the desk. "You think this is *funny*?"

"Get to the point."

Potter took the newspaper and read from it. "In the early hours of this morning, an unidentified British man was the toast of France as he tracked down the missing Parisian girl, Henrietta Dupree, blah blah blah. The Parisian police possessed neither the intelligence nor the resources to rescue her, et cetera. Yet, one man from England was able to extricate Henrietta and six other victims."

Potter flattened the paper in front of me. The photo, my part specifically, was not that clear, taken on a phone, most likely. At a push, friends and family would recognize me, but I wasn't going to be signing autographs as I swanned around the city's watering holes. If I was ever freed.

"You should feel honored," Potter said. "The French press are not usually given to praising the English."

Shortly after that photo was taken, I was thrown to the floor and

Bertrand knelt on my spine, demanding to know where Fanuco was, threatening death, jail house beatings, big dirty penises in my mouth and rectum.

"So you're a hero," Potter said sarcastically. "And you have some very good lawyers."

"I do, don't I?" When I was allowed to make a phone call, my only recourse was Park Avenue Investigations. I reminded them that, even if I'd done wrong, I was entitled to "all the legal clout PAI commands," and emphasized the company's reputation may be in danger.

Potter stood and gathered his papers and picked up his jacket. "Yes, very good lawyers indeed. Keeping your name out of the press. For now. You are being bailed until a hearing in four days. Providing the hero angle plays well in the French media, you will likely be represented by the best money can buy."

"Cold-hearted capitalism has its uses."

"Indeed. Just do not get involved in anything else in the meantime."

I gestured to the newspaper. "No mention of dozens of bodies, I notice."

"Not yet. But it'll come out soon enough. Maybe you'll be a hero twice."

He waddled out as if late for another appointment, and a couple of uniformed officers entered immediately. I did not see hide nor hair of Pierre Bertrand as I was escorted from the building.

Both the police and the foreign office declined to offer me a lift, which was particularly galling because a marked police car followed my cab back to the Grecian. They had rather miraculously found my wallet in the quarry and returned it to me, so I was able to pay the driver. Back in my room, I peeled off the tracksuit and dumped it in the waste bin, slipped into the hotel bathrobe, and sat on the bed. Sleep nagged at me, and I had not forgotten about the hire car parked illegally on a footpath outside The Golden Lion, although that may already have been taken and burned out somewhere. Maybe that's where the younger Vietnamese men went.

I could address neither of those issues yet.

I placed a video-call to Jess via my iPad. In the PAI lab, she looked tired, but not as bad as I felt, which she was quick to remark upon. I told her there was some trouble and added the requisite, "But nothing I couldn't handle."

She knew about Harry by now, but kept focus, and updated me on the credit card check and confirmed that the trail matched almost exactly that of Gareth and Sarah's known movements: activated in Leeds, spent on in Paris, then on a number of purchases in Ho Chi Minh City, Vietnam's former capital, previously known as Saigon.

"Thanks, Jess," I said. "I really owe you for this."

"Yes, well, I expect more than a P45. I want dinner and the most expensive wine on the menu."

"You'll get it."

"*When*, and only when, you clean yourself up."

The smile felt alien on my face, like a breaking scab. "I'll even buy a new suit."

That seemed to satisfy her. "Anything else, boss?"

She had done as much as I could have hoped. But I needed a different angle.

"If I find Sarah, I still need ammunition," I said. "Work on Curtis Benson himself, specifically his monthly shipments and anything else about his pint-sized bulldog."

"It isn't a lot to go on," she said.

"You've worked wonders with less."

She said, "Gee, thanks," and hung up.

On the surface, it was likely the pair travelled together, but there was no trace of their plane tickets on either card. They could have bought them on the clones made by *Madame Rouge*, but Sarah and Gareth had crossed paths with Sammy LeHavre and the Vietnamese gang-masters. Was it dumb luck that I'd gotten so deeply involved, while Sarah and Gareth simply took off to the same country those people came from? It was impossible for so many lines to intersect so randomly. There was more to this.

Someone knocked on the door.

I put down the iPad and peeked out through the eyepiece.

The receptionist.

She checked one way down the corridor, then the other. She'd seen me come in wearing the hideous tracksuit but my shaggy hair was still filthy, as was the five-day stubble grown in two-and-a-half days.

I opened the door and she said, "This is for you."

I accepted the brown envelope, holding it with my thumb and two fingers. "What is it?"

"A boy dropped it off and gave me fifty euros tip to leave it out of our register."

Ah, I knew what it was now. I thanked her and she went on her way, and I emptied the contents on the bed.

Fast turnaround.

I examined the passport and credit card. Said my new name aloud: "Tomas Gerard." I repeated it a few times, getting the feel of it on my tongue. A French name, of course.

I twitched the curtain to check on the police car. They made no secret of watching me. Thanks to Roger Gorman's desire to protect his share price, as opposed to protecting *me*, he'd hired the priciest lawyers in Paris to look after my case, but with this surveillance I could not simply up and leave.

In the bathroom, I showered for twenty whole minutes, the water cocooning me in heat, in steam, washing over my aching limbs and joints. After, wrapped in the robe again, I opened my new passport to the photo I supplied to *Madame Rouge*. It was taken in the days when I was still traumatized by my experience in Thailand: shaved head, dark goatee, a stud in my ear—my attempt to look like a dangerous guy, a true hard-man.

When the shower-mist cleared, I snipped at my hair with scissors until it was as close to my scalp as I could make it, then covered the remaining patchy growth in shaving foam. I used a razor I bought in reception to remove the final layer of bristles, a couple of tiny nicks but they would heal in an afternoon. I applied more foam to my face and shaped my advanced stubble to match the passport—a scratchy circle of hair around my mouth, darker on the chin. Not quite as thick as I'd like, but it appeared intentional rather than scruffy.

I looked at myself afresh: slight bruise to my face, my hand strapped, and my ribs discolored. Mikey's work still bloomed the size of an orange around my sternum. The head-shot in Tomas Gerard's passport sported a piercing that had healed many years ago, but the smooth pate and rough goatee, combined with sleep-deprived eyes, made me look like an utter scumbag.

Good. As far as I can get from smart, well-groomed Adam Park the better.

I applied moisturizer liberally on every shaved area, dried off and stood naked in my room with a bottle of water. I was about to get dressed, when the phone rang, making me jump.

The British caller said, "I'm Carl Walker from CQP Solicitors. I've been retained by Park Avenue Investigations to oversee your defense. I will liaise with local experts—"

"What's the catch?" I said.

He *harrumph*ed before replying in a clipped, business-like way. "That when your defense is complete, successful or otherwise, you will relinquish all authority over the company and sign full chairmanship to Roger Gorman."

"Thought so."

"Well?"

I sipped the water.

"Mr. Park? Are you there? I need you to agree to this before you engage my services."

"*Mister* Gorman seems to forget I already have a healthy bank balance. I can already afford the best defense possible. I won't be giving up anything to *Mister* Gorman."

His turn to pause. "Sir, we have considerable expertise in—"

"I don't care. I'm out of the cop shop, and that's really all I needed from you."

"If you don't use us, sir, your funds will be frozen. Your private funds—"

"You're fired," I said with a laugh, and hung up. Not even Roger Gorman could freeze my personal accounts.

I itemized my equipment again, before securing it in my pack: iPad, which was fine; the remaining smartphone and the nuts-and-bolts Nokia; gaffer tape, which is something every traveler should carry (no better tool for patching-up torn rucksacks); my miniature tool kit; my precious camera and binoculars.

I dressed in cargo pants, a long-sleeved cotton shirt and a pair of walking sandals, heaved my rucksack onto my back, and examined my reflection. I was some distance away from myself, both inside and out.

I left enough cash on the bed to cover my bill, then lugged my rucksack to the lobby and selected a free map from the dispenser. I unfolded it and held it up like a dumb-ass tourist. Outside, I kept it up but not so much that it obscured my face. I pretended to be confused by the directions, and headed toward the Metro, folding the map badly as I went.

I listened.

No car engine.

No footsteps.

Nobody followed.

I warned myself not to get too excited as I reached the Metro and, unmolested, caught the shuttle to *Charles de Gaulle* airport.

Without incident, I purchased a first-class ticket to Vietnam on the cloned card, intending to repay the money directly to the real person's account as soon as I landed. I now had four days left to reach Vietnam—a communist country about which I knew hardly anything—and locate a man and a girl who may or may not wish to be found.

Unfortunately, the only flights from France, every one of them, stopped over in Bangkok.

ASIA

VIETNAM

Chapter Twenty-Seven

I thought it would have meant more to me, being back in the city that drove me to grow from lean to strong, to seek out people who need helping, and taught me more lessons than I could have hoped to learn otherwise. Had I commuted to the city itself, perhaps the vibrations of my past might have shook something loose. For now, I remained in the embrace of Bangkok's airport, a sprawling town-sized structure with amenities to service every whim. At one point I found myself staring out the huge windows at the distant city, willing myself to grow scared or angry, but it was just a place—a speck of dirt on the global map. Technically no different than any other place. It wasn't as if the soil retained homeopathic traces of my blood, filtering it out through veins beneath its surface, to infuse with my psyche. I may as well have been gazing at a photograph of Milton Keynes. Eventually, someone bumped my leg with their case and I snapped myself away, and paid for a much-needed massage while I waited for my connecting flight.

I landed at Ho Chi Minh City Airport on Tuesday evening, eight hours ahead of France and the UK. It was sparse and clean, and virtually deserted but for pairs of soldiers roaming with dogs. I was one of a dozen or so people waiting patiently for luggage and our footsteps and voices carried high into the metal fixtures and echoed back at us. Once I collected my rucksack, I wrestled with the visa-on-arrival paperwork, breezed through immigration control, and finally stepped out into the Socialist Republic of Vietnam.

And it was hot. Not warm, but *hot*.

Local time was seven p.m. and the sun had long-since left the sky, yet the air clung damply to my skin. I'd been hotter in the past, but humidity always takes some getting used to. When I travelled through India and Thailand, the taxis were sweatboxes on wheels, so the air-con in the one I snagged was a refreshing surprise.

I asked the driver to take me to *Pham Ngu Lao* in District One, the street on which, according to the data Jess had mined, Gareth's ill-gotten credit card first transacted a two-night stay in the *Saigon Backpacker Hotel*.

The barefoot driver said, "English?"

"Yes."

"Ah. David Beckham, yeah? You like him?"

I couldn't help a smile. David Beckham: universal ice-breaker. "Sure," I said. "Good footballer."

"Old, though. Lost pace."

Like a pub conversation back home. I said, "He's retired now."

We drove in silence for a minute or two, the dark dual-carriageway zipping by outside. He said, "You know Wayne Rooney?"

We chatted like that for the next half an hour, passing through small pockets of civilization—settlements of twenty-or-so buildings at a time—with empty stretches of darkness in between. Each mini-town was active, with kids playing in vests, sinewy men smoking or drinking, and every place without exception owned emaciated animals; pigs and goats, cats and dogs, ribs showing beneath their fur. Many displayed tiny birds crammed into cages, and when we slowed I could hear their pained chirps while men, women and children paid them no mind.

The driver also enjoyed his horn a little too much. Every time we approached a moped or pushbike or piece of rust on wheels he'd honk loudly before overtaking. Sometimes we'd get a honk in reply. We passed a *lot* of mopeds. The driver's football talk was almost constant, pausing only to tell me no one called Ho Chi Minh City by its official name (christened after Vietnam's North Vietnamese leader). So I got it into my head that I was in *Saigon* now. Ho Chi Minh City was for when dealing with officials.

Soon, the surroundings grew taller and more solid. Fewer breaks in the buildings and the road was less dusty. We pushed into a box junction at traffic lights and stopped. To my right, a line of— literally—hundreds of mopeds waited for a green light, revving as if about to commence a race. One scooter held a man, woman and two kids. All except the man wore crash helmets. Another moped-owner rode with some sort of grass-like vegetable piled on the back, towering higher than he was. Others were young people wearing face masks, like surgeons.

Adam's Smug Travel Tips #23: In South East Asia, face masks are used, not for health reasons, but to keep the sun off people's faces because, unlike in the west where a tan is considered attractive, lighter skin is desirable here due to the notion that peasants working the fields are cursed with darker looks. You even get lotions that claim to help bleach skin pigments.

The lights changed and the race launched en-masse and surrounded us on all sides. Horns beeped and honked like a fight could break out, yet the parade flowed on. The driver kept his eyes forward and asked who I thought Manchester City might sign next. We inched forward and swung into the throng, which parted lazily with each blast of noise. No one died. No one got hurt. And after much maneuvering between barely-protected riders and cy-clists, he eventually deposited me outside a bar on *Pham Ngu Lao*.

Recalling a word both Anh and Fanuco said back in France, I asked, "Do you know anything by the name of Giang?"

"Giang?" he said.

"Might be a bar, a restaurant, a street…"

He told me he hadn't heard of it, and charged me twenty US dol-lars for the journey, which is far preferable to the local currency, the dong. Yes, *the dong.* Despite the country's violent history with America, the people still preferred the simple dollar (about twen-ty-three *thousand* dong to one dollar). I paid him, retrieved my rucksack, and stepped out into the sauna of Saigon's nightlife where, even on this insignificant crossroad after eight p.m., the motorbike procession was endless. Whenever the lights changed, dozens, maybe hundreds, droned by, chugging fumes into the air, so it made crossing the road look impossible. I didn't have to face that right now, though.

The Go2 Bar, from Jess's list, would not have looked out of place on the corner of a New Orleans street, a canopied awning over tables and chairs on the pavement, open windows and dark wood furniture. Inside the bar, I ordered a Diet Coke, where western faces mingled with what may have been locals or tourists from neighboring countries.

I chose to sit outside.

A tall, skinny waitress in denim shorts and a Go2 t-shirt skit-tered out with a menu. "Pizza is good," she said with a strong accent. "Burgers good. Noodles very good."

"Just the drink, thanks." I pointed at the glass, smiling like an id-iot.

I made a mental note to try to learn some key Vietnamese phrases. I should have done so already but, on the plane, sleep had been far more pressing.

As she was about to depart I asked her to wait, and showed her some photos of Sarah and Gareth that I printed out at Bangkok Airport.

She shook her head. "No, don't know."

I asked her if she'd show the photos around for me. "To your colleagues," I said.

"Coll …? What?" Her English was passable, but not conversational.

"Staff. Waiters. Waitress. Show them?" I handed her twenty dollars.

"Ah, yes." She took the photos and sizable tip, and placed the menu before me, then disappeared inside.

From what I could tell from my perch, Saigon's District One was nearly all tourism: groups of young girls, probably students on gap years, giggled past; older men in denim waistcoats hanging around on powerful motorcycles; couples, arm in arm. Music beat out from various colorful-fronted bars, and gaping shops flogged t-shirts and hats, knock-off designer names alongside local Vietnam-orientated merchandise. Already, the never-ending honking and droning from the traffic blended into the background, and my ears zoned in on nearby conversations about where people had been and where they might go next and how much they loved Vietnam and how they missed real tea.

The waitress returned with the photos and said, "Sorry, no one know these people. One guy say maybe the man was here, but not the girl. He don't know when. You police?"

I left another ten dollars and hit the street. *Pham Ngu Lao* was a narrow road with a pavement on one side, the other open frontage and a dusty channel on which people walked and traded. It was reminiscent of the *Kao San Road* in Bangkok, but without the persistent haranguing from flyer vendors. For the length of the street, I was left alone except for an eighty-ish man selling cigars and packs of postcards from the vantage point of his wheelchair. I smiled and shook my head and tried to go past, but he shifted his chair into my path, face sagging as if I insulted him. It took me a few seconds to remember that, like many poorer nations, people in Vietnam see tourists as wealthy phantoms, gliding through their lives, taking a break from paradise. When we wave off a five-dollar tea towel or ten-dollar elephant statue, they simply cannot understand why; if we have money to burn, *all of us*, why not buy a flute or hat or whatever they are flogging?

I put my hand in my pocket. "How much?"

He grinned toothlessly. "One dollar. You like Manchester United?"

"You know the Saigon Backpacker Hotel?"

"Of course! I know all hotels, hostels, guesthouses. You go down there." He pointed past a vegetable stand, to what looked like a narrow alleyway. On his hand, only his thumb, index and little finger remained, the rest having healed over. I bought a pack of postcards from him for a dollar and gave him a second dollar for his trouble, but he thrust it back in my hand and shook his head like I was stupid and held up his little finger. "No, no. *One* dollar."

The Saigon Backpacker Hotel was located a hundred yards from the main stretch. Each alley, I realized, was an extension of the road, not a new address in itself. This particular passage was litter-free but coated with a layer of wet grime. Three foraging rats fled as I trudged toward the hotel with its white sign and blue writing that no doubt once lit up.

In the tiled lobby, the air was thicker. I noted the usual book-exchange in a corner beneath one of four wall-mounted fans. Whenever the oscillation twisted in my direction, the cold air brought goose-bumps to my sweat-filmed skin. Two girls manned the reception desk, both aged between fifteen and twenty, with flouncy dresses and flowers in their hair.

The one wearing glasses stood and said, "Help you, sir?"

"You speak English?" I asked in a voice so tired it surprised me. Must've been the heat.

"Many in our city speak English now. And French. And sometime little German. Saigon is very modern. We like English. Good English."

It pays to speak the language of the tourist.

I said, "Do you have a room?"

"For how many nights please?"

"I'll pay for three, but I may leave sooner."

"For three nights, sir, thank you."

I went through the booking-in procedure, handing over whatever they asked for. They checked Tomas Gerard's passport against my face and against a list of some sort, and told me they would keep it until my departure. I didn't object. It was standard practice in plenty of countries, and no one questions security procedures in Vietnam. Ever.

When it came to paying, I asked if they remembered my friends who stayed a couple of weeks ago. "I don't suppose you have their room? They said lovely things about this place."

She opened the book. "What name?"

"Isabella…" Damn it. Suddenly, I was drawing a complete blank.

"Isabella and Joseph," said the girl.

"Isabella Laurent and Joseph Coulet," I said. "Of course."

"They check out two weeks ago." As she came across a note, she frowned, slid my passport to one side. Out of my reach. She said, "They had to leave."

"Why did they have to leave?"

"Trouble," said the girl with glasses. "Police came."

"They were arrested?"

"Not arrest. Just … sir, we cannot talk about them. Their room is not available."

"Did they do something wrong?"

The girl adjusted her glasses. "We were not working that day."

I thumbed three twenties and placed them on the counter. "Can I ask who was on duty when the police came?"

The girl pushed the money back toward me. Would not meet my eye.

The other girl handed me my passport. "No rooms. Very sorry."

I took the passport and money. If the police wanted Sarah and Gareth's activities to remain confidential, I could waste no more time. I needed to move. And move I did.

Chapter Twenty-Eight

My French SIMs were not working, presumably cancelled by the authorities when I absconded, although there was no shortage of phone shops around the corner from *Pham Ngu Lao*. I bought a genuine iPhone from an elderly lady with one leg, and she was happy to accept an Adam Park credit card (I figured now I was outside Europe they couldn't touch me). I added two hundred dollars to the SIM. It wasn't fully charged, but stored enough juice to set up my Outlook account, then call Jess on her personal mobile. It was mid or late-afternoon in the UK so I thought she was still at work.

"Where the hell have you been?" she demanded.

"You still okay?" I said. "No one suspects?"

"*Everyone* suspects. The police interviewed me. Gormless Gorman told me I'd be in deep shit if he caught me helping you. You are in *trouble*, mister."

"What do you have for me?"

"Where *are* you? And what is that *noise*?"

The honking went on, and on, and on. I couldn't hide it. "I am in Saigon and what you can hear are the residents of Saigon heading home from work."

"Saigon? Figures. So you'll want some info on Mr. Delingpole's spending habits? Or should I say Mr. Gallway?"

"I just came from the backpacker district. He and Sarah checked in together at a cheap hotel, and Gareth drank in at least one bar. They were *here*. I need to know the most recent spend."

She paused and I heard typing. "The Rex Hotel."

"Really?" I said. "The most recent place is called the Rex?" It sounded familiar but I couldn't place it.

"Last night," she said.

"*Yesterday*?" So I was closer than I hoped.

Jess continued. "Lots of smaller transactions last night too, and a lot of nights before that. Doesn't look like he spent enough to stay the night in the hotel. Drinks, maybe food."

"He's using it for living expenses. We got lucky on that earlier hit, but I guess he's started using cash in the hotels so he can bribe them to stay off the grid. No questions asked if they're suspicious about his passport. But why? What's he *doing* here?"

"Holiday?" Jess suggested.

"This is more than a whim, more than simply fancying a new country. Vietnam, it's too random. It's the sort of place I would have visited. Heck, I'd come back on holiday myself, but…" I was losing myself in the place. Back to the task at hand. "He's enjoying himself," I said. "But it's not a pleasure trip. It has a purpose."

"I can't be in DDS too long. They must be monitoring me. Besides, I think this is entering your area of expertise and leaving mine. I'll email you a full list. Okay, it should be with you now."

My phone bonged to indicate I received it.

I said, "Anything else regarding Benson?"

Her voice changed. Hushed somehow. "I'll call you back on this number in half an hour."

I hung up and Googled the Rex Hotel, and realized why it rang a bell. It was pretty famous if you liked Vietnam War movies. It was also the hit furthest away from my current position, so I decided I'd make my way there by way of the list, geographically rather than chronologically. But that meant surviving the roads.

I had read about how to do this, but it was counter-intuitive to say the least. Although the flow of scooters and motorcycles and the odd car appeared constant, I waited for a gap sufficient for me to step into, not an actual break in the stream. Then I walked into he melee. And I kept walking at a steady pace. The riders seemed to sense my movement, my intent. Their action couldn't even be described as "swerving." They flowed, and other road-users eased round them. I was a pebble in a river, its current gushing around me.

I made it to the other side, heart beating faster. A minor thrill that I could never forget, that of mastering a new trick for traversing a foreign land.

The route from *Pham Ngu Lao* to the first bar was a straight line then a short dog-leg, so it wasn't a stretch to say I was walking where they walked. Seeing what they saw. Dodging the slew of tourists and locals. Waving off a t-shirt vendor. They would have done all this too.

I entered Purple Jade with my scruffy gear, shaved head and goatee, and took in its cozy booths and live piano, and realized it was geared toward business clientele. Gareth spent a hundred dollars here, and looking at the prices they seemed inspired by London or New York rather than the two-dollars-a-drink in the Go2 Bar. It was conceivable he'd made some friends and bought a round with a spot of food, but I flashed the photos of Gareth and Sarah to the bar staff and the manager, and no one recognized either.

Next up was Insomnia, a retro-style place with modern, comfortable seating and prices more akin to a backpacker on tour. It advertised musical comedy and served a mean virgin cocktail, but alas, no one could recall Gareth or Sarah.

The bars I entered gave a stark contrast to what lay outside. Clean, air-conditioned places with mid-to-high-priced drinks, their designs reflected any metropolitan watering hole, then back to the streets caked with fumes and disabled locals hocking more cigars and postcards and the odd bit of Vietnam-themed tat. I found myself buying four cigars from four different sales-folk, just to keep moving; a couple of purchases could feed them for an evening at least.

The final bar I tried, *Saigon đêm,* was air-conditioned but it more closely resembled the bar in France in which I'd been drugged and carted out to the countryside to die than the swanky lounges I'd explored so far. The entrance took me down a staircase below street-level, and the patrons were all Vietnamese. I paced slowly through the thick cigarette haze. Each man I neared turned toward me, then feigned indifference once I passed. I was suddenly very aware of the rucksack on my back, which advertised that I was carrying all my money, cards and documents. Deeper into *Saigon đêm* were two booths, both occupied by fat middle-aged men in shirts and ties with much younger women sat on their laps in skirts and crop-tops. One of the men, when he noticed me, adjusted the gun on his hip. Then I noticed more guns, in shoulder holsters, on hips, and even slung on the back of a chair. The only women present I took to be prostitutes, including the one in gold leather bolero top and blue hot-pants who sashayed toward me as soon as I got to the bar.

"You American?" she asked, slurring her words. Her eyes were glazed, hinting at more than alcohol in her blood.

"British," I said.

"Ah, British. We like British."

I had four hundred dollars in one pocket, fake passport in another, an iPhone in a third. My real documents were in my bag along with credit cards and an iPad.

I showed her the photos. "Wonder if you've seen these people."

She leaned over them, then in toward me. "I see *you*, baby."

"Aashka!" called a young skinny man from a Formica table. He levelled a look at her that left no room to argue. "*Lại đây!*"

She ambled over to the skinny man and sat on his lap, kissed his neck while he watched me, his hand clasping the girl—Aashka's—buttocks.

The heavyset elderly barman stood still, eyes boring through me. He shook his head and folded his arms. I nodded understanding. The room's glare weighed heavily upon me as I retraced my path toward the staircase. A chair scraped.

I stopped.

Some guy with a gun in a shoulder holster weaved toward a dim W.C. sign. Most of the patrons lost interest in me, although a couple of the more disgruntled men lingered. I took the first of the stairs and emerged into the stuffy street.

What the fuck was Gareth doing in that place? Drugs? Was Sarah with him?

Traffic had eased, but I was sticky beneath my shirt and the rucksack dragged me down more than before. It was after ten, and I still had three other places to try, but I figured I should make my way to Gareth's least likely transaction: The Rex Hotel. It was the most out-of-place establishment, so it could have held the key to his odd bar-crawl.

A twenty-minute walk away on *Nguyen Hue Boulevard*, The Rex Hotel was the focal point for American and western journalists during the war, and the scene for regular press briefings by the US military. As the war progressed and the briefings bore less and less resemblance to facts relayed from embedded journalists in the field, the sessions became known as "Five O'clock Follies." The rooftop bar would serve GIs and war correspondents during downtime, where they could enjoy a beer or cocktail whilst observing the flash of artillery ghosting over the horizon. Today it is a five-star establishment with around three-hundred rooms, two ballrooms and swimming pools, a gym, spa and six restaurants. The hostesses who greeted me in the lobby were pristinely garbed in red and gold, with perfect hair and jewelry. Figuring I needed some sort of base from which to operate, I saw nothing wrong with a little luxury, so checked in to a standard room and dumped my bag, before heading straight back out.

The rooftop bar presented a bird's-eye view of the surrounding streets. The traffic's raging torrent had calmed to a steady stream, but the horns still tooted merrily twelve stories up. The *Saigon đêm* aside, everything seemed so relaxed, despite the cacophony of noise. Even the hawkers acted friendly more than pushy. The beer itself was another testament to communist imagination in that it was titled *Saigon Beer*, but it was as nice as any Budweiser or Heineken and so refreshing after an hour or so traipsing about with my rucksack I thought I might start dribbling.

I showed the photos around the bar staff, but didn't get a single hit, although I was informed that over thirty staff worked here, so they couldn't say for sure. A shift change was due in an hour. There were worse places to spend an hour than watching over Saigon at night.

Jess called and I could tell by the background noise she was in a coffee shop or pub. She said, "Curtis Benson's shipments go to a Bahamian island called Lana. They are plastic-packed and the official documentation lists them as medical supplies. Nothing that requires additional paperwork or permits, but the island's only hospital is a wreck. Population of fifty-thousand, and a mortality rate more in keeping with the middle-ages."

"How is Curtis Benson interested in this?"

"I don't know," she said. "Before he was … taken, Harry said he suspects Curtis Benson has people on Lana. Possibly shipping heroin or coke out there to boost his titty-bar income."

"Sounds sensible, but it's still guesswork."

"Want me to stop guessing?"

"No, your guesses are usually more accurate than most facts." I waved my empty at the waiter in his spotless waistcoat. He nodded. I came to a decision about something that had been preying on me a while. "Don't take any more chances on PAI property. I wondered what Roger meant by saying you'd be in deep shit, and I realized he can file a criminal complaint against you for aiding a fugitive. And he'd do it too, just to hurt me."

A ping sounded on the other end.

"Hold on a sec," she said.

"I mean it, Jess. I can fire you when I get home and you'll walk into another job, but not with a criminal record. Especially in some cyber-crime—"

"Shut up."

I did so. "What's wrong? Are you okay?"

Shuffling on Jess's end. "Just a sec, I need to check someth—" Her words cut off. It didn't sound like anyone else was present. Then she said, "Oh. Em. Gee."

"What is 'oh em gee'?"

"O.M.G. Oh my God. He's active."

"*What?*"

"He spent thirty dollars in a bar."

"He's spent money in a lot of bars. Why is this so special?"

"Because that ping was an alert I set on my phone. He *just* made the sale. Right now."

"Right now?"

"Five minutes ago!"

"Shit, where?"

"The … I can't pronounce it. The Saigon… *Saigon dêm.*"

Oh, wonderful.

The waiter delivered my beer. I paid my bill and left a tip, and hurried back inside, handing my untouched beer to an elderly lady sat alone as I went.

Chapter Twenty-Nine

The Rex loaned scooters to their guests, but rarely so late at night. I paid yet another bribe and the duty manager opened the office especially for me, and I signed a contract putting me out two thousand dollars if I didn't return the vehicle. It took me twenty minutes, but I was back on the street, a full-face crash helmet pulling sweat straight out of my skin.

At one in the morning I was still surrounded by motorists. A thin flow, but constant. I wouldn't have wanted to try this during daylight hours. I pulled in a hundred yards down from *Saigon đêm*. Plenty of taxi-bikes queued, and people socialized outside the bar. I crossed my fingers that Gareth hadn't left yet.

When freeing my gym-friend's daughter from that pimp in London, a rage had swollen within me, before exploding to life all over someone I deemed deserving. It didn't take a psychologist to work out that I spent a year preparing physically and mentally for any sort of attack and, when it finally happened, I panicked. Now I was about to walk into a bar full of men who looked at me the way a prison population regarded pedophiles in a shower block.

No one went into *Saigon đêm*, no one came out. Few shops were open this close to midnight, but clubs emitted muted thuds, all hosting a gaggle of bicycles, mopeds and motorbikes outside, while hip and cool Saigonians conversed and compared machines. It was more than forty minutes since Jess's ping, so I crossed the road easily, took three deep breaths, and entered the dark stair-well.

The crowd had thinned to about a dozen men, although scantily-dressed women still displayed themselves about the place. The booth where the two fat men sat earlier was now occupied by four different men and two women, all laughing as they swigged whatever the Vietnamese called Champagne.

Probably *Saigon Champagne*.

I received one suspicious look after another as I advanced toward the bar. Perhaps my dodgy-bloke appearance was putting them off. It still nagged at me, though.

Why was Gareth spending money in here?

Working on getting more documents? Did he and Sarah part ways?

I got the greasy, heavy-set barman's attention and asked if he spoke English. He did not. I showed the photo of Gareth and stabbed at it with my good hand.

"Have you seen him?" I asked slowly. Because foreigners understand English better when you speak it slowly. Next, I'd try raising my voice.

The barman shrugged.

"Like me." I gestured to my face. "English. Spending money." I rubbed my thumb on my forefinger.

Again, the barman shrugged. This time he added a down-turned lip and a head-tilt.

It was a woman who stepped forward. A different one than before, older, with green eyes and too much rouge on her cheeks. "I speak good English," she said. "Very good English. First class. You got a nice hotel, mister?"

"I'll give you twenty dollars to ask if he's seen either of the people in this photo."

She took my money and spoke to the barman, who replied quickly. "He say he tol' you already. He didn' see him."

Must've been lost in the body language. "Ask him … ask him who spent thirty dollars recently."

"Sorry, I don't … what you wan' know?"

"Thirty dollars. On a credit card."

As she spoke, the barman's attention flicked to one side then back to the photo. Someone moved behind me. A trim man in a decent suit headed quickly for the door. Tall, broad-shouldered. Short, cropped hair.

I had found Gareth Delingpole.

I took a step in that direction.

The barman held my wrist. The green-eyed girl said, "Yeah, he know him. In bathroom. Guy in bathroom."

"Thanks." I pulled free and strode toward the guy with his back to me. I called out, "Gareth," and the guy bolted for the exit.

I ran after him and skipped over a leg extended to trip me. Vaulted a table. The shouts in Vietnamese sounded loud and sharp, but I caught hold of Gareth and—

It was a Vietnamese man. Taller than average, middle-aged. A forced grin, yellow teeth. He was one of the big-spenders from the booth.

"What?" he said. "I don't know no Gareth." Good English. Suspiciously good.

"You're spending on his card," I said.

"Prove it."

"I don't have to prove it."

"Sure you do." He nodded behind me.

At least six men held guns in my direction. Mostly drunk men. It may not have been the first gun pointed at me this week, but the experience didn't get any more pleasant. I knew all six could not shoot without hitting the man spending on Gareth's card. But they wouldn't miss me, either.

I let go. The man smoothed himself down. He must have given a signal of some kind, as the posse lowered their guns.

I said, "You have a credit card."

For the first time, I noticed a sore on his lower lip. It glistened even in the dim lighting, looked like a herpes scab opened by his sudden amusement.

"You are not from police," he said. "They are not so desperate to use foreigners."

"I'm just looking for someone."

"You say you look for credit card."

Everyone around us twitched, the occasional glance at a friend, a slow-nod here, a fist-clench there. Primed to pounce at the slightest signal. I considered rushing the man and treating him like a hostage, but someone might have got a shot off.

I said, "Who are you?"

"I ask you first."

"I'm an investigator. I have no interest in causing trouble for you, but I have to ask you about that card."

His yellow smile flashed again. "I am someone who does not have to answer questions." The man took the photos off me, ripped them into four pieces, and dropped them on the floor. Then, instead of leaving as he originally intended, he slinked off back to his booth and the people there chuckled smugly.

I approached, but two other punters got in my way. I lifted my hands non-threateningly and called to the guy in the booth, "I can pay you."

He waved a hand. Simultaneously, the two punters shoved me toward the door. I stood my ground. Two more stood, this couple holding old-looking handguns. I expected taking out the first two would not have the effect of making me the alpha in the room, but rather a swarm of fists and feet would pummel me into a hospital, if not a hail of bullets.

But it was my one lead. If I was chasing the wrong guy, being here was pointless. Yet, if the man with the lip-sore was using that card, he'd had *some* contact with one of them, with Gareth or Sarah. He was a lead. One I could not allow to fade away into the night.

The two with guns stepped towards me and one of them, a guy with really bad acne, spoke in Vietnamese. I gave no indication that I understood. He shook his head like I was stupid. He said the same thing again, louder and more slowly.

"Huh," I said. "Doesn't that work in *any* language?"

The green-eyed prostitute joined the group and placed her hands on my chest. "You have to go now, mister."

"I need to ask about—"

"You ask." She patted my chest gently, held my eye. "You ask already."

The man with the card lifted a glass in my direction and swigged from it, dabbed his open scab with a napkin. The woman, now on his lap, giggled and kissed his neck. No one in this place was going to move.

I took the stairs slowly back up to the street, and the laughter of around twenty men barreled up the passage behind me.

Chapter Thirty

Half an hour later, grinning man with the herpes scab emerged alone, wobbling some. He lit a cigarette and stood beside the taxi drivers, and chatted for a bit. From behind a Dumpster-size bin, I held my new iPhone steady on the moped's handlebars, enabled the camera and used the optical zoom to observe him better. It was not as good as the phone Jess gave me, the one I smashed in the quarry, but I snapped a couple of shots anyway.

He had seemed well-respected by the other punters, or possibly feared. But his use of the card meant Gareth could have been mugged or had his card cloned, and that guy was simply the beneficiary. Still, he must know *something*. I wanted him to tell me *where* Gareth was mugged, and—if possible—what happened to him.

Once the cigarette smoldered to a stub, he dropped and crushed it and undid a chain on the railing beside him. Mopeds, motorbikes and pushbikes—all were secured there. He heaved his vehicle to one side. I couldn't get the camera to focus on the moving figure in low light. He looked around once more, then swung his leg and pulled into the road on…

A ladies' push-bike. It even had a basket on the front. Either he borrowed his wife's or he'd stolen it.

Jacket flapping behind, he merged with the traffic and I fired up the moped. I gave him a one-minute head-start, then rolled after him. Which was stupid. I caught up in seconds, and when I tried to slow down I wobbled and brought the irksome honks of a million horns. I sped up and passed my target without looking at him. In my mirrors, he didn't appear too perturbed.

The road bent to the right and ahead of me was a flat street lined with offices and banks, turns feeding off it every few hundred yards. I couldn't tail him this way. I got three junctions ahead, gambling that he wouldn't turn off one of them.

Down the fourth street, a club pumped music out of tall doors and the familiar collection of young people with spiky hair and loose clothes gathered outside to laugh and dance and smoke. Over the club's door, a black plastic sign read "*đo⊠ phòng*" in red writing. I pulled up to the young people, and when I removed my helmet I drew half a dozen curious looks and half a dozen aggressive ones. A twenty-something bloke in a white silk shirt spoke in macho Vietnamese, pointing his cigarette. I heard the word "American" and shook my head and said, "British." That seemed to placate them, but then turned their backs to me, engrossed in their own conversation.

I said, "Anyone speak English?"

No one made a move to acknowledge me. I took out five twenty dollar bills and held them in the air.

"One hundred dollars for anyone who'll lend me their bicycle."

It made me feel like such a pig. I was swimming in money, but these people, well-dressed as they were, couldn't even afford to get into a nightclub. Flashing my cash around seedy joints felt right, but playing the slick foreign savior, handing out cash for favors, it left me feeling dirty.

"Lend?" said one girl. She was pretty with heavy hips, tight Daisy-Duke hot pants and a vest. "Like, you bring it back?"

"Yes," I said.

The cigarette-pointer said something to her. Again, I picked up

"American" and he rubbed his thumb and forefinger together. She waved him off. "So, you give me hundred dollars, I lend you bike, you bring bike back here, I keep hundred dollars."

"Correct. And …" I patted the moped. "If I don't come back, you keep this."

She frowned. *If it looks too good to be true…*

"Okay," she said. "Keys first."

I gave her my keys and she unlocked her bike, a rickety-looking thing with no gears and one brake.

"Thank you."

"Welcome." She led eight of the group toward the door to the club.

I cycled back up the street, feeling the drain of two thousand dollars on my bank account.

The old bike was stiff, and I lumbered rather than rode. By the time I got back to the main road, the man with Gareth's credit card was way ahead. At least he hadn't turned off the street. I probably appeared ridiculous keeping the helmet on, but if he spotted a helmeted cyclist in his vicinity it would likely raise less suspicion than a Caucasian face.

I pushed myself hard, my shirt sticking to me as if I'd come out of a downpour. I remained about three hundred yards behind for the first mile, then he steered into a street. I reached that road in time to see him pull into an apartment complex of grey concrete.

His neighbors consisted of four residential blocks and a few shops and cafes, all closed. Streetlamps lit the road in a yellow hue, and as I left the main drag, the horns and engines sounded a long way away. Nothing moved except me. The squeak of the bike's wheel was the loudest noise.

I trundled past the complex and the entrance led to an underground parking structure. No sign of the man. I stopped at the next junction. The building was six stories. Small balconies hung over the pavement. No lights. Open windows. No air-conditioning units.

On the pavement opposite, a raised bed held shrubs and plants and a couple of trees, and made a decent hiding place for both me and the bike. It wasn't directly opposite the man's home but as uninterrupted views went, this was pretty good.

I removed the helmet. Steam literally floated above my head. I folded myself behind a bush and sat in the dry soil. I watched as a dim light on the third floor came on for ten minutes and then died.

He was home for the night.

As night faded into dawn, a chugging tuk-tuk misfired. I jerked upright, my head shifting from a horrible angle on my shoulder. I hadn't been asleep, but my body was crying out for it. Now alert thanks to that squirt of adrenaline, I crouched in the bush for another hour, traffic growing steadily, but there was no movement in the apartment. Commuters passed by, the occasional glance my way made me feel ridiculous, and proved this wasn't an effective hiding place after sun-up. Most of the women wore traditional gear—long, colorful *áo dài*, the silk tunic over pantaloons, while the men seemed far more westernized in shirts and trousers. Three schoolgirls in dazzling white *áo dài* and conical leaf-hats giggled as they saw me emerge from the bushes to continue my "surveillance." I use the term loosely, of course, because I was behaving like an amateur right now.

Out in the open. Taller by a head than ninety-five per cent of the foot-flow, with every person on the street giving me a wide berth. If the grinning fraudster on the third floor happened to look out, I could expect a posse of faithful barflies trotting up the road, *settin' fer a lynchin'*.

Or something.

I crossed the road and popped into a clothes shop and browsed for an *I Love Vietnam* cap or some such, but this wasn't a tourist area. Instead, the excitable old lady behind the glass counter placed a *non la* on my head, a cone-shaped hat much like the schoolgirls were wearing but this one was made of straw rather than leaves. I bought it and went to a café and sat at an outdoor table, where a bored teenage girl in shorts and a vest asked in Vietnamese what I wanted.

Without thinking I said, "Coffee, please."

"You wan' drip coffee or Nescafé?"

"Nescafé?"

Inside the café, behind the counter, sure enough, jars of Nescafé instant lined up behind the sweaty bloke with a red, bulbous nose and the approximation of a chef's outfit.

"Drip coffee please," I said, whatever that is.

Back home, the proliferation of American sitcom-inspired coffee-shops gave me great places to take prospective clients who didn't want to meet in the office or in a wine-bar full of hooray-Henries, and also to take Harry if I wanted to watch his jaw hit the table when he saw how much a venti soy latte cost. He called me a coffee snob, which I did not take as an insult. Actually, he once fainted at the price of his white-chocolate and raspberry muffin. True story.

My drink this morning arrived in a metal filter placed on top of a large espresso mug with a jug of what appeared to be milk beside it, only thicker. Cream, perhaps? I must have looked as green as any first-timer, as the girl lifted the top off the filter. The coffee slowly dripped through to the cup.

Aha! That's why they call it "drip" coffee. Good detective work.

While it dripped, I watched the apartment complex, a fruit and veg stall setting up between us. When my filter was empty, I watched what the other coffee-drinkers were doing. They poured in the white gloop, which turned out to be condensed milk, testing it for taste. I copied them and sipped. It set my mouth alive with sweetness and the kick from the coffee was like a thunderbolt. I drank it slowly and when my target failed to emerge, I ordered another along with something from the menu called *Xoi Lac*. It was the only thing I dared try to pronounce.

More waiting followed. I could call Jess to see if she could run a list of people registered at this address, but it would take hours and might not even work. I had no idea what systems the government used here. It's not like hacking is an exact science, either. One government agency is not like the one in the country beside it, which can be like an English-speaker trying to order breakfast in Vietnam without pointing at pictures.

Adam's Smug Travel Tips #45: Take a chance on food. Even if you don't usually like "foreign food" back home, you might surprise yourself.

My breakfast was a sticky rice dish with roasted nuts and strong garlic, which was nice enough but my stomach flipped at the second coffee. I needed the loo, but didn't dare risk losing the guy for a day. It was Saturday when I left England, and Benson set the deadline as midnight Friday, which made today Tuesday or Wednesday, I wasn't sure. I was ahead of the UK here, so if I was experiencing Wednesday morning, Jess and Caroline and Jayne were still in bed on Tuesday night.

Then something caught my eye. In the periphery, over my shoulder. An actual *car* trundled up the road. I had seen only a smattering of them in the country, and this one was moving slowly.

It was a police car.

The men inside, one mustachioed, the other young and clean-shaven, slowed as they neared the café. I bowed my head to my cup, and pretended to drink. The last thing I needed was to draw the attention of the local constabulary. Any serious examination of my documents would mark me as an illegal, and I didn't dare think how a communist police force would treat me.

The car passed at a leisurely pace and stopped outside the complex. It gave three blasts of the horn. No mistaking it for a polite moped-driver. The man I'd been following stepped out wearing a suit and tie and checking a gun under his jacket. The two uniformed cops greeted him and he climbed happily in the back seat, then the car drove away, honking into traffic.

I bowed my head, closed my eyes, and howled. Inside my head, of course. Not literally. My credit card thief was a fucking *policeman*.

Chapter Thirty-One

That bar, full of men with guns. Close-knit. Protective. Wary of strangers. *Saigon đêm* was a cop hangout. Blow off some stress after work with booze and birds. Why not, it was a free country. Well, as free as any dictatorship, I suppose.

I checked the iPhone to see if I could ask Google about nearby police stations, but alas I'd been using it for more than a couple of hours, so it was dead.

I kissed goodbye to my two thousand dollar deposit, cycled back to The Rex, and slunk up to my room, dust and sweat forming a kind of soup on my skin. It wasn't even nine a.m. yet. I showered while the phone charged, then used to the hotel's Wi-Fi to research police stations in Saigon. District One's main station was on *Duong Pasteur*, and for once my luck was in. It was close to the Fideco building and the main Bank of Vietnam headquarters, both of which I could actually see from the rooftop bar. About five minutes' walk. I dressed in khaki shorts and a microfiber shirt and, rather than carting around more photos, I snapped a couple of shots onto the iPhone, now at a quarter battery, and set off.

The police station dated back to before the war, and could easily have been mistaken for a bank were it not for the police cars and bikes parked out front and the various officers and patrolmen coming and going in their green uniforms with red epaulets. A couple of them nodded my way as I entered through the arched doorway and approached the front desk, a plain table with two older men behind it. An army of fans redistributed the hot air, but there was no air-conditioning that I could detect. I stood before the reception desk and one of the men—White Beard—looked up at me once, then back to his paperwork. His colleague, a clean-shaven wrinkly chap, didn't even look up.

"Hello," I said. No reaction. I used the iPhone to look up a translation. Lots of replies so I tried the easiest-looking one: "*Alô!*"

White Beard looked up again. "*Alô*," he said. Then some more things I didn't understand.

"Speak English?"

"No." He went back to his paperwork.

I brought up one of the photos of the man I was looking for, one I snapped outside the *Saigon đêm,* and placed the phone in the path of White Beard's pen. He stopped and laid his pen flat. He spread his fingers on the desk and gave me his attention with a smile that didn't seem altogether genuine. "*Làm những gì bạn?*"

"I'm sorry," I said. "I don't speak Vietnamese."

He waved his hand behind his partition, indicating a vast open-plan area where people who I assumed were suspects or witnesses talked to men in suits, at desks dotting the cauldron of a work-floor. I assumed he was highlighting how busy the place was.

I pointed at the phone. "I'm looking for this man."

I mimed binoculars and pointed again at the phone. I felt like such a dick, but it was less than forty-eight hours since I learned I was coming here. Charades were all I could rely on.

White Beard picked up my phone but gave no indication he recognized the man. He pressed the *home* button and showed his colleague, who shrugged. Another policeman came over, and then another. White Beard pressed buttons and went online. There were no apps or anything other than what came pre-installed, but he was finding plenty to amuse himself. The younger of the two new guys told him to do something, and he did. A roar of laughter from the trio. I tried to snatch the phone, but they pulled it out of reach. They were playing some pre-installed game.

"Come on," I said. "I just need to—"

"You are looking for me, I assume?"

I turned to the voice. The rangy frame, the yellow teeth, the wet sore on his lip that he wore as casually as a tie-pin. Yes, the man I was looking for stood right there, not a drop of sweat to be seen. His badge said *Thiếu tá Công an* in small letters.

I said, "I can't do anything to you here. You see that, don't you? I'm not looking for a fight. I need information."

He tentatively shook the hand I offered and I noticed his neat fingernails, his dry palm. "I am Major Giang. Lanh Giang."

"*Giang?*" I said a little too eagerly. "Did you say your name is *Giang?*"

"*Major* Giang," he said. "I am a senior officer here."

... a bar or a restaurant or the name of a song... No, none of those things.

It was a man.

Just like that, the "Giang connection" was right in front of me.

Chapter Thirty-Two

Major Giang growled a couple of orders and White Beard handed back my phone. I thanked him and asked if we could talk somewhere.

Giang said, "Is this about the same thing as last night?"

"Yes, but I do *not* want to do anything that will damage you. I need answers."

"I do not think that is something I must provide." He signalled to the men who commandeered my phone and they came towards me.

I said, "I have proof," and displayed my email on the iPhone, a list of bars and transactions on Gareth's fake card. "It wouldn't take long to get this to your commanding officer."

No reaction.

"All it takes is a rumor," I said. "The odd bribe here and there might be tolerated, but hundreds of dollars on a credit card stolen from a British national? They'll screw you up, and your career will be ended. You know they don't need undeniable proof, just enough for a strong suspicion."

The cops escorted me to the door.

Giang said, "*Khoan đã!*" which dismissed the men. Quietly, he said to me, "There are not many policemen who speak English, but my desk has no privacy. I will meet you somewhere I think there will be no ears."

"My hotel isn't far—"

"Neither is the war museum. Meet me there in one hour. Inside the gate. A little cooler for you, and not too far to walk."

I agreed and made as if to leave, but Giang did that tough-guy thing and stopped me.

"And Mr. Park..." He dabbed at his sore and flicked a dot of something off his breast pocket. "Do not record me, do not bring any friends, and do not try to mess with me. Right now you are an inconvenience. Be more than that, I will make sure you regret it."

I found the War Remnants Museum by flagging down a rickshaw and taking a ten-minute ride along the streets in the shade of the skinny young man's red-fabric seat. He jogged at a good pace, his back wet, his bare feet hard and scaly. I gave him a ten-dollar tip, which he accepted with a great big smile.

Until the mid-90s, the War Remnants Museum was known as the American War Crimes Museum, and a Huey greets visitors as they enter the reception garden, lending a taste of what is to come. The Vietnamese call the Americans "invaders" while the Americans think of themselves as "liberators." Every story in the museum was told, naturally, from a North Vietnamese perspective.

Further into the gardens, an F-5A fighter canted at an angle, a Japanese couple posing beside it, their phone on the end of a selfie-stick. A dozen-or-so tourists perused anti-aircraft guns, a second jet, a decimated US Jeep. Under the first awning that skirts the outer path, framed pictures of what they called "American Atrocities" dominated the walls and glass displays; burning children, the charred corpses of babies, beaming GIs posing with dead freedom fighters (not the "Viet Cong" or "Charlie," strangely enough). As I digested the mechanics of one of the most horrific weapons ever deployed in modern warfare—*napalm*—Giang managed to approach and stand beside me. We were alone under the awning.

"I fought for the South," he said. "A foolish boy who believed US propaganda."

"You think communists invading from the North was propaganda?"

"No, I think teaching that communism is evil was propaganda. That was the great lie. Paranoia repeated today with Iraq and others—anything not democracy must be defeated. Unless the oil price is threatened." He ran his fingers over the glass protecting a photo of helicopters fleeing Saigon. "When the imperialist invaders fled, I was enrolled in a school where I learned the truth about our war."

"What truth?"

"That America wanted a base in South East Asia. They failed to get a foothold in Korea because the South insisted on ruling themselves. When the Party flocked south in Vietnam, it was the perfect excuse. It was the same with the French, here and in Cambodia. But we repelled them before, and we repelled the Americans after."

"Repelled. Big word for a guy born and bred in a third-world country."

His yellow smile spread again. "You were raised in a corrupt system. You call us third-world because iPhones and flat screen TVs are still new to us. Your system is full of wealth and technology, but it feeds lies to its young, and glorifies the rare American victories during the war. But me, I spoke fluent English by the time I was fourteen. When I was fifteen, I fired an M-16 for the first time. Killed three men two weeks after my sixteenth birthday, three good men who wanted to free Vietnam from tyranny. Did you know, ninety per cent of Americans believe they won the war?"

"I don't think it's that many." I turned away from the images of napalm victims. "Are things really better under communism?"

"Not at first. The US licked their wounds and, like bitter children, they imposed sanctions. But look at Vietnam now. Since Mr. Clinton lifted those sanctions, and allowed us to play by the same rules as everyone else, we have grown strong. Soon we will be like China. The Vietnamese Lion will roar."

I didn't know enough to argue, quite frankly. I understood communist principles in an abstract sense—you don't smoke as much dope on as many beaches as I did without getting into the odd discussion or two—but in practice it comes down to the people running the show. Communism didn't work due to human nature. We believe that the person running the factory deserves better remuneration than the person sweeping the factory floor. Unless you are the person holding the broom, of course.

"The credit card," I said. "Where did you get it?"

Giang produced a small box with a wire antenna. Raised his eyebrows expectantly. I lifted my arms to the side and he swept my body, the box beeping slowly. It squealed when it detected my phone, which I handed over, and he completed the check to his satisfaction.

"I will require compensation," he said. "How much shall we say?"

"I probably don't have to pay at all, but let's call it a show of good faith." I gave him an envelope stuffed with large bills. "I'm on a tight schedule. We'll say two hundred dollars cash for the information or I go to your superiors."

Both sides "winning."

Giang pretended to consider it, then took the envelope. "Let us walk."

So we strolled the museum. Giang insisted on giving me his version of the conflict whenever we were near other people. When we found the section dedicated to prisoners of war, a school trip streamed by, and when Giang showed his police ID, the boys' and girls' faces lit up like they'd met a pop star. He smiled and ruffled some heads, and when they moved on, he asked me if I had any children.

"No," I said. I was tempted to add the laddish joke, "none that I know of," but it was hardly appropriate.

"I have five," he said. "Two boys, three girls. The girls sleep in one bedroom, the boys in another. My wife and I pull the sofa out at night."

"While you drink champagne and buy rounds for your friends. And judging by that thing on your lip, romancing of a lot of women who aren't your wife."

"I do not spend all the money on myself. I wish to send my oldest boy to university in your country, once I have educated him in its propaganda. I do not think all my children will go, but one is enough. He will get a good job and buy us a bigger house."

Giang stopped to point out a black and white photo of an emaciated North Vietnamese soldier, nude in the bottom of a pit, being urinated on by four GIs, one of whom was smoking a cigar. He said, "This is what the west did to Vietnam for too many years. If I can improve my life by taking something from a western bank or British criminal, I will do that."

"You got it from a criminal. This guy?" I showed him the photo of Gareth.

"The man in your photo looks very much like him."

"Tell me what happened," I said. "Everything."

And he did.

235

Chapter Thirty-Three

Gareth Delingpole, or Joseph Coulet as he was known on his passport, arrived in Saigon three weeks ago with his young lover, a woman who went by Isabella. They stayed at a low-key place called the *Saigon Backpacker Hotel*, paid cash, and relinquished their passports. However, due to the discrepancy between the stated nationality and the language they spoke, those passports were flagged upon arrival by the People's Security Service, Vietnam's answer to MI5 or the FBI.

Thiếu tá Công an Lanh Giang, or "Major" Lanh Giang, as the official title translated, worked for the Vietnam People's *Police* Service, who tackle local matters, so when the flag flashed through to the switchboard, it was Major Giang's duty to take action. He immediately set up surveillance on the western couple, who dined on cocktails and in fancy-pants restaurants, who held hands and kissed in public, who laughed with each other and their fellow westerners. Alone, the man read car magazines, while the girl sketched incredible pictures of the city. Always, though, the man flashed a credit card around like it was a magic money generator. The major sent in a rare female officer to discreetly check the card as the waiter processed it, and saw it was registered to a Mr. Gallway, not M. Coulet, which confirmed the suspect was an illegal immigrant. This, in turn, meant a significant conflict of interest for Lanh Giang.

Some years ago, Lanh Giang and his team—before his promotion to major—raided a packed, steamy factory cobbling together fake designer handbags. He became separated from the group, and found himself in an undocumented extension that led to a tunnel tucked away through which the senior factory-masters could escape. The factory owner himself was ducking into the tunnel, ready to escape, but the fleeing man gestured to the desk, upon which sat a small pile of cash.

With another baby on the way, Giang's hesitation, his temptation, turned to need. The factory owner vanished and so did the pile of cash. Giang was promoted to Major, and all seemed well, until the factory boss reappeared a year later.

He had since extended his reach beyond Vietnam's borders, and traded workers with colleagues in Thailand and Cambodia and China, exporting individuals with electronic aptitude in return for those skilled in needlecraft. That, inevitably, progressed to the sex trade and an increase in the boss-man's profile. He mostly sent girls away to Russia, Western Europe, Britain, and France. He was behind a "Thai Brides" website that shipped sixteen-year-old Vietnamese peasants to lonely men willing to pay a handsome sum, sent domestic slaves to the Middle East, and supplied sex workers and strippers to international "businessmen."

People like Curtis Benson and Vila Fanuco.

The now-rising criminal possessed a recording. Grainy phone footage, taken whilst the lens poked out of his pocket, revealed Giang's choice, and threatened to end his freedom, and crush any hope of his children leading a better life than him.

So Major Lanh Giang did as he was told. He passed information, made nice, worked hard. His career flourished and his family was left alone. Then the first "perk" came his way.

After liberating evidence from a locker in the police station, and doctoring the paperwork to blame a new recruit, he passed on the incriminating garment to an intermediary in a dark, smoke-filled bar with more strippers than patrons. Whilst waiting for the all-clear from the man in charge, he was taken to a back room where a beautiful young woman unzipped his fly and—once his fake resistance gave out—showed him a glimpse of the finer side of life.

It all unraveled from there.

The next time he did a favor for these people, the reward went further. He still loved his wife, of course, but these girls … they became a semi-regular pastime. Money came in the form of small bills, quantities that made a huge difference to his life, and his university savings fund. These girls, this money, it was symbolic of the new, global Vietnam, the country they all loved so fiercely.

So, when Giang ascertained the People's Security Service's suspect was an illegal immigrant, his first call was to the man who thanked him for the information, but told him firmly that they knew all about the couple, and ordered him to back off. More difficult, though, the man also instructed Giang to make the Security Service back off too.

To fulfil these orders, he made himself look incompetent. He signed off on an operation that saw officers raid the *Saigon Backpacker Hotel*. As ordered, he took the foreigners' belongings himself, and logged only a couple of items into evidence. He apologized to his superiors for the error, citing his enthusiasm to impress the People's Security Service as his excuse. He would later face a disciplinary hearing and be fined a week's wages.

When Gareth and Sarah returned to the vicinity of the hotel, it was Giang himself who approached, and told them they could not go back.

The three of them travelled to The Rex. Gareth waited in the bar with Sarah, drinking beer and Diet Coke, Sarah raising and lowering the soft drink with a mechanical alertness, not touching Gareth, looking at everything around the place, everything except her boyfriend. When they were called to the penthouse, they got as far as the lift when Sarah made a dash for the door.

Giang grabbed her and squeezed her arms until she stopped struggling, and shoved her into the elevator car. He had no idea what awaited her, but he was now more involved than ever, so he dared not screw up.

The penthouse was sparse but clean, with a view over the city that ended a half-mile away due to the brown haze that hangs over the buildings all day, every day. The man who greeted them was not the boss who held Giang's life so tightly, but a lieutenant who rarely got his hands dirty, relying instead on his two cousins, trucked in from the hills to aid his business.

Gareth said, "She's here."

To Giang's surprise, it was clear Gareth knew these men, and had been expecting this meeting.

"Is that my stuff?" Sarah asked, pointing at the bags Giang unloaded that morning.

Gareth looked curious too.

The lieutenant told Giang, "The client chooses what things they keep. Sometimes, it makes the transition easier. Less panic if they have familiar clothes and shoes. Or if they have valuable items, the new owner keeps them."

He then indicated one of his cousins should pay the Englishman. A briefcase came out and the cousin laid it on the bed. He released the catches and opened the lid.

Gareth's mouth curled into a smile.

"Ten million?" he said.

"As agreed," said the boss.

Gareth fanned one of the packs of money.

Sarah watched, eyes darting around the room, trying to take it all in. Numbly, she asked, "What is this? Why are we here?"

Gareth just said, "Sorry," and closed the briefcase.

The two men flanked Sarah, and one of the cousins yanked her wrists behind her back, and the other injected her in the neck with something that made her unconscious in seconds.

Gareth said, "You won't hurt her?"

"No longer your concern," the man in charge replied.

Giang was ordered to escort the Englishman out. In the corridor, he asked Gareth why he sold the girl, who clearly had a lot of affection for him.

Gareth shrugged. "She was gonna ditch me as soon as she could. One night in Paris, she came back late and drunk. I knew she'd fucked someone in the toilets or some alleyway. Besides, I need the cash."

Giang was not a bad man. At least, he didn't think so. He played a system that others would exploit whether he did so or not. But now he had stepped beyond that, directly assisting a terrible crime. So he took great pleasure in telling Gareth that he was holding ten million *dong* in that case.

Gareth said, "Yeah, so?"

Giang waited for the doors and composed himself. He told Gareth, "Ten million dong is less than five hundred dollars."

Gareth said, "Fuck off," and chuckled as if Giang was going to join in. When he didn't, Gareth said, "Take me back up there now."

Giang didn't move. "When you made your deal, what was the choice?"

"The guy in Paris, he said ten thousand US or ten million Vietnamese. Come on. I want the dollars."

"Mister," Giang said calmly. "You made a deal with a man who wants to take your girlfriend away. Do you really think they will say 'Fine, no problem?' No. If you cause trouble for them, they will kill you. They will take back their ten million dong from your corpse and spend it on pizza and beer."

But Gareth's blood was up, and he swung the case at Giang, made a charge for the penthouse. Giang pistol-whipped the Englishman and dragged him into the lift, sat on him all the way down, and frog-marched him out of the hotel, flashing his ID as he went. He drove Gareth, bleeding in the backseat, out of the city, and left him on a dusty road next to a motel that Vietnamese used when visiting Saigon. He told the foreigner to stay there two nights, then leave.

That was two weeks ago. Giang did everything in his power to save the man's life.

Last Monday, a corpse was discovered on a rubbish tip in the east of the city. Giang caught the case purely by luck, and found a Caucasian male with a shotgun blast to the chest, which took off half his jaw. He carried no ID except a credit card in the name of Gallway. What remained of his face, his build, and the fact that he was still gripping a briefcase containing ten million dong, led Giang to identify the body as the illegal immigrant the People's Security Service were looking for. He remained in a morgue, unclaimed.

Giang even took a photograph on his phone. It was low-res, the flesh raw and brown, but it was detailed enough for me to see his face, and accept the truth.

Gareth Delingpole was dead.

Chapter Thirty-Four

During the tour of the museum, Giang had bought us ice creams. I was finishing mine as we emerged onto the street. He got to the top of the cone, and dumped the rest in a bin.

"You think that's okay?" I said. "Selling foreign girls to slave-traders?"

"It is supply and demand. If they did not supply, the demand would remain and someone else would help them. It is not my business."

"This guy, Gareth, his body had nothing else? No USB drive?"

"Nothing that I saw. I had no interest in him beyond what I told you."

So Gareth Delingpole saw the opportunity to make some money, and since he viewed his wives and girlfriends as his property, he would believe he was justified in selling Sarah.

Death by shotgun blast was a light punishment compared to what I wanted to do to him.

Back in France, when Gareth was seeking to procure documents, Sammy must have tipped off the Man in Tan, who made his approach to Gareth and negotiated a price for Sarah. He then flew them both here for the final trade-off. The flagging of the passports meant the gang could not move in immediately, so Gareth—and Giang—spent a fair bit on the credit card in the intervening days.

Despite understanding how Sarah fell off the radar, and confirming that she was alive, I was no closer to tracing her. All I had achieved was solve a credit card theft.

And yet, if Gareth needed the money that badly, I had to ask, what happened to the cash stolen from Curtis Benson? Was that all engineered to hide the theft of incriminating data? Data that was now, presumably, in the hands of Sarah's new owner. If he could not decrypt the data stick, the item was useless, so it wasn't beyond the realms of possibility he could have thrown it away, or simply reformatted it and filled it with a pirated season of Game of Thrones to watch later.

I said, "Take me to the people who bought Sarah."

"Do you really think I'm going to say yes to that?"

"If I buy her from them—"

"She already had a buyer."

"Then I'll pay *that* buyer for her. I need you to make that offer. Supply and demand. I have the demand, they can supply her."

"They will not do it. If I suggest it to them, my position will be … compromised."

I crouched as my stomach turned at the thought of losing her after being so close. Heat blew back off the pavement. I touched it.

Hot, so hot.

I stood, a plan forming. A stupid plan, but a plan nonetheless. It worked with Sammy LeHavre and the forger.

"If you took them a customer," I said, "you'll get a finder's fee, correct?"

"Yes."

"So take me. I'm a foreign pervert looking for a young girl, a companion. I want to see her before I buy, and I'll pay top dollar. Or top dong, if they prefer."

I lost targets before, never to be seen again. I failed in my job on those occasions, and of course I still replayed events in my head, scenarios I could have conducted differently, but ultimately I always moved on. This was different. Perhaps it was the scope of the crime, a vast net cast over young women all over the world. Maybe, if I could save even one, it would put hope out there that not all was lost for the others.

Giang said, "How much will you pay me?"

"A thousand now, a thousand when we get back. US dollars, of course."

Giang made that face again, the one that pretended to be considering it, then nodded. "I will come to Notre Dame close to your hotel."

"Did you say Notre Dame?"

"Yes, on corner of *Le Duan*. Like the one in Paris. But better."

Saigon had a Notre Dame of its own. Who knew?

"Be ready," he said. "The day will be hot, and you may get wet."

I bought some watertight Ziploc bags, then walked into a bank and, over the counter, withdrew a serious amount of cash. I had to present my genuine passport and banking credentials. In one of the Ziplocs, I placed a thousand dollars, and in another I secured a further twenty thousand in large bills, the amount Giang estimated I would need to put down as a deposit on any girl I decided to buy. Twenty-thousand could possibly even get me a scrawny kid all-in, but a pretty western girl like Sarah, I'd be looking at a couple of hundred at least, which I would pay "on delivery."

Money is a luxury that has, for many years, been in abundance for me, in quantities far greater than I have ever needed. I never used it flippantly, though, never took it for granted. But now I was cut off electronically from Park Avenue Investigations, my personal wealth was all I had, and if I needed to spend it all to rescue one girl from the clutches of men who think they wield the power of God, then I would gladly give it.

And yet, would giving these men so much do more harm than good? Would it encourage more kidnapping, more hurt and suffering?

Back at my hotel, everything went in the rucksack. All my electronics, my clothes, my binoculars, the defunct phones, even my flip-flops and guidebooks. I superstitiously ensured my genuine passport and bankcards were close to the top in case I did not return, so I would not forever be known as some French tourist who vanished one day. I changed into lightweight cargo trousers and a long-sleeved cotton shirt. I placed the money in my lower trouser pockets and inserted my fake passport into another Ziploc, along with the cloned credit card and the iPhone, charged to half-battery and switched off. I then taped this little package to the inside of my left thigh and secured the emergency two hundred bucks to my right.

With the UK in the middle of the night right now, I fired up the iPad and sent Jess an email telling her the plan. An item from Roger Gorman lay unopened in my inbox. I considered not reading it, but if he was going to do anything that affected me directly, I needed to know before it stung my case.

Dear Adam,

I hope this finds you well. You have been out of contact for several days, and we are starting to grow concerned. You have used PAI resources, namely IT and telecommunications equipment, in direct contravention of our strict rules, and you have been cut off from these resources. I am sure you appreciate we cannot allow board members to break such rules when it would not be tolerated by rank-and-file employees. You are also in breach of condition 311.5 (that no investigation will be carried outside the UK without line manager or board approval) and 312.1 (that no investigator will go more than 48 hours without filing a progress report). This also applies to freelance contracts, under which you are currently operating. While we appreciate that a missing persons case can be extremely stressful, we must insist that you file a report along with your immediate location.

In addition to the issues relating to your procedural breaches, you must also report to Paris's Préfecture de Police on Friday 26th July at midday regarding your legal entanglement, for which Park Avenue Investigations holds no responsibility. A lawyer will be provided for your interview, which may lead to criminal charges being brought.

If you are suffering stress, depression or other mental illness, PAI will of course be more than happy to work with you to resolve these issues, and return you to your usual high standards of work. You must contact myself or another board member no later than midnight on Thursday 25th July.

Yours… etc.

Tomorrow. Same deadline as Benson, just twenty-four hours earlier.

It was his attempt to sound concerned, whilst allowing the subtext to wave a powerful fist under my chin. He'd obviously been advised to offer me help, to sound like the model chairman. I was *his* boss, for fuck's sake. It was definitely a precursor to declaring me incompetent. It was like this when he blackballed my desire to blackball his client list. Although I could technically veto a company, I had to prove beyond doubt that our involvement with that company would damage our reputation due to ethics or morality, like the Church of England investing in payday loans companies.

But because our company's aim was to supply corporate investigative services, it was difficult to veto *anyone.* I succeeded a few times, with firms that had been dragged through the press for tax avoidance or bribing politicians, but Gorman mostly got his way.

I had run away before in the hope that I would come up with some tactic or legal challenge, or maybe hope Gorman upped sticks to explore newer pastures. I knew now that was the wrong move. But I couldn't mount an attack yet. I had to form a defense, too, and time was the real problem here. I dared not focus on Gorman until Sarah was back safely with her sister. I was closer than I had ever been, and a corrupt police officer, *the Giang connection*, was going to take me there.

Chapter Thirty-Five

I dumped my pack in The Rex's left-luggage, and caught a taxi to Notre Dame, a small but picturesque cathedral opposite a park lined with coaches disgorging backpackers young and old. Rickshaw vendors and taxi-bike owners descended upon them like starving masses around an aid truck. It was easy to pick out the seasoned travelers from the newbies by assessing the level of terror on their faces—the scale morphed from *"meh"* to *"oh fucking shit my Christ!"*

Giang rolled up in an unmarked car, now changed into linen trousers and a V-neck t-shirt. He had dabbed cream on the sore, but his yellow smile was just as pleasant as when I first saw it. I got in, handed him the agreed-upon chunk of money, and let the air-con flow.

He said, "We will turn this off when we get close. To acclimatize you. Very hot out there."

It took an hour to get out to the freeway, such as that was, then we did not talk as he sped along at a steady fifty-five, passing through little towns like the ones I'd seen on my way from the airport. Many were poorer, where naked children played football with junk tied together in a ball-shaped assemblage, and people sat on deck chairs beside what I would have assumed were derelict houses were it not for the bright decorations and curtains in the windows and doors. The open road yielded wide, expansive views of dusty land stretching for miles on either side. We passed a one-story complex that could have been an abandoned truck-stop, at which Giang waved a hand and said, "This is where I left your credit card man," and we did not even slow down.

Two hours after leaving Saigon, we stopped for a comfort break beside a warehouse-like structure, one that served as a urinal for van drivers, policemen and British detectives alike. It was a fine way to empty a bladder. If you held your breath.

About ten yards from the stench of layer upon layer of old piss, a man with one tooth for every two centimeters of gum hocked snacks and drinks from the back of an estate car. I bought enough to keep my strength up—a stick of stale bread, some dried meat and a green banana, plus a bar of Cadbury's chocolate and two one-liter bottles of water. When risking one's life on pure hope, preparation is key, and *water* often equals *life*.

Giang showed me to the door of the main building. Invited me to peer inside.

People hunched over rows of workstations, sewing, cutting, hammering, like a cleaner-than-average sweatshop. The woman nearest me, in her thirties, had a gnarled stump below her knee and her right hand was a smooth knob. The woman next to her possessed no legs or teeth. Beyond her, a man in his forties worked with hands on the end of his biceps where his elbow should have been. No designer names that I could see on the colorful purses and wallets, the only brand being the yellow star on a red background from the Vietnamese flag.

"Cripple factory," Giang told me as he led me back to the car. "Many places like this. Government assigns jobs to all, even our cripples. Some are from American bombs in the war, some with bad birth defects. The Americans dropped Agent Orange on the banks of our waterways to burn the plants and prevent ambushes by the North Vietnamese. They didn't care that people lived there, drinking the water or washing food, spraying crops…"

"Why did you show me that?" I asked.

"To demonstrate why Vietnam is growing strong."

"By penning disabled people into factories?"

"By creating money more efficiently than corrupt capitalist societies." His arm swept aside. People got off a bus. Westerners, mainly. Tourists. He said, "We bring people here to show the evil brought to us by war, then they buy badly-made products sewn by hands mutilated by the Americans."

I almost laughed. "Guilt-tourism."

Giang smiled like we'd made some kind of bond. "But you see now? If men like those we see today can help a poor family by removing a daughter who is a burden, or a son who can program a computer, isn't that worth it? Isn't that how nations become great again?"

I said, "Can we get going?"

He seemed deflated as we trudged back to the car with our little bags of food and water. I ate the melting chocolate before we got in. It was not nice.

We spent the next hour and a half lumbering along in a car with the air-con off and my sweat glands turned up full. The roads smoothed and the verges grew greener. Eventually, we arrived in a bustling town with narrow streets, and through the car window I could smell that we were close to water. It reminded me of Cornwall except with more mopeds, more horns, and more dust. The young slouched as they walked. They sported big sunglasses and sluiced product in their hair, and wore basketball vests, smoking.

I don't know what I'd been expecting from the Mekong Delta, but what I saw was definitely not it. Under canvass awnings, obscuring most of the view, twelve-foot motorized barges lined up side-by-side, the owners ferrying tourists out into the river made famous by a thousand movies. Some were workboats, bright drag-on-faces on the front, with tractor-engine-sized rear propellers. Others were the narrow, four-man prop-powered gondolas that Giang referred to simply as "riverboats." We wobbled down a floating platform to a quiet quay, headed for a lone riverboat with a long-stemmed propeller. No one manned it.

The boat wobbled as I lowered myself into the middle seat, my broken finger jabbing at the knuckle. Giang turned a key, depressed a teaspoon-sized lever and tugged on the starter chord. The engine fired first time and a cloud of blue-grey smoke belched into the air. He gave it some gas, tugging against the current as we sliced over the surface beyond the quay. And then, revealed before me, was the Mekong Delta itself.

The water stretched to the horizon in both directions, with few manmade outposts on the nearside shore. It looked less like a river, more like a brown lake with a constant riptide. Hundreds of boats navigated left and right, and we crossed their well-established lanes dangerously slowly. The bright faces of working boats carrying both tourists and fishermen grinned at us, the opposite shore growing slowly larger as we neared. Soon, as we skirted this side, tributaries fed off the main body, with houses lining aquatic residential streets.

We navigated upriver for half an hour or so, the grumble and intermittent stutter of the engine literally the only thing I heard. When the river traffic thinned, and the landscape grew green and tall on both banks, the nose of our boat rose and we accelerated, leaving a wake like a speedboat.

It isn't often I think of my mother, her of the *no-more-compromises*. When I remember her readiness to shack us up with Stuart Fitzpatrick, I still feel the ache of a bitter child, but when I am on water like this, with the roar of a motor and the thump and bump of the hull skimming the surface, I wonder what her death was like. Did she see it coming? Did she have time for a final thought? Was it of me?

Soon, there were no other boats on the Delta. The engine quieted to a drone as Giang sought the correct route. I ran my hand over my head, feeling the sting of sunburn. Giang passed me a silly conical tourist hat. I reluctantly put it on.

He steered us into a wall of reeds, chugging slowly, his brow beaded with sweat. We eased into a tributary a mere three times as wide as the boat. Giang shouted something but I couldn't hear it. I picked up something to do with snakes, so I just nodded.

Foliage bowed in from both sides, brushing my arms at times, and we both ducked occasionally to evade the odd low-hanging branch. The sun flitted through trees, and I got the idea that, if not for the engine's volume, I'd be getting lectured on how the Americans destroyed all this with cripple-creating chemicals before it grew back again. Strong. Like Vietnam.

He had a point, I suppose. The people of this country were astounding. The disabled doing crappy jobs to keep their income, no matter how small; the young embracing a new era in their country's evolution; communism trying to outdo capitalism through sheer willpower; a proud nation, rising from the ashes and blood of a long-ago conflict that still hung like a restless spirit over their daily lives.

We slowed to a crawl, and Giang let the engine idle. We drifted while he listened to the jungle chirp and screech around us. A whistle pierced the air and Giang replied with three bursts. Another, longer whistle responded and Giang gently steered us ashore. We angled for an overhanging tree, where a skinny brown arm pushed the branches aside and we glided easily to a ten-foot pier jutting out of solid land. The arm belonged to an elderly man in the black pajama-like garb we associate with the Viet Cong, or rather "North Vietnamese freedom fighters." The old man was unarmed as far as I could tell, although his hollow eyes held on me all the way in. It took me a moment to realize his hands were missing.

Chapter Thirty-Six

Giang paused at a fork in the path and hung a left, taking us further from the river than the right-hand prong would have. The permanent shadows cast by the canopy lessened the heat somewhat, but the air remained muggy. I sipped water to keep my hands busy. The plant-life lining our route thinned and we came upon a shirtless, anorexic-thin teenager wielding an AK-47 that probably weighed more than him. He tracked us to where another sentry waited, as thin as his compatriot, his gaze equally hollow. The path opened into a square clearing about twenty feet on all sides, with three huts constructed from irregular wood. A cooking pot hung over a smoky fire in the center. Clothes dried on washing lines.

Four armed men emerged from the huts, two AK-47s, two old-looking pistols slung loosely in string-belts. Those with pistols had deformities to their arms. A man in his forties followed them out. He wore cargo shorts and a faded Manchester United shirt sponsored by Crown Paints with the name "Cantona" peeling on the back.

"Makes a change from Beckham," I mumbled.

Cantona was the only one who didn't look emaciated; he was portly, with a mop of thick black hair and a wispy beard like a fifteen-year-old's. He spoke Vietnamese to Giang, his body language all open and friendly but the tone dragged with the throaty ring of annoyance. Giang mirrored the body language but his voice raised an octave.

He told me, "They will search you."

The shirtless AK-47 boy slung his weapon on his back and patted me down. He was not exactly proficient at this. He found the larger wad of cash, and no one reacted when he removed it from my pocket. My document pack remained fastened sweatily to my leg. He handed the cash to Cantona. Clearly in charge, Cantona remained static except for a nod to one of the pistol-bearers, who took the cash aside to a tree stump that served as a dining table, and subjected it to a more thorough count.

We followed Cantona to the back of the camp, the two AK-47 boys and the remaining pistol-chap falling in line. Dead eyes at my back. Fingers poised over their triggers.

Cantona squatted at what looked like a tuft of mossy weeds the width of a dustbin lid, and lifted it to reveal stairs dropping into a jet-black cavern. He slithered into the hole, landed on the top step, then ducked out of sight. Giang went next, looked back up at me as he descended, then the dark swallowed him too.

I sat on the rim. Sipped my water. One of the AK-47s poked me in the back. I turned my head to give him a "yeah, what?" look, but was met with wide black pupils and an expressionless face. I held the boy's gaze, then slid off the edge.

The staircase led down to a narrow passage, forcing me to crouch-walk all the way. It was, I guessed, one of the thousands of tunnels crisscrossing the country, left intact after the war. When it leveled out, a candle every ten yards or so did nothing except illuminate the basic shape of the tunnel and cast flickering shadows of the two men ahead. The air felt as if someone was boiling water and funneling the steam this way. At least one person tramped behind me, so I dared not pause for breath. A brighter light up ahead gave me some hope of a reprieve, though, preparing to emerge into sunlight any moment.

I did not emerge into sunlight. In many ways, it was the exact opposite of what we think of as "light."

A room, of sorts. Lit by candles and camping lanterns. Maybe fifteen wooden beds lined the walls and gave off the stench of moldy fabric. The people here, I counted ten in all, rose slowly from these beds as Cantona urged them with a prod or a barked command. No one over the age of twenty. The youngest was hard to tell. A boy, sixteen at the most, but could have been fourteen. Men and women, boys and girls. All in sack-like ponchos that mostly covered their bodies. They stood, slouched in the gaps beside their assigned bunk, heads bowed against the low curvature of the roof. All eyes concentrated on the floor.

Cantona stood at the far end, hands on hips, a salesman's grin painted on a face lined with shadows from the dim wattage.

Giang said, "Do not think of them as human beings. It helps, trust me. If they were not here they would die on the streets. Now they have a chance to live."

A gun barrel prodded me from behind. All three gunmen—gun-*boys*—were now so close to me I was surprised I could not feel their breath. I walked the line, determined to meet each gaze, to not shy away or bury it deep down. To not think of them as human would make this easier, yes, but it wasn't something I could— or should—ever forget.

Of the ten, three were male and seven female. The males were all Vietnamese, but two of the females were Caucasian, with the high cheekbones of Eastern Europeans or Scandinavians. No one spoke, and they returned to staring at the ground once I passed.

I reached the end, Cantona and Giang in close proximity.

I said, "She isn't here."

"I told you it was unlikely."

"Ask him where they sent her."

He did, and got a short reply. Even Cantona was sweating in this box. Giang said, "He will not tell you."

I turned to the prisoners. "Who knows where an English girl was sent?"

Cantona yelled something, and Giang translated, "No talking to them."

"Sarah," I said. "Her name was Sarah."

Cantona addressed one of the zombie gun-children, who raised his AK-47 to strike me. I cowered and held up my hands. Cantona barked again, and the boy stood down. I nodded reluctantly to show I wouldn't try it again.

But one of the prisoners caught my eye. A boy, the youngest, whose thin, ragged form made an accurate guess at his age impossible. He whispered something. It wasn't loud enough for Cantona to hear, and I wondered if he'd really spoke. He did not look up from the floor, but if I understood correctly, he said, "Artist."

Giang said, "Choose. They will not be patient."

If they got suspicious, there was nothing here backing me up. Even with Giang's recommendation, I was walking a sharp edge already. To get the boy, I show no enthusiasm.

I said, "I want to ask them something. The prisoners."

"You cannot do that."

"I want an English-speaker."

Giang asked Cantona the question and the Man U fan pointed at each in turn, giving what turned out to be a quick bio. The two Caucasian girls were Russian prostitutes exchanged for an internet expert sourced from Hanoi; others were taken as debts accumulated by people in remote villages, and the boy was a rebellious factory worker whose parents could not control his unproductive nature.

"How much for all of them?" I asked.

Giang translated the answer. "It would cost about six hundred thousand. But he says you cannot have all. Other customers will come tomorrow. You said you want one item. Choose one. Or two. But you must pay a deposit for each."

"The Russian girls. How much?"

"One hundred thousand per girl. Very desirable."

"What about the others?" I forced my expression into neutral. "Are any of them worth the twenty-thou I put down? Any I can take with me today?"

Cantona didn't like that. A cheapskate diner ordering the salad and tap water. He waved as if to dismiss me.

"Then I'll take them all," I said. "One million US dollars for all of them."

Giang relayed my offer, which forced Cantona into some mental arithmetic. If the Russians were top of the line, the premium lobster, then the others were worth far less. A quick tally ran through the man's brain and he nodded.

I said, "Tell me where the funds need to go, or I can arrange cash on delivery."

On Cantona's behalf, Giang asked, "Where will you like them delivered?"

"To The Rex Hotel. Within twenty-four hours. I will arrange rooms for them all, on a full board basis, and I expect them all to have legitimate travel documents and be cleaned and clothed appropriately."

"Is fine," Giang said. "All documents are part of the package. Their belongings too, if they have any." Seemingly counting his commission in his head, he told Cantona my conditions, and the man agreed.

I had one final demand, though. "And I take one with me now."

He shook his head. Rubbed his chin in faux-consideration.

I was never much good at bluffing, as Curtis Benson would attest. But it was all I could try. If I failed, and Cantona caved too early, I was sunk.

"This one." I pointed at one of the Russian girls.

Her eyes lit up and my gut dropped. She wasn't going anywhere yet, but the hope that sparkled so brightly … her desire to be out of here no matter what I might inflict upon her … I wanted to cry. When Cantona laughed off my request, I tried one of the stronger-looking men, someone who would be of value to a land-owner or who needed a domestic to lift and carry. Giang said Cantona believed him to be worth in the region of fifty-K.

Referring to the boy, I said, "This one can't be worth more than ten."

Cantona eked-out the decision a little, to maintain an illusion of "winning" the negotiation. Through Giang, he said, "Okay. Take him," and one of the guards hustled the boy out of the room. The other prisoners deflated like punctured dolls.

I said, "Tell them they'll be free soon too."

Giang didn't need to ask. "Not a good idea. If they worry you are a bad man, they may try to run. They will be killed. You go now."

I was drenched in sweat and the air was closing around me, stink and moisture now a thick aura about my body. I stooped back into the passageway, and when I saw real daylight I started running. I grazed my back on the roof a couple of times. Sped up. I needed to get out. I hit the stairs and scrambled up. Cool, cool air wafted over me. The hole seemed even smaller as I raced to emerge, skinning my left knee as I collapsed onto the ground outside.

And there I lay, the jungle heat now a refreshing experience.

Giang and Cantona climbed out too, Cantona rather amused by seeing me there. I was actually grinning. My money—partly earned by Roger Gorman's horrible investments and vile clients—had saved ten young men and women from a life of slavery.

I was still fumbling in the dark as far as Sarah was concerned, but in the wider world, I'd finally done some good.

Chapter Thirty-Seven

Beside one of the huts, the boy was given a wash in a bucket of river water, and traditional Vietnamese clothing lay folded on the tree-trunk table. He waved at me. Perhaps he understood that I was not a predator or slave-master. Someone brought him a sack the size of a swimming bag, which I assumed contained the possessions brought along when he was taken, and which now technically belonged to me. On the surface, it was an oddly-polite gesture, but it made perfect sense. A glimmer of familiarity, of happiness. It helped keep them *compliant*.

While I was still sat on the floor, Cantona handed me a laptop computer with a Wi-Fi dongle attached to a satellite phone.

Giang translated, "You must transfer one hundred thousand dollars now, and provide proof of funds for the rest. Otherwise, his boss will not authorize him to inconvenience the other clients. The assets will remain here, for sale."

"No problem," I said.

I logged on to a surprisingly fast internet connection, but when I entered my banking passwords, none of them worked. I tried again, and still nothing.

Cantona watched me closely.

The accounts didn't respond with the "Your details are incorrect" message, but went straight to "Please contact your bank" and provided a number to ring. I asked to use the phone to which the internet was linked, and Cantona allowed it. I got through and gave my details, passed the security test, and then I learned what the problem was.

And everything I had achieved so far turned instantly to shit.

"Suspicious activity on your account, sir," said the chirpy lady on the other end. She cheerily outlined my recent transactions. "We are required to freeze all activity until you can verify your identity."

"Well, I've verified it," I said. "Please un-freeze the account."

"Oh." A pause, then, in that same *nothing's wrong* tone, "The suspicious activity is just one of the problems, sir. When we detected this, we are required to do a search on other possible accounts, to prevent further chance of fraud. And there is a stop on all your funds. Because you are not legally present in the country where the activity took place, the authorities there have declared it illegal for you to process any financial transaction in Vietnam."

"It's *my* money. I can do *what* I want, *where* I want—"

"And because there is a European arrest warrant now issued to all EU countries … I'm sorry, I can't unblock this account. You must present yourself at a bank or police station with necessary ID, and once this matter is cleared up you can access your funds again."

"Present ID? I'm in the middle of a *jungle*—"

"I'm sorry to hear that, sir."

"I need the money. *Now*. Just a hundred thousand—"

"There is nothing I can do, sir. I have to hang up now," she said, still as chirpy as can be. "I hope you manage to untangle things."

"Wait—"

But she had gone.

Roger *fucking* Gorman. He exerted no authority over my personal banking, but plenty of knowledge of financial crime. Heck, it was our specialty. When tracking someone who has absconded with funds, the best way to make him surface is to eliminate access to those funds. So all Gorman would need is proof of criminal activity (check: France was indisputable) and reasonable doubt about my financial activity (check: company credit card, company equipment), and the big cash withdrawals which my personal bank would be legally obliged to disclose when that customer was wanted on a European arrest warrant.

I stared at the phone before handing it back to Cantona. He didn't read my dazed expression, and wired it back up to the laptop.

Giang knew, though. "What should I tell him?"

Those people, underground in that furnace of a dorm.

Two guards brought the boy to me, presented him in his loose-fitting black outfit. He hadn't stopped grinning, expecting to be taken away from this place.

Cantona jabbed a finger at the laptop and mumbled something.

In a thick accent, the boy said, "He say hurry."

Cantona slapped the boy round the back of the head and used a phrase I assumed meant, "No talking."

"Do not fuck with me," Giang said.

My head fell into my hands and I rubbed my face.

Cantona and Giang exchanged words that grew in volume, bodies swinging left and right. Giang eventually shut up.

He faced me. "You must leave now."

I pulled myself up and placed a hand on the boy's shoulder. Giang gripped my wrist and shook his head.

"I paid for him," I said.

"This is not Harrods," Giang said. "Go to the boat. I will meet you there."

Down the path that led into the jungle, three guards were visible.

As if reading my mind, Giang said, "If they were going to kill you they would just do it. They do not play games."

"What about you?"

"If you go to the boat and do not look back, I will be there in five minutes. I must do something for them first. Something that will ensure we both leave safely."

When I glanced at the boy, his mouth was open slightly. One of the guards passed Giang a handgun.

I didn't move. "What are you going to do?"

Giang set his jaw, his eyes rigid, taking on a hollow quality akin to the young guards. "I am going to take you back to Saigon, and you will forget everything you saw. The only reason you are not dead is you have value. As someone who may be missed. These others, they will not. But if you make trouble, they *will* take that chance. You call it risk versus reward. I remember this from the Americans."

I still didn't move. One of the shirtless guards took a step toward me. Cantona shouted at Giang. The policeman cocked the gun.

"Go," he said. "You do not want to see this."

"*I paid for him!*" I yelled. "*He's mine!*"

"It is your forfeit," Giang said, tears brimming. "For promising money you do not have."

"I *have* it. Tell them I have it. I just need to—"

Cantona yelled again.

Giang pointed the gun at the boy, who squeezed his eyes shut tight. Giang took a breath. Cantona shouted a single word.

And I dived forward. Too fast for the guards, too fast for Giang. I slapped the gun from his hand. He whipped out a pearl-handle from his pocket. A blade sprang from the housing. I parried his clumsy attack and elbowed him in the throat. As the other guns came up my way, I tangled myself up and splayed Giang, took his knife, and used him as a shield. I gestured at the gun and the boy handed it to me and hid behind us.

In one hand, Cantona aimed a pistol. In his other, he pressed a mobile phone to his ear.

I said, "Tell him I'll kill their pet policeman."

The boy frowned. "Tell them … you kill him?" His English wasn't great.

"Yes."

As Giang gasped for breath, the boy spoke in a high tone. Cantona shook his head. His reply, through the boy, was, "They do not care. They kill us all."

Bolts racked. Barrels pointed. No negotiating. Except…

Cantona spoke into the phone, frowning at the reply. He made an affirmative grunt, then hung up with a chuckle. He barked orders at me.

The boy said, "You must kill policeman."

Giang sputtered, "No. Wait…"

Cantona talked quickly, waving his gun in our direction.

The boy said, "They do not like for him. Their boss, they say cop too greedy. He a risk. Take too many money. He bring you here. If you kill him, they trust. You take me then."

"No," I said. "I can't just—"

Giang forced an argument out, but Cantona aimed at him, which shut him up. To me, Cantona held up a hand, his fingers and thumb extended.

One of the guards yanked Giang from me and positioned him on his knees.

Cantona pulled his thumb back to his palm. Then, slowly, his little finger.

A countdown. 5 … 4 … 3…

All three guards trained their weapons on me and the boy.

Giang whimpered on the dusty ground, yellow teeth bared in a panicky grimace, the herpes sore wet and raw. He said, "I am not a bad man … I do this thing, this business … for my family…"

I thought of the hookers he'd defiled, the money he'd taken, Gareth and Sarah whom he'd handed over … all for personal profit.

Not for his family. Not for his survival. For *money*. For personal gratification.

But I couldn't kill him like this. I couldn't.

2…

The boy gripped my free hand, the broken finger troubling me. He may not have been a direct victim of Giang's greed, but if the policeman had done his job…

I wasn't a killer, though. I couldn't…

The guards aimed at us, readying to fire.

I hefted the gun. It said "Colt" on the side. I stepped closer. A thousand options flew through my mind, but all of them resulted in me and the boy full of holes.

Except one.

1…

The gun roared and bucked in my hand, and the back of Giang's head vaporized in a cloud of red and grey mist. He thumped to the ground like a slab of meat.

I killed him. Murdered a cop.

Now, and forever, I was just like them.

Chapter Thirty-Eight

I stood stock still, staring at the pulpy mess; the bone fragments, the globs of brain, and one lifeless eye, his other closed against the floor. Dust coated his open scab. Someone had taken the gun from me without me realizing. They patted me down again, this time locating the cloned credit card and passport taped to one leg, but not the two-hundred dollars taped to my other. They returned my passport but not the credit card, and let me keep Giang's knife. I folded it back up, and placed it in my pocket.

Then they marched me back to the river. As I trod one step after the other at the barrel of an AK-47, the jungle hummed like a million wasps trapped in a huge jar beyond the wall of green. My only solid thought was a vow that I would find this place again. Even if I had to utilize Roger Gorman's private security clientele, I would ensure every man at that camp died, every slave would be freed, and I would raze this place from the face of the Earth.

No fucking compromise.

We reached the pier and the boy held my hand. I moved to get into the boat, vaguely running Giang's start-up process through my mind, but the memory was of a man with half his head missing.

The young guard said something and the boy translated, telling us to wait. We stood in silence for almost ten minutes, until two men carried a six-foot parcel out of the trees, Cantona at the rear. The bundle of sacks and bin liners could only be one thing. Cantona said something which needed no interpretation but the boy did so anyway: "We take this."

The guards lowered Giang's corpse into the boat and Cantona signalled for us to get in. The boy automatically took the helm and I didn't object. I hadn't said a word since I shot Major Giang.

Major...

I killed a police officer. A father and husband. A vile predator in his spare time, but his family would never know that side of him, and would forever wonder why he left home one day and never returned.

Cantona tapped me on the head and crouched to my eye-level. He said, through the boy, Giang was going to die anyway. "Orders from boss. He stupid to bring someone here. Is better this way."

Back in that quarry, the Man in Tan asked me, "Was it the Giang problem again?"

Problem...

Again...

Cantona stood and waved the teenaged sentries back up the jungle path, and strode after them.

The boy said, "We go?"

I nodded. The engine roared to life first time and he handled it like a pro. Better than Giang, in fact. We sputtered along the narrow jungle passage, my eyes on the bundle all the way.

The boy said, "Thank you, sir."

"What's your name?" I asked, my throat dry.

"Tho," he said. "It mean long life. That is why you pick me. I have to live long life."

"I picked you because you seemed to recognize Sarah."

"Yes. Girl from England. Like to draw. She was there. Short time, though."

I needed to forget what I did back there. Concentrate on the future. I said, "What can you tell me, Tho? Who took her?"

He was silent for a moment. "Na Trang."

"Who's Na Trang?"

"Not 'who'. A place. On the sea. Take me there, I show you girl."

I found my bag of food untouched and opened the remaining water. It was as warm as a bath, but it washed over my throat, taking with it the sandy film that I couldn't swallow. I caught Tho licking his lips and passed him the bottle.

"Is yours," he said.

"Now it's yours."

He accepted with a bow of his head and necked the lot in one go. Then he asked if I might share some food, so I passed him Giang's bag. All that was left was a bar of chocolate, now virtually a liquid, but Tho unwrapped it and poured the gloop into his mouth, then let the wrapper flutter away onto the river.

My mouth widened in a nervous funeral-type smile. Among all the death and inhumanity of the past hour or so, I was annoyed at the kid for *littering*.

The boat arrowed out of the bush and into the Mekong Delta, and Tho gunned it to several knots faster than Giang. I looked back to the shore to memorize the lay of the land for when I returned to destroy all I'd seen.

Was this really what people called "sanctimonious" when I got on my high horse about morals and "doing the right thing?" Seeing humans treated like shit, and vowing to do something about it? If it was within my power, that wasn't a bad thing; it was my *duty* to act. It wasn't hand-wringing liberal guilt, either. I was going to burn everything here, and every evil person within if I had to.

I mentally marked a tree with five tall branches, all hooked like hockey sticks; three shrubs close together, which I nicknamed the Three Stooges; a rock the shape of a cake. But as we ploughed deeper into the river, the reeds got smaller. The trees too. And when I searched for more landmarks, I found none. Nothing to give a name or simile, no arrow pointing the way. The vastness of the jungle swallowed everything, and with the view's growing uniformity, it dawned on me so slowly, with such a creeping sense of sickness, that I would never find this place again, no matter how long I searched.

And I would have to live with that forever.

When we could see the other side, Tho dropped the power and let the engine idle, and prodded the corpse with his toe.

I wanted to take Giang to his family. But I could not. I'd be arrested for the murder of a man willing to kill a child in order to stay alive himself, who used women as property as surely as the traders did. I should not go to jail for that.

I did not deserve it.

With the boat wobbling so much we were close to capsizing, I took one end of the body, and Tho managed the other, and we rolled Giang into the brown water of the Mekong Delta. He barely made a splash. Rocks weighed him down efficiently, and the air that bubbled to the surface was minimal. It was only when the current turned us downriver that I realized we could possibly have said a word or two before disposing of him.

"Na Trang," Tho said. "Now we go to Na Trang?"

Eventually, we passed that same pier from which Giang launched, but carried on a few hundred meters past the town's main drag. There was no landing dock, but the bank tapered to a sliver of beach, allowing Tho to ground the boat safely next to a smaller one, upside-down with its hull in need of repair. We were at the bottom of someone's garden. That someone was an elderly man in a floppy hat. He shouted, waved his hand at us to leave. I placed the boat's key in his hand and he seemed appeased.

We skirted the side of his house and emerged into a street full of traders and stalls. A marketplace. I bought us a meal of rice and prawns from a street vendor, which Tho ate so fast it was pretty much an inhalation. The next Saigon-bound bus cost five dollars apiece, and as we waited under a simple bus shelter beside a dusty road, I counted my money, both physically and mentally.

The cloned French credit card was taken from me, and I had no access to my genuine accounts, no backup money in any form. Nothing except the cash in my pocket. One hundred and eighty dollars.

I said, "Shit."

"What shit?" Tho asked.

"Nothing. How do we get to Na Trang?"

"We fly. You have jet, mister?"

"No. And my name is Adam."

"Mister Adam, we can fly. No problem. I never been on a plane."

"We can't fly."

He slumped back. "But you rich, yeah? We fly."

"I'm not rich," I said.

"Oh," he said. "But better than hole. Many people come to see me, no one want me. Skinny boy, not much good for working."

I expected a lot of people would have been interested in him, those of particular tastes, but the customers so far had not been that way inclined. I didn't explain that, though. He could keep that tiny shred of his innocence intact.

There was no air-conditioning on the bus, and the air actually *felt* grey. The boy managed to sleep on the three-hour journey, but I could only think about death.

We were dropped a couple of blocks from The Rex, and Tho's eyes lit up when we entered the hotel's reception, but I told him not to get too excited. I retrieved my bag, and in the bar I checked the contents. Nothing out of place. My iPad was still there, as well as my genuine Adam Park passport and Adam Park credit and debit cards, the latter items now nothing but inert plastic. I possessed no more working SIM cards, and could not risk spending money on a new one.

I purchased a payphone card from reception, and ordered a drip-coffee for me and a Coke for Tho, forgetting about the prices here, but I needed a caffeine boost. While Tho kept our seats in the pristine ground-floor bar, I used a payphone to call Jess.

Voicemail.

I briefly outlined my situation, omitting the slave-trading and my committing murder, and told her I was heading to Na Trang and that I was skint. I asked her to loan me some money via Western Union and said I'd call back in an hour.

However, as I sampled the sweet coffee, I picked up on someone outside, drinking beer at a stall on the wide pavement. It could have been the sort of paranoia that follows any encounter in which a person could have—*should* have—died.

I couldn't see the man directly, but he was hunched over a laptop. His body shape and vaguely-glimpsed skin suggested Caucasian: thick brown hair and beard, black-framed glasses, a worn-looking suit. He looked up briefly, then smoothly back to his screen. No jerky movement, no panic.

Was he really watching me? Maybe his interest was because I looked like I'd been rolled through a jungle and steam-blasted; bald head, goatee beard, stubble shading through, a filthy bandage on my finger, imbibing alongside a boy in this chrome-gleaming bar.

The man downed his beer, closed his computer, and wandered away without so much as a glance.

Once we'd finished our drinks, I took Tho outside and flagged down a couple of taxi-bikes to take us to the grand-looking train station. I paid sixty dollars for two bunks on the overnight to Hanoi, which stop off in Na Trang at five a.m.

"You're sure she's there?" I said.

"Yes. The man who took her is there. He own many businesses. Is famous. I know him. I show you offices."

The train was seventies technology—clunky and chunky—but clean. It was on time, and we found our bunks in a four-bed cabin. We'd eaten at the station, and brought water and crisps for the journey, so I was ready for bed. A man in his twenties shared our cabin, a chubby guy in fake Nike high-tops and a fake Real Madrid football shirt with the name *Beckham* on the back. He nodded to me and said, "English?"

I said, "Yes," and held the same football chat with the new guy as I had three or four times so far.

Conversation faded from all parties within an hour, with Tho and the football fan both asleep. I closed my eyes and waited to be taken down into some nightmare. I expected to be assaulted by gunfire, by a head splitting, then disintegrating.

Instead, I dreamed of Roger Gorman.

Chapter Thirty-Nine

We were in a park, where the mahogany-tanned executive calmly scattered bread for a flock of ducks gliding about the water. I yelled at him that it was wrong, that he shouldn't be doing that. He carried on, standing upright in his five-grand suit just the right side of a shin-high fence. I handed him a bag of seed and told him to use this instead, but he ignored me, flashing a smile from which his teeth shone in a parody of a toothpaste ad. I screamed at him to *please use the fucking seed. Just because bread fills their bellies, it doesn't mean there isn't a better way*. He pointedly held up a slice of white and ripped it into six pieces, then tossed them in the water. The ducks gobbled it up. Sweat coated my head, and the pressure in my chest built and swelled, then exploded through my limbs. I hit him. I punched and kicked, but all he did was sway.

"This is not very professional," he said.

I woke in the bunk with sunlight filling the cabin. Outside, hills rolled by in unremarkable monotony, mist shrouding the view in grey. Tho and the other lad were up already and sharing a pan of water which they splashed on their faces and rubbed in their hair. They offered it to me and I accepted. The bandage on my hand got wet and when I brought it to my face, it stank of sewage—or perhaps something worse. I removed it and washed my slimy, broken finger, the pain less than before, but still swollen and tender to touch. Tho helped me find one of the bandages I bought in France and when I struggled to wrap it tightly enough, he unwound the fabric and bound it for me.

He said, "Okay-dokey."

"Thanks," I said.

He beamed and then the train took a corner, and all three of us could do nothing but stare. We were high up, cresting a hill, and the mist was actually clouds. We now dropped out of the sky, winding down tracks with a sheer drop to the right. Paddy fields on the flats ran on for miles into the distance. Men and women tended these fields even this early. A couple of children waved at the train. The fields disappeared into a light ground-fog, and out of the fog rose tree-covered mounds that poked up into the clouds. A rail bridge curved sharply across all this, as if designed to give travelers the perfect view of this postcard-scene.

Na Trang itself was a bit different.

When we left the concrete train station, the heat had not yet fired up, and the mild air made me want to walk a bit. Tho led the way like he knew exactly where he was going, marching to a tune in his own head. I grew more and more suspicious the further we went.

He seemed too happy, like he'd shrugged off a month of imprisonment in some of the least humane conditions imaginable. I shouldn't have worried, though.

I found it troubling how easily I'd forgotten about killing Giang. I was thinking about coffee and how hard carrying a rucksack was. Surely I should have been curled in a ball, sobbing at the fragility of human life. A normal person would, wouldn't they?

When Tho led me round a corner that led to the beach, my suspicions piqued once again. The sea was calm and children played in the shallows. Primary-school age. No parents. It was seven a.m. I didn't voice my concerns, just followed him.

He watched the sea as we wandered a promenade that felt like a ghost town: hotels, a pavement, a road, another pavement, then beach. There was no fairground, no dodgems or candy-floss van, no donkey rides; not one, single slot-machine. Roped-off areas of beach belonged to the hotels lining the front, allowing their guests to sunbathe without the constant attention of hawkers, many of which were already gearing up at the side of the road, selling cigarettes and bags of pineapple.

Tho stopped by a hotel called Cineram. Not a chain I'd heard of.

"He owns this place?" I said. "The man who bought Sarah?"

Tho didn't answer. Watching the boy, listening to his voice, the vagaries of his promises, I knew some time ago what we were doing here, and it was nothing to do with finding a missing English girl. I followed him inside anyway, into a deserted marble lobby adorned with gold fittings and a traditional Vietnamese tapestry depicting a man on a boat being towed by turtles. The woman on reception glanced up at us. She fixed a smile in greeting toward me, then lost the smile as she saw my guide.

She said, "Tho?"

"Mam," Tho said.

The receptionist rushed toward Tho and the pair hugged so tightly, she might have snapped the boy had I not fed him. It was Tho who broke the embrace. He pointed to me and said a few words, and the woman came at me so fast I flinched. She bowed, then shook my hand with both of hers. She spoke words of thanks in accented English, and I nodded and smiled in return, told her it was no problem, I was happy to help. It should have been a beautiful reunion, but I was so empty, so devoid of emotion that I could have walked away without saying anything.

Still, I said, "You're welcome."

I wasn't even angry. The boy wanted to be with his mother, and I could not hate him for that.

I turned to leave. "Good luck."

I'd taken two steps when Tho grabbed my hand, spun me round to face him, and hugged me about the waist. He said, "I am sorry I lie to you."

I patted his head. I held back tears, the effort stinging. "I understand," I said.

"I do what I have to do. I worry you leave me in Saigon."

I was already planning to return to Saigon and pick up Gareth's trail at the motel where Giang said he dropped him. But I wasn't equipped to seek out a killer in a city like Saigon. Not without funds. Not without resources. With the time difference, I had something like a day remaining on the deadline Benson set for Harry's release, and I now held little hope of making it.

"I would have done the same," I told him, although I wasn't sure I meant it. But what else could I do? Beat the shit out of him? "I'm glad you're home."

Chapter Forty

There was no train to Saigon until noon and, without any money, I didn't really know what else to do, so I returned to the beach. It was deserted, and a morning haze gathered on the horizon. I removed my footwear and strapped it to my pack, rolled up my trousers, and strolled in the shallow sea. For the first time I faced the prospect of failure, and the very real notion that I could lose the man who saved me.

Saved me. That wasn't an exaggeration. After our first case saw a teenage girl reunited with her father, he told me a few things about my own dad. That he'd been a bruiser in his youth, that Harry joined the army while dad learned a trade, and when Harry came home on leave he'd always be the one yanking my dad out of fights, holding him up on the way home, lecturing him through the fog of another hangover. My dad didn't listen. Harry was out there fighting all over the place, so where did he get off telling his friends how to live? He thought he'd lost my dad to that life. A life of anger, first sated by booze then exacerbated by it.

The next time he returned for a little R&R, my dad introduced him to a radiant young woman who worked in Marks and Spencer and sought to be a store manager—ambitious for those days, especially for a girl—and during that particular holiday not once did Harry have to intervene between two men whose fists were flying.

Within two years of meeting my mother, dad was running his

own plumbing business, owned a terraced house with four bed-rooms, and lived with a wife who adored him. Harry always had my dad's back, but it took the love of a driven woman to properly *save* him.

I listened, though. I heeded his advice. I *grew*. I became the man I was today, now lingering stock still in the sea on the other side of the world, waiting for the sun to break through the fog and bright-en my day.

Waiting.

Always waiting. Watching the horizon. Hoping for a solution to present itself.

For my dad, the solution was my mum. Until her ambition stretched beyond the house they worked so hard to acquire. She tried to keep on working after I was born, but the hours, coupled with the sexism of the seventies and eighties, it was too much for her to carry on. She retreated into herself, and while my dad worked extra jobs to keep us in that house in the street with the upside-down Union Flag, my mother discovered something better. Always looking for something better. And once dad was gone, she snatched the first shiny object that came her way. A nice house, comfortable living, a good school for her son, then expanding her reach to a canal barge, where she could do all the things she want-ed.

The mist cleared and I shielded my eyes from the low sun.

Expanded her reach...

Where she could do the thing she wanted.

I turned from the ocean, and ran with my heavy bag all the way to the hotel where I dropped off Tho. I knew how they could thank me.

The Cineram was serving breakfast, and Tho's mother, whose name I now learned was Gi-La, welcomed me back, and Tho himself beamed broadly. I asked for access to a computer and a phone, and Gi-La, a supervisor for this shift, was more than happy to provide it. I used Tho to translate my way onto an English language server based in Belize, then logged in to the personal network Jess and I set up years earlier. It didn't utilize the bespoke software I'd gotten so used to at PAI, but it accessed the bowels of the dark web without detection.

I could not navigate this world anywhere near as well as Jess, but I could poke around without fear of some digital bogeyman snatching my soul. I could also access pilfered files that went up for sale occasionally, and that included legitimate public documents as well as the sort of information our Deep Detect System could easily penetrate. When I wasn't locked out.

Land registry.

That was the key. Ownership of land away from home. Like my mother's barge, a Vietnamese criminal who could afford to spend a hundred grand a time on human cargo would own many properties both here and abroad. I was thinking of France.

It took me half an hour of conventional Googling to identify the quarry in which I fought Umbrella Man. It was owned by an ostensibly American firm called "Cargo Links Around the World," which fit with the communist mentality of naming everything in the most utilitarian way imaginable. That company was part of a chain of shipping container manufacturers that—last year—branched out into the business of transporting those containers across the globe. A decent cover for smuggling whatever cargo you choose, especially when whatever you choose will not cross a country's borders willingly.

Whoever bought Sarah was rich, and so if that's how the slaves were relocated it wasn't a great leap to think he'd be associated with this shipping firm. But the list of investors was huge. Through both dark web documents and conventional company records, I narrowed it down to eight men, and chopped a further five from there due to them being out of the country for at least the past two months. Whoever was holding her would want to receive her personally.

So three men stood out: a banker who appeared to work for the government rather than himself, yet when he was not domiciled in Vietnam he drove Ferraris around the Nurburgring in Germany and stayed in hotels that charged a thousand dollars a night; a property tycoon who made regular donations to art galleries and projects getting kids off the streets; and a mystery man, one who appeared to have no job to speak of, but whose father was a great northern military hero called Le Loi—he invested in over a hundred businesses, opening channels of trade to the rest of the world. I asked Gi-La to pop back in. She did so, with Tho at her side.

I said, "I think it's him."

"Him?" Gi-La said. "No, cannot be."

"Why not?"

"He not real," Tho said. "Is joke.

"Not real?"

"Le Loi is legend. He ride on turtles, take sword from woman in lake, fight off bad people from outside Vietnam. Many hundreds of years ago."

Gi-La hurried out of the office and returned with a colorful storybook with Vietnamese script and a man standing proud on the backs of two turtles while ships burned behind him.

"Le Loi," she said.

I looked at the investments again. All over the place. Seemingly random, but actually the timing was perfect. The injections of funds came mere months before those businesses started generating millions for the owners. I had to laugh. Through a capitalist system, the ruling party of Vietnam was taking a slice for the people, propelling private businesses into the global marketplace, before reaping the taxes that sustained this nation.

And then I saw it.

Not some clandestine deal. Not some shady government cover-up. A photo on Google Images. A donation, a philanthropist delivering a series of paintings to a charity auction in aid of street kids, commissions he arranged himself with a mysterious up-and-coming European artist. One featured a landscape along an industrial river, the freighters and cranes intricate in detail. A second presented a cityscape sketched in pencil and overlaid with charcoal, smudged just right to indicate a grim day. A grim day in *Leeds*.

But it was the third that nailed him: the silhouette of a lone woman on a cliff, water dappling behind her under a sunset so golden it could only have been real. Had Sarah's previous work not been devoid of humans I might not have noticed, and to the uneducated eye the figure might have been waving. But I saw it as a break in her signature; a secret cry for help.

Sitting back in the chair, I said, "Vuong Dinh."

"You go now?" Tho asked. "Find girl?"

I snatched up my pack and tightened the straps. "Damn right I'm going to find the girl."

Chapter Forty-One

The capital city of Vietnam is situated on the western bank of the Red River, eighty-five miles from the South China Sea. Most people arrive in Hanoi by rail or—like me—by air. The express from Na Trang cost another sixty dollars, leaving me forty in my pocket, but I arrived by lunchtime and used the internet in the airport to access Google again.

Vuong Dinh was a fifty-four year-old property developer who lived in a mansion-like home overlooking the Red River. When US President Bill Clinton opened up the unified Vietnam for international commerce, Dinh bought up derelict shops and stalled housing developments for the cost of their outstanding debts. His expansion drew the attention of the ruling Communist Party, who frowned upon such wealth, so he made large contributions to the Party itself as well as funding community projects across the region, while he built a modest empire.

Photos of Vuong Dinh on the internet were mostly official shots of him shaking hands with politicians and holding skinny orphans in the air, as well as that story from less than a week ago of him donating Sarah's paintings. After I clicked off here, I mined snaps that were clearly not posed, some paparazzi shots, some incidentals, and zoomed in on his entourage. One thick-set chap, who I would best describe as a "goon" cropped up time and again in the background; smart suit, wraparound sunglasses. It took me a few passes, but soon I was positive.

He was the man in Paris holding onto the black girl in the back room of that British-sounding bar.

I fired off an email to Jess to ask her to look deeper, and to press her on the subject of a loan. An out-of-office reply pinged back:

> *I'm sorry, I am out of the business due to a sudden bereavement. I will reply upon my return.*

My first instinct was that Benson had killed Harry. I stopped myself being sick with the thought that the out-of-office was far terser than Jess's usual prose. I dashed to a payphone and called her mobile.

"What happened?" I said.

She hesitated, groggy. It was still early morning in Britain. She said, "They suspended me. I have no access to DDS, the PAI mainframe, nothing."

"Oh God, I'm sorry."

"Yeah, no more helping out the globe-trotting playboy. My loss."

"That's not what this is."

"No? You're off doing who-knows-what while Harry is who-knows-where having God-knows-what done to him. You have two days left. Are you any closer?"

"Yes, I just need—"

"Money, sure. The problem with that is, I can't send it to your fake name because it's been flagged by the Vietnamese, and I can't send it to your real identity because there's no visa attached to your passport. So, come on, master detective, any bright ideas? Shall I strap a wad of twenties to a carrier pigeon? Should be there in, oooh, ten days?"

"I'm sorry," I said.

"Sorry? I'm suspended. Probably going to get fired and blackballed across the whole business. Harry is—"

"I know the situation. Give me a break a moment."

"A break? You want a break? Bring Curtis Benson what he wants, then I'll give you a break."

"I'll do that far quicker if you calm down and help me." Drawing looks from others around me, I lowered my voice. "Can you research something? See if you can hack into someone's personal accounts. His name is—"

"I'm being monitored," she said.

"You told me you were suspended."

"Not by Gorman, you prick. I'm under *surveillance*. Electronic and in person. I am a key suspect in aiding and abetting a wanted criminal. I can't do anything online except shop and read the news."

"Who's watching you?"

A deep sigh. "I don't know for sure. Guy in a Mondeo. And I have my own security system that makes my computers act in a particular way if there are eyes in there. I examined the subdirectories, and it looks very high-end. Possibly government."

So Agent Frank hadn't gone away completely. I told Jess everything I knew about him, and she accepted it without giving me any more shit.

I said, "Can't you do it from another computer? I'm so close, Jess. So close."

"Sorry, Adam. You used to do this without all the tech and gadgets. Do whatever you would have done before you met me."

Google Earth revealed the topography of the hills and town that surrounded the Dinh mansion, but the mansion itself was blurred out. Not many people achieve that. A map printout would have to do. I hit the print button on instinct, not thinking of the cost, and paid five dollars for my trouble.

I took a bus to Hanoi central (two dollars) and bought a detailed map (three dollars) then headed to a second bus station, where I established which service I needed. I purchased an all-day pass (one dollar—*bargain*) and had an hour to kill.

Back in England, it was often the tedium that I found most diffi-cult, but here I spent that dead hour leaning on an ornate stone wall overlooking a lake with a depiction of the great Vietnamese folk hero Le Loi. It was cooler here in the north, perhaps thinner air thanks to the altitude, so when the bus turned up fifteen minutes late I was not as sticky as before. No air-conditioning again, but the open windows gave sufficient ventilation.

In the late-afternoon, the bus stopped in a small port town called Ong, a copper-colored dot on the Red River. Copper-colored due to the former chemical factory. These days, Ong was a lumber town with a natural harbor about half a mile wide. Behind the road, the green land rose steadily at first and then steeply, with craggy rocks coated with trees. From the tarmacked road, I count-ed maybe thirty workers on the dock, loading freshly milled timber onto a fleet of barges. I drew vaguely curious looks from a couple of bristly men but nothing more than that.

I dug out Giang's knife, which I stashed in my pack for the flight, and carried it in my pocket as some sort of false reassurance. For the next hour, I hoiked my rucksack along the road, reading the map I printed out.

Trekking the longer stretches of road beside the river, I thought of Giang, sunk at the bottom of the Mekong Delta. I must have been spotted with him at some point, so that would make me sus-pect number-one. I wasn't sure my story would hold, that we travelled together, he loaned me a boat, and that was the last I saw of him. I would have to surrender to the authorities eventually, but I'd be over a thousand miles from Giang's last known location when I did so. If I ended up in jail, I just hoped my finding Sarah would lead to the recovery of Benson's true target—the USB drive.

I was still bothered as to why he'd lied about the money, though. Something to do with his Caribbean Island retreat. Trying to avoid questions from the tax man? Perhaps he was doing something similar to Sammy—hiding revenue and keeping higher profits for himself.

Having concentrated on where I was going, I hadn't noticed the clouds closing in, so I got little warning when the heavens opened and soaked me through in seconds. I protected the printouts as best I could, rounded the next bend, and found myself slightly elevated from a large house a mile away. I slogged into the forest until I hit upon a trail. When I came to a clearing with no tree cover, I dashed to the other side, and was rewarded with an unobstructed view of my target: Vuong Dinh's mansion.

The rain stopped as abruptly as it started, and I dug out my binoculars.

A wall surrounded the mansion on three sides, with a solid gate on the main road overseen by cameras and an intercom. A warning sign depicted a man being electrocuted. The wall was topped with broken glass, and the fourth side dropped to a rocky grave that skirted the river. The rear grounds were smaller than I expected but still enough for twenty-two people to play a decent game of football, and allow a sprinkling of spectators. A driveway and garages accommodated a Land Rover, a Ferrari and a Humvee in plain view. Along with kennels.

I crouched in my soggy clothes. I hadn't packed my cape or utility belt, so decided against breaking in and lobbing smoke grenades whilst silently taking out the baddies one at a time. Instead, I watched. I noted when people came in or out—feeding the dogs, a visual observation of the gate, checking the electricity supply. I jotted the time at which a van arrived and disgorged a man with brushes and poles, and mentally crossed out "*pose as window cleaner*" from my list of clever plans. That left a blank page of ideas.

I read again through the observations I made about the property and paid more attention to a phalanx of wires connecting the house to the outside world. I assumed the thickest cable, which ran from the north corner out to the cliff leading to the river, would be electrical, with a backup generator housed somewhere on the property. Several smaller wires from the south corner also spread to the river. I counted six. All shot into the rocky drop-off, beyond where I could see.

Around the mansion, all was lush and green, and the road was straight for a mile in either direction, as if they chose the site the way a king might select land for a fort. But there was one weakness. One access point.

I secured what I thought I'd need in a Ziploc, left my rucksack, and retraced my steps until I stepped out onto the road a few hundred yards from Vuong Dinh's property. I crossed into the woods the other side, and once I was far enough from the house I switched on the flashlight. There was no path, so I caught branches and brambles several times. I heard scurrying every time I paused, and maybe a few slithers. The country was surely home to venomous breeds of snakes and spiders, but most animals would rather hide than confront something the size of a man.

The drop wasn't quite as sheer as I thought, but still a long way down. I switched off the torch and used my binoculars and the light from Dinh's house to locate the junction box. It was the size of a chest of drawers, embedded in the rock outside the perimeter. All the communications wires fed over the electrified fence, then bunched into it. Out of this box came a cable as thick as my forearm and stretched over the rocks, down into the river. Vuong Dinh could run his empire from home if he chose.

I closed my teeth around the Ziploc bag and used both hands to crawl along the ground skirting the cliff, up a slight incline to the mansion's boundary. I came to the fence and swung my legs out into thin air. My feet pressed onto the ledge below. I lay on my belly and remained flat to the surface, crabbing in the dirt toward higher ground. The angle was so narrow, if I let go I would have slid and tumbled down the slope and slapped into the shoreline a hundred feet below. Hindered by my aching broken digit, my sideways-shuffling toward the junction box took ten minutes, by which time I was sweating enough to coat my face in dust, acting as unintentional camouflage.

On the flat ground, I knelt beside the box and took a screwdriver and a pair of pliers from my Ziploc and went to work, the torch in my teeth. I got it open, and had no idea what I was looking at.

Again, I needed old-school skills to solve a modern problem.

I emptied the dead phones from the bag, and found one of the more basic handsets still boasted a near-full battery despite there being no signal. I snipped the ear-buds off a set of headphones and plugged the jack into the phone, then sheared a tiny section of insulating coat from one of the mansion's wires. I wrapped one of the headphone wires around this, grounding the other on the box. The pain in my finger grew worse than the scramble along the cliff, the precision required being far greater, so I removed the bandage and let it flutter away.

Then it was a case of opening the mobile with the tiny Torx screwdriver set and bypassing the CPU so it worked like a regular phone. I held it to my ear and got a blast of high-pitched static.

Broadband or some slower internet connection.

I attached it to the incoming wire at the far end, reasoning the other lines could also be internet-based. I was correct. The final one made no real sound, but there was enough of a hum to demonstrate the line wasn't dead. I repeated this with another two phones, but they had less than a quarter of battery. In these, I pushed the speaker up full. Only the dead iPhone from Saigon went unused.

It was the clumsiest-looking wire-tap in my entire career. No way to tell if it would yield results. Over the next half-hour I considered how fortunate I was for the near-constant humidity. In Britain, even the warmest of nights would have seen me shivering after my soaking. But here, the warmth still surrounded me, dried me to an extent, and I lay there, listening to the river, and to creatures stirring in the night.

Eventually, one of the phones rang. Someone in the house picked up.

And spoke Vietnamese.

Of course they did. What was I thinking? Tap the phones, great, but then what? I didn't even have Tho to give me the gist in his own way. I didn't pick up on a single word. Nothing Anglicized, nothing remotely familiar. The line clicked dead.

On the bright side, they didn't know I was listening.

Then the lights came on. I mean *really* came on. What I thought had been floodlights were just placeholders. I ducked behind the junction box, expected to draw a hail of gunfire or pack of dogs, but the new illumination revealed another layer of foliage between the fence and the main building. I was level with the football-pitch-sized garden, but my position was relatively dark.

And that's when I saw something. Three somethings. Through the sparse bushes and thin trees, the three somethings carried trays: one with food, one with a decanter of amber liquid and a tumbler glass, and the third carried a domestic phone. I focused on the direction they were headed and pinpointed a balding man on a sun-lounger wearing a shiny dressing gown, facing the wide mass of water far below. He'd been there all along as I worked. Three hundred, maybe four hundred yards from me—was it far enough for the other sounds to have obscured my phones?

The three somethings arrived at the balding man: women. They were *women*. In porn-like French-maid outfits. One was a black girl, tall, with a sturdy hourglass figure; one oriental waif, possibly Vietnamese or Thai; and the final one was Caucasian, with dark bobbed hair, a petite frame and toned legs. I begged her to turn. *Begged* her. Would have screamed if my voice wouldn't have brought security guards swarming.

And then she did. She moved her head slightly. Although I'd never seen her except in photos, on the net and on paper, even from this far away, it could not be anyone else in this huge and varied world.

It was Sarah.

I had found her. And she was only yards away.

Chapter Forty-Two

The man in the silk robe accepted a drink from Sarah—she was carrying the whiskey—and then the phone from the black woman, while the Vietnamese girl held the food until the phone call ended. Then he ate his evening meal—steak, by the looks of it—and the girls waited, eyes firmly on the ground before them.

In what we think of as the "developed" world—Britain, America, France—there have been several instances where high-profile rich men were tainted by what seemed like irrefutable evidence, but nothing was done until a massive public outcry. I wondered how much it would take for someone to investigate a kidnapping allegation against one of the architects of Vietnam's revival, made by an illegal immigrant who was wanted on violence charges in Europe, and possibly involved in the disappearance of a Saigon policeman.

I could not go to the authorities.

While nothing else happened, I spent the time re-strapping my little finger to the one next to it using gaffer tape. Soon, another figure approached the group. It was the Goon, still mafia-sharp, still in his sunglasses.

I pressed myself flatter to the ground, a foot from the fence that buzzed with current even with nothing touching it.

The Goon stopped beside the women and clasped his hands. The man in the silk robe finished his dinner and placed the tray on the floor. The three women raised their heads, and when the man swung himself around to assess them, I confirmed it was Vuong Dinh, the doughy businessman I viewed in many press photos. He perused them, then pointed at the black woman. I now recognized her as the same one the Goon was manhandling back in Paris. I couldn't remember her name.

Vila Fanuco's favorite.

Sarah and the local girl cleared away the plate and took the phone, and the Goon escorted them back to the house. For a split-second, Sarah looked directly at me, like she knew I was there. In the harsh light I thought I could see her blue eyes. Her mouth was not happy or sad, but it was those eyes worried me, honed in like lasers on my hiding place. I even shook my head in case her condition bestowed her with some sort of super-powered vision.

Not now, I tried to convey. *Please don't give me away.*

It was only momentary, though. At the Goon's command, she disappeared with her handler behind the main building.

Vuong Dinh's robe was now untied, the black woman topless, and her head positioned over his groin, stroking smoothly up and down. I turned away. I didn't need to see that. Didn't want to think this was why Sarah got brought here.

How far was I behind her?

Two weeks?

Facing the junction box, I picked the phone with the strongest battery life, and opened the line using a code Jess taught me five years ago. The hands-free speaker rang shrill in the night, and several unseen creatures scurried away. I switched the speaker off and held the handset to my ear, and a man answered in Vietnamese. I pictured the Goon, but couldn't be sure.

I said, "I need someone who speaks English."

"Speak English? Go."

"I am an interested party in a property you recently purchased. I am willing to pay more than you did. A lot more." The second time I'd tried this trick. This time, though, I had nothing with which to back it up.

The Goon said, "Which property?"

"You paid about a hundred thousand for this property. A few days or weeks ago. You know the property I mean?"

A nose breathed on the other end. Wind hissed through the jungle. Something chirped. Something replied with a shriek.

I said, "I have half a million dollars in cash. For *you*, if you broker the deal. A further half-million for your boss."

"You are the British man. Go home, British man. Go home."

"I don't want trouble. But I'll create some if I have to. I want the girl, I want the belongings she was sold with, and I'm willing to pay enough to buy her ten times over. It's good profit."

"Her ... belong—belonging..."

"Her things," I said. "Her property."

"Hm. Yes. I call you back?"

"I'll call you in ten minutes."

I hung up and watched the garden, trying not to focus on the lounger. Shortly, the Goon crossed the lawn to where Vuong Dinh tied his gown and the black girl was getting dressed. The Goon waved her away and spoke to his boss. I heard every word but understood nothing. The Goon returned to the house.

I called the number. "Do we have a deal?"

"Her things," the Goon said. "You know her things. *Want* them."

I'd played my hand too openly. Too eagerly. "You know the item."

"She have data sticks in special pocket. No use. Broken."

Sticks-plural. I tried not to sound surprised. "You still have them."

"Girl say they valuable. But cannot break code. You break code, British Man?"

"She keeps the data sticks," I said. "I'm offering far more than it's all worth."

"Half million for girl. Half million to me. Half million for sticks."

I swallowed, as if I had any intention of paying. "Okay. Fine. I can be at your house in—"

"No," he said. "No house. You come, you die."

"Then where?"

His turn to pause. "You know how read co-ordinates?"

"Why?"

"You must take a boat where I tell you. We exchange there, at noon."

"She comes to me undamaged, with all her belongings and travel documents."

"Of course."

My mind somersaulted, searching for some sort of plan. "She holds onto the data sticks. I'll being a computer to check they're the real thing. Then I hand you your cash, the rest will be transferred by satellite phone. Clear?"

"Is acceptable." He dictated the coordinates before he signed off with the bad-guy handbook's standard farewell: "Come alone, and do not try anything."

To help him feel at ease, I said, "I'll be there."

Except, I had nothing to offer in terms of power or sex, so pretending I could offer money was the only option left. Trouble was, I had no real plan beyond tempting them to move Sarah out of that house. I'd just negotiated a deal in which there could be no winners.

Chapter Forty-Three

The Gulf of Tonkin is host to Ha Long Bay, a vast area with over two thousand islands and islets formed of limestone pillars rising individually out of the sea. With their sheer contours and thick foliage, they are more likely to be inhabited by mammals and birds than by human beings, but their beauty attracts hundreds of thousands of tourists per year, most sailing from Bai Chay Wharf. A long-time UNESCO Heritage site, the cruises are tightly regulated, although shipping and other non-tourist transports are able to navigate further out, where the islands continue almost to China. The islands vary in size from fifty-meter fenglin towers to hundred-meter lumps, all unique in shape, housing secluded bays, hundreds of caves and even sprawling markets floating around specially-allocated islets.

This was the chosen location for our exchange. A location I identified after a fitful night sleeping rough in a bus stop, Giang's knife in my hand and my pack close by. The cover of the jungle was the more obvious option, but I kept flashing back to the cacophony of animal noises, of scurrying and slithering in the undergrowth. The prospect of jerking awake with a cobra coiled on my chest flung up an invisible barrier to that option. In the morning, I communicated using hand gestures with a couple of dock workers, one of whom had an app on his five year-old iPhone that mapped the coordinates for me.

Despite the thousands of daily tourists, the scale of Ha Long Bay allows for a degree of seclusion, if you know where to look. It was one of these secluded limestone mounds where I suspected the coordinates would lead. Not a place you'd pick for a business meeting, but perfect to dispose of a body.

I had no intention of venturing out to such a rendezvous.

I caught another two buses in order to reach Ha Long City, the first Vietnamese hub I'd seen with more minibuses than mopeds. I spent five dollars on an hour's internet with strong drip coffee and several servings of something called Gat Gu, a rolled rice pancake that was sweet and delicious. I was told to nod three times whilst eating each one, a local custom I would normally embrace, but since nobody monitored me I stuffed them straight into my face whilst scouring maps in and around Ha Long City.

This was my old gig. My *Sherlock-Holmes-in-board-shorts* work. Assess the geography, check the starting point, go over the reasons for coming here; predict, conclude, then hope. When I was simply tracking a missing gap-year student, though, if I got that wrong I could attempt several other avenues. Here, I had one guess, so it had to be as accurate as any guess could be.

I finished my pancakes by nine, so that gave me extra time to reach the coordinates which, according to a quick online calculation, were an hour from Bai Chay. I guessed the Goon would bring her here by car before departing on one of the private vessels moored half a mile south of the wharf, one of which I learned from some basic online research belonged to Vuong Dinh's holding company. It was here where he hosted casino nights for clients and, it was rumored, government officials, whose luck was usually higher than the average punter.

Providing they honored my instruction and ensured Sarah was physically carrying the USB drive(s) at all times, the only snag would occur if they decided to take Sarah to the island via helicopter, but given the nature of the Bay, it would seem unlikely. This was a covert arrangement, and a helicopter would draw attention. Plus, if they wanted me to come here specifically, it made sense they'd utilize Dinh's boat.

I walked the mile south to the private pier and discovered it was part of a hotel complex, with a separate dock and outbuildings. I expected the pier to be part of some form of club where boat owners would wear pastel shades and pullovers tied round their shoulders for no particular reason, but this was a functional concrete pier that saw six large vessels moored—three junks with folded sails, a 115-foot yacht (a Derektor if I wasn't mistaken) and two lunking heaps of the sort you can sleep on in lieu of a hotel, out on the Bay itself. Workers came and went from all of them. Except the Derektor. Its name was the *Hoà bình đẹp*. I'd seen it online. It meant "Beautiful Peace."

I had developed that idiotic Batman delusion again, where I could take on whatever thugs came my way and glide out of there with the damsel now relieved of her distress.

Adam Park, the white knight.

When the Goon and his Goon-squad brought Sarah here, I planned to surprise them, start a fight, perhaps, and encourage Sarah to scream and tell everyone about her kidnapping. I'd take a beating, sure, but when the police were called she'd give her statement and I'd be arrested. But Sarah would be free and available to give Benson his USB drive.

I found a clothes shop on the complex and selected a pair of black, loose trousers, a V-neck top, and a conical hat that a legitimate Vietnamese would wear. The stooped saleswoman charged fifty dollars for the lot, but I haggled down to fifteen, plus the dead iPhone and charger. She was happy enough to throw in a surgeon-like facemask for free. The clothes fit well enough, the trousers a mere two inches short, although Giang's knife sat heavy in the pocket and the loose material made it sway against me. I switched my boots for strapped sandals and fresh air washed around my toes as I left the store.

The hotel charged me twelve dollars for up to twenty-four hours of left luggage, but they accepted my final ten. I kept my binoculars and the knife and picked up a tatty paperback from the book exchange, and—literally penniless—headed back to the concrete pier. I took a perch beside the only way in, pretending to read. The mask covered my lower face, and I pulled the hat low to obscure my European eyes. No one bothered me.

Thirty minutes later, they pulled up in big-bad gangster cars: two Land Rovers and a Lexus, all with blacked out windows. They drove really fast up a dusty driveway, just to enhance their gangster credentials. They all got out by a gate at the end of the jetty. I counted eight in total. Sarah was in traditional Vietnamese dress and clutched a small orange shopping bag to her chest, her upper arm enclosed in the Goon's paw, bringing the total number of people to nine.

I guessed I could take out three if they were surprised enough, but then I'd have five more to contend with, plus Sarah who had absolutely no idea who the hell I was. I should have prepared a better escape route than … umm … than no escape route.

It was possible, if she didn't panic, that we could make it to the hotel, but if we didn't get there we'd likely be mowed down by gunfire, or else they'd catch up and take us away and do … *horrible* things. Beating me. Beating Sarah too. They could go further than those in Bangkok and kill me this time, and I would have failed everyone.

Failed Harry.

Jayne.

Caroline.

The group came closer. A brisk walk. One girl. Of the eight men, all but one were Vietnamese. The final guy was Caucasian, a wiry, grey-haired guy in his fifties, carrying a canvas holdall.

I stood no chance. But I had to try. For Sarah's sake.

For Harry's.

The workers took no notice.

The Goon manhandled Sarah roughly along. They were almost upon me.

These men.

I gripped the knife as Sarah came closer. Prepared to strike at the second-to-last man. He was the smallest, the most nervous.

I had killed already.

I would stab him in the throat.

Neither Sarah nor the Goon spotted my eyes in the shadow of my hat. All it would take would be to move the book away, tense my legs, and launch forward. Take out the Caucasian guy fast, since I had no clue what he was doing here; maybe get another of the Goon-squad into the water before the rest were upon me.

Holding me down.

Beating me.

And just like that, my window was gone. They passed by and I relaxed my grip on the knife. I bowed my head and tried not to watch the party board the *Hoà bình đẹp*.

She had been within touching distance, but I couldn't do it. I couldn't help her.

With a shake to my hands, I folded the knife into the book and walked away.

Even if I'd acted as planned, they would have taken Sarah away before any police arrived. She would still be a captive. And I'd be dead. Or worse.

That's what I told myself, anyway.

Chapter Forty-Four

Bai Chay Wharf jostled me around as if I were invisible. Shoulders barged. Elbows dug. Rucksacks were swung at my head. It may have been because I was walking in a straight line without any sense of what to do next. I planned to earn some money by selling more phones or other possessions, charter a boat, then go to the drop, but without a new plan, I'd be killed, and Sarah returned to whatever duties awaited her back at *chez Dinh*.

The fear I suffered on the pier was a complete surprise. I'd not been paralyzed in that way for many years. Even in the quarry on the outskirts of Paris, being shot at, arrested by the French police, even holding a gun on Major Giang, I didn't freeze. I did what was necessary.

No compromises.

Between young backpackers and silver-haired tour groups, I made it to the chain-link fence along the boarding pier. The bay and its limestone monoliths were visible in the gaps between dozens of waiting boats, a mix of faux-traditional junks, modern functional barges, and luxurious cruisers. By far the most numerous were the barges. Westerners and Easterners boarded in a constant stream, but I needed something smaller. I wasn't sure I had enough time to sell my stuff.

How long would it take for them to launch the yacht? I doubted health and safety would be as big a factor as back home, but they'd still need to do *some* checks. Plot a course. Possibly inform someone of their route.

Then I spied an alternative to a fire sale.

A man all in beige, late 20s, hung around the food stalls at the edge of the seating area filled with backpackers drinking coffee, cold soda, snacking, chatting … and not paying enough attention to their luggage. Most threaded their feet through the straps so their bags couldn't be snatched, but the Beige Man assessed each one. He held a card for "Zuma Cruises" but I saw no ticket kiosk or boat by that name. He dropped the card, crouched, made a big deal of the mishap with his outstretched hand—standard misdirection—then with his other hand close to his right leg he slashed the nearest rucksack with a straight razor, thrust his hand in, and took out a passport, a wad of money, and a hairbrush. He placed the hairbrush on the floor, palmed the loot, and was on his way. The operation took less than ten seconds.

I fell victim to his type a few times. Live out of a suitcase or rucksack for enough time and it was inevitable. The key is in being prepared or, like me, get to know the tricks of these so-called "petty" thieves, although "petty" sanitizes what they do. They are just "thieves" to me. Or "scum-sucking-selfish-bastards." Many times, people I was searching for had encountered someone like this Beige Man, and was the reason they had gone dark on the family. No money, no phone, no passport. I traced one girl working in a beach bar on the east coast of India after being robbed of everything. She'd been there six weeks, trying to raise enough cash to move on, too embarrassed to ask her mum for help.

The thief skirted a chain-link fence behind the ticket kiosks and ducked behind the toilet block. I circled the opposite way around the outbuilding and approached him from behind as he counted his latest score. A couple of hundred dollars by the look of it. Some kid's spending money. Their holiday ruined. He turned as I got within arm's reach.

I said, "Speak English?" and he said, "Fuck you," and I punched him in the stomach.

He doubled over and I brought my knee into his cheekbone. He fell, stunned. I snatched his most recent acquisitions and knelt on his spine while I searched his pockets. Two thick wads of cash—one of dong and one US currency; about a thousand dollars in total. Three more passports, four necklaces of limited value, keys, and two phones. He bucked beneath me and I slapped the back of his head so his face met the dusty ground.

"I asked you a perfectly civil question. *Do you speak English?*"

He coughed. "Little bit."

"Good. I'm taking this money, and you get the rest of the day off. Clear?"

He nodded rapidly.

I said, "Where's your boat?"

"My…"

"Your boat, fuckwit. Where is it? I know you have one."

"Please, not my boat. Take money. Not my—"

I slapped his face into the dust again. Told myself I was only roughing up a lowlife. It wasn't torture. I was being practical. He robbed people of their holidays, of their wonderful experiences in this beautiful country. Besides, a slap or two was better than a Vietnamese jail.

"On pier four," he said. "Near end. Between the *Gong Lai* and *Ving Lai*. Big boats."

"Key?"

"Please, sir…"

"Relax. I'm the good guy here. I'm just borrowing it. I'll bring it back. But I don't have time to barter."

He twisted his head to look at what I'd taken from him and he pointed awkwardly at a bunch. "Key."

I let him stand, told him, "If you are lying, I will find you," to which he nodded again.

I spun him and wrapped my arm round his neck, locking his blood-flow in place, held it there until he passed out. He'd be unconscious long enough for me to get away.

I returned to the melee of people bustling for tickets and shoved my way back to where the theft occurred. I placed the passport and two hundred dollars on the table in front of a twenty-something girl. She looked understandably startled.

Adam's Smug Travel Tips #1: Watch out for your shit. Petty criminals aren't dumb.

I said, "Be more careful," and walked away.

I left the other passports and possessions with the food-hut in the hope they'd find their way to some lost property department, but I had no way of tracing the owners of the cash.

I would put it to good use.

Harold's Tours employed several touts, funneling on-the-day purchasers toward various ticket offices bearing the name, which led me to believe they were well-equipped. I went through the do-you-speak-English routine several times, until I found one tout with whom I could communicate in way not limited to him handing me a flyer and pointing at the kiosk for which he worked.

I said, "I need a GPS unit."

He still tried to sell me a tour, but I lifted my hat briefly and took off my mask. Showed him a portion of the cash.

"I'm in a hurry."

He led me to the main kiosk where he and his boss offered a rubber-encased oblong box about twice the size and three times the thickness of an iPhone. The screen took up half its surface, the rest a dial and keypad and the brand name, "Garmin."

They asked for a thousand.

We went back and forth, and agreed on six hundred, although they retailed at around three. He threw in a pier pass.

Through the security barrier, I jogged down the quayside until I came upon a barge with *Gong Lai* stenciled on the side and a red dragon painted on the front. The *Ving Lai* was moored beside it. In the water below, a motorized inflatable bobbed up and down. I climbed down the rope ladder, stepped on board, and sat down immediately as it pitched under my weight. It was actually a small Indigo, a rigid plastic hull with a powerful motor and room for between four and six people, the sort of life-raft you get on the smaller yachts, so I guessed the unconscious man behind the toilet block had stolen this too.

The ignition and steering worked more like a car than the rigmarole of the riverboats, and the Indigo fired up first time. Sleazy Stu's teachings came back to me, and I checked the fuel gauge—almost full—and noted the two gas cans strapped in the back. Satisfied, I plotted a course to the Goon's coordinates, donned a pair of sunglasses I found beside the seat, and chugged out from in between the two larger boats.

There, revealed before me, was the whole of Ha Long Bay.

Chapter Forty-Five

A fine mist gave the impression of shrouding the bay, but the sky was blue and clear. Hulking barges made of wood, painted to look like rainbow-colored dragons, dozens of them, maybe hundreds—more than I could count—ploughed through the water, a herd of vessels migrating slowly to their established channels.

I maneuvered the Indigo easily enough, though, thumping off conflicting wake from several junks and other boats. The wind buffeted my face, hat held on by string. Although I truly loved the water, I ate air more times than felt safe even for me, so I slowed to cut around other sailors, waved at a couple of happy tourists as I went. I was already off-course but in less than five minutes I was bearing straight ahead. Dozens of barges remained visible through that illusion of haze, but were far enough away that I gunned the engine and sliced over the calm water, back toward the Garmin's route, where the limestone islands seemed to go on forever.

Their number was impossible to count, stretching to a translucent horizon. Conservationists estimated nearly two thousand, so the bay must have been vast. I came to the first of them, and it towered above me, the green reaching into a sky so blue the whole scene looked Photoshopped. Then more of them materialized, giant craggy teeth spaced at odd distances, pointing upwards, sheer from the water.

I rounded those natural monuments into a stretch of open water, and what I saw made me drop off the throttle and cut the engine. The quiet of the ocean descended so quickly it startled me.

The *Hoà bình đẹp* sailed some distance ahead, as unreal as a toy on a pond. Now I'd come to a halt the sea tossed me around with uncontrolled jerks that threatened to throw me overboard, so I forged ahead slowly.

At first, I thanked God, or Dad, or my mother, or whoever was watching over me, for this slice of luck. But as I kept pace with the yacht, I realized there was no reason to be amazed by the coincidence. They, too, must have been utilizing a GPS. We were both aiming for the same destination, so it would actually have been odd *not* to cross paths. Now the question was what to do about it. A six-inch blade didn't make me a pirate.

Judging distance on water is harder than on land. The sameness of it all is what does it. The actual size of the yacht helped, and the abundance of landmarks towering over the waves allowed me a bit of perspective. I estimated they were about two nautical miles away. Yet, even with that knowledge, the yacht appeared to be standing still, so gauging the correct speed was nigh-on impossible. I couldn't risk becoming an obvious tail, either.

I edged forward in slow increments, but their yacht still didn't appear to be moving, until it veered left and cut across perpendicular to my route. I let the engine idle and bobbed up and down, allowing the current to shift me left, where one of the smaller limestone mounds lay motionless, its sheer sides rounding off to a green mop of hair-like foliage. The *Hoà bình đẹp* was definitely heading that way, but that was not the atoll on which we were to make the deal.

Then it stopped dead, and waited for several minutes.

With no clue what I was planning, I sped the Indigo toward them. Kept the pace steady but not flat-out. The islet next to which they had seemingly anchored grew larger.

Something else floated in the water. A long, flat structure on which huts had been built at wide intervals, on which people in conical hats and loose clothing roamed, giving the thing scale. Closer, its wooden frame became apparent.

A solid platform.

As I advanced much closer, I discovered the yacht's launch moored to a jetty, a sleek motorized boat like a mini version of its parent.

The floating structure was a *marketplace*. They'd stopped to go bloody *shopping*.

Three other boats disgorged passengers and, now I was close enough to see faces, I realized the market extended along the islet in a dogleg. Two of the other boats were tourist-packed, while the final one appeared to be another private vessel, smaller than Vuong Dinh's.

I pulled my hat low and my mask up and guided the Indigo into one of the spaces for smaller craft. A walnut-skinned woman greeted me and called for my line, which she kindly tied off, and I climbed up a couple of feet onto the surprisingly sturdy gangway.

Around fifty or sixty people shared the space, shoulder-to-shoulder, browsing bananas, pineapples, bread, crisps, bottled water for a dollar per liter, dried meat. I shunted through the crowd. Mostly Japanese and Caucasian features, a couple of the Japanese and a few of the vendors wearing surgical-style masks like mine. I figured Sarah was on the boat, but if I was going to trim the odds, I should know the lay of the land.

Down in a shallow net in the floor, eels slithered over one another. Four more nets next to them, all containing a different variety of fish, flopping and slapping in the water. A middle-aged Vietnamese lady in an apron pulled out one eel and, on a bloodstained block, *thunk*ed off its head with a cleaver and dropped the rest in a bag for a tall man in chef's whites. The smell wafted up, fresh and full-bodied. I twisted to get away from it, and came face to face with the last person I expected to find here.

Sarah.

She still clutched that orange shopping bag to her chest in that same desperate way. Two men stood either side of her, making no effort to blend in, while the Goon—still in his suit and sunglasses—bartered with a man with no legs over the price of a bag of apples. I feigned interest in the eels, but something must have drawn Sarah's attention, because she lingered on me, as if studying a painting. Did she remember me from the hotel pier?

While most people's short-term memories filter out incidents of zero importance, those with an eidetic memory would instantly recall a stranger out of place. I held her eyes. Lowered my face-mask and smiled. She took a deep breath and her mouth turned up slightly at the edges. I hoped she understood.

The Goon opened another negotiation. Sarah resumed that that neutral look, although her fingers kneaded the carrier bag. It contained very little.

I stayed two stalls behind. Through the comings and goings, Sarah looked at me again. I concentrated on examining an octopus that an elderly lady presented to me in a plastic water-filled pot. Its legs whipped around and I nearly dropped it. The chef took it from me and he gestured for the lady to bag it.

I shifted to an empty stall, where two giggly British girls chatted about some guy the blond one met in Hanoi and how she hoped to hook up again in Ho Chi Minh City.

"Excuse me," I said. "Would either of you have a pen I could borrow?"

The brunette forced a smile as she took me in. Taped-up fingers, Vietnamese clothes, conical hat. I did look pretty ridiculous as soon as you realized I was a northern British bloke. With a quick glance to her friend, who nodded, she fished in her bum-bag and gave me a sparkly pen.

"Any paper?" I asked.

"No, sorry." She shrugged at her friend.

The friend shrugged too. "It's all on the boat."

I had to get to Sarah somehow. See if she could break away whilst on board the yacht. When their guard was down, she could jump overboard and I'd pick her up and be gone before they realized she was missing. She just needed to know I'd be there, waiting.

But there were no stationers on the market. I scanned around again and found what I needed. A pineapple. A price tag tied around the stalk, a cardboard strip, displayed "$5" in black pen. I paid the five dollars without haggling and took the price tag and handed the world's most expensive pineapple to the blonde girl.

She said, "Umm, thanks?"

I wrote on the strip, *"When the boat leaves, I will follow. Jump when you can."* I signed it *"A friend,"* which I hoped she believed. Now all I had to do was get it to her.

I handed back the pen and said, "I'll buy you an octopus if you slip this to that girl over there. The men can't know."

"Oh, pu-*lease*," said the brunette. "What are we, schoolgirls?"

The blonde said, "Yeah, we're twenty, not fifteen."

"A bit of advice, mister. Girls don't like it when guys play games. Especially older guys hitting on young girls. If she likes you, you'll know."

Their love lesson complete, the two uber-wise girls returned my pineapple and sashayed off.

I picked up a second pineapple, and spent time bartering this one. It confused the woman, since I hadn't quibbled before, but we went through the routine as the group came back along the gangway. Having pounded her down to four dollars, I backed away and dropped both fruit into the group's path.

One of the guards kicked one accidentally. When he bent down to pick it up, I knelt to collect the other. As I did so, I slipped the label into Sarah's carrier bag. She caught the operation but no one else did.

So only I could hear, she said, "It's a trap."

I stood back up with my five-dollar pineapple and the shorter of the two guards returned my four-dollar one, and they all moved on, my disguise clearly more effective than I'd realized.

Some trap.

So it had been a trick to lure me here. Or maybe simply an attempt at counter-surveillance. The Goon kept looking out to sea, perhaps checking for an out-of-place boat waiting for the yacht to resume its journey. He hadn't expected me to come ashore.

Sarah pointed to some bottled soft drinks, but no one wanted to stop. She pulled away and was about to cause a scene when the Goon acquiesced and bought the drink for her. As he passed her the bottle, he tried to smile. He seemed genuinely disappointed as she rearranged her bag to accommodate the energy drink.

Once the Goon stepped away again she used the cover of movement to read my note. When finished, she let it drop into the water between boards and tried to find me again through the mass of shoppers. Five stalls away, examining another octopus, I gave a thumbs-up, and Sarah nodded minutely.

The vendor, however, thought the thumbs-up was for her, so I ended up paying ten dollars for a live octopus in a bag of seawater.

Back toward the dock, I wandered past the eels and fishery and I sat on the boards next to my boat, tossed my sandals on the deck, and dangled my legs in the water. I used Giang's knife to cut pieces of pineapple. The sweetness and juice satisfied a thirst I hadn't noticed until it hit my throat. I tipped the octopus into the sea and it floated there for a second, as if anticipating a trick of some sort, then it flexed its tentacles and shot down into the deep.

The group of four passed the octopus stand.

Nothing to do now but wait. I planned to give them a head start, which shouldn't be a problem given the speed they'd established so far. When she was ready, she'd jump. I would accelerate and scoop her out of the water. Their yacht was faster in a straight line, but I could zip between the outcrops, disappear, and find my way back to any part of the Vietnamese coastline. I congratulated myself on its simplicity. No going in half-cocked this time. Harry would have been proud.

They reached the eels and the fishery.

Son, you need to plan when you go in, and plan to get out.

With hindsight, I should also have planned for what happened next. I recalled all Caroline told me about her sister. How, when feeling stressed, her personality would regress, fold back in on itself and emerge like a robot, a mind lasering in on solving the problem before her. She would analyze her immediate aim in life, and simply act. Without emotion. Without further thought. Today, she had a savior in sight. Three men around her. Her white knight, her Batman, a mere ten feet away.

A promise of rescue.

All she had to do was get away.

Sarah lunged for the eel vendor's meat cleaver. Before either guard could react, she swung it and the blade gouged into the short one's neck. She yanked it out and blood sprayed flat and wide like a hose with the end nipped.

The people around them screamed and scattered, dozens splattered red. One woman crouched by the fish and splashed water on her face to wash out the fluid. The chef dropped all his wares and dived into the sea. Several followed him, some unintentionally as they got caught up.

The only person sprinting *toward* the mess was me.

Sarah went for the other guard. He grabbed her wrist and she tried to knee him in the groin, but he was ready for it.

The Goon placed his bags on the floor and drew his gun just as I got to him. I shoulder-barged him low in the ribs. Although he felt as solid as a bag of cement, he staggered over the boards and splashed into the water. The second guard let go of Sarah and launched at me. Without breaking stride I punched him in the throat and landed my heel in his solar plexus. He tumbled backwards and down into the eel enclosure, where he thrashed about and screamed for help.

"Come on!" I grabbed Sarah's hand and led her to the Indigo.

The Goon surfaced and his hands gripped the platform. No gun that I could see.

I lowered Sarah to the deck, the cleaver and carrier bag still in her hands. The Indigo fired up and I pulled into open water, looking back to see the Goon adjust his wraparound sunglasses as I made off with his prize possession.

"I dropped my drink," she said.

Chapter Forty-Six

Crashing against mercifully-small waves, the Indigo launched into the air every few seconds. Each time, the craft wobbled as it landed but I didn't dare ease off. My two-handed grip fused my fingers to the wheel, the little one hurting like hell. Over the wind, the crashing spray, and the engine, I had to yell to be heard.

"*Are they following?*"

Sarah held her bag between her legs and wrapped both hands around the rail, one of which was covered in blood. Her face was streaked too, her expression completely neutral. After a quick look back, she said, "Yes, they are."

"*How far behind?*"

"I don't know. Who are you, please?"

I eased off the throttle enough to glance back. The yacht faced us, moving, but it was nothing but a white gash in the water, not close enough to shoot at us. I dropped the speed some more, and steered to the left, between two islets two hundred yards apart. The yacht disappeared from view.

"I'm Adam," I said. "Caroline hired me to find you."

"Caroline did? That was nice of her." No sarcastic inflection. Just matter-of-fact.

"I'm sorry I have to ask this right now, but do you have a pendrive? A USB stick?"

"No," she said. "I have a few." She showed me the orange carrier bag, containing a pair of red high-heeled shoes, a mobile phone, a toiletry bag, a couple of matchbooks and six USB memory sticks. Mostly black, but one red one.

"Which one is Curtis Benson's?"

"Oh, Gareth deals with all that. Have you seen him?"

We passed another limestone outcrop, then turned South East to create a wide arc and throw them off our trail.

"I don't know where he is," I said, worried that telling her he was dead might freak her out. "I haven't met him." I waited for a reaction, but didn't get one. "What did they do to you there? At the house?"

"Cleaning, a bit of sex, some dancing. They were teaching me to cook, too."

"A bit of sex."

"Yes. A bit. Sometimes once a day. I've only been there ten days, though, so I don't know if that's normal."

"With Vuong Dinh?"

"Eight times with him, once with Kwong, and another man did it too. I didn't see him again."

"Who's Kwong?"

"The man you pushed in the sea. With the suit. It's a nice suit."

"Are you okay?"

"They said it was my job now. I had to. Or they'd hurt me. I didn't want to get hurt. I didn't want to do the sex, either, but it's my job."

I didn't know if it was better or worse that she had this condition. It allowed compartmentalization, but at the same time it made her easy to take advantage of. A choice between sex with someone she didn't like or getting hurt was simply a mathematical calculation for her. I expected the other two slaves were not quite as together.

"I'm going to take you home," I said, and smiled as reassuringly as I could.

She actually smiled back, although it appeared to be a learned reaction rather than instinctive. She said, "I'd like that."

An insect droned by my head and I swatted at it.

"So, we'll set down on a beach," I said. "Hide out for a bit, then make our way—"

Another insect zipped by and I pulled my head away in annoyance. In doing so, I caught movement in my peripheral vision. Out on the ocean.

"Shit!"

It was the launch from the *Hoà bình đẹp,* closing in. Three men on board, one with a rifle aimed this way. The muzzle flashed and I fell sideways. The bullet/insect impacted the seat.

I pulled Sarah to the floor, told her to stay down, and crawled back to the wheel. In a crouch, I increased our speed and zigzagged as much as I could. I may not know much about guns, but it was a safe guess that shooting from a moving boat was not particularly accurate. I veered hard to the right and a series of tiny explosions raked the water as they engaged some sort of automode. I took us through an archway of white stone and pulled a left for cover behind an island, but their boat was more powerful and equally maneuverable.

Sarah said, "You should go faster."

"Thanks."

But the throttle was as open as far as I dared and the craft almost capsized with every jerk of the wheel. I skirted the island as the gunfire resumed. White chips and dust erupted under the battering of stray bullets. One of them would hit home eventually.

I ran us behind a pair of rocks that resembled two rabbits kissing, dropped our speed to a crawl, and spun a one-eighty to face the way I came. When I heard the other motor rise in volume, I accelerated. Suddenly, we were in a game of chicken. Their reaction was instinctive. They spun aside. The gunman stumbled and his long-barreled weapon tumbled over the side.

I raced toward a cluster of smaller islets where I reduced speed due to the proximity of the obstacles. It gave me time to think about what I just did, and what I saw on their boat: the sniper was the Caucasian guy who boarded with the holdall, pasty white, so he likely hadn't been in the country too long. Also of concern was what I *didn't* see, which was the Goon. He wasn't on board. Just three mini-Goons. The two on the marketplace were tough but not well trained, but the guy with the rifle, travelling so fast and on water … you don't get that close to your target without some serious range-time.

I had been correct. They knew who I was and why I was there. They probably knew my funds were frozen and that I planned to take Sarah away from them. I would have been murdered out here, my body never found.

It was, indeed, a trap.

The pursuing boat roared out ahead of us. The sniper now wielded a handgun and let off round after round. I yanked the wheel left and fled between a valley of seaweed-covered rocks, pings and cracks sounding either side.

I blasted out of the valley and into the path of a second motor-launch, piloted by the guy who fell into the eels. Kwong—the Goon himself—held a gun on us. He fired and my left ear stung. Blood sluiced down my neck as I accelerated right. Two more rocks touching. Another archway. A deep one; a tunnel. This one much lower than other escape routes I tried. I ducked right down to avoid a head injury.

Ha! Too small to get their launches through.

The dark tunnel afforded more cover, and was cold and damp.

The exit was a welcome sight as we burst into sunlight. I guessed the two touching islands were big enough to give us another head start.

Not for the first time this week, I was wrong.

The cave led to a lagoon, completely encased by sheer limestone rock. The only escape was where we entered. They had pushed us into a prison.

Chapter Forty-Seven

The island interior was a sheer white donut. Vegetation grew thirty feet above sea level, where the angle formed a steep hill. Several inlets, but no adequate cover.

Sarah looked up at the rock face. "Are we safe now?"

"No," I said.

A flock of birds took flight high up at the sound of us.

Sarah said, "We shouldn't have come in here."

"No. We shouldn't."

"So why did we?"

"I need to think."

They couldn't get their launches in, but they could swim. And we were unarmed. Except for a meat-cleaver and a six-inch knife.

Sarah said, "What now?"

"Now…" I didn't have an answer. "Look for a cave. Any way to get out of this boat."

Sarah said, "There."

I followed her finger to a narrow horizontal gash in the limestone about seven or eight feet above the water. The lip was coated in bird shit.

I said, "We could hide in it but they'd find us eventually."

"The birds," she said.

"What birds?"

She swept her finger up the green hillside to the spot where a flock of fat sea birds perched. "When we came through that tunnel, birds flew out of there, where *those* birds are waiting. The droppings. It has to be connected."

At full speed, it took a minute to ride over there. Looking directly up, the gash was easily wide enough for Sarah, but I'd have to squeeze through, if I made it at all. The problem was that it was higher up the limestone than I estimated. At least four feet over my head.

The chug of a motor echoed through the tunnel.

I cupped my hands and crouched so she could step into them. She held her bag in her teeth and I boosted her up to the feces-coated entrance, heaved my hands up to shoulder-height, and she secured her arms on the ledge. With a final shove, I raised her feet right over my head and felt her land on solid ground.

"Thank you," she said.

A dinghy arrowed out of the tunnel; a small inflatable they must have carried on board. Bugger. Kwong and the sniper were both riding this one, positioned behind the Eel Guy and a Driver. Firearms came out—snub-nosed machineguns. They'd be here in less than a minute. In range in less than that.

I tried to jump to reach the cave's lip, but the boat just bobbed deeper. I opened the cupboard, hoping for flares at least. Nothing.

I called up to Sarah, "Toss me the matches."

"But they're mine," she said, clutching her bag.

"Give them to me!"

"Why?"

I poured the spare fuel out onto the Indigo, on the sides, out into the sea. It would have been great to toss a few containers in the water and aim a flare at them like James Bond, but that's not how flammable fuel works, unfortunately.

Sarah said, "Oh, I get it," and threw down a book of matches. They were from The Rex.

I struck one and set fire to the others and—standing on the nose of the Indigo—threw them on the floor. The fuel ignited unspectacularly at first, and then it caught with a *whoompf*. Flames obscured me from the approaching boat, but they wouldn't stop bullets. Limited visibility was the best I could do.

"The cleaver," I said.

She threw it to me. I caught it by the handle, but it slipped, headed for the water and I grabbed it in a panic. The blade sliced my right hand. Not deeply, but it was another wound for the collection. I bled freely.

The first bullets pinged into the rock.

I took the meat cleaver and hacked into the limestone at my chest-height. It did little with the first blow, but on the fifth, the blade sunk in. I jiggled it loose and swung again. Deeper this time. Slippery with my blood.

Heat seared at my back now. A pop sounded, the inflatable giving in to the flames. More gunfire, this time impacting the boat and chipping into the cliff around my legs.

A final swing and the cleaver's blade jammed in up to the handle.

Sarah said, "They're nearly here."

I backed up close to the flames, then ran toward the rock. I couldn't leap, exactly, but I threw myself and gained air thanks to my momentum. Pushing off sent the flaming boat backwards and the approaching gunmen unleashed a barrage upon it. My foot landed on the cleaver's handle and my thigh pushed upwards. I got my arms onto the ledge, but they sunk into bird shit. I started to slide. I dug in my fingers, and jammed them in to the smallest of ridges. My foot again found the embedded cleaver. I flexed my toes to give me more leverage. Sarah held me by the upper arms and tried to pull, but her brain quickly calculated the odds of success and she stopped.

A burst of bullets battered the rock over my head. I heaved again, fingers straining, but it was no use. Then the cleaver snapped.

All that stopped me from falling was Sarah. She hugged a larger outcrop and wrapped her legs around one of my arms, which I held onto. I dangled over the sea. Unable to move. Then Sarah did something that seemed odd at first. Unable to actually lift me, she tangled her body around the rock, wedging herself fast between this outcrop and the cliff-face. Then she squeezed her legs together and bent at the knees. She'd turned herself into a human lever-system. I rose up the face and rolled onto the gooey shelf.

The dinghy arrived. The Sniper opened fire, bullets hitting the soft rock. No ricochets. On my belly, I helped Sarah unfold and we both crawled into the cave. The last we heard was the Goon yelling.

Sarah made it through into a wider cavern. She calmly offered her hand and I waved it off, wiggling sideways through the two immovable slabs. The upper section curved out a couple of inches, trapping me there.

I had to pivot. My head stuck out into daylight. The four men inside the dinghy looked up. Kwong smiled, raised his gun, but I was gone by the time he got off his first shot. I jiggled backwards, feet-first, like a caterpillar, and made it through.

I sat up. Bumped my head on the ceiling, but I could move again. I tore a sleeve off my outfit and wrapped it around my cut hand. A bright white pinpoint through the tunnel suggested Sarah's logic had been correct. There was another light source up ahead. We crawled towards it through a trickle of freezing water.

"Do you know what's on those pen drives?" I asked.

"No. Gareth made copies. Lots of copies. But he couldn't get the files to work. He told me to look after them. So I did. When the men put my clothes into a suitcase, I made them give me this bag. My shoes are important too. Gareth bought them for me."

The *dead* Gareth.

"Nice of him," I said.

"He said they made me look like a slut when I danced."

"Like I said, nice." The new light was closer but I was getting a bad feeling about it. "The money, Sarah. How much money was there?"

"I didn't want to take it. Gareth said we should. He told me Curtis owed him wages. I thought it was a lot for a doorman."

"How much?"

"About five thousand three hundred pounds."

A fraction of what I'd been told. So Benson really was onto another scam. Something he'd pay dearly for, were it exposed.

Sarah said, "It was enough to start again somewhere. But Gareth said the pen-drive was more valuable. I supposed that's why he made copies. So he could sell them all and we'd be happy. When do you think he'll be back?"

His body would be a pale, bloated bag of rotting organs by now, slowly disintegrating in a Saigon morgue. I didn't think now would be a good time to mention this.

The hole was the size of a football. Plenty for a bird to fly through, but not nearly enough for a man. Or even a skinny eighteen-year-old girl. In the beam of sunshine, Sarah's expression gave little away except that we should continue up the passageway. There really was no choice.

Because some caves are formed by geological shifts and others by water erosion, they are more varied than anyone can predict, but the stream dappling gently around us marked this as the latter. So when we no longer had to crawl and could actually stand up, it was more happenstance than luck. Another meager glow slowly materialized ahead. When we reached the light-source, I almost forgot why we were there.

The passage opened into a cathedral-sized cavern, a luminous layer of some green organism coating the roof. Several dripping holes in the cave's shell emanated an otherworldly radiance that rippled shapes against thick shadow, revealing a network of natural walkways and slopes. The draught on my skin made me shiver, and the air tasted damp. Both ends delved into darkness, and either could have led deeper into the island or stopped dead meters beyond the reach of the nature-made spotlights.

A couple of the holes up above flickered. Muffled voices sounded. Vietnamese. A head and shoulders leaned into the cave fifty feet over our heads. A torch came on and swept around. We ducked behind a boulder.

I gestured for Sarah to stay where she was, and moved silently back to the corridor. Listened. A hollow breeze gusted. Nothing that sounded like a man slopping his way up.

No noise but the voices above.

We had to chance it.

I beckoned for Sarah to join me, but before she could move, a gunshot exploded through the silence and impacted above my head. I dived behind the boulder, with time to see the head and shoulders hanging through the roof were equipped with night-vision goggles. Several more shots rang out until an American yelled, "*Cease fire!*" The sniper called, "You're stuck, Adam. Give up the girl and we'll leave you a boat. Go home, don't come back."

Lying bastard. Why bring along a mercenary sniper if they were happy to take her and run? Were that the case, they would have said "no" back at the house.

She was bait. For me. The troublemaker.

Sarah hugged her bag like a teddy bear. I wondered how much she'd value it if she knew the truth about Gareth.

The American sniper called, "Come on, Adam. You know we got you."

I wasn't going to give up Sarah, so there was no point negotiating. But he'd said there was no way out...

I darted back toward the passageway. Waited. The first thing to pass my hidey-hole out of the entrance was the barrel of a snub-nosed machinegun. Eel Guy was holding it the way SWAT officers do on American TV shows, which at least *looked* correct.

I summoned that feeling, that focus I achieved in Paris when faced with Michelin Man and Butterball. I grasped the gun barrel, whipped him round to open his body up, and drove my fist into his solar plexus. The air gulped out of him and his eyes bulged. My knee came up to his jaw and shattered it. He fell, unconscious, and I took his gun. Searched him for other weapons and found none.

I took cover behind the boulder again. The gun had a safety catch and a switch that ratcheted from "1" to "3" to "auto." I'd read enough books to know this meant single shot, bursts of three or full automatic fire. I selected "1" and popped up over the boulder and fired at the roof. My cut hand and broken finger flared under the recoil.

The heads all pulled back outside and shouting commenced.

"Go," I said.

Sarah looked at me dumbly.

"The tunnel," I said. "Go."

"Why?"

"To get away."

"There's no boat," she said.

More flawless logic. Where was she when I needed a clear, uncluttered brain? Oh yeah, imprisoned by these guys.

The sniper's head came back out. "Is he dead? Our guy?"

"No," I said. "I'm the goodie, remember? You're the baddies."

They returned fire and I hunched back down. My eardrums stung from the noise—so much louder than outdoors. I made a mental list of who we were up against: the Goon—Kowng—of course; outside help in the form of a sniper; Eel Guy, who wouldn't wake up for a while; then the other two mini-Goons.

Four left.

I said, "Stay this side of me."

I squeezed off a couple more rounds without aiming. The recoil nearly made me drop the gun, but the people disappeared again. We ran to the side, into shadows. Bullets gouged into the rock all around us before we made cover.

"Light," Sarah said.

A tiny point an indeterminable distance into the cave. It looked like the passage quickly got smaller. The light source could be the width of a grapefruit or big enough to drive a bus through, I couldn't tell.

A rope dropped through one of the holes in the roof and a coil landed on the floor; plenty down which to rappel, but I'd be able to pick them off easily.

"No," I said. "We'll take them here."

The first of the mini-Goons descended. I aimed. My hands shook. This guy on the rope, I had no idea who he was. He might've believed *I* was the bad guy.

I pushed those thoughts away and pulled the trigger. The gun bucked against my shoulder, my hearing in one ear numbed, and my shot cannoned into the dark.

"Not as easy as it looks is it?" the sniper said.

I fired again. Missed.

The sniper laughed. "I'm guessin' you ain't fired a gun before Paris. Here."

A volley of gunfire battered the rock and I covered up with my hands. I managed to peek around and the mini-Goon was already halfway down. I fired blindly again, which was met with more laughter. That made me fire up at the sniper, who mockingly pushed his head and shoulders further into the gap.

He said, "Come on, buddy, you can do it."

I fired again. Not even close.

Sarah said, "Adam?"

The sniper's arm came around and a handgun fired. "Like that," he said.

Sarah said, "Adam."

"*What?*"

"Me," said Kwong.

I turned slowly. Kwong held a snub-nose machinegun on me one-handed, a large handgun on Sarah. He was in arm's reach. All I had to do was rush him. But his other hand was a problem. A bullet would pop through Sarah's head at a single flick of that trigger.

I held the machinegun to one side.

The sniper called, "You got him?"

"Yes," Kwong said.

The mini-Goon landed and his friend also slid down the rope, followed by the sniper. One at a time, they sauntered over. I stood beside Sarah, under Kwong's gun.

He said, "You bring no money?"

I shook my head. "I have money. I just don't like to spend it if I don't have to."

"He's bluffing," the Sniper said. "Our friends in Europe say his accounts are frozen and the boys in the jungle took everything he had. Kill him. Let's get the girl back to the house."

"Do not give me orders," Kwong said.

The greying sniper held up his hands up in a sarcastic surrender.

Kwong said, "Take girl away," and the two mini-Goons came for her.

One of them went behind Kwong to get to Sarah, but the other passed in front of the gun. In that split-second, I did not think; I somehow assessed the situation, and simply acted.

I shoved the mini-Goon into Kwong himself, bundling them both over. The other mini-Goon swung a gun my way. I redirected the barrel to my left where the sniper was raising his handgun. The gun spat fire and the hammer rattled on full auto, flaying the sniper's chest into red mush.

The second man I killed in two days.

I rammed my elbow into the mini-Goon's throat and kicked the side of his head as hard as I could. He was out of it.

Kwong pushed his subordinate off him and I aimed the acquired gun.

I said, "I don't think I'll miss from here."

Kwong relinquished his weapons. Sarah picked them up. The final mini-Goon's too. Three machineguns and a handgun.

"He came from down there." I indicated the light Sarah spotted. "Let's go." When she didn't move, I said, "What are you waiting for?"

She said, "To shoot them."

"We don't do that. We're the *good* guys."

"But they will kill us," she said.

"They won't. That's the only way out of here, unless they can monkey-climb that rope."

"What if they do?"

"Then we'll deal with them."

"No," Sarah said. "Kill them now."

Mission mode.

Logic.

Survival.

Shoot them dead, and we live for certain.

"Why won't you kill them?" she asked.

"Because they're unarmed."

"That doesn't make sense. I told you what they did. It was wrong to make me have sex. They shouldn't have told me it was my job. It wasn't my job. We should kill them, or they will make me do that job again."

She hadn't compartmentalized as much as I thought. It was a normal reaction. A victim, yearning to feel safe. Some might call it revenge, but for victims of sex crimes, it was logical; a necessary step in order to be free.

"When I was a lot younger," I said, "I was in a situation. I was asking questions in Bangkok of men who didn't want to answer them. When I made trouble for them, I was taken somewhere, and three men beat me. I promised them I'd stop asking questions. I meant it too. Just being in that room. No escape, no choice. But they carried on. Even when I begged."

"It isn't the same thing," she said. "They gave me a job, forced me to—"

I shouted, "*It is the same thing.*" My voice echoed through the silence, Goon and mini-Goon watching, kneeling, hands on their heads. Quietly, I said, "It was the same thing."

She shook her head, her lip out. Not stroppy; more confused.

I said, "They cut off my clothes. In between beatings they took turns with me. From behind. I bled. I was forced to … have them in my mouth too. They held my jaw shut and made me swallow. When they were all done with me, they beat me some more. Then they left me on a beach."

I had never told that part of the story to anyone. Not even Harry or Jayne. And no, I was not blind to the fact that this may have influenced my affinity with those in need of rescue. It started as a personal form of revenge, but mutated slowly into empathy. Okay, occasionally it delved into sanctimonious moralizing, dragging me into that superiority zone that Harry so often cautioned against.

But we are the sum of our experiences.

I came to know victims of rape and violence through my work, and while I thought I was helping them, in reality *they* were helping *me*. The reason I eased off my training was partly Harry's warning about me truly hurting someone one day, but also because I made a choice. I would not let those men in Thailand define me. Because that's what women did all the time; they found the strength to carry on.

"We're done with them," I said.

Sarah said, "Okay," and wandered off into the dark.

Chapter Forty-Eight

The gap out into daylight would have granted access to a horse. It was angled backwards so it was clear from the outside but not the interior. The path Kwong had taken was obvious, a beaten-out furrow in the shrubs and waist-high grass skirting the side of the gentle rise, over which we saw the inlet where they moored the launch. They had strapped a ladder to a gnarled, old tree branch on the upper section of the island. We were almost to the tree when I heard a sound like a buffalo hurtling through the brush.

Kwong landed a shoulder in my chest and slapped the machinegun from my hand. So monkey-climbing ropes was part of his skillset.

I rolled with it and sprang up. A fist like a hammer slammed into my face. Nothing broke, but stars burst and the world went sideways. He fell on top of me and we grappled like wrestlers until I levered my head back and smashed it into his nose. It crumpled and, for the first time, his sunglasses finally fell off. I pushed him away and rolled up onto my feet. Still dizzy, but just about with it. We exchanged a series of blows, each blocking the other a dozen times. He was tough but slow. I was disorientated, unable to focus properly.

Sarah picked up the gun. Kwong hadn't seen it yet.

I allowed him in closer. It made him over-confident. I stepped inside, locked his arm for leverage, then spun him over my hip into Sarah's line of fire.

"Now!" I said.

She didn't do anything. I looked again, and the mini-Goon had snuck up, grabbed her from behind, and hit her head against a rock. It drew blood. Still conscious, she threw the gun my way. It slid over the side and down toward the sea. The mini-Goon acquired the other firearms Sarah was carrying.

I froze. Released Kwong.

He gave an order, and the guy holding Sarah pointed. She got on the ladder and, without even looking my way, she climbed down it, her precious bag still held in one hand. The mini-Goon followed.

The six-inch knife was already in my hand.

Kwong said, "When we get back to house, she is reward for ending you. Mine. Mr. Dinh is very generous."

I went for him. He barely flinched. He evaded the blade and blocked any misdirection I attempted. His foot glanced against my knee and I stumbled, dropping the knife. He punched me in the jaw and I couldn't stay upright.

As I lay there, he searched the ground. Found my knife. He grinned. He'd also found his sunglasses and folded them and put them in his pocket. He advanced on me. I crawled to the cliff edge. Below, Sarah climbed into the boat with the mini-Goon.

Then I saw the machinegun knocked from Sarah's hands. It was six feet below, nestled on a tuft of mud and sticks. A bird's nest. Too far away.

Kwong reached for me.

I pitched over the side. Landed on a ledge but no closer to the gun.

Kwong saw what I was planning. He swore in Vietnamese.

I crawled further forward and leaned right over.

Kwong slid down the ladder like a fireman.

My fingers touched the gun.

He leapt onto the launch, pushed Sarah to one side and crouched beside a cupboard.

Further still, and I was almost there. Almost.

Kwong took out a rifle and slapped home a magazine.

"Fuck it." I shoved myself forward. My stomach lurched as I dropped. I grabbed the gun. Scrabbled at the limestone cliff as I plummeted toward the sea. I bounced off the side. Somersaulted involuntarily. I landed hard on the flat rock they used to steady their ladder. The pain in my ribs forbade instant movement, but it was close enough as I found my feet.

Everything hurt: my finger, my hand, my ear, my face, my ribs, my knee.

The Goon's rifle was bolt action and he'd only just slid it back. He clicked it home.

I opened fire. Full-auto. So close a blind man could not have missed.

Kwong crumpled in a bloody heap. I turned it on the mini-Goon and he dropped as soon as the first volley hit him. Then back to Kwong for the final time, filling him with holes. I felt nothing but the recoil of the *ratatatatat* as death spewed forth, concentrating only on controlling the vibrating weapon, until the magazine clicked empty and my ears rang in the silence.

The two men lay there. Two corpses. Nothing but bloodied slabs of meat, tenderized and slaughtered out of necessity.

I stepped onto the boat, and without even noticing my ribs, I rolled Kwong's corpse and tipped him over the side. I did the same with the other guy. It was only when Sarah came and hugged me in a rather mechanical way—another learned reaction—that I felt the damage inflicted upon my bones and muscle.

I started up the motor. I was tempted for a moment to head back to find the yacht, but I didn't chance it.

Keep yer eye on the prize.

I headed on a bearing that I assumed was shore, and accelerated towards dry land as fast as I dared.

Chapter Forty-Nine

Dry land was a beach. My orientation was way off and, without the GPS, we had no sense of location. I estimated we kept going for two hours. Peopled littered the beach, a couple of kayaks topping the waves, so I guessed civilization was close by. Besides, fuel was low. Vietnamese families stared in wonder as we hobbled and lurched out of the swish, blood-smeared motor launch. My knee wasn't badly hurt, but my ribs and my hand gave me real trouble. I looked like a hunchback as I hobbled up the sand and onto a rural road that led into a town about a mile away. It took us another hour to get there on foot.

As we traipsed along, I told Sarah all of it. Start to finish. Well, most of it. Caroline hiring me. Curtis Benson hijacking my case. Lily and her escape. Vila Fanuco and Henrietta Dupree and Pierre Bertrand. I told her how I found the slave sale in the jungle, and I did not sugarcoat what Gareth had done.

"That makes sense," she said. "I'm very upset with him." She then told me in detail how every step I'd taken mimicked her and Gareth.

He persuaded her to open the safe as a sort of game. When she objected to stealing the money, Gareth proposed on one knee and convinced her to come with him to Paris. He spent a lot of time away from her, and told Sarah to make friends, look "normal." Gareth introduced her to Kwong on their fifth night and he took photos of her and sent them somewhere. Gareth told her they were for the IDs, but it seemed to me they were also for evaluation purposes. Kwong paid for their flights and they travelled first class to Saigon where they had to find their own hotel but still had a lovely time. Until Giang took them to the strange men in The Rex. She woke up in a hot cell full of other people. She was allowed to draw and paint, but she didn't stay there long, as Kwong showed up and took her away, and delivered her to Vuong Dinh who told her about her new job. She still didn't understand why Gareth ran out on her.

When I revealed he had been killed in a dispute over money, she simply asked me what we were going to do about Vuong Dinh. We would do nothing except tell the British consulate, and they would work with the Vietnamese, although if we knew the nationality of the other people in that jungle prison, we could advise those countries to add their weight. There were two Russians, but beyond that I wasn't sure.

She said her suitcase was on board the yacht, so I entertained the possibility that they believed there was a chance I'd deliver the million dollars, but the sniper's presence indicated the likelihood was slim. If non-existent is "slim."

Eventually, she let me have her bag.

I fished out one of the USB sticks. "They're all the same?"

"I don't know," she said. "Gareth bought them in the airport before we left for Paris."

"And you held onto them?"

"Yes. He asked me to."

I took out all the drives and gave her back the shoes. She tossed them in the first bin we came to.

The town boasted a small medical center rather than a hospital. It was quiet, hot and stuffy, and the triage unit resembled a worn-out council office. There were three people with large but seemingly non-urgent cuts and a young boy cradling his elbow, his mother fretting on a mobile. Body odor and disinfectant mingled without quite masking each other. When it was our turn, the doctor—a sixty-ish woman with grey hair who spoke passable English—saw that I was the most hurt, but I insisted she see Sarah first. While the examination took place, I noticed an ancient-looking computer through the door of an unmanned office. Nobody saw me hobble in.

The computer was active, with no password lock. *Windows 95*.

I logged-on to the super-slow internet and brought up the British consulate in Hanoi. I spent ten minutes trying to get through on the office phone and eventually spoke to a low-level administrator. I gave a brief outline, that Sarah Stiles, missing from the UK for over a month, was kidnapped and that I had freed her. I gave my real name and told the skeptical chap to look both of us up, then come get us.

"Do not use the local police," I said.

After I hung up, I placed the pen drives—six of them—on the desk and found the PC's USB slot and inserted the first stick. The windows explorer box popped up but the drive was gobbledygook. Although the operating system was ancient, I didn't think it was hampering the file. I took it out and tried the next one. Nothing. The fourth yielded a result. It asked for a password. I tried "Benson" and "Curtis" and "Blazing" and "Seas" and even "Password," but I suppose it would be more creative than that.

Instead, I felt in my pockets and was pleasantly surprised to find the only thing that survived the journey was my international phone card. I called Jess. While the phone rang, I logged onto a server only Jess and I knew of, and clicked-and-dragged the USB icon across. It wouldn't decrypt but it would copy everything verbatim. The slow connection didn't even register one percent by the time Jess picked up.

I told her not to speak, just check out "the server." Then I asked her for Curtis Benson's number. I lost my phone, I said, but didn't elaborate. Her own voice caught as she spoke. She clearly wanted to ask why I sounded like death, but it must have been close to Benson's deadline. Perhaps a little past it. I was so disorientated I couldn't even think about that. It was two p.m. now, so it would be seven a.m. there. I'd either missed it by a margin or killed it by a whole day. When Jess relayed the number, I disconnected and called the man himself.

He said, "You got good news for me?"

"Yes. I have your drive."

"You got my money? You got my employees?"

"You don't need any of that," I said. "You know it and I know it. I have the USB drive with whatever data you lost. That's the real endgame here, isn't it?"

"You so smart, Mr. Detective. Listen." Silence. Then a scrabbling noise. Then a man groaned. "Speak."

"Adam?" It was Harry. Voice hoarse. "Adam, is that you?"

Five percent.

"Are you okay?" I asked.

Benson said, "He's fine. Where you at? I'll send someone."

I almost laughed. "I'm still out of the country."

"You got about sixteen hours to get back here, then. With my money. With my burglar-girl, and her dumb-ass boyfriend."

"And the USB drive?"

"Yeah, and anythin' else they took."

Eight percent.

"Can we stop pretending?" I said. "This is what you need, why you were so desperate to get them back. Let Harry go. I'll be there as soon as I can. I might have to Fed-Ex this, but you'll get it. Besides, Gareth is dead. You can verify it, I'm sure. The Saigon police—"

I heard a metallic *click-clack* on the other end.

Benson said, "That was a Beretta. Nine millimeter. You know what that does?"

"I know what it does."

"It's aimed at the old fucker's head. 'Less you can give me some guarantee you'll be back by midnight with everythin' I asked for, I'm killin' him now and takin' that blonde computer geek a' yours. And she dies tomorrow. Same time. You ain't back then, I take someone else."

"Please, give me one more day. Don't kill him. It won't change anything."

"It'll make you understand when I give you a fuckin' deadline, you meet the fuckin' deadline."

Harry grunted. Muffled, Benson told him to kneel and stop mewlin'. I yelled at him to stop, but he wouldn't answer. It was the end for Harry. I had nothing, except twelve percent of an encrypted file.

Twelve percent of a file I knew held the key to all the secrets, all the lies.

A large, firm hand folded around the back of my head and slowly pushed my face onto the desk with a strength I could not fight against. The other hand relieved me of the phone and a familiar voice spoke calmly and loudly.

"Mr. Benson, do not shoot that man."

A pause, and evidently Benson came on the phone.

The person holding me down said, "Good. Adam is correct, is he not? The file is all you need?" A pause. "I do not care. I can verify the item." Argumentative noises in the earpiece. "If you harm the man without due cause, I will destroy you. Understood?"

It clearly *was* understood, because the man replaced the handset and let me sit up. He pulled the USB drive out of the computer and the file transfer was abandoned at eighteen percent.

"Hello, Adam," said Vila Fanuco. "You've had an interesting couple of days."

Chapter Fifty

Back in the waiting room, Fanuco presented my rucksack to me. I asked how he knew where I was, where my bag could be found. He said he had people watching Vuong Dinh's yacht following chatter picked up on his home line. Then he showed me a custom-made tablet computer with a map and a red dot over the medical center.

He said, "They made her swallow a beacon. She didn't tell you?"

That answered a number of other questions too. Like how they could track us in open water and through the cave system.

I said, "She wouldn't have told me if I didn't ask."

"She will shit it out in a day or so. But now I have to decide what to do. She is someone else's property."

"She's a person."

"Bought and paid for."

"By your competitors." I handed back the tablet. "What do you care?"

"They are no longer our competitors." He smiled. That illusion of too many teeth again. "The events in Paris granted us a ... merger of sorts. That is to say, they are willing to surrender the territory in Europe if they can participate in our network."

"So you're here, what, inspecting them?"

"A consultant, you might say. Their holding camps are crude but effective, as you can attest. You know, the boys at the one you visited, they laughed all day after you killed that police officer." I shushed him and he waved me off. "No one will listen to this. And I certainly do not hold it against you. I told you, didn't I? You are a dark reflection of people like me. I saw in you the ability to kill."

I felt something sink inside me. "It was you, wasn't it?"

"Me?"

"On the phone. The guy who ordered me to kill Giang."

Fanuco rubbed his chin, a proud grin creaking through. "You should be thanking me."

"Thanking you?"

"If I had not prepared you with Major Giang, do you really think you would have been able to survive out there?" His face came close to mine, his breath hot. "How many did you kill?"

"Four," I said.

"I heard five."

"Sarah killed one of them."

"Ah, yes, we come back to the girl."

I shifted in my seat. Pain flared in my ribs. "She's going home," I said. "She'll be leaving with whoever the British Ambassador sends to collect her. You don't have connections that deep, I assume."

He sighed. "You assume correctly."

"I'll be arrested as an illegal immigrant. Maybe the consulate will get me freed, maybe not. But whatever happens, they already have Vuong Dinh's name." I hoped for some tell in Fanuco's expression but no anger or annoyance broke through. I said, "Secrecy is paramount to your operation. That's the reason you guys used me to retrieve the data. Why Benson dressed it up as something else. Because if he had a detective hunting down a memory-stick, it might draw attention from the law. But wanting revenge for a robbery is mundane day-to-day stuff for a sleazy strip-club gangsta. Can't have MI5 knowing there's evidence out there pointing at a world-wide club for smugglers. *Right?*"

He gave nothing away.

I said, "Vuong Dinh's name will be all over the place. The British won't let it lie. The kidnapping, forced labor, and sexual assault of one of their nationals. It will make the news, and they will pressure the People's Security Service to investigate."

Fanuco tapped the pen-drive thoughtfully on his chin.

I said, "You could kill me and take Sarah, I know that. But isn't Vuong Dinh a liability now he's out in the open?"

He brought his face so close I could smell garlic and chili on his breath. "I am actually allowing the Vietnamese security service to track down and close many outlets that I do not consider secure. In exchange for certain … permissions for legitimate businesses being fast-tracked. I have not yet decided about Mr. Dinh."

A thought occurred. "The girl Sammy LeHavre gave to them in Paris, they said she was your favorite. What was her name?"

"Marie," he said.

"Vuong Dinh has her at his place. Or he did when I was last there."

Fanuco patted me on the shoulder, a happy gesture. "Well then, that is settled. Vuong Dinh *was* a valuable client. He will be an equally-fine sacrifice."

I nodded, actually feeling something good for a change.

"And you, Adam. Like in Paris, you will be the hero of this piece." Fanuco gently squeezed my leg. "Work for us."

"For you?"

"*Us*. A resource. Investigative services. For when things go wrong. Like data removed from a trusted location." He winked. He actually *winked* at me. "We could take care of Roger Gorman for you, without hurting him of course, and put you back on your throne. Where you belong."

I ignored the offer, mainly because I was so tempted by it. "I'm surprised you don't simply kill Curtis Benson, all the trouble he caused."

"We are not the mafia," he said. "We do not go around 'whacking' people for misdemeanors. We help one another stay alive and out of jail. Mr. Benson helps many of us, independently. If we need an outlet for more cargo, or if we have excessive money to launder."

I could have pointed out Benson's monthly packages to the Caribbean. Might have changed Fanuco's mind about "whacking" him. Although Mikey might have an objection to his boss being offed by a foreign business associate, and blame me.

I said, "So he's basically an outsourcing center."

"In this case, yes. Occasionally, with lowlife people like him, there are mistakes. You, Adam, could help us rectify those mistakes."

"You deal in misery and death and—"

"You feel no guilt now, but unless you commit to your true self, those deaths will eat at you forever." His voice softened. "No matter how much good you think you are doing."

"I don't need it."

"They will revisit you in your sleep." His voice remained quiet, his gaze distant. "Trust me. They will."

"I've slept fine," I said. "When I kill one of you, it isn't taking a human life. It's saving dozens."

Vila Fanuco took back his hand and stood. Coughed the catch out of his throat. "I respect that opinion, of course." He glanced to the door where two Vietnamese men with guns in shoulder holsters had arrived without my noticing. He said, "You will answer these men's questions. You will do so honestly, without mentioning my name. Then you will be lost in the communist paperwork system, and allowed to go home on your real passport. Once I have verified the contents of this pen-drive and ensured no copies have been made, you will return it to Curtis Benson by midnight on Saturday—your new deadline."

A rush of gratitude flooded my chest, then I instantly felt a terrible, crushing guilt about its source. An evil man was doing me a favor, keeping me out of jail, sending me home, saving my friend's life.

I said, "What about the French?"

"The government came to an agreement with your company's lawyers, although the decision is more to do with the public. Pierre Bertrand issued a statement that he forgave your actions in kidnapping him, although he is still pursuing *moi*, of course. Whether you want to be or not, you are the hero out there. Your name is censored for now. Human rights, you see. But it will come out eventually. "*Investigateur Angleterre*," they call you now."

Detective England. It had a nice ring to it.

Sarah stayed with me while my left ear was glued shut and they stitched my hand. The ear would forever be missing a nip of half-moon from the top but I could probably get it sorted with surgery. They reset my little finger yet again and gave me an injection while they bandaged my ribs and issued a small bottle of prescription painkillers for a week. I was not looking forward to the flight home. I changed into clean clothes from my rucksack and asked to use the office again.

In all the rush, the one person I hadn't called was Caroline. I let Sarah do that. I could hear the squeal of delight in the earpiece, and Sarah even smiled in a genuinely happy way. The men with guns waited patiently. When the lawyer from the consulate arrived, he brought with him a serious-looking woman in a suit way too hot for a Vietnamese afternoon: the British Ambassador herself. She thanked me coolly, and although she assured me that Sarah would be afforded every privilege associated with being a diplomatic guest, I got the impression she was not happy about my departure with the security service guys.

My goodbye with Sarah was perfunctory. A robotic hug, then the uniformed men handcuffed me and led me out.

My interrogation took place on the way to the airport, a voice recorder capturing all. I avoided mention of meeting Major Giang, but other than that omission, I told them everything, including the shootings on Ha Long Bay. They would already know about the market incident, I thought, so leaving that out could have caused delays. Plus, Fanuco said he already struck a deal with them, and if he was confident they would stick to it, I would happily defer to his judgment.

They escorted me to the airport's check-in, where a ticket waited. I would be flown to Bangkok again, then on to Dubai, and then Amsterdam and—finally—Leeds/Bradford Airport. I wouldn't have to go through London. Or Paris. If all went well, I'd arrive at ten a.m. local time.

I dropped a painkiller at the bar, chased with a cool American beer, and the chemical washed through me. Even my broken finger numbed. Jess had wired me a couple of hundred quid, which I was now able to collect. The first thing I bought was three Vietnamese drip-coffee kits, as if I was returning from holiday with souvenirs.

I finished the beer and slipped off the stool, and found Vila Fanuco sat in the corner. I approached and he held out the USB drive. I didn't take it.

He said, "Looks like Mr. Delingpole tried to copy this before he was killed, but the copy destroys itself on replication."

I took the drive. "Clever-clogs, that Curtis Benson."

"So, if you managed to get the copy to your lady-friend, it would have been unreadable."

"I had to try, you understand."

"I do," he said. "But if you try again, there is now an alarm built in. As soon as you go online with the copy, it will tell me. And I will find you. And I will kill you. Understand?"

"Sure."

"You sound casual."

"Because I have no intention of copying it. I get this to Curtis Benson, Harry goes free. End of story."

"Thank you, Adam. It has been a many years since anyone trusted me like this."

I thought about that, and about some idle research I conducted online in a quiet moment between buying my drip coffee kits and hitting the bar.

I said, "Vila Fanuco. That's the name you chose."

"Yes," he said. "I chose it."

"Fanuco. It's completely made up. No meanings anywhere."

He hesitated. "It has meaning."

I nodded. "I guessed it had meaning *to you*. But not in my Google search. Something to do with your family?"

His lips pressed into a line. "My children. Be careful where you go with this."

"Okay. I'm sorry." My finger still ached from the last time I pushed him. "Vila," I said. "It sounds Spanish or South American. But in Czech it means 'to protect'."

He stared at nothing. "It means 'to *desire* to protect'. To *aspire* to be a protector."

Whatever this man once was, *who*-ever he was, that person was not sitting beside me now. That man was dead. This one—who broke my finger and killed God knows how many—he was all that remained.

He said, "My warning to Mr. Benson only protects your friend regarding this data stick. If you have other business with him, it is no concern of mine."

"That's it? As long as I don't piss him off any further, you're all out of my life forever?"

"Yes. It is that simple. Bon Voyage, *Investigateur Angleterre.*"

It all seemed pleasant enough as I left him there, waving, smiling, sending off a friend on holiday. Perhaps he was satisfied at my promise to cooperate fully. I could not tell one way or the other if he knew that I was lying my arse off.

UNITED KINGDOM

Chapter Fifty-One

I landed at Leeds-Bradford Airport a few hours earlier than Fanuco intended. He'd planned the route based on the longest stopovers to minimize the risk of my missing connecting flights, but I switched the route to a riskier but faster one. It was overcast at five a.m. but refreshingly cool.

At Bangkok airport, I thought a courtesy call to Curtis Benson would ease my anxiety at Harry being held yet another night, but he said, "You wanted to stop bullshitting, so stop it. Bring me the things I told you to bring, or I gut your bitch."

"I have one item," I said. "The one you need."

He went on a rant about how he'd fuck me up, kill my friends, et cetera, et cetera, but I was woozy from the painkillers and another beer, so it washed over me. Finally, he said, "I want *everything* I asked for. The guy's dead, fine. But I want the girl, and I want anythin' else she's got with her—*anything*, even if you think it ain't what I want. Bring it all, or bring a mop and a shovel, 'cause that's how you'll be takin' the old bastard home."

I tried to remind him about Fanuco's deal, but he hung up. I hoped it was a futile gesture on his part, because even if Fanuco had been serious about "destroying" Benson, it would only be an act of vengeance. It wouldn't save Harry.

I called the one person I could think of.

"What have you done now?" Jayne said.

"It's not me," I said. "I will get him back. No matter what, Jayne. I'll get Harry back."

"Tell me what to do."

So I told her to dig out Harry's contact book, which I knew would be a literal book rather than electronic. I told her who to look for, and what I needed. It was an absolute punt, what sports fans might call a "Hail-Mary" play, but I needed to know for sure.

Jess switched my flights online and although I experienced a squeaky-bum time-window in Paris, the connecting flight got me to Leeds-Bradford at four a.m., and I collected my pack by five. In arrivals, Jess and Jayne waited. Caroline would have been there to greet me too, Jayne said, but she departed in the opposite direction to support Sarah while she helped the Vietnamese with their pursuit of Vuong Dinh. I still intended to return there myself, regardless of Fanuco's warnings, and destroy the camp where I found the boy, and which traded Sarah into bondage.

I had other friends I could call on, but it didn't seem fair. I would keep this tight.

The pair looked tired, especially Jayne, who understandably seemed older than when I left. Jess hugged me and took in my appearance—the bruised face, the bandages—and faked ambivalence. Jayne stood there, watching, wrapped in her multicolored knitted cardigan.

She said, "So."

"I have the item." I showed them the pen drive.

"But not the girl. He wants her for some reason."

"He might just be being thorough, or he might just want her gone. Make sure she doesn't say anything to harm whatever he has going on. I just don't know right now."

"You can't simply hand that over."

I pocketed the USB stick. "I'll exchange what I have for Harry."

"And then what?" she said. "You think I'm going to let you flounce on in with no advantage?"

"What's the alternative?" I said.

She put her hands in her pockets and turned toward the exit. "Harry wouldn't want you getting killed in such a stupid way. Let's go to work."

Jayne drove us to my apartment in Harry's ancient Land Rover. On the way, I gave them the outline, the bare highlights, including the shootings in Ha Long Bay, although once again, I omitted the detail of Major Giang. Not that I was ashamed; he deserved much worse, but … there was something nagging at me. I still felt that pressure on the trigger. My inability to say "no."

It wasn't *guilt* as such, but I'd work it out in time.

Inside my apartment, Jess took out her laptop, plugged in a wireless dongle, and said, "I'm still officially on suspension from PAI but I managed to send those MI5 bugs on a wild goose chase through an automated server sequence. I used this cloned 4G connection to keep working on Curtis Benson."

She then treated me to a run-down of all she discovered over the past day-and-a-half. She demonstrated the path used to track Benson's packages—the spreadsheets, the ghost-manifests, the different signatures in the same hand—and eventually revealed their final destination. Not quite what I'd been expecting, but all good stuff.

Just not enough to secure Harry's release by itself.

She removed the 4G dongle and, offline, she examined the pen-drive that Fanuco warned me not to copy, which she didn't. But she did try to open it.

"It's too much," she said after ten minutes. "I definitely can't copy it. I can't even break this encryption without an algorithm a million miles long, and even then not in a day. Sorry."

Meaning we couldn't even take a screenshot of each page and

keep it as collateral. Which left us with Harry's contact in the West Yorkshire Police.

"*Retired* contact," Jayne said. "Which means he was calling in fa vors to get this. Expensive favors, so when you get your mountain of gold back, I'm sending you a bill."

She presented us with CCTV stills obtained via two blind contacts, and also a copy of a plane ticket. I looked at them carefully, and everything shifted.

I mean *everything*. I checked and re-checked the date-stamp and examined the photo carefully. It was impossible.

Well, im*probable*.

The ticket was in the name of James Pickering, not someone I'd come across before. But it was a two-stop deal, landing in Heathrow on Thursday morning. Yesterday. It originated in Bangkok. The CCTV stills, though, were what really set me on edge.

Walking into the United Kingdom via Heathrow's arrivals lounge was none other than Agent Frank of MI5. No luggage, a hoodie and jeans, but there was no mistaking his doughy physique and square head. He'd been the guy watching me in The Rex. He'd followed me all the way. He was willing to trail around the world to find that USB stick, and on a fake passport to boot. Something was very wrong with that.

"What does it mean?" Jess asked.

"It means things are more complicated than I thought." I was tired from the flight, and I ached all over. I dropped a painkiller and rubbed my head.

Jayne said, "You thinking hard there? Because I really need you to have a plan. Harry's dead in sixteen hours."

"I'm thinking hard," I said.

"Don't you get flippant."

"I'm not being flippant. I'm thinking."

"You did this—"

"HARRY BROUGHT ME INTO IT!" I was stood face-to-face with the older woman. I lowered my voice. "I was happy out there, surfing, jumping out of planes, rock climbing..."

"Hiding from the world."

"Maybe. But I was happy. Isolated from all this shit."

"A real renaissance man," she said, turning away. "A travelling man. A man with no home to speak of."

"I can make my home anywhere."

"Anyplace but where it matters," she said. "Where it counts."

"Jayne," Jess said.

"No," Jayne said. "It's true. All this being 'in the moment' or whatever he calls it, he doesn't think. Just acts. Adam ... Harry taught you to keep your head. Stay away from the rough stuff. You shouldn't be bandaged up like the mummy's curse. Shooting people in the middle of the ocean ... while my Harry is held who knows where."

I said, "I just stopped running away."

She slumped in a chair and buried her face in her hands while Jess hugged her. She didn't cry.

Jess said, "Okay, can I make anyone a tea?"

I thought about the drip coffee kits and felt even sillier than when I bought them. I declined the tea. We weren't going to get any further like this. I had come up with a last-resort idea on the various planes, and those photos of Agent Frank allowed an actual *plan* of sorts to glimmer to life. It worked well enough in theory, and even then only if my newly-birthed guesswork was correct.

Unfortunately, it meant placing a call Roger Bloody Gorman to schedule another meeting.

Chapter Fifty-Two

When I entered Roger Gorman's office, Jess waited outside. Roger was seated behind his desk in a shinier suit than usual and his big pasted-on smile dulled the room down no end. He offered his hand but I relegated him to the same corner of my life in which Sleazy Stu resided. He didn't leave it hanging the way Stu did.

"Well, that's gratitude," he said. "Our lawyers get your charges dismissed and—"

"My funds are still frozen."

He waved that off. "A technicality, I'm sure. They are frozen for the police investigation. Nothing to worry about if you have nothing to hide."

"Who's investigating me?"

"Oh, I think it's the Serious Fraud Squad or some such. It's more to do with your unofficial use of company assets, which may—probably not—result in embezzlement charges."

"The Deep Detect System," I said. "That's why you got Jess out of the building. So you could wipe any trace of it from the system in case the authorities want to poke around."

"Smart fella." His smile was genuine this time. Smug rather than warm.

"Temporarily, I assume?"

"Better not to have that thing on the company servers at all. Don't you think it would be advantageous to outsource the running of such software? Somewhere with no extradition?"

"So you finally trusted a source outside the UK?"

"Reluctantly, yes. Perhaps you'd like to move out there and man the department for us."

"It's okay," I said. "I have a better deal for you."

"Really? Seems to me that, right now, you have absolutely fuck-all to offer." The smile shone, and it was the first time I'd ever heard him use the word "fuck." It made me want to punch him. He said, "The psychological evaluation will show erratic, irrational behavior, your current injuries suggest violent tendencies, and your actions in running around with company equipment prove you are mentally-incompetent to hold any power of attorney."

"And you keep on paying me fifty-one percent share of the profits."

"Huge profits, Adam. With your authority gone, I don't have your misguided hippie conscience weighing us down. It's just a matter of time until I force a buyout."

"Right," I said. "And yet, when the fraud charges against me are dropped and I get my own lawyers and psychologists to challenge your findings? You know your play is tenuous."

"It's not water-tight, but I'll find a way. You don't have the stomach to take me on, Adam. We both know that."

"Maybe we don't have to go through years of this. What if we both come out on top?"

I placed a manila file on his desk with several sheets of A4 within. I'd prepared them before coming here, which ate up more time than I wanted to spare.

Gorman speed-read it. "Is this real?"

"Bring in the lawyers. But make it quick. You have thirty minutes to decide. I'm on a pretty tight deadline." It was already eleven a.m. Thirteen hours.

He made a call and within seconds four dour men in suits joined him, taking turns to examine the document. Nods aplenty followed, and a need to draw up a preliminary agreement mooted and the most junior of the four dour men departed to prepare it.

I said, "Just so we are clear: I take full charge of this company until midnight tonight. I get a free run of all PAI's systems and clientele. You cooperate fully, no matter what I ask. If I need help from someone you shouldn't be in business with, you will still provide it. Everything you tell me is confidential. I cannot reveal it without surrendering all my liquid assets back to you as a penalty. You. Do. Not. Question. Me. You just do it. Okay?"

"Okay," he said, still stunned by my offer.

"In return, you buy out my share of the business for twenty-two million pounds sterling, around half what it would be worth if you go the forced route, not including any legal fees or bribes to dodgy psychiatrists. This is not a negotiable amount. Okay?"

"Okay. It's … a surprisingly … good deal. Why are you doing this now?"

"I said don't ask questions. The price is up to twenty-*five* million. You got that?"

The dour lawyers all nodded and made notes.

"Twenty-five million. You pay that and use whatever contacts you have to get the fraud case dropped and my other assets unfrozen."

"Done," he said. "And you relinquish all title and deeds at midnight."

"Under the final condition you change the name of the company and all mention of me from its books, nullifying my non-compete agreement. If you can live with this deal, I can live with it, but I take full control right now. Objections?"

"No." Gorman stood and came round the side of the desk. Gestured to his chair. "It's all yours."

"Jess!" I called.

She entered, curtsied, and said, "Yes, sir?"

I said, "You're no longer suspended."

"Good to know."

"You're fired."

"Thank you," she said, and left the room.

Naturally, there were clauses that forbade me from altering the structure of the company, meaning I couldn't fire Gorman and the rest of the board, then appoint my mates as trustees. I could, however, hire Jess as an outside contractor investigating the movements of a suspicious individual in a blue Ford Mondeo, and who travelled to Saigon to spy on me in The Rex Hotel.

But that was just the jumping-off point for my new hypothesis. Jess called me a nutter and asked if I thought the moon landings were faked too. Yet, to me, with all I'd seen, and Curtis Benson's insistence on my returning more than the USB drive, it was the one thing that made sense. We now had twelve hours to prove it and use Agent Frank against Benson and his little pit-bull.

Park Avenue Investigations employed a team of six full-time investigators, although in truth two of them were covert communications specialists recruited from the Royal Signals whose work rarely saw an official stamp, and never ventured inside a courtroom. They were currently out on a job that I didn't want to know about, and three others were out of town. That left Phyllis Dunleavy as Roger Gorman's representative to approach XenoTrope Security, for whom we did a job a couple of years earlier. She was a lawyer by trade, well presented and greying gracefully. More accustomed to forensic accounting, when I outlined what I required from her today and how her relationship with the XenoTrope board may benefit us, she almost danced a jig.

Jess lifted the block on her own PAI account in minutes and

delved into Benson's financials at a level she could only dream of on a domestic machine.

Meanwhile, I studied the flights in and out of Ho Chi Minh City over the past three weeks. There was no other James Pickering, although I did find Gareth and Sarah's French alter egos with ease. I cross-referenced the names with those arriving back in England on a predetermined set of dates, and entered them into a database that excluded women, couples, families and men older than fifty and younger than thirty. It was over a hundred people.

Phyllis was gone an hour when she called me. "I'm sending you a little prezzie," she said.

When it came, the image confirmed my theory in less than half a gigabyte of pixels.

Phyllis's mission was to utilize technology that XenoTrope, once upon a time, temporarily lost to a disgruntled technician who wanted to sell it to the Chinese, and they recruited PAI to retrieve it. The technology was a piggybacking algorithm, completely legal but highly confidential. They'd been contracted by the government to improve facial recognition software and to that end, XenoTrope was granted free access to all UK airport, seaport, and railway camera systems, something it was felt the general public would be less-than enamored by. Still in its infancy two years ago, it had now improved exponentially. Phyllis's pitch was for them to trail a live subject, one who would be incognito, possibly in disguise.

They picked out Agent Frank on the date that hoodie-Frank appeared, the one that Jayne sourced, and used that as a model to whizz through every face that entered Britain over the past four weeks. It picked up on Agent Frank in a bald-cap and glasses and a passable moustache. He came in via Heathrow ten days ago. But this wasn't the image I was interested in.

It was Agent Frank's companion whose face now occupied the terminal in Roger Gorman's office, and made me wonder if the moon landings really could have been a hoax. He was travelling with none other than Gareth Delingpole.

Three days after his murdered body was supposedly found on a Saigon garbage dump.

Chapter Fifty-Three

Agent Frank obviously got to Vietnam ahead of me and—with far better resources—pinpointed Giang as a bent copper, then rewarded him for his help in faking the photographic evidence by passing on Gareth's credit card. He didn't care if it would lead me to the Major. The death of one suspect sent me after another, while Agent Frank was free to interrogate Gareth alone. His second trip to Vietnam meant either Gareth gave up nothing or Sarah was holding the thing he needed.

I floated one option: "What if Agent Frank is dirty?"

"Okay," Jess said. "MI5. No problem."

I left her to it in a smaller office, while I synched into Xeno-Trope's system to run more facial-recognition scans on the country's infrastructure. Unfortunately, the system wasn't a magic portal. You needed to manually set which systems you wanted to scan, and then input date parameters and the acceptable range of accuracy. While Phyllis remained at XenoTrope working on train stations, bus stations, and law-enforcement, I took the motorways, which yielded nothing. Phyllis snagged Frank in Leeds a number of times, including one with me in frame on the night I sent Lily on her way, and this morning at Leeds-Bradford Airport at eleven-fifteen. Around the time my original flight should have landed.

Only Benson could have tipped him off as to my itinerary.

Jess rushed into Gorman's office. "Gareth's house in Birstall. It's been empty since they ripped off the safe, right?"

"Right."

"They why, ten days ago, did the 'leccy turn back on."

"Electricity?"

"And gas and water." She smiled. "Am I a genius? Come on, you can admit it."

It was seven p.m. I packed a bag of kit I thought I might need, and Jess drove me in Harry's Land Rover. Back at my apartment, Jayne collated all the evidence on Benson and held onto the USB drive. If we were in danger of missing the deadline, she insisted she would deliver the drive herself and explain I was still trying to trace the "other item" that I was now sure was related to Benson's packages to the Caribbean. The USB drive, I figured, showed payments from the nameless network to Benson, the money laundered through his clubs, but it likely showed Agent Frank's back-handers too. Hence his interest.

Two separate threads, wound together.

Jess and I hurtled through the Saturday evening traffic, out to Gareth's street in Birstall. Jess parked on the main road. I handed her Harry's Taser, showed her how to press it into a subject and zap manually. She tested it and seemed scared that I thought she might need it.

"Well," I said, "you told me you wanted to be more than my Felicity Smoat."

"*Smoak*," she said. "DC Comics, Adam. If you're going to take the piss, get it right."

We walked toward the house, the kitbag in my hand. An Asian family at the end of the road was holding a street-party, a wedding or some celebration in which orange scarves waved and music blared, but we didn't need to venture that far. Gareth's house was a large red-bricked terrace, with an external cellar door down a damp staircase. The basement window was caked in grime. Jess tried the door, but it didn't budge.

"Solid," she said.

The music wasn't loud enough to conceal breaking glass, but I'd brought along my trusty roll of gaffer tape. I attached lengths of tape to the panes, took out a hammer. Dull cracks sounded with each swing, but not enough to carry over the party. A firm swipe with the claw end embedded it in the tape, and I pulled out the remaining pane. I repeated that with the other three and kicked in the squares of wood that once connected them. I shone a light inside.

Boxes. Four dining room chairs stacked. An old bedframe.

"Hello?" I called.

No reply. I folded myself into the window, ribs jolting with each readjustment as I took care not to cut myself. I dropped to the stone floor. More pain. I called again and got the same response.

Jess landed behind me, hands on my shoulders. I asked if she was okay and she bit her lip. Nodded. I found a pull-string and a bare bulb turned on in then musty storage space.

Then I heard a scrape. Jess did too.

"There," she said.

A wall ran along the side of the stairs, and when we found a recess at the far end, it turned out to be a spacious under-stair nook, the sort you'd expect to find firewood stored.

In place of logs, however, lay Gareth Delingpole.

Someone wrapped him in a duvet, tied it with rope, and gagged him. He wriggled like a maggot, eyes bulging. I ripped off the tape.

Gareth said, "I don't care if he's a spy, I don't care! He can't do this to me. He's fuckin' crazy. Come on. Untie me."

"We aren't police," I said, and dragged him out into the open by his feet.

Jess and I stood over him, arms folded across our chests. Gareth blinked a few times until I decided to untie him. He unshelled himself from the duvet and got shakily to his feet wearing only a pair of filthy briefs. He stank of shit and piss.

"Who are you?" he said. "Are you with him? You his bosses? Cos I wanna file a *big* fuckin' complaint."

"You are Gareth Delingpole," I said. "What happened with the guy you came back to England with?"

"Who the fuck *are* you?"

I slammed my forearm into his cheekbone and he staggered to the wall.

I said, "Talk."

He came back towards us and said, "That cunt held me here for two *fucking* weeks. If I didn't tell him anything, I'm not telling you."

I hooked my left fist into Gareth's belly, concealed the little finger's pain as an angry snarl.

I said, "Tell me what you told him."

Gareth wheezed on the floor. "I told him to go fuck himself. Now I'm telling you too."

My next blow was an elbow that demolished his nose. Blood dropped down his front and he lay on his back.

As the blood seeped, he laughed. "You think this shit's gonna work?"

I knelt beside him. "No, Gareth. Not at first. You're a man without feeling. All you know is your own cowardice. Sure, you'll hold out. For a while, anyway. But you'll give in eventually. Thing is, the guy who brought you here, I'm guessing he used those 'non-invasive' techniques. Did he water board you, Gareth?"

Gareth wiped his nose. "And hit me a few times. It don't work."

"No, you've been to prison. You know how to take a beating. And you're a clever bloke, right? Cleverer than anyone believes. Like most sociopaths. And that's what you are, Gareth. A sociopath. You're special, aren't you? You *deserve* to hold power over people, whether it's the women you abuse or authority figures you laugh at because they can't get what they want. That's why Agent Frank's techniques didn't work. You know waterboarding will end eventually. You knew that guy was on a deadline."

"Yeah, he made that mistake. Told me what he was after when he found me. Torture only works if you think it'll go on forever."

"So. He kept you alive here. The duvet stops you freezing at night, but from the smell I'd say he didn't provide a toilet. He keeps coming back to work on you, though. It's something he needs. Something other than the USB stick I got off Sarah this week."

He seemed shocked at her name at first. Then, with bloody teeth, his rat-like stubbornness grinned through. "You're a fuckin' psychic. Congrats."

"No, a man like you will always resist basic pain." I grabbed his wrist and twisted him into a lock that left his arm raised and his face pinned to the floor. Gripped one pinkie. "Say goodbye to this little piggy."

"Like you're gonna do that. Even the spook didn't dare."

"The 'spook' is in danger of being exposed as bent. He couldn't risk hurting you properly. It's more evidence against him."

I applied more pressure to the finger.

"Hey," Jess said. "We didn't discuss this."

"It's necessary," I said. "He won't talk to us without it."

"And what about you? Can you come back from ... *torturing* a man?"

"I can't come back from losing Harry. Not when it was in my power to save him."

"You don't see the hypocrisy?"

It wasn't easy to argue back. But we were running out of time. I said, "Maybe I was wrong all these years."

Gareth laughed and blood and snot bubbled out of his nose. "Good cop, bad cop. Fuck you both."

"Gareth, if we were sat here a week ago I would have just offered you money. That's what you wanted all along. Stealing the USB drive, this 'other item' Curtis wants, selling Sarah. I'm betting I could offer you twenty grand and all this would go away."

"Call it fifty and you got a deal."

"That's what I mean. Greed. You abuse women, you treat them like property, and if I give you money I just encourage you to keep on going. That much cash, it makes you attractive suddenly. Flash it around and a particular sort of woman comes running. You get her under your control and it starts all over again."

"Hey, okay, thirty. I'll take thirty."

"No, Gareth. I'm through pushing money toward the filth of society. My money isn't for the likes of you." I firmed my grip on his pinkie. "Last chance."

"Fuck you," he said again.

It wasn't until I arrived at this moment that I was certain I could go through with it. But every word I spoke to him was the truth. Maybe there was more of a moral grey area inside me than I realized.

To Jess, I said, "I'm sorry."

I twisted the bone and a tiny snap sounded, followed by Gareth's animal-howl. I shoved his face into the duvet to smother it, knelt on his head to keep it there. I'd never done anything like this before, and the motion crept through my hands. But if beating him and waterboarding didn't work, what choice did I have?

Jess looked away, a hand to her mouth.

I said to Gareth, "I don't care about the MI5 guy. Just tell me what Curtis Benson wants. Tell me what you took aside from the USB stick."

I released his head and he screamed, "*Fuck you. I didn't take anything else! I told the guy I'd given what he wants to Sarah, told him she had it, that's all I'm telling you. Fuck you. Fuck you!*"

I kicked his face into the duvet again and snapped his ring finger at the knuckle. Quicker this time. Easier.

I said, "I know Sarah didn't have it. I met her." I closed my hand around his next digit, cracked this sideways too. "I'm taking a hammer your toes when I get done with your hands. It'll end when I run out of ideas, and not before."

"Like I said…" Drool strung from his bottom lip. "Fuck you."

"Damn it." I held out my hand.

Jess hesitated, made a noise like a squeak. Her face remained stone, but her usual honey complexion had paled. She handed me the Taser.

I pressed it into the base of his spine, set it low, let go of his arm, and pressed the button. He danced on his belly as the voltage ripped into his nerve cluster, shooting out through every extremity. After five seconds, I let go. He slumped, no resistance left.

"It's in my locker," he said, gasping. "At my gym. But I didn't steal it. It was mine. I swear. Benson'll pay for it, though. He'll pay." When my expression didn't alter, he said, "Figured I'd give him the stash when the funds cleared."

I zapped the Taser in the air.

"Okay," he said. "I'll take you. Leeds Pride Gym."

"Great, thanks," I said breezily. To Jess, I said, "You know that gym?"

"Yeah," she replied. "But this … this isn't what I agreed to."

I frowned.

She said, "I was okay you roughing him up, but this…" She gestured to the mangled fingers. "It's too much."

She didn't say another word, just shook her head, and helped me tie Gareth up again, and we maneuvered him back out into the night.

Chapter Fifty-Four

Back on the street, the revelers partied on. Bhangra music chimed and thumped, colorful fabric spun and swayed. And I slunk out of Gareth's back yard, encouraging him along with his arm in another painful lock, all the way back to the Land Rover. No one saw us, or if they did, they didn't think it was worth breaking away from the celebration. I'd dressed him in the t-shirt and tracksuit bottoms Jess found scrunched in a corner, then blindfolded him with a rag from his own cellar and bound his hands with gaffer-tape.

Shortly before ten p.m., we parked outside the upscale Leeds Pride Gym and I asked Gareth which locker was his. He insisted on coming with me. I squeezed his injured hand and he squeaked out the number 890, plus the combination: 22, 5, 11. I used more tape to bind his hands behind his back, strapped his feet together, and hog-tied him on the floor of the back seat. I zapped him into unconsciousness with the Taser on a higher setting, a blanket shielding him from casual observers.

Inside, I told the receptionist I was thinking of moving gyms and asked if I could have a quick look round. She offered to give me the tour if I'd wait ten minutes for Rudy, but I said I'd rather look around myself if she didn't mind. She did mind, clearly, but to appease a potential customer, albeit a bruised and disheveled one, she allowed me in.

Through a busy, modern gymnasium, I entered the men's changing room and identified locker 45, a half-sized cupboard with a combination lock. None of the naked and half-naked men paid me any mind, so I was left to work.

22…

5…

11…

It unlocked first time. I slid out a full sports bag and unzipped it on one of the benches, removed two dirty towels, a couple of damp socks, a stinking t-shirt, and a pair of shorts that made me want to wash my hands before continuing. All designed to make the casual thief move on to the next locker.

I checked the zips—nothing. Flipped the bag upside-down—nothing but a couple of crumbs sprinkled out. That left the contents themselves. I hated Gareth even more right then as I rummaged in the shorts' pockets, finding more nothing, which left the socks as the only hiding place.

"Hey," said a gruff voice. It was a member of gym staff, taller than me by an inch, biceps bigger by six. "Aren't you the guy Rachel let through to look around?"

"Yes," I said, turning a sock inside out. "And this place is a mess."

"You better leave, mate."

"I don't think so."

This last comment drew looks from the other men. Most were flabby office-types. I doubted they'd get involved.

"Out," the gym-guy said. "Now."

The third sock yielded a piece of plastic the size of a postage stamp. A 64GB SD card. The sort you'd use in a digital camera.

The gym-guy stepped toward me. "Put that back."

I placed it in my pocket.

He said, "Are you deaf?"

I pulled out the Taser and, as I did with Gareth, zapped him. He folded in a heap and I turned to the collective gasp of office heroes and said, "If you all rush me at once, you'll get me down. But some of you will go first. Anyone up for that?"

A few shook their heads, but most stared. Good.

I washed my hands, left the changing room, and returned to the Land Rover. Gareth hadn't stirred. I booted up Jess's laptop and accessed the DCIM folder on the card. While Jess drove, I unveiled the deep, dark secret.

Photos of Agent Frank meeting with Curtis Benson. Nearly a hundred of them, taken with a good zoom. Crystal clear. Dozens in an Indian restaurant I recognized as being close to Blazing Seas. Then a load in a park in the city center, the two men back-to-back on a bench like in a 70's spy movie. A series from a popular coffee shop. Each location revealed a collection of snaps, exchanges of envelopes and, in one instance, a briefcase. The final set showed both men at the club while it was empty—in which Benson was clearly animated. It was date-stamped Friday 14th June. According to Lily, back when she danced for me, Benson confiscated something from Gareth around that time. Sarah and Gareth broke into the safe on Sunday 16th.

I copied all the photos across to Jess's "Pictures" file on the hard drive. No encryption here to worry about.

So, Agent Frank knew Curtis Benson personally. Taking bribes, passing on information to the worldwide network of which Vila Fanuco was a prominent member. No wonder Agent Frank was so desperate for me to find them. He did all he dared to extract information from Gareth, which only pointed him to Sarah. But I think Agent Frank knew that wasn't true. Which meant Frank wasn't all the way psycho like those paying his back-handers, and he was unwilling to commit the sort of atrocities I was now able to perform, leaving him one course of action.

Jess was one of the best tech-heads I'd ever met, but she wasn't trained in counter-surveillance, so I couldn't blame her for what happened next.

As we descended a slight hill and entered the inner ring-road's longest underpass, Agent Frank made his move, and his blue Mondeo clipped the rear offside bumper to send us into a fishtail. Jess gritted her teeth and fought the wheel, correcting course with a squeal of tires. It was more of a nudge than a genuine attempt to crash us; an assertive way to get our attention. I glared out the window as he gesticulated for us to pull off at the next ramp.

"Keep going," I said.

We shot past it and I told Jess to pull in front of him. It'd be harder to send us off-balance if he was behind rather than at the side, but he predicted our play and sped up. Jess swerved back into the left lane. Agent Frank turned his wheel, but Jess was forced to brake anyway as a little yellow Fiat Cinquecento signaled left to exit the ring-road. The Mondeo hit the Fiat. The smaller car went into a spin, bounced off the central barrier, and landed across the two lanes. An articulated lorry slammed on its airbrakes and—spewing steam from its wheels and hydraulics—its trailer jack-knifed, blocking the entire road. Miraculously, nothing collided with the tiny Fiat.

Now all the traffic was in front of us it was easier to hold Agent Frank at bay by blocking his attempts to pass. A groan from the floor hinted that Gareth was coming round, but he was fairly harmless in his position. Still, I ejected the SD card from the lap-top and pocketed it. I considered swallowing it, but a glance at the time showed two hours until midnight.

Jess said, "Adam?"

"You're doing fine," I said, as the frustrated Agent Frank tried to pass again.

"*Adam!*"

A wall of stationary traffic greeted us maybe ten seconds ahead.

No exit ramp. This section of road was set into a valley of sheer concrete. Agent Frank was too close to us; he would not have spotted the traffic jam.

"Brake," I said. "Now."

She landed both feet on the pedal. We screeched to a halt. Agent Frank rammed into us. His airbag exploded in his face, and the impact first pushed me deeper into my seat, then slammed me forward into the dashboard. Jess was wearing a seatbelt, so she fared better than me—just winded.

Ribs screaming, I fumbled the door open. Taser ready. But Agent Frank was there; pretty spry for a guy with middle-age spread. He punched my wrist, releasing the Taser and slammed my head into the Land Rover's door. I literally saw stars, staggering to balance.

People from the cars in front were on the tarmac, watching a man in a suit hitting another man, who already looked like shit. They watched as Agent Frank swung a foot into my ribs. They watched as I screamed and dropped.

Jess climbed out of the Land Rover, pleaded for help, told Agent Frank to "*Stop, stop, just stop!*" The dirty MI5 agent drew a gun on her and she fell silent.

He said to me, "Hand it over, or I give our press officers a real fucking challenge in making her look like a psycho who deserved a bullet."

I propped myself up on one elbow. "Hand what over?"

He cocked the weapon. "Give it to me. I'll tell Benson it's safe."

"You'll get it to him by midnight?"

"There's a bigger picture you're not seeing."

"I'm seeing a dirty cop, whatever way you spin it."

Agent Frank gave me a rueful look, then bent down and pistol-whipped me across the right temple. The world tilted sideways and vomit rose in my throat. While his hands explored my pockets, he spoke to me. I couldn't hear properly, and I couldn't be sure the words coming from his mouth were real or if I was passing out. The words, though, if true, meant things had changed yet again.

When he found the SD card, he said, "Thank you."

And through a blur of red-stained vision, I watched him reach into the Land Rover and take the laptop.

"I can't be seen with Benson," he said, "and his club's gonna be busy right now. I'll let him know as soon as I can. And I'm sorry about your friend. I really am."

He took off, back the way we came, away from witnesses, away from us.

I lay there on the road, a failure. A failure for Jayne and for Harry, and for myself. I had nothing with which to bargain. I waited for the darkness to take me, which I knew would be shortly, no matter how hard I battled to stay awake.

Chapter Fifty-Five

All my muscles contracted and my limbs straightened in unison. A prickling sensation shot through me. The intensity increased and I opened my eyes to Jess's smooth face leaning over me.

"What was that?" I asked.

She held up the Taser, depressed the trigger to set off the blue electrical spark. "Lowest setting."

"Jesus, that thing'll be out of batteries soon."

"Thought it would bring you back more quickly than CPR."

"No kiss then?"

She bent in and kissed me full on the lips. It lasted five or six seconds and I wondered if Harry had been right about her. But what was five seconds? A sister would kiss her brother if he came-to after being beaten unconscious. No tongue, either, which was a bigger confirmation of Harry's full-of-shit-ness.

"He took the laptop too," she said.

A Saturday night crowd of motorists and revelers rubbernecked nearby, but no one ventured too close. Sirens sounded.

"Fuck," I said, and slumped my head on my knees. "He's dead."

Jess put her arms around me, and my head moved automatically from my knees to her chest. It was nice. Warm. Soft.

"Adam," she said.

"Don't try to make it sound better. I've fucked this up. All of it."

"Here." Without trying to budge my head, she showed me her

phone. Like the one she issued at the start of all this, a five-inch screen. "You know I told you I got round the surveillance by using a wireless dongle?"

"Right. So they couldn't trace it immediately."

"It was attached to my laptop when you copied the photos."

"The one Agent Frank stole. Yes, I get it."

"You don't," she said. "Otherwise, you wouldn't still be head-fondling my boobs."

I lifted my head under my own steam, ribs objecting in no uncertain terms. "What?"

"Moving anything into my 'Pictures' folder automatically uploads them to our cloud server when I'm on an internet connection. The 4G dongle was still attached, so the photos uploaded." She flicked the phone to her internet-storage folder. "Look."

The latest entries were photos. Around sixty of the hundred-or-so that I copied. Not enough time to send them all to our server, but plenty to prove to Benson I was in possession of the disk.

I said, "It might be all we need."

"So go."

I took her phone and braced myself against the pain as I stood. I kissed her full on the lips and when I pulled away she giggled through a huge grin and had to adjust her glasses.

"Thank you," I said, and turned toward the crowd, but the sirens getting ever louder gave me pause. "Better to untie Gareth and tell him to run. Remind him he's still a wanted man."

She nodded, and I headed into the crowd, away from the blue flashing lights converging on our spot. It was ten-thirty.

It took me twenty minutes to cross the city to my apartment. Twenty minutes of wheezing and aching, of staving off bolts of pain from my ribs, my head, my hand. Twenty minutes of looks from the nightlife of Leeds, of people eager to either get out of my way or hit me in the face. But I made it just as Jayne was leaving.

"Good Lord," she said. "I'd about given up."

"Give me a minute," I said.

We went back inside. I drank water out of the tap and splashed it over my face. I told her what happened, and she didn't outwardly judge me for what I did to Gareth, but I expected we'd be due a heart-to-heart pretty soon. With an hour to go, she held out the USB stick.

"You can't just hand it over," she said.

"I won't. We have Benson's extra-curricular payments, we have his dirty agent. Those things he can keep." I was dog-tired and hurt everywhere, but I could see the finishing line at last. "I've made mistakes, but this makes everything right."

And then the phone rang. My landline phone.

Jayne said, "I thought it was disconnected."

"It was." I picked it up and listened.

Mikey said, "Turn on the computer you keep under your couch. Your instant messenger has mail."

He hung up. Jayne asked a bunch of confused questions about how the hell a cut-off phone-line could be reactivated like that. She asked what sort of people these were, how it was even possible.

I folded out the screen and it booted up immediately; asleep, not powered down as I'd left it. So someone broke in here this afternoon.

The IM icon blinked. I accessed it. A live video-feed commenced. A shaky camera focused on a door with a colorful glass inlay. A gloved hand reached from behind the lens to open it via a battered metal knob. Inside, the camera faded in, adjusted to a grim storage room with a fridge, sink and a black & white telly. Piped music echoed through streets in the distance, and I got the impression this room was located a long, long way from Leeds.

My phone rang again. Jayne handed it to me, my eyes glued to the screen.

Mikey said, "You thought she was safe, eh?"

The camera whip-panned to a sofa in the far corner, where a man all in black, his face hidden by a balaclava, held his hand around a young woman's throat. Her hands were bound behind her and she was gagged. Tears streamed down her pixie-like face. Lily Blake.

They found her.

"We heard what you did in Vietnam. You even think about that shit tonight, those men will gut your princess and fuck the corpse. You got that, pretty-boy?"

I watched the screen a moment longer before closing the lid.

"Meet me at my office," I said. "It's deserted."

"You're volunteerin' to go somewhere without witnesses?"

"You could kill any of us at any time. Why should it matter? Bring Harry, and I'll bring the data stick, along with the photos your boss is so scared of losing."

Muffled discussion on the other end. Mikey said, "Okay. But remember you ain't playing for one life now. Do not think for one second you can fuck us on this."

Even though I now did not expect everyone to survive the night, I promised him no more delays, no tricks, no attempt to double-cross them.

I was lying again, of course.

Chapter Fifty-Six

Whilst waiting for Benson and Mikey in Gorman's office, I checked on the progress of my money. By eleven p.m., twenty-five million pounds sterling had flowed into my personal bank account, Gorman happy to hold up his end of the contract. I filed documents with the bank to ensure the taxman kept his nose out of my business for another year, and spent a little more time communicating with Jess about our ever-evolving plan. Like the business with Gareth, she did not approve, but agreed if Benson made a good-enough case to kill me, he'd have the sanction to do so. In these circumstances, it's easier to ask forgiveness than permission.

Then I perched on the edge of Roger Gorman's desk-cum-penis-extension, the boardroom table broken up and retracted into its false wall. His Oriental-inspired rug made the room seem less spacious somehow. As I sat there, looking out over the softly lit snake of the River Aire, I pondered if I had truly crossed an irredeemable line in Vietnam. And with Gareth. Jess clearly thought so. If she was right, I was about to cross another.

In the car park below, a people-carrier pulled up, the sort parents might use to take the kids on a trip, or transport friends to the airport. Mikey led Harry out by the arm. He staggered—disoriented, confused. Sometimes, given his take-no-shit attitude, his Army background, it was easy to forget he was pushing seventy.

Benson stepped out too and, as they approached the building, disappearing beneath me. They would take the elevator up to the lobby. They would not have to bypass the shell of the building below, its construction equipment, the scaffolding, the plastic sheets snapping in the light breeze.

I made my way to reception, where I could hear the intercom buzzing. As I walked, I thought about the day my dad died, how my mother sat outside the morgue with me, tears on her cheeks, sad that her husband was no longer with us, yet even as a child I intuited it wasn't all-out grief. There was something else there. I cried real tears, but it was a buxom nurse who comforted me. For years I couldn't understand how I knew what my mother was feeling. It wasn't sadness, not in the sense most would feel at the passing of someone you'd sworn to love and honor forever. A sense of relief, perhaps, no longer bound by doing the right thing and fighting for a marriage she and Sleazy Stu killed three years earlier. An end she had not envisioned, but an end nonetheless.

Benson, Mikey and Harry entered reception. Harry perked up as he recognized me, unhurt physically but his eyes were glazed. Mikey cut the cable tie binding his hands and he fell towards me. I hugged him properly, afraid of dropping him. He seemed as healthy as I could expect after five days as a captive. Or was it six?

"Careful," I said. "I've got you."

"Horse tranqs." He sounded kind-of smug. "Shot of adrenaline'll wake him up."

As I walked Harry to Gorman's office, he slurred indecipherable words like a drunk. Wielding a gun too bulky for his compact frame, a suppressor making it even more comically big, Mikey followed a few feet away. Once inside the office, Harry squinted to focus.

"Adam?"

"I'm here, mate," I said. "Stay calm. We'll get out of this."

Benson snorted. "Where's my drive?"

I lay Harry gently on Gorman's overstuffed leather couch and took the USB drive from my pocket. Laid it on the desk.

Benson's attention held steady on it. "And the other items?"

I clenched my good fist to stop it trembling. The gash stung. But in a good way.

"I wanted to talk about some other stuff first." I gestured toward Mikey. "You might want to do this in private, *Curtis*."

"I can stay, boss," Mikey said. To me he said, "And it's *Mr. Benson*."

"Is that really your decision to make, little man?"

"I think I can guess what my boss wants, pretty-boy. Although, not so pretty now, eh?" He laughed at his own joke.

I looked at Benson. "You gonna let him talk to you like this, Curtis?"

"He's my most valued employee," Benson said. "He stays." He took a gun from his jacket and pointed it at me. "Talk."

I felt an odd sense of pride. My actions in Vietnam made them scared of me. They needed the extra leverage in Lily, tracked her down somehow, and now they were far less sure of themselves.

I had earned a reputation.

"Let's see what I can do about Lily." I presented Jess's mobile phone.

I let Benson watch the first set of files speed over the screen, PDF documents Jess copied to a remote server, same as the photos.

"First," I said, "we'll talk about your monthly care packages. You bundle up a whole load of cash the first Monday of every month and send it via Marley Holdings—your shell company. They leave Liverpool and, through some seriously creative accounting, they don't actually arrive. Except, packages of medical supplies *do* arrive. They go to St. Clarence's Hospital on the island of Lana where, coincidentally, one Dorothy Benson resides. A seventy-two-year-old lady with severe dementia. You know her, don't you?"

Benson's eyes flicked to the USB stick on the desk. "What does this have to do with my data?"

"It demonstrates that you are supplying a hospital with a lot of money on a monthly basis. Not just medical bills, but a whole lot more. That facility isn't exactly pristine, or it wasn't until just over a year ago, when it upgraded its facilities."

Photos on the phone showed before and after pictures of St. Clarence's: filthy interior, damp walls, grotty bathrooms. Following these were images of the standard you'd get in the most private hospitals or spas.

I said, "You had your mother committed here, but you couldn't stand to have her suffer in those conditions. So I thought—I *thought*—you started skimming off the top. The money you were laundering, it would show short each month. Accounting issues, unforeseen bills, the odd bribe you needed to make."

It was Mikey who spoke. "I do the books for him, arsehole. Money ain't missing. I ain't helpin' him scam anyone. 'Specially not the people who send us these girls."

"I know. It was my original theory. I was wrong. Things have changed, but the motivation is still the same."

I showed a photo of a much younger Benson with Dorothy. Then I swiped to a photo of Dorothy in a hospital room surrounded by tubes and wires, then of her in a garden with a couple of orderlies.

"This is your boss's *mother*," I said. "He's using money from some very powerful people to fund the upgrade of her living conditions."

"First," Benson said, "it benefits the whole damn community

over there. Second, that money." He jabbed a finger at the screen. "It's my *cut*. My legitimate cut. Only reason it's in cash is 'cause I choose not to pay tax to our bullshit government."

"Curtis Benson, big bad gangsta-man, sends his wages home to Mommy."

Benson didn't find that amusing. Mikey did. He said, "So you thought you got yerself the upper fuckin' hand, huh?"

"At first. And you're right. He is *not* skimming extra from the smuggling networks."

Benson picked up the USB drive and said, "Right. So you're fucked in that respect. Where's the other item?"

"Right here." I indicated the phone.

"What's on it?" Mikey asked, adding respectfully, "Boss. If you don't mind my asking."

"Blackmail shit," Benson said. "That bitch Gareth was trying to blackmail me."

"Yes," I said. "But not in the way I thought. Gareth Delingpole spent all the money before I could find them. It was far less than you said because you'd already shipped a ton of it off to St. Clarence's. *This* is what you need to satisfy your paymasters." I indicated the USB drive. "I'll hold onto the other stuff until you release Harry and Lily."

Benson said, "Hand over the phone. Now."

Mikey said, "What's the big deal? The data stick is what's important, right?"

"I made a copy of that disk. I placed it on an SD card, like you get in a camera. Burglar Girl and Thick-As-Pig-Shit took it along with my money, and this drive. They were together. I want the backup copy."

"Bullshit," I said. "It can't be copied. You have your orders to release Harry on return of that data. So don't be stupid, Curtis. You don't need Lily. You don't need us. It's over."

Benson firmed up his grip on the gun. "I should kill that fuckin' stripper just to piss you off."

A glance at Mikey was all I needed. Benson thought he'd escaped Fanuco's instructions on a technicality, that Lily was his upper hand. But I saw how frightened he was.

"You don't really know what's on that card," I said. "Do you?"

"I don't care," Benson said. "I know he was gonna use it to get more money outta me."

"Because if you did know, you wouldn't let your pint-sized bodyguard be present."

Mikey said, "Keep up the jokes about my height, pretty-boy. Remember I took you out when you was at full strength. Reckon a schoolgirl could kick 'yer ass right now."

I kept my attention on Benson. "You think it's accounting documents?"

Benson said, "Hand over the phone."

I showed him the first photo. Him and Agent Frank in the Indian restaurant.

Harry stirred, conscious of guns.

I said, "Don't worry. They won't hurt us."

"Don't be too sure," Mikey said, coming close for a look.

"It's nothin'," Benson said. "Business."

"And this?" I swiped to a snap of him and Agent Frank exchanging envelopes.

I should have seen it from the shape of the envelope, but it wasn't until Agent Frank told me how wrong I was that it made any sense. When he leaned over me on the road, searching my pockets, he insisted he was not corrupt in the way I thought he was.

"This man," I said, "is Agent Frank McCabe of the Serious Organized Crime Squad, working out of MI5. I thought he was dirty, but I was wrong about that too, wasn't I? It was a mystery to me how a lowlife hoodlum managed to smuggle so much cash out of the country, but now I see it. In exchange for MI5 and HM Customs turning a blind eye—"

"Fuck you," Benson said. "Nothin' here shows this."

"Agent Frank McCabe is not passing *you* information. You aren't giving *him* bribes. *You're* leaking *him* information so you can keep exporting money to your mother's hospital."

Another glance at Mikey, and I knew he was processing all this.

I said, "And Mikey is not aware his boss is an informant."

Lily was out of danger now. Me and Harry too. I couldn't keep the grin from my face. I was fairly sure my eyes were sparkling.

I said, "The law making inroads is the reason Fanuco and his mates let me investigate on your behalf instead of going after the drive themselves. Because you've fed MI5 operational details. This USB stick, unencrypted, allows you to redistribute the laundered cash to its rightful owners, and could end the network, stem the flow of people and drugs and weapons."

Benson held the gun out at arm's length.

"These photos are on a secure server," I said. "Me, Harry and Lily, we all walk free tonight, or this all goes to Vila Fanuco, along with everything I know."

"It's bullshit," Benson said. "I swear."

"It's not," I said. "And you know it."

Mikey said, "He wasn't talking to you, pretty-boy."

Striking as fast as a cobra, Mikey disarmed Benson and pointed the silenced gun at his boss, the other at me.

"No," Benson said. "Please. I can explain."

Mikey raised his gun and shot Curtis Benson through the head.

Benson's corpse dropped like a sack of wet sand and blood fountained out of the wound for a second before slowing to a trickle.

Mikey turned to me and said, "In case you hadn't worked it out yet, Benson ain't my boss. I'm his."

Chapter Fifty-Seven

The connections were all there. Primarily Bosnia. Fanuco, running the black market in his old neighborhood, would have encountered soldiers trying to keep the peace. He and Mikey probably met through some mutually beneficial deal in those dark times. No reason a business relationship couldn't be established there and then. Mikey the muscle, Fanuco the brains. The details were irrelevant, though.

"I want this done right," Mikey said. "I want it clean." His voice was reasonable, calm. Like Fanuco's. "But someone might have to do somethin' they don't wanna. Don't make that person be me."

Benson's blood had spread all around his torso and was pooling closer to Mikey's feet. He tossed Benson's gun aside, the magazine toward the corpse.

"Benson was fairly new to our network," he said, again reasonably. "I'm supposed to babysit for a year, make sure he knew the way we work before lettin' him loose on his own. Thing is, no one coulda guessed some fucking retarded girl would crack a safe he claimed was top a' the fuckin' line. We mighta' killed him anyway fer losin' it, but might not. If it came back clean. With no blowback. But you, not-so-pretty-boy, you're fuckin' blowback."

"How do I get Lily free?" I asked. "She's nothing to you."

He picked up the USB drive. "Let me be honest. Vila likes you.

Dunno why. But he says you live, so you live … 'til you create a direct problem. Tonight, though," he said, his voice shifting down an octave, "might be a direct problem."

My eyes found the data stick.

"You gonna stop fuckin' around? Stop playing the big-man, like you've got some sorta free will?"

"Yes," I said.

"So when I test this, I'm not gonna find an empty drive or nothin'?"

"You can test it right there." I indicated the laptop on Gorman's desk.

I spun the machine around, active already. He plugged in the USB drive. He would have to approach from that side coming off the rug. I had one chance at this. My leverage was almost gone. Once he verified the data was real, he could shoot us both and head off for a curry and a pint.

I asked, "How did you find Lily?"

"When your money got cut off," Mikey said, as he studied the decryption software, "it cut her off too. She figured you'd set her loose so it was safe to update Facebook. She wasn't happy. Said you dumped her like everyone else in her life." Blue light from the laptop screen danced over his face. "But no matter how pissed you are, you don't update fuckin' Facebook, otherwise, you can bet the people lookin' for you are gonna stake out that souk in Tunisia where you been spendin' all yer time."

As distractions go it wasn't particularly ingenious but I knew he'd have to work the computer to authenticate whilst talking to me. I moved slowly round the desk as I talked.

"Who's holding her?" I sat in Gorman's chair.

"Locals. Paid 'em a couple a' hundred dollars." He looked up at me, suspicious, gun still firm in one hand. When he was satisfied I couldn't see the keyboard, he hit a few keys to disengage the first password, then used a combination of Alt plus other keys, and then finally another password. His face lit up with a white glow. The gun and its suppressor wilted.

A woman's voice said, "Okay, I've got it."

Mikey frowned. "What—"

I brought up my hand, pressed the end of a nail gun into Mikey's forearm, and pulled the trigger. A six-inch nail *thunked* out and pinned him to the desk. He grimaced, but held onto the gun. I shot another nail further up his arm, and another into his leg.

"Fucking cunt-bastard," Mikey said through clenched teeth.

It didn't take much to remove the gun from his hand.

"I'll find you," he said. "The stripper-whore's *dead*!"

"No you won't." I took a few steps back. Raised the gun.

He took in my plan. Benson's body lying on the rug. "Thought there was something off about that. The way it felt."

"Plastic sheeting," I said. "Took it from the building site below and lay it under the rug. Got this lovely nail-gun from their lockup too."

"Smart," Mikey said. "But stupid. You can't kill me without re-percussions."

"Sure I can. *You* decrypted the drive for me."

"Right," Jess said through the speakerphone that I left open from the start. "It's all through."

I explained the computer on which Mikey accessed the drive was paired with one on the PAI network, and right now every bit of information was being copied and stored on a server in a faraway place, right next to where Gorman stashed the Deep Detect System. No need to decrypt the file if someone else has a password.

I said, "Me and Harry and Lily, we go free, or you all go down."

A buzzing sounded from Mikey's jacket.

I said, "I'd get that if I were you."

He answered with his good hand and tried to sound like he was still in control. "I know. I'm on it. Yeah, fucker copied it." He listened. Held out the phone. "He wants to talk to you."

I aimed the gun at Mikey. "Hang up."

"It's Vila. He ain't happy."

"Hang up," I said.

He obeyed. From Gorman's drawer, I took a set of carpenter pincers, another item liberated from the site below. I dropped them on the desk, careful to remain at least two arm-lengths from Mikey. He used them to pull the nail pinning him.

I said, "Step back."

Again, he obeyed, cradling his oozing hand and glancing backwards where he was planting his feet, a limp prominent. His eyes lingered on Harry, slouched twelve feet away on the couch.

"Stop," I said.

He did so. "You guess what I'm thinkin'?"

"That you can get to Harry, yank out one of the other nails as a weapon, and use him as a human shield to get away. Close?"

"Spot on." He nodded, impressed. "I told Vila he was full of shit about you. A pretty-boy playin' at tough-guy shit. Way you attacked me last week, that was one clumsy fuckin' technique."

"Out of practice."

"Yeah. Now look at you. Guess Vila was right. You got a fuckload a' cold in you."

"I'm not like you people."

"Sure y'are. You put this setup together in *one hour*. You were never gonna back down about the data stick, and I'm guessin' there ain't one security camera workin' in this place."

"Actually, we shut down the city center. This building, anything controlled by the council, anything linked to the same network the council uses. Mysterious bug."

"Smart-arsed bastard. And you got plastic under this rug, ready to get rid of our bodies. Me an' Benson. All 'cos you can."

"No," I said. "I did it because I knew I couldn't be safe from you. Once you got that disk, I was dead, and so was Harry. Everyone else you threatened too. Jess, Lily, Jayne. All of us. That's why I have to do this. Call it pro-active self-defense."

He tried to flex his pierced hand. "You don't know shit, Park. I was gonna walk outta here with that and you'd never hear from us again. Vila *genuinely* fuckin' likes you. It's weird, I know. But he saw what I'm seein' now. Stone-cold killer. You always were, I guess. Just took somethin' special to pry it loose."

During the years I spent sculpting my body into what I thought of as a fierce machine, his words would have given me nothing but encouragement. I'd been itching all of that time to fight, to hurt, to kill. But now, holding that gun on Mikey, having planned his murder with as much conscience as arranging the funeral of someone who was already dead, I pushed the logic on myself again. *He* was a killer.

I had no choice.

Beside Benson's corpse, Mikey said, "This'll look great on your CV next time Vila has a job vacancy."

I edged forward, close enough to not miss. Added pressure to the trigger.

"Adam Matthew Park, what in fuck's name are you doin'?" Harry had found his feet. His body was still shaky but that drunken slur and foggy expression were gone.

"Harry, you don't get it," I said. "He's a killer. He *will* do the same to us, first chance he gets."

"Two wrongs, Adam…"

"He's willing to *kill* a girl. To punishing *me*."

"Don't give you a right to kill him. *Adam*. You've won."

Mikey said, "He's right. You got your copy." He adopted a whiney girly voice: "*If I die or go missing or anyone I care for is taken, the file goes public.*" Back to normal: "Right?"

Mikey was unarmed, stood on a sheet of plastic, a blight on everything good and decent. If my soul was the price of cleansing this world of him then so be it.

Harry said, "It weren't self-defense the last time I talked you outta killing someone, and it ain't self-defense now."

Jess was right about what I did to Gareth. But I would get away with it. Just like I could get away with killing Mikey. But what then?

Harry stepped toward me shakily. "C'mon, son."

"But Lily…"

Harry's face set itself hard, his lines far deeper than mere days earlier. "If you kill this man, he'll have done far, far worse to you."

"Spare me the clichés," I said. "I've killed already. I did it because I had to at first, but I didn't care. I didn't enjoy it, Harry, but I didn't hate it either. It wasn't difficult. They're right. This is who I am."

"But it *isn't* you, son." He came closer now, circumventing Mikey in a wide enough arc to avoid offering the smaller man a hostage.

"I'm damaged enough now for it not to matter. It won't haunt me."

He made it to my side. Placed his arms around my shoulder. The gun didn't waver. He said, "But you doing this … killing him? It will haunt *me*."

Mikey's smile was forced. He didn't know what I was going to do. I wanted to prolong it, to make him suffer. But I lowered the gun. Mikey breathed out. Harry nodded sadly.

"You know, pretty-boy," Mikey said, "you had me going there a while."

Harry pulled away from me. "You ain't that damaged after all."

"I damn-near pissed myself," Mikey said. "No-one done that to me since I met Vila the first time."

"I'm honored," I said.

I weighed the gun in my hand. Savored its power. One squeeze of one trigger.

"Tell me," Mikey said. "You were serious, weren't you?"

"Yeah," I said. "I was serious. Get the fuck out."

"I have that drive? We still need what's on it. Even if it ain't private no more."

I stood aside, ushered Harry out of Mikey's reach and Mikey limped forward. Removed the USB drive, and pocketed it. He used the pincers to remove the other two nails, teeth gritted against the pain.

"Damn it," he said. "This fuckin' hurts."

I shrugged. "I'd say I was sorry, but I'd be lying."

"Yeah, look at the pair of us. Couple a' fucked up psychos."

"He's not a psycho," Harry said.

"Oh, he is," Mikey said. "If it weren't fer you he'd a' done it. Right, pretty-boy?"

I neither confirmed or denied it.

Then he threw the computer at me. I batted it away, but he was already on me. A nail in his hand slashed at the gun, knocking it to the floor. An elbow landed in my ribs and I curled up low and punched his injured thigh. He staggered backwards, losing the nail. He came at me empty-handed, a ferocious howl on his lips, eyes bugging, all pretense of normalcy gone.

I returned a couple of good shots, my own blood rising, my elbow connecting with his jaw, the uppercut pinging a couple of teeth out. Yet he kept on coming, alternating strike zones, up, down, side-to-side, so I could predict nothing. No defense for it. When I finally gave in and dropped to the floor, beaten and exhausted, only then did he take a breather.

The lights of Leeds swam through Gorman's huge window, and the river that runs through it blurred. The shimmering mass of water. I tried to focus on the room. Thought Mikey was looking for something.

Harry found it and was pointing it at Mikey.

"Give me the gun, mate," Mikey said.

Harry held it firm. "No."

Casually, Mikey said, "Fine, have it your way," and picked up two of the nails he'd discarded. "Be more fun this way anyhow."

"Don't," Harry said. "I might not have killed anyone recently, but I know how."

"War's different."

"Not too much, I reckon."

I pulled myself up, every muscle in my body resisting. I felt blood on my face, down my back.

"Wait," I said.

"Don't worry," Mikey said. "I'll keep my end. Won't hurt the cunt. But I'm turnin' you into a fuckin' kebab."

He rushed at me again. The gun spat with a metallic clunk and he bucked virtually in mid-air.

The recoil knocked the weakened Harry over and he dropped the gun.

Mikey landed on his back, but he was up quickly, the bullet high enough in his chest to avoid his heart and lungs. He stared at it. Insulted that he'd been wrong about someone else that night.

I dived for the weapon. Mikey dived too. But the new wound in his body was enough to give me the edge. I rolled away and held the gun on him.

Harry sat up slowly, gaze working between us. He sighed heavily, the way he did on those rare occasions he had to admit he was wrong.

"Fine," he said. "I shouldn't have stopped you before."

I remained strangely calm. "Difference between you and me,

THE DEAD AND THE MISSING

Mikey? Is that if I kill you here and now, I won't ever do it again. You, on the other hand, you'll go on and on and on."

Mikey said, "Yer bluffing."

I took one shallow breath.

Harry closed his eyes.

I said, "No more compromises." And I fired a very quiet bullet into the back of Mikey's skull.

The spray covered half the couch and a large section of the wall. Hardly any of it landed on the rug covering the plastic.

Chapter Fifty-Eight

I don't know how long I stared at the two dead bodies on my floor. The clock showed ten to midnight. It would be Roger Gorman's floor in a few minutes.

I placed the gun on the desk. Harry consoled me on what I must have been through to bring me to this place, to turn me so cold and so clinical. He told me he loved me, and that he was proud of what I'd done.

Outside, Harry's Land Rover pulled into the car park. I helped Harry to the lift and escorted him down to the ground floor. As soon as she saw us, Jayne leapt out of the ancient vehicle and ran like a lovesick teenager and swept her husband into her arms. Harry grinned and tried to kiss her but she pulled back and said, "Get off me, you old fool." But she saw how much he needed the affection and gave in. "Fine, quickly then."

The pair kissed. For a few seconds.

"Happy?" Jayne said.

Harry's grin remained. "Very."

"He's a bit weak," I said. "Get him home. Rest. Malt whiskey."

As she took him away, I heard Jayne say she'd get him to a doctor and I heard that kind offer rebuffed in no uncertain terms. It hurt to smile, but I did so anyway. I was going to have to break my agreement with Roger Gorman in a major way.

In Monday's edition of the Yorkshire Evening Post, and the inside pages of a few national newspapers, a story would run about how some anarchist group crippled Leeds City Council's ability to control their CCTV network. The bug also knocked out a number of online security systems whose servers tied into the many businesses that partnered with the council and the police, and this resulted in the neutralization of burglar alarms, as well as dozens of fire prevention systems. So, while the blaze at Park Avenue Investigations triggered an alarm to the fire service, the CO_2 jets protecting the mass of servers malfunctioned.

Had that floor been equipped with water-based sprinklers, gravity would have sucked the water through and doused the flames before they took hold. But because Roger Gorman valued the dearth of information and computerized knick-knacks so highly, he'd only installed the CO_2 system, which is supposed to smother the flames and preserve the microchips and diodes and terabytes of data that water would destroy.

One thing the newspapers would not report, however, would be the lone man standing a quarter of a mile away, watching the business he'd spent his whole life building up burn in a beautiful orange ball. The fire engines arrived within fifteen minutes, but the flames already gripped deep in the oak paneling, spreading fast to the rest of the property.

Investigations into the blaze would reveal that arson was the cause. They would uncover the bodies of Michael Durant, a private military contractor turned mob-enforcer, who murdered his boss after trying to kill Lily Blake, a dancer at the club with whom he'd grown obsessed. To evade his troubling attention, the dancer herself fled to the continent on a false passport. Indeed, this was not the first example of such behavior from Mikey.

One Sarah Stiles also confirmed that he was an obsessive stalker, hence why she, too, had fled after robbing the safe in desperation with her then-boyfriend Gareth Delingpole. And when Sarah's story built into one of human trafficking and the white slave trade in South East Asia, the bodies in Park Avenue Investigations were soon forgotten. The foreign office announced the arrest of property-tycoon-cum-sexual-predator Vuong Dinh, and for a while the Vietnamese even took over from Muslims as the right-wing press's bogeymen-*du-jour*.

Early Sunday morning, before a single press story broke on the subject, I met a traumatized Lily at Leeds-Bradford airport, her transport a private jet laid on thanks to my newly released funds. She was freed via a begrudging phone call from Vila Fanuco, acting under my orders. He was now cooler on the idea of us working together, but he said he trusted that I would keep that data secure. He didn't fear me, though. That much was clear.

I took Lily to the hospital and posed as her boyfriend to get to her bedside, and was promptly introduced to her mum, who rushed up from Lincoln. Although they'd not spoken in a couple of years, Lily found it in her heart to forgive whatever prompted such animosity and agreed to move back in while she recovered. The rather well-to-do woman was surprised her daughter was dating a beaten-up man in his mid-thirties, but swallowed any judgment and limply shook my hand.

I'd changed of course. Showered, scrubbed raw, put on a slick Armani suit for some reason. I guess I needed to offset the bruises with a respectable wardrobe.

Lily and I talked in private, her mother taking the hint to go get a coffee. She'd left on an overnight ferry from Plymouth to Bilbao, and loved the onward train to the south of Spain. Despite the cramped conditions she was mesmerized by the landscape and was welcomed so warmly by more experienced "backpack-people," as she called them. She avoided hotels and took advice from her new friends and booked into hostels and stayed up late talking and drinking and talking some more. She'd been so happy to listen to other people's adventures, and although she never fully revealed her own background, she once confessed to being a stripper, and everyone cooed about it sounding exotic rather than sleazy. She hooked up with an American mountain-biker named Kurt, and went with him to Tunisia, where he was due to cycle some route in the Atlas Mountains. When my money stopped flowing to her, she couldn't resist Facebooking that I ruined her holiday and dumped her like a sack of shit. This was when her phone automatically checked her in at the souk in which she was drinking with her new beau. When the men took her, they did so quietly, and Kurt thought she'd done a runner on him. She replied on Facebook to say she'd fill him in later, but no—she would not run out on him.

She'd see him soon.

I kissed her forehead and told her I'd take care of her. She could travel as long as she wanted.

After the hospital, I took a walk to my office building. The top floor was a gaping black frame atop the glass-fronted structure. Police still worked alongside investigators. A black-and-white car guarded the entrance, a uniformed man and woman on duty. I met Roger Gorman at the edge of the cordon, in the courtyard below the charred ruins. He was wearing a red tracksuit, the first time I'd seen him without perfect formal attire.

"Adam, thank God," he said. "I thought maybe our little rivalry had driven you to suicide."

They'd extinguished the flames and found bodies. Unidentified at this stage.

"Sadly not," I said.

"Please, Adam, I am not a monster. I may not like your hippie pacifist nonsense, but I value human life."

"Just not brown people's lives, huh? Not the kids your clients sell guns to in war zones around the world?"

"See?" he said. "Hippie nonsense." He frowned as if registering me for the first time. "Good God, what happened?"

"I was in a fight last night. Celebrating my windfall. Thanks for that, by the way."

"You're welcome." He looked up grimly. "They say the whole place was gutted. The computers, the servers. All our records."

"It was stored remotely, though, right? In the cloud or something."

"I'd … not gotten around to it. Besides, the confidential nature of what we do … it's too risky to leave it in the hands of some Apple or Google university graduate."

"So no secret backup?"

"Yes, we had backups, but—" He waved his hand upwards. "They were all in-house, at the other side of the property."

"So Roger Gorman, businessman extraordinaire, still hasn't quite moved with the times." I'd known this, of course, but this needling of him was my first fun in what felt like weeks. "I don't suppose you knew you could purchase server space in, say, Brazil or China, which would serve as your own personal 'cloud.' Run it yourself for minimal cost."

"No," he said. "I did not know that."

Not that it would have done much good against Fanuco and his network anyway.

"You know," I said, "if everything was on those servers, the whole business—your clients, your accounts, your results—that's going to put a dent in your future."

"It might do that, yes."

"You'll more than likely lose a few investors."

He faced me fully. "What are you getting at?"

"We floated on the stock exchange some years ago, right? I mean, the brokerage side of the business did. I know the private investigation section is separate, but the real money lies in the other stuff doesn't it?"

He now spoke slowly. "Yes … So…?"

"I'm wondering what this will do to the share price."

His mind worked. He'd obviously been informed of the fire this morning. "The share price."

"You don't have a business to run, Roger."

"But … but it's more than bricks and mortar. It's *me*, it's the others who manage that place, the investigators, the software…"

"All gone."

Gorman sat on the ground, head in his hands.

I said, "There is no Park Avenue Investigations anymore."

I walked back toward the train station. He would know I had something to do with it, and he'd call the police to tell them. But it wouldn't matter. The man I arranged to meet at the coffee shop on the concourse would see my alibi held strong.

Before I even reached the train station, he placed a hand on my shoulder. "You did a fine job here, Adam." The voice was unmistakable.

"Hello, Vila," I said, figuring first-name terms was a two-way street by now.

"Mikey was a valuable asset."

"He enjoyed the violence too much. He was a liability. I did you a favor."

"Perhaps."

"And he was supposed to be watching Benson. He missed that the guy was a snitch."

"But he was still a friend."

"You don't have *friends*."

He gave me a pleasant smile. His dark woolen coat and the suit showing beneath made him look like a reporter. I handed him the USB drive. Simple. Just like that. I expected a fanfare.

I said, "I assume I'm safe now."

"I did not think you would take such a chance. But I believe you understand the situation. We are like ... Ronald Reagan and Mikhail Gorbachev."

"Mutually-assured destruction." I felt a shameful swell of pride. "Good."

Fanuco chuckled quietly. "If you even come close to our business again, you will be killed. If you release this information, you will be killed very slowly. Your friends, your little girlfriend…"

I waved him away. "Okay, okay, I get it. No need to labor the point."

Fanuco nodded. "How is your girlfriend?"

"She isn't my girlfriend. And she'll live. It's not the first time Mikey hurt her."

"Your other friend, then. Sarah, is it?"

"I don't know." I couldn't imagine her fear, the simple terror of all she'd been through. Mission mode might carry her through. "She'll be okay."

Fanuco raised his collar. "Well, if you ever tire of this life, we will have work for you."

I told myself to be disgusted at his suggestion, that I should be fighting his offer, but having witnessed the brutality of his kind first hand, I could not stifle a smile. I had survived. I couldn't really say I won, but I had survived.

Vila Fanuco offered me his hand. "Farewell, Adam. I hope we meet again."

I left it hanging there, wondering if I shook it, would I be viewing him as human? Would it make him a person as opposed to a force of nature dedicated to violence? Would it make me want to be his friend?

"Not me," I said. "Not ever."

And for the final time, I walked away from him.

Epilogue

Sat on top of the *Miss Piggywiggy*, I pulled my coat tighter. A frying pan smoked beside me as it cooled. July and August had gone, and September was approaching its end. Aside from some follow-up questions about the France business, I did not hear from any law-enforcement agency, so by now I figured I was in the clear over Benson and Mikey. The Vietnamese tourist industry, with help from Sarah's true-crime book on her ordeal, helped douse the anti-Vietnam flames, and the poor and the EU resumed their place in the sights of the gutter-press. The book changed my name and did not once mention specifics of Vila Fanuco's business. At least, nothing that would endanger it.

Endangering the business would be left to the drip-drip-drip of anonymous tips that Agent Frank would receive, courtesy of the decrypted data. Enough to point them at the correct people, but not incriminate me in supplying the information. It wouldn't end the network entirely, but it was better than nothing.

A compromise, I suppose.

Lily was one of the people who—during the week following the fire at PAI—discovered her bank account bloated to the tune of around a quarter of a million pounds, her share of Gorman's fee for Park Avenue Investigations. I did not believe I deserved a penny. The people who lost their jobs as a result of the business going under did, though, and so the investigators and administrators and researchers all received a cut of the loot.

After I rejected her proposal to rebuild the business from the ground up, Jess reluctantly used her money to move to London where she launched a boutique electronic investigation service, one that would work freelance for law. She would stay away from Fanuco, but other than that, she—and Phyllis from PAI—made a formidable team.

I allocated half the pot to that unofficial redundancy package, while the rest remained in a trust I set up to provide sustainable projects in war-torn countries. It wouldn't change those countries overnight, but a school, a hospital, a freshwater well … anything that can be maintained by the indigenous population was something worth investing in.

I used my remaining money to hire an American private security team called Black Lion to sweep the area of the Mekong Delta along which I believed the network's holding cell was situated. Over the course of a fortnight, helicopter searches identified a number of camps, but most were illicit alcohol dens or refining cocaine. But then, in the final few days, as my account dropped below seven figures for the first time in years, they located it. I did not enquire, exactly, what tactics they used, or if anyone was left alive; a crumb of deniability to which I treated myself. All I knew for certain was a total of thirteen young people were deposited at various embassies in Hanoi, and returned home to their countries of origin. No arrests were made, and Fanuco never enquired after me.

It left me a modest amount on which to live.

On the *Miss Piggywiggy*, I examined the pan and ascertained it was safe enough to return below. I stepped into the galley and Lily said, "About time."

Caroline Stiles tended sausages and bacon on my grill while Sarah poked at a pan of baked beans with a wooden spoon, trying to stop them sticking.

"Come on, Adam," Caroline said. "Eggs aren't going to fry themselves."

"Gimme a break." I rinsed the pan with cold water, dried it, and applied more oil. "It was her fault I got distracted."

Sarah placed a mocking hand on her chest, so shocked. "I merely asked you to demonstrate how to break a stranglehold."

I said, "How's Harry?"

Caroline broke a second egg into the pan. Sarah answered for her: "He's okay. Auntie Jayne wouldn't talk about you, though. Even though Cazzy asked. Right?"

"Right," Caroline said. "It's a lot for them to take. You know?"

I took the pan of beans from Sarah and stirred them. I had seen the older couple only once since Jayne took Harry away that night. Harry fought in a war, but Jayne never experienced such stress, and was suffering from what Harry assumed was post-traumatic stress. I thought he probably was too.

I said, "Yeah, I understand."

"Maybe they should go on holiday," Lily said.

"Just because you've got a bit of cash, don't let it go to your head."

Over the past couple of weeks, she and I planned a route for her, one that would take her from country to country, avoiding France and Vietnam. She decided Kurt was a nice fling, and would meet up with him if their paths were to cross, but no more.

"Anyway," Sarah said, "you can't go too far. Not if I'm meeting up with you next summer."

Caroline said, "Sarah?"

"Sorry, Cazzy," Sarah said. "But I'm not going to let what those men did keep me locked up."

Caroline looked horrified.

Sarah said, "I'll be nineteen by next year. And Lily and I'll be travelling together."

I was so proud of her.

Sunday brunch was ready in a few more minutes, hash browns coming out of the oven, along with black pudding and soda bread. We sat around the table and Lily told Sarah excitedly about where she planned to go first. She would skip Paris…

"Obviously," Sarah said.

Adam's Smug Travel Tips #10: Planning ahead is not against the spirit of backpacking. At least book accommodation one stop in advance, and that way you do not end up sleeping in a railway station amid gangs juggling flick knives and cops patrolling with Dobermans.

Lily detailed her route from Balboa in Spain, south through Portugal and then back up through Madrid, Barcelona, *maybe* the south of France, and on—

A knock sounded at the door. Every one of us jumped and fell silent. Sarah edged behind her sister, while I took Lily by the hand and guided her to one side. From behind the fridge, I took a military-grade Sig-Saur, ensured it was loaded, cocked it, and snapped on the safety.

I obtained it on my final visit to Gareth Delingpole, once I tracked his new identity to a bedsit in Bristol. I broke in and searched the place, and found the weapon behind a loose skirting board. When he came home, the cops were waiting, and Sarah's testimony, along with Agent Frank's highly-selective account of those weeks, was enough to send him down for twenty years. I kept the gun, though. Spent weeks practicing flicking it off and dry-firing it, and had it down pat. And that's what I held now, wondering who the hell was at my door.

The knock came again. "Hello? I know someone's in there. I can hear you."

"Relax," I told the women. "I know who it is."

Nobody relaxed as I opened the door, gun behind my back.

Sleazy Stuart Fitzpatrick, Mr. Moneybags, peered into the cabin. "Hello, Adam." He was dressed in his rich-guy-on-a-day-off attire.

"Give me a minute." I closed the door in his face. Lily took the gun from me and I exited the cabin into the bracing morning air once more. I faced Stuart Fitzpatrick and said, "Okay. Hit me."

"One hundred and sixty-four thousand."

"Why do you keep doing this? You know I'll say 'no'."

"I heard your business went under," he said, not quite answering the question. "I thought maybe—" He raised an eyebrow. He wasn't taking the piss, but it felt like it. He walked around the side of the barge, stroking a hand along the brass rail I fitted last week. He said, "This is new."

"A lot of it is," I said.

He noticed the fresh paint on the roof, fingered a spot of solid gunwale that was rotting the last time he came by. "You've been working on it."

"I've had some spare time."

"What made you spend it on the boat?"

I shrugged. "Seemed like the right thing to do."

"And you plan on keeping this up?"

"Well I'm not planning on working for folk like you anymore. And I'm not in the missing persons business. Maybe I'll sell my flat and open a coffee shop."

"Adam. Are you seriously telling me that you're going to stop neglecting your mother's boat?"

"It's a barge. And yeah. When it's ready I'll take her for a trip somewhere. Sometime."

He smiled. "I know you and I will never be friends, Adam. But that doesn't mean we have to be at each other's throats."

"We're not at each other's throats."

"We're not mates. Some might say we dislike one another."

"While you keep trying to buy this thing from me, we always will."

Sleazy Stu seemed old now, older than he was. He could have retired years ago, sold his company. But people like him don't retire. They don't give up. So what he said next was a real surprise. "In that case, I rescind my offer."

"What?"

"I no longer offer you a hundred and sixty-four thousand for this barge that's worth maybe thirty." Stuart completed a full circuit and he stood at the gangplank. "Of all the things I bought your mother, this, the thing she paid for herself, was what she loved most of all. Only used it twice a year, but she loved it." He returned to shore. "The fact you were letting it go to ruin was killing me, Adam. But promise me you'll take care of it, and you'll never see me again."

I said, "I'll ride her for as long as I like. If I ever get bored of her, I'll let you know." I was surprised how easily the smile came to me.

He nodded and, satisfied, he started to walk away. I stopped him, though. I ran this moment through my head a hundred times since I decided to work on the barge. I didn't know if I'd go through with it. But I did.

I held out my hand.

He looked at it. Like he wasn't sure what he was seeing. Then he shook it. I made it brief.

We didn't speak and this time I let him leave, his gait hesitant, like he was expecting me to call him back, to "one-more-thing" him. Maybe even invite him in for brunch. That didn't happen. We'd stopped playing silly games over my mother's memory, but friendship was perhaps too much.

I waited until he was a good distance away, then opened the newly-restored door, and descended the steps, returning to my friends where we would enjoy a perfectly normal Sunday brunch, before returning to our normal lives once more. Where Sarah would start university, where Caroline would continue bonding middle-managers via paintball matches, where Lily would set off to see the world.

And where I would decide what to do with the rest of my life, hopefully—in time—without the need to keep a gun behind the fridge.

* * * Adam Park returns in **A Desperate Paradise** * * *

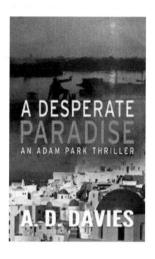

When the mother of a dead aid worker believes his death has not been investigated properly, Adam Park travels to the Greek island of Paramatra to delve into an alternative suspect. With the cops there struggling to cope with the influx of refugees from warzones across the Mediterranean, Adam must battle corruption, and ruthless smuggling gangs, all amid people so desperate they will do anything to reach the paradise of the west. If he cannot stay the course, and dig out the truth, a murderer will go free, and Adam will fall prey to the same evil.

His First His Second

Meet Detective Sergeant Alicia Friend. She's nice. Too nice to be a police officer, if she's honest.

She is also one of the most respected criminal analysts in the country, and finds herself in the grip of a northern British winter, investigating the kidnap-murders of two young women—both strikingly similar in appearance. Now a third has been taken, and they have less than a week to chip away the secrets of a high-society family, and uncover the killer's objective.

But Richard—the father of the latest victim—believes the police are not moving quickly enough, so launches a parallel investigation, utilising skills honed in a dark past that is about to catch up with him.

As Richard's secret actions hinder the police, Alicia remains in contact with him, and even starts to fall for his charms, forcing her into choices that will impact the rest of her life.

In Black In White

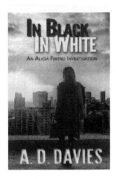

Meet Detective Sergeant Alicia Friend: cop, analyst, cutie-pie. She acknowledges she is an irritating person to have around at first but, when given a chance, all her colleagues fall in love with her. She can't explain it, but it's how she works, how she gets her best results.

And it is exactly how she must work when a British diplomat is murdered on US soil, and the UK Ambassador orders her to observe the FBI's investigation.

Soon, the murders expand to encompass a wider victim profile, each confessing their politically-motivated lies on camera, and Alicia shows why her superiors overlook her quirks, and consider her one of the best minds in her field.

Drafting in her old partner, Alicia imposes her personality on the investigation, and expands the focus from a politically-charged arena to the madness of a psychopath who cannot seem to stop.

Three Years Dead

When a good man…
>Becomes a bad cop…
>>But can't remember why.

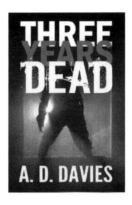

Following an attempt on his life, Detective Sergeant Martin Money wakes from a week-long coma with no memory of the previous three years. He quickly learns that corrupt practices got him demoted, violence caused his wife to divorce him, and his vices and anger drove his friends away one by one. On top of this, the West Yorkshire Police do not seem to care who tried to kill him, and he is offered a generous pay-out to retire.

But with a final lifeline offered by a former student of his, Martin takes up the case of a missing male prostitute, an investigation that skirts both their worlds, forcing him back into the run-down estates awash with narcotics, violence, and sex, temptations he must resist if he is to resume his life as the good man he remembers himself to be.

To stay out of jail, to punish whoever tried to kill him, and to earn his redemption, Martin attempts to unravel the circumstances of his assault, and—more importantly—establish why everyone from his past, his former friends, and his new acquaintances, appear to be lying at every turn.

Project: Return Fire

An inadvertent trip through time...
A battle to decide the fate of mankind...
One chance to set things right...

By Antony Davies & Joe Dinicola

Deep in the Juras Mountains, Johnathan Santarelli's team of Army Rangers investigates a radioactive anomaly. Suddenly Santarelli and his men are transported back to 1945 in German-occupied territory!

Far from their loved ones, the Rangers want nothing more than to preserve the timeline and get home, but when an elite Nazi unit captures future technology, and the Rangers are confronted with younger versions of important people from their present, they question if this trip was a coincidence after all. Before long, the U.S. team realizes it has a higher duty: stopping the Third Reich from turning the war in Germany's favor.

Before they return home, the team must battle the Nazis for the future of time itself...

17268056R00246

Printed in Great Britain
by Amazon